EXPOS
ALL
VILLAINIES
by
S.J. Haxton

EXPOSED TO ALL VILLAINIES by   S. J. Haxton
Published by Boswell Book Publishing
ISBN 978-0-9929293-1-2
Copyright © S J Haxton July 2014

COVER DESIGN by Claire Chamberlain
www.clairechamberlain.co.uk

EXPOSED TO
ALL
VILLAINIES
by
S.J. Haxton

Printed by

TJ International,

Padstow

Dedicated:the unknown,
un-named women and children at
Pendennis Castle
in 1646

The Castle's Prologue

On an August morning when a sea mist shrouds the Carrick Roads, muffling the cry of the gulls, look to the headland. In the moments before the hazy sun dries the dew or the mewling buzzard has flapped its lazy circle high into the air, a castle, squat and solid, rides the fog like a phantom. Pendennis Castle endures. It had stood for a hundred years before a bloody civil war between King and Parliament focused military minds at this Western fortress at the entrance to the river Fal. The granite walls survived both the war and a brutal siege lasting five months with barely a scratch; the citadel outlasted both monarch and Commonwealth, unstirred by the passions of politics, impassive, as it would stand through the reigns of the kings and queens to come.

However, the granite of Cornwall is remarkable, inspiring legends of glistening auras round isolated tors and mystic properties of stones that record the past then speak to those who would listen. In the ambiguity of the murky dawn light perhaps what seems to be the whisper of a stirring breeze are the stones of Pendennis murmuring their memories of an August long ago, when one thousand loyal hearts chose to come to Pendennis to make a stand for their King. Two hundred of these desperate souls were women and children.

Three women's voices still echo through time. One runs from her past, one fears for her present and the third has an uncertain future.

The girl with eyes the colour of honey is older than her years and has come the farthest of the three. Her past will brighten her future but she does not know that yet. A wheaten-haired wife stands by her hero, busying herself with the distraction of a routine one hundred and sixty three days old. The wind catches her words of reassurance to the young and the sick but only the walls hear her weeping. There is a woman with hair the colour of a sunset. Constantly her slate grey eyes look to the north over the water. This harbour has felt many tides while she watches but still she looks for a wake, a dark head in the water and she listens for the howl of a hound. The castle holds these three women. They have all made their choices. They have more choices to make.

Linger a while and hear their voices before the mist lifts and gulls' cries make them indecipherable once more.

I Grace: Bristol 1640 – 1641

Fortune is a wheel of great magnitude. I have had much time to reflect on the turns of the cycle in these six…nay, not even six years. Five years and some months ago I was a naïve innocent with not a worry in my head save which bodice best matched my favourite skirt. Through four of those years this land has raged with Civil War. The wheel turns.

Father's prosperity was at its height in 1640. His ship, the *Content*, first berthed in her home port of Bristol that Christmas morning. It seems inconceivable now that he, a moderately successful merchant, had been able to keep the purchase of a ship a secret, let alone the circumstance that led to it, but he did. We had had no hint of the windfall that had blessed the Godwynne enterprise. My mother Ann was ill, her latest pregnancy troublesome, so she had taken little interest in the latest commercial transactions. My eldest brother Henry was in London, my youngest brother Edward was at the school at Frome Gate while I should have been shadowing my mother at her domestic duties. What were we to know of commerce?

Even now, I clearly remember father pacing the length of the room, back and forth, in front of the blazing fire, gradually revealing the full the extent of his mercantile triumph. It stemmed from a part share in a cargo, an astute sailing master of the vessel and Letters of Marque for King Charles. Some might call it the proceeds of piracy. The King was pleased to take his percentage of the profits at least.

Thus my father, a pirate one might say, bought his own ship. 'My ship': we knew the implications as father spoke. 'My ship' meant one not shared with other owners as was the norm for merchants who could not afford to risk everything in one vessel. 'My ship' meant that there was the capital and the confidence to spend it. My future was vested in that ship in so many ways.

Pasco Jago was the sailing master who brought the *Content* on that un-seasonal first voyage from Dartmouth, where my father had purchased her. I heard Pasco say,

'There's many who'd kill for command of the *Content*' I doubt he knew his ability to prophesy.

Christmas Day, after prayers, saw us at the quay admiring the tall masts and neatly stowed canvas, appreciating the way the *Content's* shape gave her the appearance of a well-stuffed goose, plump and full of good things. I have known many ships and have even sailed myself since then, but none have been as pretty as she.

The Twelfth Night celebrations at our house in Wine Street that year were the most cheerful of any in the community. I doubt I shall ever know the like again, though the night also marks so much that I do not care to commemorate. We had the usual feasting, as always cramped but, with guests universally adopting the custom of wearing disguise, much of the merriment of the evening resulted from that fact. Wine and ale flowed in civilised moderation, the talk eddying around gossip, commerce and modest ribaldry. There was even debate on the policies of the King, and England's increasingly angry House of Commons.

I remember father mediating a heated discussion in which Rob Yeamans, his oldest friend and my godparent, challenged Will Barber, the gloom-mongering gunpowder maker, when he claimed that repeated orders for barrels of his best grade by 'a well-connected aristocrat in Radnor' meant the King and Parliament would come to blows. Master Yeaman insisted that the rule of Parliament would prevail upon His Majesty's good sense even if the monarch's need for cash did not. Father always tried to sit on the proverbial fence - until Parliament hanged my godfather.

Crossing the crowded room to my mother's side, I stumbled. In that moment, I glanced up under the cowls of two monks. I did not recognise the faces but those eyes, one pair an icy grey and the others as blue as summer sky, were looking into my future. I remember a hand gripping my elbow to steady me. Then the figures moved on into the throng, only the blue eyes looked back.

Tradition dictated that the city mummers would perform their silly antics, adding to the frivolity. Ned's closest friend Tom Shewel played the Turkish Knight while Ned heckled mightily from the staircase. The gathered fellowship, many with ancestors from across the Bristol Channel, harmonised the Welsh ballad 'The King' at midnight to mark the passing of the season,

'Old Christmas is past; Twelfth Tide is the last,
And we bid you adieu, great joy to the new!'

There was no great joy for the New Year. The first dawn of 1641 had barely broken before my mother was dead along with her stillborn babe. My father was distraught with grief. It must have been the hardest task for him, to have to send the letter to London. I believe he truly felt it would be kinder to ask a favour of the merchant with whom Hal had served his apprenticeship and for whom he was now an agent: Master Hill duly released my brother for a brief spell. Father hoped to lessen the pain if he could break the news himself so Hal was not told why he was called home but it was a great mistake to make.

When Hal arrived from London for the funeral, he and father argued. You could hear it all over the house. My brother, never the humblest of my siblings, had changed. He was harder because living in a house where there was no kindness to apprentices had made him so. He was defiant and challenged my father's authority. I believe Hal's sorrow was deflected into anger and he felt the man before him had caused all his sadness as well as our mother's death so he needed to inflict revenge. Nevertheless, what he said to our father was as unforgivable as it was terrible to hear,

'You just could not leave her alone could you? You disgust me! So eminent, so prosperous but you are no better than…an old goat!'

Hal did not return to the house after the funeral. He never came to Bristol again. Weeks went by and neighbours kept telling me that 'in the fullness of time your grief will pass and life will return to normal. Time heals all things.' The clichéd words echoed hollowly in my ears. Nothing would ever be the same. I missed my mother's calm, loving presence every moment of every day and my father was sliding deeper and deeper into his grief, encased in invisible armour. He was sharp and distant. I think he could find no solace with us his children for we reminded him of too much.

By default, I became the mistress of the house. Our steward Matthew Allerway was dependable and loyal; Jinty James, the woman who had been my mother's maid became my mentor. I suspect that some of the other servants became resentful. How else was I to manage? Edward and I rarely saw father.

It was early summer before my father decided to join us for an evening but he did not tell us he was coming. I remember Ned and I were laughing because Ned had picked up my lute and was lazily plucking a version of Kemp's Jig in a minor key. It sounded terrible, so I threw an empty silver bobbin at him. I missed but I hit the house-cat curled up behind the hem of the wall-hanging.

At that moment, father flung open the door with a merry 'Huzzah!' as he used to do. We had not heard his footsteps. Any levity in his eyes vanished for at that instant the startled puss launched itself across the room reaching the door at the second it opened. The timber crashed back upon its hinges, bowling Kitty into the fireplace.

I remember an instant of deathly hush after the animal stopped yowling. Whether father was angered by the dumbstruck expressions of alarm on our faces or the discovery of a minor domestic brawl we never knew. As the door juddered to a stop in his grasp, his tone became icy,

'Am I in a mad menagerie? My daughter behaves like a hoyden and as for my son's musical talent, I find little to recommend your further studies in the gentlemanly arts, Edward. Perhaps it is time your energies were more usefully directed?'

Barely two weeks later, on Edward's fifteenth birthday

Father signed the papers for my brother's apprenticeship. Ned had hoped for a chance to go up to Oxford but instead he followed father as Hal had done and was presented by Master Richard Hill as apprentice to the worshipful Guild of Merchant Adventurers in the City of London. He told me that he felt as if he was being banished.

Edward had been gone ten days. As I breakfasted, there was a thunderous banging at our door. I was stunned when my godfather Robert Yeamans dashed in, his cloak swirling, his doublet buttons fastened lopsidedly in his haste. He was waving two pages covered in a tight handwriting, which I recognised instantly. My heart was thumping in my chest as he pressed them into my hand. I read:

My good friend,

These last months have been such that our deep affinity has been tested to its utmost, my regret being that the fault has been all my own. My mind is affected by the most infernal of darkness, and I believe that I must seek to shed some light upon my unhappy circumstance. This I cannot do here. Memories crowd upon me too closely.

I am to take ship with the Content on this morning's tide as she sails and, as I have so instructed, will be at Avonmouth by the time you receive this letter. I intend to act as factor to my own ship and will execute all necessary transactions. My steward Matthew Allerway has instructions for the management of the house under the auspices of my daughter. God willing, monies will be made available on a regular basis as I intend to continue to trade, primarily through Andrew Voysey in Dartmouth, with less profits but good staple returns. I regret leaving Grace. As her godparent I would ask that you advise her as you have advised me and with the same affectionate esteem as that in which I hold you.

Henry Godwynne

Despite the crippling mal-de-mer that had prevented his career as a master mariner, and however unlikely it might be, it seemed that my father had run away to sea.

II Hester: Bristol 1641 – 1642

I blame her father for all my troubles. If that man had done his duty as a master and a father and done what any right minded gentleman does when his wife dies, he would have married again to a respectable widow and then I would not have come to be where I am now. Who else is there to blame?

Look, all a girl wants is a post in a household where servants and masters know their places and all is respect and...oh, what's the word? So that you know where you are with everything, stable. But what did he do? Got all maudlin and rowed with his eldest, chucks his other son out too then takes to the seas. The eldest was already apprenticed in London when I was first employed at the Godwynne's in Wine Street.

I'm trying to work out when that was; I'm one summer younger than my sister Sally and she was born in the year before this King came to the throne. What was that? '25? Then I am ...oh I don't know...girls don't get schooling. No lass in Radstock needed to know numbers, just wanted strong arms for hard work and for giving the mining lads a black eye when they took too many liberties on the way back from the inn.

I do know that it was some-when in the Autumn when I walked to Bristow - it only took me three days though I admit I did dawdle a little but 'twas as much because my shoes weren't the best as anything else. That was after my Pa threw me out when I wouldn't take my mother's place in his bed. She'd been dead years but he had Meg then Sally till they got men of their own and a belly full of babe. Not necessarily in that order. That weren't for me; I'm a good girl. And I wanted to see more than the doorstep of some Radstock hovel.

So anyways, I got to the city and at the hiring fair wore my clean new pinafore and brushed my hair and got myself a scullery maid's post and cared not a ha'pence for my old days. I still say the day Master Godwynne took himself off was the start of my troubles. A household with no master will never prosper. Any servant will tell you that. Old steward Allerway did his best, but there was bossy Jinty James who made sure the mistress needed her at every turn then when the wife died got her claws in the daughter too. I'll give her what's due though, the daughter learned fast and even I was wrong-footed when she called me into the parlour that day.

It would have been better for me if that laundry lad had kept his mouth shut when that old shrew Jinty questioned the counting of linen. What was it to her that a few napkins went missing? And how was I to know that Allerway kept account of every last splinter in that household? I'd have thought he'd have better things to do than worry overmuch about catchin' and checkin' the washed linen when it came from the launderers once I'd put it away. That house had enough in the coffers that they wouldn't miss 'em or that pair of gloves I had hidden under my pallet and I could have sold them for a couple of shillings to put away for a rainy day. But they had the boy bleatin' "it is me master's reputation what depends on it" and so they swept their beady eye on Hester Phipps. I should have realised it was serious when I was faced with them all.

'It has come to my notice that there is linen missing from the press and I wish you to make a full explanation,' says the daughter.

'I'm sure I don't know what's missing nor what's not,' I said-'for 'tisn't my job.'

She didn't let me finish. She knew as well as I did that for sure it was my job. She said I'd got a 'slovenly tone' and was 'impudent'. I'll tell you, that made me stand up straight. She really sounded like her Ma then. It was a bit of a shock. I had caught on that I was in trouble though. So I thought 'I'll bluff' but it turns out that wasn't a clever plan.

'Well,' say I, 'It is often that I've had to straighten out and iron crumpled napkins, and them all to be folded away proper and all, ma'am, so I do my duty.'

I reckon she had planned to trick me – you know what she did then? She set a trap and I fell right in.

'Is their work returned neat and tidy?' says she. Well, I knowed that the bundles were always returned tied up and sealed but I waited a moment, then sounding polite as anything, knowing I'd got to do my best, I told her that I was sure it all came back all loose in the basket. She looked hard at me. So I started to cry, real tears and all, I just couldn't stop myself. But it didn't help for when I put my hand in my pocket for my kerchief a bit of launderer's ribbon came coiling out at my feet.

'Hester Phipps,' she says in her Mistress Godwynne voice, 'I accuse you of pilfering from the property of your employer, abusing our trust thereby, and being an impudent common thief!' The steward called the Captain of the Watch and they dragged me out a-screeching, off along the crowded streets to Castle Hill and the gaol. The watch gave me a black eye for swearing at a gawping gang of the city militia boys coming the other way to the drill ground. Wonder how many of them are rats' food on a battlefield now, eh?

So, there was I in Bristol Gaol. I came to hate rats in Bristol Gaol. The place was infested with them. There was nowhere to get away from the stink and the noise and the filth. And the rats. I hate rats but I tell you, I could eat a rat now I'm so hungry.

Everyone thought I would hang with my accuser's pa being one of the city's influentials, the Aldermen, mayors and all; they're mostly traders, rich merchants and the like. I never did find out why I didn't fall the gallows' drop. Not I. Guilty I was found, but instead I was sentenced to slavery in the plantations in the New World.

I can't count how many months I was in the prison cell, but I know when the frosts came I felt it. My ragged skirt didn't thaw for three days in the middle of the darkest months. I didn't catch my death though. Radstock girls are made of stronger stuff.

Even behind bars, we heard the soldiers' talk, heard that the old fort was being fixed up and that the King was right out of favour. Now, I b'aint a clever woman but I know when things are unnatural, and men against their King, that's going to cause trouble. We didn't know it then but there was a storm brewing alright.

Well now. Storms; maybe it's storms that I should blame all my troubles on? Come the spring in '42 there was I on this ship, with dozens like me, all chained like animals between the barrels and bales of cargo. Down the river Avon we went bound for...somewhere. I was so sick when we left the calm waters of the river I had no care for where we were going. I wouldn't have minded if I had died there and then.

We kept close to the coast as far as I could tell though I had no idea whether we had reached Bridgewater Bay or Hy-Brasil. We were dragged up on deck for air once a day. I think that it had happened three times. If I could bear to look up, all I could see over my left shoulder was a dark grey line above dark grey sea under a pale grey sky. About the same colour as my face I reckon. Then, in the afternoon, the storm broke.

I'd thought there was something amiss. The sailors had been doing superstitious stuff like touching their collars and some even crossed themselves. Nobody whistled. The singing stopped as well. Not that you could have heard anything above that noise. I'd never heard anything like it and I'd swear even the cannons I've heard on battlefields since don't sound the way that storm did. It grew till it was a shriekin' and a howlin' and the hull was slamming into the waves like hitting a wall. The planks were groaning, and all of us chained were praying harder than we have ever prayed before. I hardly ever prayed. I started that day and have prayed every night since. I forgot being sick, I just prayed.

And my prayers were answered though I couldn't know it when I heard the screams from the main deck above us, for there came a crashing smash and water gushed in from a hole in the side where rocks were grinding the planks into splinters. What was I to do, for my wrists were chained? But perhaps the Bo'sun didn't fettle them right, or maybe my bones had shrunk so small from lack of food, or perhaps God was listening to me but, panicking, I twisted and pulled and the irons slipped off. There was nothing I could hang on to and I was swept with bales on the surge of water up through a shattered hatchway and into the sea. I couldn't tell 'ee how long I tossed in the waves. I remember nothing until sharp rock cut my hand and the pain brought me to my senses.

I could see a lantern swinging in the dark. I think I was groaning. Hands pulled me up and the next that I knew I was on a stone hearth and wrapped in a ragged blanket with sheepskin beneath my head and two small children, wide-eyed, watching my every move from a settle and a woman with a foreign accent speaking soothing noises as I struggled to awake.

None but me survived the storm. There would be nobody to gainsay me when I, Hester Phipps, became the only survivor of a ship not full of convicts but one carrying a lady and her servant; the newly respectable, upright, hardworking, decent Hester Phipps. Well, once I had some clothes on my back I would be decent. And which foreign shore had I been wrecked upon? Cornwall, I was now in Cornwall.

III Mary: Cornwall

Cornwall, the county of my birth: I have lived here all my life and I never wish to be anywhere else. Where else should I be, for I was born into the great Carew family? My grandfather was Sir Richard Carew, the author and chronicler of this Duchy, this isthmus besieged by ocean with its tors and moors and rugged cliffs, the legendary land of King Arthur. There are those who scoff at Cornish fables, but live here for any time at all and I defy anyone not to sense the magic in this land.

Penwarne where I was born sits on the south coast, with its mellow stones and deep-hedged lanes, a soft, gentle landscape to nurture us. Our ancient manor house with its fine, tall windows nestles in a secret valley, hidden from the elements and seaborne raiders, wrapped by the folded landscape as in a shawl, but barely a mile from the coast. My father once bade the stable-hand build us children a swinging seat in the woods, overlooking Portmellon cove, where I would watch the azure sea and think of Tristan and Isolde.

Perhaps I am fanciful, a romancer. My papa always called me his 'little dreamer'. That is as may be but I found my own 'Tristan', my very own hero, my childhood sweetheart. Still, I must not dwell on my romance, though it is that tale which brought me to this fortress.

I am proud to be Cornish. Penwarne, my home and happy haunt of childhood, was where my brother Richard (whom - the family always called Diccon) and four sisters were indulged with ponies and pets and I was spoiled just as much as the rest.

My mother died in '31 when I was only seven years old, leaving papa with his brood. Even though the grander Carews at Antony oftimes suggested it, he never remarried, so I had no stepmother to chide me as I grew, only lessons with a tutor engaged to school my brother. With my mother gone the tutor took on additional duties, paying attention to the intellectual needs of the daughters of the house. Master Cobb had little interest in us girls though. When I missed lessons to tend the small assortment of creatures, which perpetually needed my care, nobody paid much heed.

Of course I learned my numbers and to read and write, but I preferred spending time in the barns feeding orphaned lambs or learning from the stable-boy how to nurse a baby hedgehog or tend the broken wing of a dove. These tasks engaged me more than Master Cobb's classes. I could hear that his lessons in Rhetoric only taught my sisters to argue with intellectual overtones to cover their spitefulness.

Great things were hoped for Diccon; to go up to Oxford then the Inns of Court and return to a gentleman's life at Penwarne, but it was not to be. My brother was not destined for the law. Since then Cornwall has become accustomed to losing its young men. However, that is quite enough of my childhood tittle-tattle; I meant to tell of this land.

This is a place where the gentlefolk are known to one and all. They run this county, the great and the good, the justices of the peace and the crown's officers. The Carews are as influential as any and as proud. It might seem to the outsider that every great household is tied in kinship with their neighbour or their neighbour's neighbour. My grandfather married an Arundel from Trerice; his father married an Edgcumbe from just round the coast. The network runs out like a spider's web. Some might marry across the Tamar and beyond, but mostly it is our marriages which are the bonds that bind the grand Cornish families together. Mostly.

In the main, the gentlefolk all speak English now. Cornish is no longer a language for parliament or courtroom, though the canny landlord might keep an ear open for any lack of respect hidden in a kernowek phrase. Thus, gentlemen and women converse in English when they sit in each other's parlours and debate the perilous state of the nation as they have done this last decade and more.

Nonetheless, Cornwall is no backwater, for all the distance from London. Our members in Parliament have grumbled with the rest at the King's meddling with taxes, with the Church. There was a time when county squires might have spoken their mind to guests around their table at supper, in their hall or that of their 'cousin' and never believed that a difference of opinion could sever their kinship. Now all is not well in these British Isles where families, villages, indeed the whole country, are torn asunder. Amity and respectful debate have been replaced by the cold steel and conflict of civil war. King's men see Parliament as rogues and Parliament sees the King as an unruly ruler. Cornishmen and women think: who will look after the Cornish, King or Parliament?

It is four years almost since this war without an enemy began. Four years since I could have been celebrating my betrothal, dreaming of my wedding day and blushing as the nuptials were planned. Instead, my marriage became a battle ground as brutal as Lansdowne, as bitter as His Majesty's present sorrows.

Now I am here at Pendennis Castle where all seems a lost cause. If anyone should ask why I, a young gentlewoman, should be with those who Parliament name 'the most desperate persons, the violentest enemies', besieged and near starvation, I will tell them that it is because I defied the great Carew household, and I became a war-bride.

IV Grace: Bristol 1641 – 1642

After the initial murmur of servants' speculation about a 'bad master', matters settled into a routine in our household when father left. For sure the businessmen and members of the Society of Merchant Venturers of Bristol grumbled in scandalised undertones for a while. A daughter should not have been running matters in Henry Godwynne's absence for under their rules she could never inherit such an enterprise, but my godfather Rob Yeaman seemed reassured that all was going according to the Godwynne plan. However, in May news of the despised Lord Wentworth's execution proved a more significant topic of conversation for city aldermen. As the summer wore on, the commercial sensitivity to rumblings of trouble in Ireland and the consequent threat to Bristol trade pushed old, local gossip into oblivion. I missed Ned especially in that summer.

In early September a consignment of currants, tuft taffeta and silk rugs bore witness to father having at the very least survived sea-sickness to reach the Levant. I took great interest in watching portions of the cargo appearing as the clothes on the backs of our Bristol acquaintances. Always it seemed that just when we began to speculate on his whereabouts, a cargo of Bordeaux claret or Holland linen would arrive on another Bristol-bound vessel to reassure me that father was alive. Nonetheless, the end of October still saw no return of his ship, the *Content.*

Occasionally I walked out with Rob Yeaman's daughter, Elizabeth, a manservant discreetly nearby to protect us. It must have been in November that I first met my husband to be. It was certainly in late autumn. The dank smell of fallen leaves underfoot is so evocative.

Elizabeth and I were enjoying watery sunshine in the afternoon near the bowling green on the open space of the Marsh. Several groups of young men were making the most of the last of the afternoon light in a rough game of bowls on the muddy grass. Elizabeth, not having brothers, was embarrassed at their proximity, and I remember I was laughing at her discomfort when a stranger's voice behind us sent a shiver of unease down my spine.

'Mistress Godwynne! Well met! It gives me great pleasure to see you again.'

The northern accent was not quite Scots; at first I could not identify it. There was the polish of an education but the tone disturbed me. His straight, mousey hair was slick, flattened by the plain broad-brimmed hat which he had doffed, and there were alarmingly translucent grey eyes above a broad, full mouth. I had a distant recollection of the tall, thin figure but could not place him.

'Ship's Master, Bartholomew Fenwick at your service, Mistress Godwynne!'

I introduced Elizabeth to cover my discomfort, but when Fenwick bowed again he did not take his eyes off me as he continued, 'I have had considerable dealings with your papa through Sailing Master Vickery...'

Then I recognised him, recalling the same eyes in a room festively full; one of the monks who had been wearing deep hoods on Twelfth Night. I resumed the courtesies, politely enquiring after his voyaging and yet I was so disturbed by that disconcerting stare. As one of my father's associates he was due all respect, but I wondered, did he know of father's travels? While I knew that I should tell him, I was reluctant to enlighten him as to the extent of father's absence. Of the blue eyed man I made no mention at all.

Eventually he declared,

'My vessel, the *Providence* trans-shipped a cargo bound for Plymouth and I have business up this West coast. So, providentially, we are thus met!' I could only reply that father was not at home at the moment, and imply his return. I found later that Master Fenwick was not deceived, but he let me offer him hospitality and I steered a bewildered Elizabeth in the direction of home with him in step beside us. Faithless friend, she made some excuse and left. The manuals of good manners explained how to entertain one's visitors, but I had not yet learned an effective way to remove them.

When Jinty bustled into the room I nearly wept with relief. Behind her a servant carried a tray bearing a delicate dish of wafers, a neat pewter flask and three blessedly small glasses. My indomitable saviour firmly commandeered the faltering conversation, placing herself at my side. She made it quite plain she expected to stay, explaining formally that the household was much altered since his last visit. Only later was I to discover just how much he already knew.

Anyone observing might have been amused as the pair of them sparred verbally, crowing about respective maritime connections. I just sat, silent, heartily relieved when Fenwick, with heavy courtesy, thanked us for our hospitality and took his leave. I remember Jinty, saying,

'To what did we owe that I wonder? And in which hole did you find him?' I replied that he had found me, and it troubled me. With well-timed humour, her hands to her lips and an expression of mock horror on her handsome, rounded features, she exclaimed with a shriek,

'Well, my word! I do believe you have had your first wooing, Mistress Godwynne!' It seemed the only thing to do was to laugh.

For some weeks there were no unexpected visits. As the sailing season ended, and business was quieter, I confess I was a little lonely. That Christmas saw few festivities in our home but in the city there was a minor bout of un-seasonable unpleasantness when Dot Kelly, a Puritan, defied the law and convention by keeping open shop on Christmas Day, then accused some city elders of boycotting her premises. The end of 1641 and Twelfth Night saw the traditional ribaldry in the halls and parlours of our acquaintances. If it was directed with a little more malice than in previous years nobody cared to remark upon the fact. It seemed to me that the tensions between neighbours in Bristol now very accurately began to mirror the stresses in the whole nation.

I wrote to Edward but he was already developing a hard edge. His letters, less frequent, were full of troubling stories of rioting apprentices. I wondered at Ned's jubilation at the London mob chasing the King from his capital. He also seemed to have developed a profound admiration for a new friend, Nehemiah Wharton, in St Swithin's Street. Ned passed on one small piece of news of Hal who had sailed to Antwerp to engage with the foreign trade but Hal never wrote.

Two short letters from my father were reassuring in tone but at no point did he intimate either his feelings or a date for his return. February's snow passed and in March came news of a diverse cargo of bolts of plush and lucrative bales of tobacco, a credit to father's stamina as well as our coffers. On the same day Parliament made Denzil Holles Lieutenant of the city of Bristol: he promptly commenced to recruit for a campaign against those individuals and their adherents who Parliament had decreed traitors. Our steward brought reports of the Puritan faction in the city loudly declaring their support for Holles and on Matthew's advice we decided to clear space in the cellars and stores, making room for some prudently stockpiled provisions. I was glad of father's commercial success because if you walked around the city you could see Trouble carved in the masons' workings, the city council investing in stone, mortar - and munitions.

It was early in April when I saw Master Fenwick again. Jinty or Matthew might have given my excuses to an unexpected caller but as they did not I was given no opportunity to avoid him. Fenwick had dressed to impress in a new suit of yellow-green velvet that did nothing for his complexion, his breeches spilling into creaking bucket-topped boots. He entered and immediately assumed control, stalking past me and arrogantly striding to the deep, high-backed chair that I considered my father's.

'I do believe that providence is the most generous of graces, for providence did bring me to Bristol and providentially you are not engaged elsewhere, Mistress Godwynne.' With hindsight, it was on that day that first I ever saw hidden depths in Bartholomew, though I did not recognize their nature.

The monologue droned on, but when the man claimed the superiority of seafarers from the north-east it was too much. I was provoked to speak up on the behalf of local mariners, Jinty's ancestors included, concluding with Master Cabot sailing from Bristol with Bristol merchants' wealth backing him. At the mention of Bristol money a taut smile stretched across my visitor's face. Looking back, I should not have contradicted him. He has a long memory.

An uncomfortable tension hung between us like a cloud, while a disturbance outside rumbled in the passageway then erupted into the hall. Matthew entered briskly, bowed briefly to me and Bartholomew Fenwick. Then taking my visitor by the elbow, he politely but firmly announced that the household was being forced to curtail the present hospitality. I was stunned to silence as the startled Fenwick was ushered out of the room. It might have been badly done but I did not care for seconds later an astonishing vision stepped through the door. In the swirl of a faded, salt-encrusted cloak stood a man with grisly beard, his greying hair caught back in an unfamiliar tarred pony-tail. Henry Godwynne, my father, had come home.

He should not have been able to appear like a phantom, without anyone being told of the arrival of the *Content*. But the ship that moored that day alongside St. Austin's Back was not the *Content* but the *Ann of Bristol*. That day we celebrated my Father's safe return and the renaming of our ship.

But there are those who say that changing a ship's name will change her fortunes. Perhaps the first to suffer was her sailing master John Vickery, who was found lifeless on Priory Slip one week later, murdered by unknown hands.

I will wager there are few folk who have seen the bodies of lifeless men washed up after a shipwreck but I saw too many in those next days and weeks. I helped as villagers laid them out in the dead house by the lychgate of Morwenstow church when the sea gave the corpses up. There weren't a scrap of anything of value on the bodies - not as I'd wanted anything like, as a mermenta morry like they say. But you might have thought there'd be something to salvage.

Anyway, they buried them in the graveyard, me and the few villagers as wasn't carrying the coffins standing in as mourners, sheltering from a biting wind in the covered gateway as the pine boxes were lowered into one big grave.

So there was I, Mistress Hester Phipps, now a young orphaned woman from a good family in Gloucester, wrecked at the mercy of the sea. I decided to keep my name - that was the only bit of my old life I was intending to keep - so if I weren't traced to Bristol then good riddance to the past.

And at first I thought to myself, Hester, you have found yourself a new billet, for I discovered I was bedded down in the only inn for miles. The woman who had soothed me was Kat Conybeare. She was the innkeeper's widow and the girls were all that was left of his family. The sweating sickness had taken him and his two boys in '39; she were struggling to keep the place. So, for my bed and board and some moth-eaten clothes I set to helping around the place. We were merry enough for a few weeks too, if they would but speak in plain language and not in the Cornish tongue.

Then her cousin Thomas Yeo from Kilkhampton barely six mile away moved in. He said it was to help run the hostelry and keep his cousin safe, but I'd seen the looks, the moon-eyes and the way he sloped around after her. I've seen that a hundred times. I don't think he liked me. If I came in the room he would stop and glare, and there was no proper talk when I was in the company, as they'd be guthing an' hething and I could understand not a word.

Now, I can't say what gave anybody the idea that I weren't who I said I was, but about three months after the wreck, Kat hauled me to one side in the tap room and in the gruff tone she used when she weren't speaking Cornish she said,

'In these parts people do value honesty and I do consider that you have truth that is undisclosed here' - she was calling me a liar - 'and you know full well that the Good Book sayeth the bread of deceit is sweet, but after, the mouth shall be filled with gravel. Now, I will have your truth.' I know a peevish woman when I sees one, so I says,

'I cry your mercy, dear Mistress Kat, but I did not know what honest and kind souls had rescued me, and I did not mean to swerve from goodliness.' Then I span her the yarn of me, the hard working housemaid, wrongly accused of theft and sentenced to a life as a slave. Sometimes you just have to speak how you believe it to be and not dissemble. But I could tell it was time to move on. After that if I met Tom Yeo in the yard he would spit on the ground and growl 'gowek gast' and turn his back on me, and around the tavern the girls would scuttle away every time I came by.

I decided that if I could make my way to a town, I could find work in a good household and never worry that anyone would know me. So Hester Phipps could start anew-and there'd be no more 'mar pleg' this and 'meur ras' that. I had to bide my time though, and I laid my scheme well. One evening in July I wrapped a loaf, a patched underskirt and a spare shift in the new apron I had been stitching and laid it behind a fallen gravestone by the churchyard wall. On the next morning, the day of Kilkhampton Fair, Kat and Tom mounted up on the old mule, her on an old-fashioned pillion pad, and the pair of them rode off early to catch the best of the town revelry.

I will admit I was sore tempted to run just as soon as they were out of the door but I waited long enough to know they'd truly gone and would be right out of sight. Straightway I took a few shillings that I reckoned that I had earned, telling the eldest child that I was away to fetch the milk. Then I collected my bundle and set off fast to the highroad east.

It was two days before the Sunday service and sermon in the church. I weren't in down on my knees behind a pew nor beside my bed with my palms together, but that morning I was praying hard to Him above. What I prayed for was a ride to my destination for I was Bideford-bound.

VI Mary: Cornwall 1640 – 1641

On reflection, to ride about Cornwall and Devon to the homes of the Carew 'cousins'- for every relation is a Cornish cousin - seemed to be a major pastime in my childhood. My sisters and I had been happy to visit sunny house on the hill, to mingle with our young cousins at their home, above the river near Antony. Papa and the Carew men would talk of money or land matters, while in the gloomy parlour our brother Diccon and the other boys undertook to complete the Latin tasks given by 'Sir Uncle'. That is what we called Sir Richard Carew.

Diccon, my Carew cousins and Jack, Richard and Nick Arundel, our relatives at Trerice, were of all of similar age and all like brothers. We younger children thought them all very fine young gentlemen. Then there was the cheerful clutch of Tremaynes at Heligan, barely four miles from Penwarne. Lewis, less than two years younger than my brother, would chivvy all of his siblings and us Carews around the garden at their pretty manor when neighbours congregated on long summer days. He called me his Carew Chick for he said my golden hair was the colour of a newly-hatched hen. I loved him for his gentle ways and thought him the handsomest of all the boys even above my own brother. I told not a soul for even sisters can be unkind to dreamers. I missed my mother but I was not unhappy until my brother's death, until papa's illness. Then I seemed to leave all childish notions behind me.

Nobody had been able to dissuade Richard from a military path, certainly not papa. He could not when his own youth had been on the battlefields of Europe. That was where he was renamed 'Carew the One Handed', when the injury from a cannon ball at the siege of Ostend back in Queen Elizabeth's day took his right hand. Like father, like son. When the tiny contingent from our district straggled off to join the King's army at the Scottish border in the early summer of 1640 the heir to Penwarne led them. He was brandishing a new pipe, cheerfully telling the lads that they would do their duty, joining the ranks of King Charles' army to show the Scots what real fighting men were like. The cannon shot at Newburn took Diccon's hand. It took his arm, aye, and took his life. He was not even twenty-five years old and now lies buried far from the soft Cornish countryside that he loved.

The news of Diccon's death shocked papa so much that he took a fierce seizure. It left him with much paralysis all down his left side rendering his good arm useless and leaving his speech incomprehensible. Though Sir Uncle had some extraordinary notions on medicines and remedies and directed a favoured physician to encourage his brother's recovery, it meant that the Carew family network took hold of our affairs.

While papa struggled to regain some of his faculties, the girls of Penwarne were sent to stay with our relatives. After Diccon's death, I rarely saw Lewis for there was no call for him to visit the Carew outposts and if we met at all I found myself tongue-tied and clumsy. However, Lewis saw only the girl he had known in his boyhood and I was to discover that he had kept that girl close to his heart.

Thus, we sisters were trundled between homes linked to my family, between Antony, and gloomy Petrockstowe, on rare occasions to my mother's cheerful family at Drewsteignton. We spent happier times at Trerice, but the best times were at Penwarne though they were few. It was a gypsy existence and it would take domestic disobedience for me to escape it, a waywardness that might seem even worse in the context of my upbringing.

There are many families in the east of this county who prefer to worship in the plain manner of those who are known as Puritans, and the Carews can be counted in that number. This in itself is no barrier to old friendships even should men be of different inclinations, which is why this war between countrymen has come at such a cost. My Uncle, despite leaning toward Puritan teachings, was nevertheless uncomfortable with men being in conflict with the King, yet my aunt and her staunchly Puritan family believed His Majesty to be in league with the Devil. When my cousin Alexander, announced his stand against King Charles he and my uncle were at odds from the outset. I am sure old Sir Uncle broke his heart at the news that his son could so betray the monarch. His heart certainly seemed to bear a heavy burden those last months. This Civil War breaks heads and hearts across the land.

Even before these dire times, as I grew to be a young woman, I was under no illusions: with papa being so ill Uncle Richard would oversee any matchmaking and bossy Aunt Carew expected me to be another pawn by which Puritan zeal, a political allegiance and a marriage could be fulfilled in one move. Should anyone think that a young woman of respected family might be in control of her own destiny then they have more romantic notions than the old troubadors.

As 1640 turned to a new year, my sisters and I were invited to Trerice Manor for Twelfth Night. We had spent a gloomy Christmas at Antony. Papa was not yet well enough to have us back at Penwarne and my Aunt's Puritan strictures meant there was little marking of the season. While I still grieved for Diccon, I was looking forward to joining festivities at Sir John's handsome home. The Arundel family were less constrained by Calvinist sentiment; they planned to congregate and celebrate in the traditional manner. I hoped that perhaps others of the young gentry fraternity of the county - one in particular - might find their way to hospitable portals of Trerice. Alas, a rare heavy snowfall in the preceding days curtailed all the festivities. Nobody could travel and though a thaw began to set in on the 5th January, it came too late to resume the plans. Deep gloom pervaded the house for we girls all felt the disappointment. However, late on the 6th a messenger did arrive. He brought a letter, for me. I still recall the thud of my heart as I hauled my skirts about my knees and ran to the room I was sharing with Agnes. The letter was from Lewis

Tremayne, a singular thing indeed.

I am too tactful to repeat to anyone exactly what he wrote, though I could recount it word for word and had it learned by heart within the hour. Suffice to say that Lewis Tremayne was declaring his long-held affection for me. He said that although it might be perceived as inappropriate, our childhood affinity gave him some hope that if he should he ask my father for my hand in marriage it would be a proposition kindly received. He hoped that I would wait for him.

I sought seclusion and remember praying that none of my sisters would come to find me, Candacia especially, as she had seen the messenger arrive and her spiteful curiosity would be consuming her. I was not ready to divulge anything at that point for my mind was whirling like a spinning top.

Would papa recover for Lewis to ask for my hand? Would he say that Lewis was a worthy fellow? At least Lewis could not be accused of impulsiveness for his proposal would depend upon the outcome of a war abroad and papa might think I was yet a little young. I rehearsed a conversation in my head, dreaming that his recovery would be swift, his reply kind and that if it was my wish, when Lewis asked for my hand he would be as welcome as a long cherished friend should be. I believed, if that could be so, at that moment nothing could mar my future.

Fate was not to be so kind. Papa did not recover fast. Although my uncle Sir Richard did not consider the matter of my marriage a pressing one, Aunt Carew had begun a strategy. The Hoblyn brothers were contracted for Bridget, Grace and Ann once each had reached an appointed age. Candacia was too young yet so her attention was turned to me. At first, she did not see matters as urgent as the strife and tensions we now suffer were merely an unpleasant speculation by radicals. She was sure that all loyal subjects would swear the Oath to protect the King, Protestantism and the privileges of Parliament. His Majesty could then be persuaded to compromise with his Commons, all would be well and a match could be sought for me where most advantageous. My hopes were the last thing on my aunt's agenda and directives on potential bridegrooms from her brother Samuel were firm and frequent. Dick Rous of Halton, three years older than I, was rejected as too youthful though his Puritan credentials were impeccable. Francis Buller was too old and not appreciative of the honour being offered. The lists were made and discarded with no reference to me. Lewis Tremayne was not in her catalogue of suitors.

The King and his Parliament wrangled all through '41, His Majesty resistant to any compromise. By my next birthday, I knew that Lewis was in Ireland with Sir Richard Grenvile suppressing rebel Catholics. By the spring of 1642 His Majesty had fled London and was on the march, gathering his forces while Parliament's Committee of Safety was securing funds from London merchants to supply rebel regiments across the country. Aunt Carew was undeterred and merely used her influence to ensure passes for her messengers to travel in an increasingly tense countryside.

The unnatural matter of a civil war was formalised on 22nd August with the raising of the King's Standard at Nottingham. On that tragic day my cousin Alexander galloped away from his ancestral home after a furious quarrel with his father. We could not help but hear the angry words shouted behind the door of my Uncle's great chamber and I was scurrying past the threshold as Alexander strode out. I remember glimpsing Sir Richard's face, which had turned almost mulberry hue he was so angry. He reached up to the linen-fold panelling between the window bays and hauled down the wedding portrait of his eldest son and with a pen-knife from the desk cut out the face and body of the heir who had so fiercely defied his father and declaimed against the Royalist cause. My aunt was stunned to an uncharacteristic silence by the raging invective against her husband.

As she tried to sooth the quaking old man, I quietly gathered up the painting of that handsome face, the full falling ruff and silk-sleeved buff coat with its red silk points.

Rolling up the canvas, I took it to the library, wrapped it in my neckerchief now spotted with tears and tucked it in the oak box designed to keep the household Bible.

Thenceforward Aunt Carew's efforts to find me a husband redoubled, her negotiations made more complex by politics - national and household. She did not openly argue with her husband, but, like Alexander, her Devon relatives had declared a fierce Parliamentarian partisanship and my aunt would not deny her leanings. I suspect that, for her, the nuptial conferences were some distraction from the sad concerns within and without her four walls but most reputable families seemed to be preoccupied. The Coswarth family politely declined to enter negotiations with the excuse that it was inappropriate to consider such matters given the 'current uncomfortable fortunes of the county'. For that I shall be eternally grateful.

By November, we knew of at least two Cornish gentlemen, Richard Arundel and John Robartes, who had faced each other on the battlefield of Edgehill. Of Lewis I heard nothing. All I could do was wait.

VII Grace: Bristol Spring 1642

I was to discover that to wait was never an option for Bartholomew Fenwick, for whom luck was something a man made for himself - with a little help from one's friends in the shadows.

Father and I were the chief mourners at the funeral of sea captain John Vickery. He had never married and what other family there might have been were in his home town of Bridgewater. A gentle, sober man, he had kept to his ship and to the one love of his life - the sea. There were few others save the crew of the *Ann* to miss him. However, Jack had piloted my father through the first dark days of his own voyaging and they had become close. He would be a hard man to replace.

Father had insisted his friend's body should rest at our house before the interment so that morning in late April we followed the coffin in the quiet, before the bustle of business began. Several ships' masters, some of the crew and a handful of men who frequented the inn in which Vickery occasionally had been known to recruit sailors shuffled self-consciously past the grave once the coffin was lowered. Following at the rear was none other than Bartholomew Fenwick, cursorily paying his respects to the muddy hole. He lingered. In that moment my heart sank lower than Jack's coffin. The offices over, my father was thanking the parson, both men moving to leave the churned ground. Fenwick purposefully blocked my father's way to the lychgate, opening his conversation,

'Good morrow, Master Godwynne, Mistress; yet so sad a time for us to meet again.'

I took my father's arm, forced to follow polite convention.

'Good Morrow, Master Fenwick. Father, this is the gentleman about whom I have been telling you so much.' I sensed rather than saw my father's mood alter; perhaps he was recalling my unladylike description of our ejected guest as the 'fellow in the goose-turd green suit'. He bowed politely in response.

'I am glad to remake your acquaintance, Master Fenwick.' Hearing the element of irony in my father's voice I looked at my feet, pursed my lips to suppress a betraying smile. Father continued,

'Do I recall our introduction on Twelfth Night? It is a while since then, near eighteen month past!' Both knew very well that there had been no introduction but my father continued, 'Master Vickery spoke highly of you, and I am glad that prov...' He faltered as his foot felt the nudge from my shoe beneath my skirts finishing, 'It is good that Fate had you here in Bristol to bid your farewell to your friend'. Fenwick nodded, tersely adding,

'It would have grieved me had I not been able to witness his passing'. That man's callous play with words makes me shudder even yet. My father was relaxing, but I suspected that this situation had been managed and not to our advantage. It gives me no satisfaction to say that I was proved right.

Aware that this was not the place for social or commercial pleasantries, with horrible predictability my father, courtesy overriding my unspoken disapproval, invited Fenwick to breakfast with us, just as I had feared. Fenwick looked self-satisfied.

I had rebellion on my mind as we made our way out of the churchyard nevertheless I dutifully took on my role as hostess. I have discovered an aptitude for feigning civility in these last half dozen years but that day it resulted in a devastating headache, forcing a tactical withdrawal, and I was asleep when our guest took his leave.

In the next few days father re-established his commercial contacts, encouraging me to continue my accounting in the 'shop' as I had done while he was absent. It became the norm for us to be examining lists and ledgers together. At other times, I attended to the household business, which would have been my mother's concern. However, the pressing matter of a new sailing master could not be ignored for long, nor could the increasing pressures on the city by the Lieutenant whose recruiting drives for the municipal militia harassed any able bodied Bristol male.

Fortunately, for my father and the business of the ship, sailors and fishermen were exempt. Matthew had protested to the town guard when our groom appeared with a rusty old breastplate and instructions to restore it to pristine condition. The recruiting sergeant had sneered. Matthew was warned. His objections would be interpreted as a sign that the household's loyalties were in question for it had been taken for granted that Parliament's and a Puritan manifesto were synonymous with Bristol's. Anxiety became palpable, especially amongst those like my father who hoped to remain neutral in the conflict between Parliament and the King, which was surely now inevitable.

Another untidily scrawled letter arrived from Ned, full of enthusiasm for his new pastime as a member of Nehemiah's company of soldiery, one of the London Trained Bands. With Sergeant Wharton's intercession, he was proud to announce that he had contrived a place in what he deemed a superior regiment of mainly butchers' and dyers' apprentices. He had met with Hal in late March but they had a strong difference in opinion over the King's right to demand the magazine and arms kept at Hull but he thought our brother was again abroad.

Father kept his own counsel on Ned's soldiering.It did not surprise me that my brother had taken to this volunteer force for he had always loved the rough and tumble of schoolboys' games but I felt a shiver of foreboding when the beat of the militia's drum echoed round our city wall.

My father spent some time at the quays and on board the *Ann of Bristol*. On the last day of April, as he and I sat in companionable silence after breakfast, he put down the knife with which he had been paring the wrinkled skin from an apple and taking a deep breath, leaned towards me. He began quietly,

'Grace, I wish to speak with you about a topic I do not take lightly.' I had no idea what was to come, waiting attentively until he cleared his throat and continued, choosing his words with care,

'I do not wish to seem disloyal to my friend's memory, but Jack understood better than most the practicalities of maritime trade. Developing the Godwynne enterprise was often a topic for our conversation at the helm or in the cabin.' I still had no idea where the conversation was leading but now I began to sense some uneasiness in my father's tone.

'Jack never mentioned Fenwick to me, but I have made diplomatic enquiries and there seems to be enough information around the quaysides about our Northumberland friend'. I would not have chosen the word friend. Perhaps he felt a need to justify his decision to himself as well as to me and he pressed on, 'He is experienced, an excellent seaman. I want to appoint Bartholomew as sailing master of the *Ann.*'

There was a silence. The clatter of the scullery and raised voices in the street echoed in the void. I could say nothing. My father continued swiftly,

'Captain Fenwick has not been to Wine Street since the day of the funeral but that is not to say I have not been in conversation with him. I have asked him to dine with us tomorrow. Will you do me the kindness of being our hostess?'

Bartholomew Fenwick arrived as the church clocks chimed the middle of May Day. From early morning, the militia had marched around the city, displaying their manoeuvres in front of the Corn Market, the drums and trumpets fraying my nerves.

The day is now a blur in my mind; how did the conversation over the meal progress from small talk to affairs of business, from general to specifics or, later, from commerce to the delicate matters of the heart? By the end of the afternoon, my father had pressed Master Fenwick to stay for supper. By the end of that supper Captain Fenwick was the new sailing master of the *Ann of Bristol.* Along with the command of a new vessel, Bartholomew Fenwick had been given permission to court Grace, daughter of his employer, Henry Godwynne. Me.

VIII Hester: North Devon July1642

I do think the Lord was looking after me that day, for at Hartland a handsome packman with a jolly smile sat me on one of his mules. I rode like a queen all the way to Bideford, except that a queen wouldn't have had the smell of un-cured hides that crept into every fibre of my clothes.

It was a route someway along the coast and misty in patches, especially near Clovelly. The packman's name was Isaac Lerwill and we passed the time with him talking of the preparations for some fight if the King and the Parliament could find no way to sort out their differences.

Now all this was a bit of news to me, for Kat and Tom Yeo spoke little of any matter but to do with my work and other conversations were in Cornish, which I did not learn fast enough. So I listened close. It seemed my new friend gleaned all the latest information as he travelled about.

I did once believe this to be too remote a place for such reporting but many gentlemen travel about with their servants. And where do the servants catch all the gossip if not at the tables of the inns and servants' hall wherever their master may go? And then they pass on what they know to men like Isaac the packman who carries word about better than any crumpled book. A news-sheet nor book b'aint any good to me who cannot read.

Anyway, he told me that the gentlemen of Parliament sent some number of demands to the King. The Parliament, says Isaac, first politely asked the King to make sure all the laws against all popish troublemakers were enforced. From the way he gave this out, all puffed chest and head up, I think my handsome packman was a Puritan by inclination, which I later found is a strong church in the Bideford district. He went on about how parliament demanded to control much of this and more of that; but I was dozing only saying 'Aye' and 'Nay' where he seemed to need it. But I did sit up when he announced that Parliament men declared they should control the army. Had it come to blows and Hester Phipps not know about it?

So I politely said to Isaac,

'What does the King reply?' a'cause I weren't going to let him see me as some backward bumpkin. Isaac told me,

'His Majesty replied "I think not" to all those clever gentlemen in London'. Isaac told me the His Majesty said a bit more than that about ancient traditions and ancestors and all. I understood none of it for my view is to leave all the politicking to the educated folks.

But Isaac, he got me to thinking. It seemed to me that there were those who were saying the King is tyrannical and bad for not giving up his control. And there are others who said His Majesty is commending that we leave matters as are for they provide a proved way of rulership. Now if the King is like the father of us all, does he not know what best fits the nation? Or do we defy our fathers? I suppose I did. But I said nothing of that to a North Devon packman.

What I did say to him was that there are some grand men somewhere who need their heads bashing together for then they would soon sort it out. But Isaac told me I was a foolish lass for surely the King was defiant and too proud and to prove it he had now a new army collected from up north and reputed to be made of regiments full of foreigners and Catholics. 'Are there enough Catholics to make an army?' I thought, but I did say nothing in case Isaac Lerwill decided he had let me ride far enough.

'There's to be a falling out!' he pronounced. He sucked his teeth then for this was a serious declaration, 'heads will be split by the swords of those great men before the summer is through'. Isaac the packman had a nasty habit of sucking his teeth when he was contemplating hard, and making a squeaking sound that made the lead mule jittery. He had pretty teeth, but it is a trying habit. I nearly lost my seating at that last remark. He was right though.

We took nigh on all day to cover the distance from Hartland and it was late in the afternoon, but nowhere near sundown when we reached Bideford. Isaac seemed to think that I owed him something and I bet he was planning ale and a backroom fumble on a tavern bench. Not a very pure inclination I thought, and I'm not that kind of lass - and anyway he reeked something awful. No matter his pretty looks, I had no intention of lingering with Master Lerwill, packman. So I kept a lookout for the outskirts of the town. When I could smell we were nearing a tannery I swung my legs over the mule away from where he was leading her and slipped off the sackcloth saddle. I was hellish stiff from sitting akimbo and I had blisters where a girl should not have sores, but before he realized I had gone I was calling my thanks, limping quickly down the hill into Bideford town. I bet he sucked his teeth then!

I needed to find a bed, and work, for this place was going to be no more welcoming than anywhere else to a poor girl. Though I had the few pennies in the pocket tucked tight inside my skirt the coins would go no way to keeping me for any time. But Hester Phipps has never been shy of work and resourceful is my watchword, so I set off downhill towards the quay.

The town felt all of a fluster. Where men-folk had finished their Friday trading they were purposefully creating barriers at the top of the town, others strengthening the shutters that hung before the narrow shop-fronts all down the hill. It took me no time to reach a wide river, fast-flowing and muddy, a quayside running across of the bottom of the High Street. I took in the view. Across on the opposite bank, tucked below a hill was another but much smaller town, shipwright yards and small quays lining the river-front. To my left I could see masts and rigging in a jumble and to my right, past a few gardens stretching to the riverbank, I could see the longest bridge I had ever seen in my life and every one of its arches was a different shape. I gawped a while, trying my numbers but losing count of how many piers there were to keep this miracle standing.

That evening on the widest part of the quay there were boys doing some marching about with broom-stales on their shoulder instead of weapons. They were foolish in their soldiering and untrained. I stood watching on the sly but laughed out loud when the 'officer'; a gangly lad in boots that were too big for him called for his army to do some clever move and each turned a different way to the next, knocking heads and hats all about. Some old men sitting outside one of the nearby inns jeered, shouting that the friends of the Bideford Brigade should be more a-feared than their foes. A dark-haired boy, one of the older lads and well built turned about and caught me looking, grinned and winked one handsome eye.

Handsome boys: how was I to know they would bring about the end of my stay in Bideford? I wasn't, now, was I. I wandered on, making my way back up through alleys and along lanes and eventually came back down to the opposite end of the stone wharf where a few boats were working the river making the most of the flooding tide. I got dizzy from watching the rising water eddy fast upstream so I sat a little way down a flight of steps that led to the river to let the feeling pass. I'd never let on to Isaac the packman that I had any vitals with me and so we'd eaten nothing all day. I pulled a piece off my loaf to tide me over and wrapped up the rest. In the shadows below the quay the evening air was cool; I was beginning to miss Kat's chimney corner.

I watched a bent grey-haired man on a small fishing boat while he prepared nets. There was a boy too who I took to be his grandson. The boy seemed a bit moon-touched for he kept piling sea-shells one on top another then taking the heap apart, laying the shells in a neat row then starting the stack again. The boy ignored me but the man saw me watching and called out,

'Do ee lack zumm'at, maid?' He had a stronger dialect than Isaac, and I had to think hard before I was sure of how to reply. 'Don't be shy, Hester', I said to myself and called back that I hoped that the wives of the hard-working yeomen of the town would be looking for a clean and tidy lass to set her hand to earning her keep.

'Where might I apply?' said I boldly. He stood with his head on one side. I think it was a good job his nets smelled worse than my skirts or he might have smelled more than a rat for all my fair words. His voice drawled, so strong was his accent, but I caught on quick.

'Ye'll vitch nort this o'clock on a Vriday,' he said, measuring me up. 'What canst 'ee do?' The water was rising fast and his head and shoulders came up now level with my knees.

Now, I do learn quickly, and remembering the lesson that Kat Conybeare taught I called down without falseness,

'I cook and sew. I can scour pots and wash good linen with care'.

'Can'ee gut a vaish? Mend a seine? You b'aint kivvy norn a Popish sort?' I was thinking on my feet and one thing I could tell was that he wouldn't wait for an answer, even though I had no idea what he was talking about so, nothing ventured, I answered in what I hoped sounded like a Devon voice,

''es Sir, and I am a good child of God's pure church, twice on Sundays'. He nodded but said nothing more. I smoothed my skirts and pulled my bodice straight, tucked my neckerchief into my stomacher. I no more thought I was fibbing for I was sure that I was a pure child and could be so twice on Sunday if needs be.

I thought the fisherman had dismissed me but after a moment he flicked a jumble of net onto the pile at his feet then leaned and touched the boy so very gently on the shoulder and made several gestures that seemed to mean 'Pack up and come!' Painfully slowly the lad carefully gathered up his shells into a holey piece of blanket which he slowly wrapped while the older man waited patiently. Then he picked up the child, set him upon his shoulders and climbed the few steps onto the quay. I waited at the top of the steps, and I will confess I could think of nothing to say for 'twas a tender moment and caught me unawares.

Anyway, the fellow just gestured to me with a twitch of his head and set off up a narrow opening and when I seemed to linger, he beckoned with one arm not even looking round as he strode away. 'Come along, Hester Phipps!' I told myself 'Nothing ventured, nothing lost and if the floor is too hard then tomorrow you shall move on!' so I picked up my bundle and ran after them.

IX Mary: Cornwall Autumn 1642 - July 1643

After news of Edgehill reached us it seemed that the whole county, already uneasy, was sent into a furious turmoil in those last weeks of '42, like a rookery all of a commotion when a buzzard is near. Mount Edgcumbe had quietly readied for months to protect the Rame peninsula. It had been fortified by Piers' tenants though nominally the family pronounced themselves 'neutral'. Saltash bristled with defensive barricades. Across the Lynher from our Uncle's place Henry Killigrew busily fortified his new-built house at Ince with the same bright bullishness for which he is so well known. Further west the disruption put men's tempers up and made for unsettled times, as gusty winds will make hounds jumpy and uneasy. The Cornish had not yet joined together, nor discovered their own strength.

Sir Uncle laid in more powder for the fowling pieces, bade my Aunt be more frugal with provisions and contributed a box of silver plate to pay Royalist troops. When she objected he exploded in a shocking outburst, raging at his wife to hold her tongue. Then, barely three weeks into '43 my uncle was taken ill, affected by an ague. Aunt Carew indiscriminately removed all perceived threats to his well-being. Hasty arrangements were made and my sisters and I returned to Penwarne where I thought I would be safe from nuptial negotiations while Aunt directed all her attention to Sir Richard. For all her zeal, she would discover she could not protect him.

January's gales, ripping the tiles or thatch off many a roof, even battered into Penwarne, normally so sheltered. Wind swirled round the folds of the valley and brought down a swathe of trees in Galowras woods. Nevertheless, it is an ill wind that blows no good, and as the storms eased and January passed my father showed the first sign of recovery, a little feeling returning to his cheek and to his limbs.

One morning quite late in the month Charles Trevanion, whose estate lay to the west of our parish, rode breathless and windswept, into the barton. My father insisted on being carried down the stairs into the hall to receive our guest. Low winter sun filled the room through the high, leaded windows. The servants set my father close to the fire and my sisters and I, anxious for news, fussed with cushions and refreshments and made ourselves generally indispensable. Charles, only a few years younger than my father, stood in stark contrast - vigorous and straight-backed. With the innate courtesy for which the Trevanions are known and loved, he spoke with my father as if the conversation was not in fact one-sided, pausing to acknowledge any tiny gesture or sound from his host. He was in a buoyant mood.

'I have news! Great news!' he exclaimed. 'How much have you heard these last two weeks?' He took a small flick of my father's fingers as a sign, and assumed correctly that we had heard little.

Continuing earnestly, he said,

'Just over a week ago three Parliamentarian men-of-war taking shelter in the lee of the Lizard, in sight of Pendennis, were captured by Nick Slanning's fleet! What a Godsend, for it provides His Majesty's army with armaments. And cash too for Sir Ralph Hopton to settle the back-pay of the soldiers…there's nothing more likely to raise their morale!'

Our neighbour acknowledged an imaginary comment from his old friend and continued, 'Timely resources, John, timely indeed but barely compensating us for the capture of one of Nick Slanning's privateers with its own cargo of muskets and cannon. Worse still, Tom Viel, you know…he is cousin to Bevil's wife, Grace. He was on board, disguised as a sailor. Now Parliament's news-sheets brag of their capture of a Royalist spy smuggling illegal weapons and as yet we have no word of Tom.' I knew the Grenviles would take this to heart for one of their own in such danger would be hard to bear.

Charles paced in front of the fire, his breeches steaming in the heat. His momentary brooding fled he became animated again,

'But no, wait, John, there is more!' There followed an astounding account of a battle barely two days previously, near Lord Mohun's home. It had been a stunning victory for the King's Cornish army led by Bevil Grenvile and Hopton, with Charles' son John at the head of his own regiment who then pursued routed parliamentarians from Braddock Church to Saltash. It was so poignant to see a father's pride beaming from Charles' face. To my mind this battle barely fifteen miles from our door had brought the war uncomfortably close.

'Now Nick Slanning wants me to consider the possibility that I might be appointed as Vice Admiral of the South Coast! He says his duties extend him too far and his inclination is to march with his regiment rather than stay Governor at Pendennis. Men are flocking to the Cornish units and Nick is recruiting Dartmoor tinners as well as Cornishmen,' declared Charles, with a flourish.

I wondered then how Gertrude, Nick's wife, would view his plans with two small daughters in her household and a baby on the way.

Small gestures from Papa and extensive but considerate commentary flowed from our guest. As he prepared to take his leave, I could restrain myself no longer and asked what had dominated my thoughts from the moment the Braddock fight was mentioned.

'Master Trevanion, Sir. Is there any news of any of our cousins, any Cornish gentlemen injured?' Then, despite my effort at discretion, my concerns spilled forth 'Is there news of Lewis Tremayne? Was he present at this encounter?' I could not bear the thought of Lewis in Cornwall and my not knowing. With a shake of his head our visitor replied,

'My dear, we lost nobody! As for your neighbour young Lewis I have heard nothing. To the best of my knowledge he remains with Bevil's brother Richard and the forces in Ireland.' I could not keep from blushing and saw Candacia watching, narrowing her eyes and pursing her lips, always a sign of trouble. When my father gave an indistinct mumble and a clumsy shrug of his shoulder our guest diplomatically drew his visit to a close, with a promise to return with more news as soon as may be. If he had no news of Lewis then I would find no ease, no matter what he said.

My Aunt, her confidence in the stability of my Uncle's health restored, had initiated new negotiations for marriage on my behalf. This time it was with James Chudleigh, now a Major General in Parliament's army, one of the Devon family from Ashton to whom we were already related by marriage. He was a young man excellently connected to other great Puritan families but just as the tentative conference began my Uncle, may he rest in peace, let go his tenure of this life.

The countryside being all beset with troops meant there was little opportunity for a fine funeral for March saw hectic campaigning in the county and my cousins' arrangements had to be measured by the turbulent times in which we living. Nevertheless, Aunt Carew took mourning seriously and consequently, and with her regretful apologies, the Chudleigh family were informed of our tragedy and matters were set aside.

As the spring of '43 dressed the hedges with brilliant bright green foliage and a mist of bluebells and ragged robin, our Cornishmen learned what their unity could achieve. Mining muscle and a bloody-minded spirit, which Parliament have called malicious, made their mark on their enemies but the successes also brought tragedy. One Arundel will tease me no more at a Christmas feast. They buried Sir John's eldest son, Jack, at Launceston in April.

And although 'A Grenvile! A Grenvile!' was the cry of the men following their hero up Stratton Hill, charging over and over until powder was near gone and men had fought for eight solid hours, the consequence of the King's victory that May morning would play out all summer. The confidence and pride of the Cornish regiments soared and our men were keen to march east for their monarch - with tragic results.

Yet, look hard enough and in every bad situation one will find good. The fluctuations of fortunes forced the rejection of my latest potential suitor. Whether she was in mourning or not, my Aunt was mortified to learn that Major General James Chudleigh and his father, who had been commanding the Parliament's army that May day near Stratton, had switched sides to fight for His Majesty. This she took to be a most personal and shameful slight to the Carew name. I, on the other hand, was doubly content for my loyalties were with the King and my heart was with Lewis.

In early July another hill saw another fight but this one was far from Cornish soil and at Lansdowne the nominal victory for the Royalists was bought at a terrible price. Sir Bevil Grenvile fell gravely wounded, dying as he led his troops. I recall I covered my ears as the parson reported the fatal blow of a poleaxe to that gallant head, the rumour that his young son John Grenvile, younger than me by nigh on four years, had been placed upon his father's horse to lead the enraged and reckless Cornish army to win the day on the escarpment near Bath. That tale has become the legend that all here believe.

Each Sunday, as Reverend Trewick gave out the latest ill tidings, I would feel sick. Though the name for which I listened was never spoken, eventually there came tidings of one name we did know; the Grenvile's coz, Tom Viel. It seemed that Parliament had wasted no time in hanging him.

X Grace: Bristol Summer 1642 - May 1643

My impending marriage was hanging over me like a black cloud but as a dutiful daughter does, I bent my will to that of my father. I truly believed he would know what was in my best interests and those of the family business so there were no romantic trysts in the wooing of Grace Godwynne. I could not count how often Bartholomew called, dined, and was closeted in my father's 'shop', scouring the accounts and records we so meticulously kept. I was not invited to join him. He and I did converse and, with Jinty as an escort, walked sometimes to the quayside. She was barely able to conceal her dislike of my suitor. We would discover that the feeling was mutual.

One boon was that Master Fenwick was often away, sometimes for weeks. Merchants including father, were anxious to have their vessels trading as the tensions mounted ashore. As I pored over accounts and ledgers I was aware of how much less adventurous the *Ann of Bristol's* trading pattern had become compared to previous years. Fenwick's recommendations persuaded my father that regular coastal trade in metals mined in the Mendip Hills, coal from Wales and timber or limestone were where steady profits were still to be made.

All hope of a peaceful settlement between the King and his ministers gone, there was a constant fear that troops would overwhelm Bristol. War of any kind was bad for trade. Civil war would destroy the commerce that was our lifeblood and neither the city council nor the merchants wanted to contemplate the prospect of soldiery within the town walls. The citizens' wives, about their daily business, now would huddle in nervous groups at the market stalls or street corners and Matthew brought reports of petitions for peace by the populace. More than one alderman disguised his own concerns by claiming that he spoke for the vulnerable women and children. I believe that the naïve souls, even my father, hoped for reconciliation between our King and his Parliament and believed that neutrality was sustainable.

Daily we heard the city militia drums. I thought of my brother Ned while rumour upon rumour spread of armies massing to attack us; one week it seemed the King was about to force our Mayor to open the gates, the next a Parliamentarian general was to meet with Aldermen who were hot in that cause, but each time excuses and adjournments delayed the occupation. Diplomacy and prevarication were characteristics of Bristol attitudes that autumn. Fenwick would press my father for a date for our marriage while I advocated discretion in view of the tense times and difficult circumstances. Once I wept that I was yet too young, too embarrassed at the thought of being wife to any man and even that I lacked a mother's gentle encouragement in the expectations of the marital bed. It was an unkind tactic and a lie as I knew well enough what men and women were about and I had Jinty caring for me at every step of my journey to womanhood. Nevertheless, the lie held and Fenwick was put off again.

Late October frosts had started to bite when one afternoon the pill warner hammered on our front door, bellowing '*Ann of Bristol*!' and I knew that Bartholomew would again be at our table that evening. All around the city, the messengers' black news of the day was on everyone's lips, 'Kineton! Battle! Edgehill!' and every time I closed my eyes I could only see Ned's dear face. Surely the apprentice boys would not be outside the walls of London, not in real combat? Dear God, the very thought of men in battle in England, fighting not foreigners but their own kind seemed the stuff of nightmares. It seemed unthinkable.

Rob Yeamans and my father, with Jinty's cousin Alexander James, Will Fitzherbert and Edmund Arundel had been closeted in the 'shop' for nigh on two hours and though the door was thick oak planking, I had heard raised, persuasive voices as I passed. The merchants were still conferring at suppertime, so were invited to eat.

As the town crier called seven of the clock, we sat down together. An air of conspiratorial tension pervaded the room as Fenwick, newly arrived, was introduced to the other guests by my father,

'Alexander James is the new Master Elect of the Society, Will Fitzherbert the Treasurer... have you had business with other members of the Merchant Venturers? Will Bevan perhaps? Edmund Arundel tells me you carried correspondence to his cousins at Truro so you know each other...and this is Rob Yeamans, my old and trusted friend as well as my associate through commerce.' Each received a peremptory nod in response. I sensed Bartholomew was not surprised that we had company.

'I do not wish to cause offence, Henry,' started Master James, 'but is it fitting that Mistress Grace be party to....' He paused, embarrassed, then plunged on, 'and can we be sure that Captain Fenwick is of our mind? There is much at stake, for Robert, for us all and we must be sure of our position. There are enough who have made their allegiances clear and they are not in our camp!' Alexander swept his gaze around the table, stopping at Fenwick, the challenge as powerful as loaded cannon.

'Alex, be still. Bartholomew is soon to be my son-in-law and naturally has my trust.' With a gracious flutter of Bartholomew's eyelids, the compliment was acknowledged but there was no deference to the other men around him. Father continued, 'Grace will dine with us for I will not send her from her own table. What we discuss is as much her future as this city's. Only Matthew will wait upon us and I would trust him with my life.' Alex took a mouthful of wine and swallowed hard.

My godfather, Rob Yeamans, took up the thread of their debate, briefly outlining matters for the benefit of the two newcomers and what I heard shocked me to the core.

'You know that there was a proper fight, a pitched battle near Kineton barely two days ago. Who won is not yet clear though the King is said to be making for London. The reality is that both armies will aim to sweep west to take Bristol now that it has come to blows, and we must look to our best interests.' He looked around. 'It is no longer the time to sit upon a fence and hope that these men of action will leave us to our trading. They will not and we already feel the tightening of our belts. Who do we want within our walls? Are we prepared to succour rebels against our King?' Edmund Arundel took a deep breath, following Rob's thoughts,

'The King's interests are ours, but there are men of influence in this city who will open the gates not to His Majesty but to that rebel, Essex, just as they have opened their coffers every time Parliament has asked them.'

'Aye, and forced us to open ours,' muttered William Fitzherbert.

'I have heard they have already sent to negotiate with Essex' second-in-command,' agreed my father, the food on his plate cold and forgotten. I was shocked for this was the first indication my father had given of any Royalist disposition.

'I knew that you would see sense, Henry. Well, then we must act.' Rob paused, frowning pensively, then continued,

'Whilst I was Sheriff I was given a Commission by His Majesty to raise troops and it is to my shame that I have not yet discharged my duty...' Evidently shocked, Arundel interrupted him,

'What, man? You should have told us before this day...'

'I had not yet thought it imperative – but, gentlemen, now the time is coming when we need to be prepared, to be ready to act!' declared Rob. 'We must have a plan in place to protect our city, ourselves, our families and our livelihoods. My own wife is newly with child again, terrified by every rumour that she hears and at me daily to secure her safety and that of our offspring.'

I knew of that for Elizabeth had told me how her mother became so agitated that she put her well-being at risk. I had recognised my friend's fears too well.

'The only way is to convince the Mayor and council that we must open the city gates to His Majesty's troops who will then protect us against the privations of the rebel forces. If we do not it will end with blood being shed over our walls!' pronounced Master James emphatically.

The air in the room seemed to freeze; I felt tears well in my eyes and my throat tightened for now I saw the stark truth. My family would be split, made enemies by this war. Fenwick, smoothing a hand over his slicked hair, sighed,

'Gentlemen, am I to understand that you propose to force the city to accept Royal troops, in defiance of the House of Commons and Militia Ordinance? Do you think that wise?'

'I knew he was troublesome, Henry! He is not one of us!' cried Alex James, 'I say we leave off this talk until we can be sure that our partners are trustworthy!' If only Master James had insisted that his fellow conspirators trust his instincts at that moment. But he did not.

Bartholomew narrowed his eyes and looked at each man in turn. When he reached my father he held his gaze, then,

'Gentlemen, gentlemen' that persuasive voice sighed, 'I am not a man to betray my purpose once engaged upon a course. I can see which way the wind blows here and my fortunes are linked with your own. I only assess the risks of any enterprise and test the tide to see whether ebb or flow will hamper that enterprise.' Always words with that man, cunning with his use of insinuation and allusion.

Thus, warily at first, began the debate of a possible plan to open the city to the King's forces, the company becoming increasingly animated. There were, Rob said, plenty more merchants, tradesmen of the city, sailors and wharf-men too, who had intimated their support. How long would the plan take to prepare? How long did they have before an army threatened the city? What tactics could be used to put off Parliament's men? Where would the Royalist army be billeted?

When Matthew brought new candles I begged to be excused. I went to my bed more ill at ease than ever. Something in the atmosphere prickled at my senses, an alarum that I could not identify. I slept fitfully, dreaming of rows of men all dressed in the same scarlet coat, marching up our street as one until a cannonball knocked them down like a child's game of skittles. Each man had the face of my brother Ned.

Ultimately, it was not the men who forced the pace. For all the talk of peaceable mutual accommodation, the Aldermen and councillors had no chance to resist the forces of Parliament. Colonel Essex arrived, threatening that Royalist armies approached to starve and lay waste to the city. The wives of half the council, including the Mayor's wife Madge Aldsworth and Mistress Ball, all terrified of bloodshed and the destruction of their homes, succumbed to the scaremongering. They begged, bullied and embarrassed our city elders to agree to allow Parliament's troops in for our 'defence'. The city soon swarmed with loud soldiers already hardened by Edgehill and all looking forward to a city billet, stout defences and a comfortable bed.

At home, Matthew was uncharacteristically volatile about the news, muttering darkly about parliamentary impositions and expectations. Despite his concerns, we considered ourselves fortunate in only having to find lodging for four troopers.

Even more fortunate was the timely departure of the *Ann of Bristol,* along with her odious ship's master, for with the occupation came requisitioning of vessels. If the *Ann* had remained in port she would more than likely have been taken up for the Parliamentarian fleet. The ship found a part cargo of indifferent wool from desperate merchants in Cirencester. Also loaded were several unmarked barrels from father's 'shop'. False bottoms hid coin, with which Fenwick had been trusted to trade wherever he could turn a profit. With the weather on his side, the man to whom I was pledged in marriage departed in haste. I failed to shed one single tear.

The 'shop' was of great interest to the new authorities. Inventories, cargo lists and every capacity to 'lend' financial assistance were assessed. A note was made of visitors and the source of any correspondence was noted, including the single brief sheet that I received from Edward, battered and over a month out of date. Nevertheless, the troopers in their

51

heavy leather coats and boots, slung about with carbines and bandoliers of powder, were less loathsome than Bartholomew Fenwick and civil enough. Except, that is, when they were in their cups. On those occasions, Matthew would sit with them, listen to their woes, sympathise at their bitter resentment of the new military governor, Colonel Fiennes. The steward would nod and murmur encouragingly and top up their tankards, they calling him a worthy sort of fellow.

Jinty reported on the growing numbers of incidents of unpleasantness on our streets. Our potboy was spat upon as a 'Papist rat' because his hair had grown below his collar and one morning I came down to find her and one of the maids scrubbing at the front door, old eggs and shells staining the woodwork and the step, yolk dripping from the overhanging timbers of our upstairs rooms.

'You'd think folk would have better things to do with eggs, and food so costly!' Jinty fussed, but I could see she was disturbed, and from that day I was no longer allowed to walk abroad, with or without an escort. My father remained tight lipped about the provocations; we never spoke of Rob Yeamans or his collaborators.

The winter of '43 was dry and cold and both armies were on the march early, well before the campaign season. The army of the Parliament's Western Association would need provisioning and Bristol would be expected to supply them. My father began to seem distracted, distant. I feared that he was slipping again into the melancholy that beset him after the death of Mama. How innocent I was then.

For it transpired that, after that night at our house, my father, godfather and many other Bristol men of good reputation had indeed taken their plans forward. Prince Rupert and an army of King's men now moved apace to secure our city with Rob and many others ready to smooth their way. The guardhouse in Wine Street, just a few doors away from our own, was to be at the heart of the action and the disenchanted troopers who lodged with us had undertaken to be part of the scheme.

Our inscrutable steward had played his part and at the Yeaman's house messages and plans had been smuggled to and fro beneath the demure folds of my pregnant godmother's gown. The midnight guard was to secure each of the city gates, the Royalists assembling up at Christmas steps and round at St Michael's Church. As the design unfolded the church bells were ready to ring, signalling to the King's army to the north of the city, who would then swiftly ride into Bristol un-opposed. Matthew and my father, the like-minded soldiers, sailors from the quaysides and dozens more individuals all had white bands to tie on collars and hatbands to distinguish them. Houses were to stand a white handled broom in their doorway to mark out allies in this mad enterprise.

Later some would be heard to say that Governor Fiennes knew of the plot all along, others would throw blame onto some goodwife who could not stop her mouth from running away with her. The consequence was the same: the plot was betrayed. The Royalists would pay dearly before they took Bristol.

The trials were pretended justice. Even Matthew faced an examination by the Council of War, which left him ashen, deeply distressed but free, from which I understood that he had devised a covering tale, which the officers could not shake. Matthew saved us for certain, though the soldiers billeted with us moved out under guard two days later and eight others took their spaces.

I had never seen a man hanged before. The gallows, especially built, stood not at the castle but in Wine Street, in the shadow of the Market House, at the level of our parlour and opposite the home of the 'rebel ringleader'. As soldiers tormented Our Lord with spears, so did they torment a man before my eyes that day when they hanged Robert Yeamans, his oldest friend and his god-daughter kneeling at a window as tears washed silently down our faces.

XI Hester: Bideford Summer 1642

On the face of it, the fisherman's cottage was a good enough place to settle and I thought, 'No need to move on, Hester'. And the simple lad with the shells, little Abel, took to me which meant that his pa - for despite his ancient looks it turned out that's what he was - was more inclined to let me stay on a'cause of there being no woman in the house to care for the four other children. I wasn't to have things that easy though and I worked from dawn to dusk in the home or on mending stinking nets or gutting the fish hauled in on the quay.

Fish was what we ate. Day-in, day-out. Along with the pottage that stayed on the hearth from one week's end to the next. I got so that I would have given my eye-teeth for a coney or a jugged hare. But it was a roof over my head and my bed beneath me; the bed was no more than a thin straw mattress and a blanket in front of the fire, but as long as I made sure we had dry kindling and some wood to burn I was comfortable enough.

I sometimes found little Abel curled up beside me of a morning, and he said nothing, being dumb and deaf too, but we managed well enough with the signs he understood and a few more that I taught him, and I could make him laugh. Not a proper laugh but a huffing kind of snort, which was a happy enough sound to make the old man to crack his broken-toothed grin when he heard it. I doubt if he'd grinned much since Goodwife Judd departed this life three years gone. So, there was I with Ezekiel Judd's brood to see to, fish and fire to tend and settling into the Bideford ways.

Old Judd was strict though and solid in his faith and would have us at prayers at the break of dawn and each one of his children were named for the church. Make-Peace and Zeal-of-the-Cross, were the boys though I shortened them down to Makey and Zeal. I shortened the girls' names too when their pa wasn't around to clip me for it. There was Joy-to-Come, the eldest and Hope-for-Good who was barely one year older than Abel. I reckon Old Judd ran out of notions for names when Abel came along. Makey and Zeal went out in the boat with their father for there was no money to pay for their schooling but neither seemed to worry about the lack. I began to teach Joy and Hope some little stitch-work for I told them if they were ever to rid their hands of fish-scales they would need an honest skill to their name. Well then, those maids were quick to learn so we made Abel new breeches and a shirt and made him snort his laugh over and over. I did like to hear that laugh; he was a dear lad, and no mistake.

Bideford was getting used to new ways alongside the rest of the county for the packman's forecasts came right and the King and the great men in Parliament were truly at each other's throats by the time the herring were running. Bideford was ready for anything that was to come. All the barricadoes were finished by September of '42, and there was a fort planned across East-the-water ready to hold town and bridge for Parliament, for the Puritan zeal I had heard in Isaac the packman's words was just as strong on these streets. This commotion betwixt King and the Parliament had the district on edge. Torrington, a town of demons if you believed all the Bideford talk, was full on the King's side back then and I could see old rivalries hid beneath the nation's hullabaloo, old grudges to be settled in the skirmishes between the thick Devon hedges.

We heard word from over South Molton way that when the Earl of Bath had come collecting troops for the King's army the townsfolk had sent him packing. The locals would have none of it. If you ask me, I think it was probably more about the big feast that the town Mayor laid on for the gentleman when the townsfolk were scrimping and making do with lean rations. They'd not be too happy at the expense but there, what do I know? Ezekiel told me some tale of the same town militia murdering one of their officers back a way and all a'cause he was a bit heavy on the orders and they a bit swift with the heavy hands. All very uncivil if you ask me.

Bread was up in price again and we were all feeling the pinch. It made every man, woman and child jumpy. Barnstaple merchants were uppity and puritanical, Bideford tradesmen all anti-popery. Soldiery rode to and from Barnstaple to Bideford, and out to Appledore, guarding the rivers, checking shipping. And every day down at the quayside the boys with their polearms, now a few more pikes than pitchforks, would go marching and making more of a band of soldiery than they did when first I arrived. But I truly never thought that they would need all that training.

I would watch them often enough for it was harmless entertainment and the dark lad with the roving eye would puff himself up when he saw me about. It was coming up to Christmas, (though many a Bideford house did not mark that popish feast) and I was following the family one afternoon, after church, Abel riding on his pa's shoulders, when I saw the militia-boy up ahead of us. So I dawdled a bit. The family went on and just as I was level, he turned about. Stepping up boldly, he took off his Sunday-best tall hat and bowed. The lads with him all snickered.

'And where does this little maid hide her pretty face?' he said, cheeky as anything. I told him to be off and play with his weapon and not bother a lass but he just laughed and made a lewd jest about his weapon that had me blushing as I walked on but smiling too. Another man with not very pure thoughts, but handsome as anything there was no doubting. He knew it too. Close-to up I could see his eyelashes were longer than a lady's and dark so that his cow-brown eyes looked fringed. His lips would twitch up to grin at every chance.

I should have seen he was too good to be true. Apprentice Shipwright Antony Jones was his name. How was I to know that Antony Jones was the apple of one Susannah Edwards' eye and she a little madam with a nasty side to her nature, and not a girl to turn the other cheek? I wasn't.

The weeks passed well enough and, if I was at the cottage alone with the boy Abel, Master Jones might come by on his way from the shipyard. He would tarry just a little too long.

I started having Susannah and her little crew of town girls, all barely old enough to have their courses let alone courting, pushing me and jostling at the market stalls every time they could. If Antony waited to speak to me after church on a Sunday, on Monday I would find the pitiful bits of laundering that I managed to hang about the narrow alley in front of the cottage all smirtched with ash.

That riled me no end for Old Judd would find me a clip about the head if he saw it. As if I didn't have enough to do between making ends meet and the halfpennies stretch to the occasional sheep's heart to break the boredom of the endless fish and keeping the hearth stacked with enough cricks to warm us all night and all the other woman's work. The last thing I needed was a spiteful doxy causing me trouble and me having to do the wash all over again.

By primrose time in '43 the uneasy truces, which we heard of but did not believe in, were all over and the fighting was for real. Many of the town militia had been part of the Parliamentarian army that marched with Barnstaple men to bite the heels of the King's men surrounding Plymouth. Antony was bitter that he had not been in the Bideford brigade, but not for long for he cheerfully convinced himself that he had been left in charge of the town's defences and spent March bragging of just that.

Our fort across the water was nigh on finished by then and more and more often we would have a squad of dragoons and the smart young officer, Major-something James Chudleigh, come inspect the works and the barricadoes. And a rare sight he was too, not much over five-and-twenty years old, with his fine chest armour glinting in the sun. A few female hearts were stirred to know that such a splendid, godly fellow was protecting our district. Antony tried so hard to get his officer's attention. He managed that in the end, only too well.

Now we being a port, there were boats to-ing and fro-ing. One morning not long past Easter, Makey came scampering up from the quay crying that there was some hullabaloo about the town, that an invasion was certain and that the terrible Cavalier soldiers were coming to take the women and slaughter all the men and bring in a Welsh army. Folk said that their boats were already seen east of Hartland Point. That set Hope and Joy off screaming and it was as well that Abel was out fishing with his pa and Zeal for he would have shaken something terrible to know them so afeared. To see what we could learn, we scurried out of our back lane.

I told Makey that he could protect his sisters and me better for being the strong and silent type and I scolded the girls to stop their row or they would call down the bad men on to us all. I was anxious to know the truth of this for I heard rumour and tall tales enough at the inn or the market stalls, aye, and from Master Jones, so we pushed our way along Allhallows Street to the bridge.

It turned out there was no invasion by sea but some silly plot muttered by a man in his cups in an inn the night before and overheard by one smart lad. I could guess who! The news had set the watch on their guard, but from then onwards it seemed daily that the soldiery in the district multiplied like never before. Then at the end of April we saw all but a handful of our militia march across the bridge and away to join the main Parliament army on its way to chase the Royalists into Cornwall.

With them went Antony Jones, sergeant and eavesdropper-extra-ordinary. On his hat-band he had a bit of old ribbon, fluttering like a lady's favour in tales of knights of old. And who gave him her bit of ribbon? Well, I did of course. And a kiss to keep his daft brown poll safe bewhiles.

Next day the segs in some girl's heel scraped a weal down the front of my shin while I was jostled and jitted at the bakehouse, and later I found a little slip of dirty linen at the bottom of my basket. 'Twas a mud scrawl, a little drawing of a dark haired man, formed of stick arms and legs but carrying a flag and sword. The other figure wore a skirt, her hair loose and scraggy. I guessed it was supposed to look like me but it was no flattering portrait. All around the picture of me there were little lines, all pointing to the body, each with a spot at the end. I b'aint a girl with much lettering or learning but I could read the note as well as if I had been a scholar. For all I was certain it was just the work of Susanna Edwards it made me jump a bit.

Little Abel shuffled up to my side and pulled my arm down so that he could see. I was sorry for he gave a little squeak and hobbled to the hearth, pulled the bag I had stitched for his shells from its hook at the fireside, and started stacking and re-stacking his treasures very fast. He did that when he was upset or anxious and sometimes he whimpered too. He was whimpering that day. Hope was watching while she worked her drop-spindle. She jumped up to grab the drawing from my hand, but like lightening dropped it again, as if she'd been burned. With a great gasp she hissed,

'Here is witchcraft!' Now that's not something you want to hear spoken aloud. But I told her it was merely some silly corrosy from a bloggy wench who deserved a whipping. Yet she snatched my hand and pulled me down. Once I was on my knees she bade me pray with her.

If you asked me I'd say that I b'aint the superstitious type. I know I'll cross my fingers and touch wood for luck and I won't whistle. But I don't believe a sailor wearing an earring will stop him drowning for I've seen superstitious men a plenty who have drowned. Funny though, my knees when I set down on them quick had new pains in them as if there were hot pins pressed through, which was strange enough as I'd reckoned I was too young for rheumaticky trouble.

Anyways, not wishing to offend Our Maker - nor turn away goodwill - I humoured Hope, even though I thought one mistress Edwards weren't the type to heed her prayers, then I shrugged off Susannah's little nonsense as a silly girl's prank, gave my knees a rub and went out to fix hooks to the mackerel lines with the boys.

Antony Jones did not come back that summer nor ever. He has a grave but his family cannot tend it for who of them can get to Launceston where the boy and so many others died fighting over some stupid bridge? Our glorious Major-

General Chudleigh became a turn-coat in May after the Stratton fight, and by the time the ships started bringing news of the loss of Bristol to the storming army of Prince Rupert, I had a battle of my own and one that I daren't lose.

XII Mary: Cornwall July – August 1643

July '43: we heard momentous tidings, news that weighed more heavily on the county than any yet that year, delivering a blow too close to home. I remember I was hulling raspberries when my sister Agnes stumbled into the larder. I can still see my fingertips stained as if bloodied. She was weeping and I was immediately filled with dread. I had to shake her by the shoulders to get any sense from her. That was where I learned of the fearsome siege at Bristol; how the King's western army had stormed a city which was surrounded by formidable Parliamentarian defences. And I learned too the names of men who would never see Penwarne again.

A Royalist news-sheet had come to us through the hands of Portmellon fishermen who fed the King's privateers with information and fresh provender, receiving intelligence and the occasional cask of Geneva spirit in return. Agnes's hand was shaking so fiercely that the rough paper tore as I snatched it from her. The crumpled pamphlet made ghastly reading. I scanned as swiftly as I could for Lewis' name, finding nothing but line after line defining how vast the undertaking of the offensive on the city had been.

Word would quickly spread through the servants' quarters and many had relatives in the King's army. Agnes had collapsed onto the cold slate floor, sobbing. To make all seem under control I calmly washed my hands, briskly bidding her get up and collect the household in the hall while I went to father's room. I knew something needed to be said. However, here was a quandary: someone should enlighten the assembled staff and of course, all that normally would be father's role. However, my sisters were as likely to faint as stand up before anyone, let alone with such news to convey. It might not be fitting, but it seemed to me that I had little choice.

Tapping gently at his door and entering quietly, I knelt by

his bed. He was awake. Once the waiting manservant had respectfully stepped outside, I explained carefully the outline of what I had learned, asked my father if I might address the Penwarne folk, to read from the pamphlet, if only to scotch rumour and to reassure our people with what little information we had. I received a slight twitch of the wrist, which I knew to be approval.

I do not know how I managed: it was one of the hardest things I had ever done but I knew the haunting anguish that was the consequence of my lack of information. These men and women, most of who could not read, were reliant on gossip or hearsay. They were our people and deserved to know the truth. Stepping into the great hall, a framework of light thrown onto the floor through the tall mullioned windows, without preamble I falteringly began to read into the silence. I remember little except arbitrary details such as the sign by which the King's armies should be recognised were green colours, boughs or the like, or that every officer or soldier should wear no band or collar around their necks. I recall thinking that the short summer nights were shorter still for those soldiers at Bristol's fight for the first attack came before dawn at 3 o'clock.

When I read out that the scaling ladders were not prepared and proved ineffective against the walls and ditches of the fortifications, old John Watty cried out tremulously that it had been the same at Isle de Rhé in '27 though the others around him shushed and bid him be still, anxious to hear the worst. Grenadoes and wild-fire, fire-pikes and petards assaulted our senses as the words leaped from the page. Hearing of the four miles of defences Silas Butland muttered that it was the 'self-same distance of the lanes between Penwarne and St Ewe church', to which someone else whispered,

'Nay, even further.'

I related how outer defences were breached but how there followed the fierce fighting through streets and into in the city which saw ambush from houses and cavalry charges along narrow lanes, cannon fire from the enemy, bombardment by the assailants. On another flank, water-filled ditches five feet deep had prevented the Western Army overcoming the defences but where despite all obstacles, the Cornish contingent had thrown themselves forwards, 'with courage and resolution as nothing but death could control'. I could not recognise the voice from the back of the hall but I caught the words "reckless more like" and thought then, how should courage be defined?

The defenders had not been able to manage the broken walls and from house to house, street to street, the Parliament's men had finally been beaten inside the old town, even though desperate women stopped up the Frome Gate with woolsacks to prevent their 'enemy' breaking through. Margery, Silas' wife, gasped and clutched her fists to her mouth, crying out at the horrors of this war that now even the women were driven to fight. We were shocked that day but since then I have come to understand the desperation which makes the weaker vessel take up club or cudgel.

Secret Royalists within the city had stopped ships' guns from firing upon the King's army. The second sea-port of the land was now in the hands of His Majesty King Charles but it had come at a terrible cost. As I continued to read the eulogies, our servants dropped, one by one, to their knees, one or two even crossing themselves as in days of old. There was a cold, dead stillness about the space despite the streaming sun.

For the news-sheet stated in stark black print, that father's old friend Charles' beloved son, John Trevanion, had died of terrible wounds. And with him in that first mad charge across Temple Mead had been the bold, daring Nicholas Slanning, newly knighted.

First Diccon, then Jack Arundel, John Trevanion…so many of our young men gone. And Nick was hardly any older than they were. Gertrude Slanning now tells how her birthing pains began the moment that he took the fatal hurt. At her husband's funeral John's wife, Anne, confided to me that she saw John's spirit beside her bed at midnight on July 26th. The spectre had a gaping wound in its thigh. How could she have known that it was on that day that they stormed the ramparts?

Nick Slanning never saw his son, while the heir to the Trevanion's estate is a hollow-eyed boy of eleven years. May God forgive me, I must confess that I breathed a sigh of relief when Agnes had gasped their names and not another's.

Cornishmen straggled back across the Tamar that summer to lick their wounds and many families grieved; more sermons were followed by growing lists of men lost to our villages and towns. And in Mevagissey I saw the blacksmith's wife wait week after week, going to the church daily to ask if there was news. Twelve months on she still could not tell whether her man lived or died for he was but another pikeman amongst the thousands. She wept that she would have been better to have left her home behind, taken her children and, marching behind the drum, become a camp-follower. Then, be it wife or widow, she would at least know which. I listened and I learned from the blacksmith's wife.

XIII Grace: Bristol July – August 1643

We listened to the church bells that rang out across the city as the Royalist army collected the corpses from the trenches outside the city walls. It was hard to celebrate a victory with so many dead or injured and the new role of our home was as much officers' hospital as hostelry for the first three weeks of August. I learned much about salves and binding wounds from the army surgeon whose frequent and attentive visits on his unceasing round of ministering could not save the slim, wiry form of one Sir Nicholas, who was carried to our hall, weakly laughing that he was so used to bullets that he had assumed they could not hit him. In the few days that I tended him he spoke to me of his beloved Devon, his wife, his daughters and the fort on the Fal that he pledged could hold out for the King for a twelve-month if needs must. How ironic! We now find his promise was a little empty.

He wept often for his friend Jack, for Colonel Trevanion had given us no time to tend his wound, though I held his hand as he slipped from this world.

The city, overflowing with troops, was also the Royal capital for a time that summer. The King rode into streets thronged with citizens cheering or hanging out of the windows. There was no sign of reluctance in the loyal toasts despite the depredations in the first hours of the Royalists' triumph. We were fortunate being away from areas deemed full of 'malignants' where the looting was at its worst. Military occupation has an ugly face no matter which side is in charge.

His Majesty made discreet visits to some of those who had demonstrated their loyalty. Jinty was buoyant at the prospect of His Majesty stepping over our threshold. I wondered how the cook would manage to find food to suit royal tastes on our meagre supplies. However, the entourage did not call at our home, entering instead at the Yeamans' doors where a tactful veil was drawn over the conversations therein.

Prince Rupert, on the other hand swirled into our hall like a whirlwind. He called primarily, he said, to set Boye upon the lazy laggards who would lie in bed under bandages, but as I cleared away a bowl of soiled dressings I caught a look, the cares of a lifetime flashing across a young face. He sat or knelt beside each mattress, quietly comforting or more vociferous, according to each man's need. I heard him rudely sarcastic about a Colonel Digby in one sentence, promising to lend a treatise on astronomy in another.

Wherever the Prince went his dog followed, a swift white shadow with a mane-like coat around his head and chest and hind-quarters covered in a short curly fur. As the Prince sat beside one officer's bed, the dog sat close to his hip, one paw resting upon the front of a booted royal foot looking intently into his master's face while the Prince absentmindedly ruffled the miniature ringlets in the hound's hair. They looked so out of place in the dismal conditions that I laughed aloud, a sound that surprised me - and the Prince too. He looked up sharply, the dog on its feet and alert in a moment.

'Madam, do you mock me - or do you mock my companion? For the former I would have an abject act of contrition, for the latter...I can think of nothing short of close imprisonment in the darkest dungeon for such a slight!'

He stood away from the bedside, and I feared he would knock his head on the beams for he was taller than any man I knew. I was horrified, unsure how to apologise for I had heard that this nephew of our King, come from the continent, was arrogant, sarcastic and rude. However, a split second after I reached the lowest curtsey I could make, a huge bellow of laughter rang out. With hand held out to raise me, the most charming, broad smile spread across the handsome features of this foreign dignitary,

'Boye! Here! Pay respect to this lady for she tends our good friends in her house!' at which the dog promptly sat, and raised a paw.

'Shake his paw or else he shall be mortally offended!' the Prince muttered to me, behind his hand, as if to keep the words from the hound between us. I did so and laughed again. I had never seen a dog like this nor one who could perform and said as much.

'When he was a puppy and I a prisoner I had months, nay years, to teach him such tricks and he is a rare breed which learns fast, though the claims by our enemy that he is also a necromancer do overestimate his intelligence!' I laughed again. 'My brother Maurice taunts me that Boye has had more hair-cuts than I have which I suspect is true, but that hair keeps him afloat. You should see him retrieve duck when we are hunting!'

I was still over-awed by this exuberant Prince in our house, the contrast with the military and the mischievous in him reminding me of my brother Ned. Was it possible that this man might ride against my kin if London was attacked?

'No hunting today, lad. Come, Boye! Mistress…I am sorry I have not been introduced. Your name?' asked our visitor, wrapping his cloak about him and moving towards the door as I stammered,

'Godwynne, your Highness. Grace, your Highness'. The Prince paused, head cocked to one side.

'Ah, your father - he has a ship, yes? He was with Master Bevan and the merchants who offered their service to His Majesty the King. The name. I remember well. I am surprised that you are still within your father's walls, for a woman of your uncommon looks and attentive nature should be wooed and wed by now!'

The irony of Prince Rupert's observation was not lost on me that day and I avoided his gaze. After another of his characteristic pauses came another bellow of laughter. 'Now, I must away to a Council of War! Good-day Mistress Godwynne!' he said, briefly acknowledging me with a flourish of his hat. Then taking leave of his officers, he bounded down the stairs two at a time, Boye close at his heels. As he reached the foot of the stairwell he called over his shoulder 'You should get a dog for a companion,

Mistress Godwynne! Get a hound!' and then was gone.

As men recovered or not as the Fates decreed, Bristol became the hub of the King's supply organization. His Majesty and his army moved out to besiege Gloucester so conditions in the city eased a little. Nevertheless, a spell of heat made us all fearful of plague even though the garrison now contained a fraction of the Royal forces. The small fleet of merchant ships that the Prince had remembered so astutely were now called upon to perform; the *Ann* was signalled out for an uncommon service.

Father, with Captain Fenwick, was ordered to attend upon Sir Ralph Hopton, the Deputy Governor. Both returned in brisk and business-like mood. My betrothed, however, could not contain his self-importance.

'It seems, Mistress Grace, that our banns must be delayed again for I am to be sent from your side on no less a matter than an urgent Royal commission. It requires more to reduce the city walls of Gloucester than the King expected, the citizens being intent on holding out. His Majesty is sending me to Antwerp for a mortar, a field gun big enough to bombard them into submission'. I shuddered to think of it - those people were our countrymen - but Fenwick continued, 'and it is *my* ship...ahhem!... your father's ship...which has been entrusted with the task of swiftly transporting the said artillery. We sail within the hour!'

My father seemed not to notice as Fenwick corrected himself, but was indeed enthusiastic about the mission, heading straight to the 'shop', assembling papers and some bags of coin, speaking rapidly as he worked,

'It is part of our duty to our monarch because the *Ann* is as swift a ship as any, and has one of the best Masters and a well seasoned crew. I will send a letter with you for my son Hal for I believe at present he should be in Antwerp.' He sat down and snatching up pen and paper, wrote quickly while voicing his thought aloud, 'You have the letter of introduction to Cornelis den Bogaerde? Hopton seems sure he is unsurpassed in this specialist field; foundry-work for such huge guns is uncommon. Hal may well be staying with

Elias Trip's son, who should be able to assist matters regarding acquisition of gunpowder. Certainly he will be invaluable should you need to re-provision the ship. Have we had time to take stores on?'

He did not wait for an answer but sealed up the package, intently running through arrangements for the ship's voyage.

'Planning the passage can be done on board, but there is no time to delay Henry,' Fenwick interjected brusquely, 'We have a slant; fair winds and the tides are with us. The *Ann* must sail now to make the most of them'. He almost pushed my father from the room but this professional arrogance did not seem to offend, the merchant deferring to the seafarer. Even then, I doubted that Bartholomew had been truly sincere in his regret at our separation for my betrothed swept past me with no acknowledgement at all, and the pair hurried off along Wine Street and down to the quayside at St Nicholas Back.

For two weeks, father's only topic of conversation was speculating on the progress of the mission. He was on the quay daily, seeking out newly arrived vessels for reports on sea conditions and prevailing winds. With each report he re-visited his copy of the charts, estimating courses. I remember saying to him that he should have sailed with the ship for he would have be less disquieted by the seasickness than the waiting. All I could hope was that we would have news of Hal. I did not dare hope that he would pay us a visit.

At last, the *Ann* delivered her alarming cargo in the depths of the night. Our household was set astir by messengers to and from Hopton's headquarters and the eventual arrival of Fenwick and a small group of dishevelled travellers. My brother was not with them but instead, in a faded cloak and with salt-stained boots, was a man whose blue eyes I instantly recognised.

As I directed the servants now rushing to bring ale, bread and cold meats I sensed something was amiss. There was an uncomfortable atmosphere between Bartholomew and the stranger, though it did not seem to touch the other men. The newcomers were introduced; the blue-eyed man was presented only as Sark, an expert gunner deployed specifically for this mission. Nevertheless, I knew there was a deeper association than that for my memory was not playing tricks and he did not take his eyes off me.

My father fired question after question about the voyage, the handling of the ship and the mortar and ammunition, quite oblivious to the tension or to the polite convention of introductions. It was the man, Sark, who seized a moment as my father swallowed a mouthful of ale. He stepped up to my father and bowed slightly, thick dark hair falling forward to frame a sun-browned face.

'Master Godwynne, may I offer my deepest condolences? I am so sorry for your loss.' It came in a rich, clear voice somehow at odds with the rough exterior of the man. I glanced at Fenwick and caught a look on his face that shocked me to the core. Furious but fleeting, there was a flare of rage, visceral and brutish. Then just as swiftly, his sycophantic features slipped back to their norm in a split-second.

'I beg your pardon?' father faltered. Fenwick moved to his side, elbowing the stranger out of the way.

'Enough! Sark! This is hardly the appropriate time. Henry, I was waiting for a private moment to break the tragic news.' Bartholomew glared again at Sark and the glare was met with an expression that was in no way contrite or apologetic.

'Appropriate time for what…?' My father must have had none of the sense of foreboding that was sweeping though me.

'I would have waited until we were alone but I now have to speak.' His tone was quite brash, and he glanced again at Sark. 'It is with the deepest regret that I have to tell you that your son, Hal, was taken by a sudden accident during the voyage.' My father's face turned ashen. Inexorably, Fenwick gushed onwards with his terrible report,

'Of course, I immediately punished the sailor who was so careless. He'll be careless no more. However, your son could not sustain the injury and his body failed. He was not strong. He died within hours. Nothing could be done. We had no choice but to bury him at sea.' Almost as an after-thought he added, 'I am sorry for your loss, Henry.'

The room swam for a few seconds, until I felt a firm hand on my elbow.

'Mistress Godwynne! Hey! Assistance here for the lady!'
I looked into a face not hidden by a monk's hood this time: the blue eyes were saying something that I could not translate. The dizziness past, I stammered,

'I thank you, Master Sark.' He pulled away suddenly abrupt.

'Not Master, I am no mariner. Just Sark!' was the gruff response.

Another pounding began at the front door, urgent and unsentimental. Despite any individual heartbreak the night's business of war would continue. By dawn the blue-eyed man Sark, the oxen and the wagons delivering the King's ultimate persuasion to his recalcitrant subjects in Gloucester were well beyond our city walls and my father and I were left to come to terms with our loss.

XIV Hester: Bideford August 1643 – May 1644

Come the autumn, different soldiers held Bideford, now for the King, though the changing sides made little or no difference to me, apart from Old Judd's grumbling a bit louder about God's retribution. Boats arrived with troops and sailed again with either more or less men, and sacks and barrels of food that would have been better in our bellies than the soldiers'. The ships made the townsfolk nervous too. We were guessing that once the King's army had triumphed at Bristol it was bound to be the other west-country ports that they would have their eye on. Even with its fort, Appledore could never have held out against the full might of an army; did Bideford have any more chance with all their guns set up in the East-the-Water battery? The local brigades made a stand at Torrington, but 'twas hardly a battle. Once the Royalists took Barnstaple it was 'Colonel Digby this, Colonel Digby that'.

Goodwives at their stalls on market day fussed, greatly perplexed, anxious that a basket of onions was sold for next to nothing to the quartermaster of the ungodly troops billeted in the town and fort. Old men who sat outside the inn on the quayside muttered about the scarcity of their tobaccky, but puffed away at their pipes just the same. We survived day to day, seeing prices grow higher week by week. It took more and more imagination to taste any meat in the broth that simmered over the hearth for there was less and less to go in it. And I was even more heartily sick of fish.

I hardly thought then that I was being ungrateful, but that's come back to taunt me now I have little but limpets and horseflesh to eat.

By September '43 the boys of the town wore a different colour band round their hats, but they practised their marching and wheeling just the same, only the voices shouting the commands had a different accent. For those who could tell the difference, there was another signature on the papers we needed to be able pass about the countryside - not that I went far. My knees began hurting something terrible.

Come Barnstaple Fair time, I could barely walk but I was determined to see it. And I'd been promised a ride to the town on the back of a wagon full of sea-coal. Old Judd was none too happy about the risk to my soul from the dark forces of the Devil and all his minions and he forbad the children to come with me, but since I was taking a basket of samphire and some pickled mackerel to sell and fair day being Friday he grudgingly let me go.

There I was on top a clean-ish sack to stop my skirts getting dusted, Dan Edwards sitting one side of me and one of the Huxtable boys the other with a pottle of cider to share.

'Where's your sweetheart Mary Trembles then?' I asked Dan, but he just laughed.

'There's prettier mermaids in the sea where my line is a-danglin'!' he said, so I cuffed him about the ear for being a dawcock, but he could see me blushing there was no doubt.

I quickly sold the fish so we could wander the quays to see the dancing bear, acrobats and jugglers. I b'aint never seen so many stalls, though Dan said there were half as many again before the war. I thought it looked like a small town, all flappy in coloured canvas, folk with trays and baskets calling their wares and selling stuff you'd never see the packman carry and all manner of things I could never see me needing, but it was summ'at pretty to see. I bought a fairing for one farthing for little Abel though I thought to myself that my master would likely have me damned for selling my soul for a trinket.

The very memory has me springing to tears again, but Abel was such a dear fellow and I did love to hear that little waif laugh, Lord bless his soul.

By the day's end, I was so sore that Dan gave me a pick-a-back to where we said we would wait for the wagon-ride home. I could barely set one foot in front of the other. Dan held my hand all the way to Eastleigh, letting go then, all awkward like. I should have known that the word would get around despite us slipping off the cart before Bideford's bridge. I told him to make himself scarce in case Old Judd caught me with a lad. That meant I had to keep a hand on the wall to help myself, clopping home up our back lane. I was never so pleased to see the cottage door as that day but little Abel did like his fairing.

The autumn was wet and the lad suffered with such wheezing in his chest that there were days that I thought he would never catch a breath again. Joy and I baked a c'oction of onion and honey in the oven and we gave the lad the juice but it made no difference to his ragged cough. By Michaelmas my wrists were beginning to ache too, so bad that I would wrap rag smeared with tallow and mustard around them at night. And it did little or nought to help. But I told myself, 'Hester, you have done nearly half a season mending skein nets, so 'tis no wonder your poor hands are suffering!' and I thought no more of it.

I would have been wiser to think no more of the Bideford boys either but I did and Daniel was my downfall. Or I should say that his sister Susannah was.

I was certain that she had done the silly drawing I had found in the basket. I had burned the thing but Joy and Hope had taken the matter to heart and every night since, when they were at their prayers, I could hear them breathe the words 'deliver us from evil' with just a tad more feeling than the rest of the lines.

Winter came on, though if I do remember right it weren't too bad. Christmas was commonly kept very quiet in a town like Bideford with more private devotion than public display, but '43 was enough to offend even the least puritanical burgher. Parliament might have passed a law and cancelled Christmas but our town was full of a swaggering, roaring Royalist soldiery. And they weren't to be denied their season's frolics. I couldn't tell how many new soldiers we had, for Barnstaple took most of them, but I would guess that there were perhaps half as many in the garrison in Bideford town as there are here at Pendennis now.

The language in their songs might have made many a

goodwife blush, but catching the jollity on the north wind blowing down Allhalland Street, I 'fess I was a little maudlin for the old days. I got to remembering some of the old festivities at Twelfth Night. It's the truth that Wine Street saw some rare times over yuletide and even back at Radstock my pa would play the fool for the mummers. Old Christmas, King and Queen of the Bean; there was none of that at Ezekiel Judd's.I didn't join in the revels. I'd have had to be mazed! If I wanted to keep my place at Old Judd's hearth I knew better than that. Mind, I decided in '43 that I bain't cut out to be a Puritan.

The season of good will must have fired Daniel Edwards up and he thought he would try his luck where Antony Jones had failed, bringing me a length of ribbon the colour of moss as a gift for New Year's Day. I was flattered 'tis true. Which girl wouldn't be? I knew it must have cost him nigh on a day's wage. The trouble was green's not my favourite colour. But it was the colour of Mary Trembles' eyes for she'd got a jealous streak in her that would sour the milk in a dairy. She'd set her cap at Daniel, even if he never knew it, and her best friend in the whole of Devon was none other than that Susannah Edwards, and she was my lovesick loon's brother. So now add to their little group of friends the town busybody Temperance Lloyd, a strange biddy if ever I knew one, and before long I had a barrel full of trouble rolling my way.

Being a straightforward sort of lass, I thought once the grieving for poor Antony was past they would have forgotten me, what with the coming and going of the soldiers and life in general turning a bit upside down. Anyway, the jostling and nastiness at market had stopped. Mind you, I had not been gadding about as much. Joy had been doing more of that work for me whiles little Abel had been poorly through the winter and my time was taken with tending him. And my legs still hurt.

Came the spring and the longer evenings, Daniel even ventured to the cottage to ask Old Judd's permission to walk out with me, though all he got was an invitation to pray with us for guidance from the Good Lord. I knew even though his pa was churchwarden before the war, Dan didn't have praying on his mind. The look on Dan's face was like he'd been hit with a skillet and it did seem so funny, though I got a beating for giggling after the door was slammed in his face.

But now where'd I got to?

May Day passed with no festivities due to the soldiery being on the lookout for some Algiers pirates who, rumour had it, had escaped from Launceston gaol. I heard talk that Mary Trembles spent her days weeping and moaning to Susannah, and anyone else who would listen, about how she was affianced to Daniel. I am sure that was a big fat lie for she was as skinny as a rake and not his type. She was saying as how I was stealing him away which was a fib too for I gave him no encouragement at all. If Old Judd had got even a breath of me and any boy I would have had a whoppin', especially after Dan had lain his intentions out at our cottage door. All her tales of us fumbling in the bluebell woods was a lidden too. Beside, Dan was taken up into the militia as well as his work, so we hadn't a church chime to share betwixt us.

Still, Susannah was having none of it and told her ma. Goody Edwards went to the sergeant-at-arms who had recruited her son. He went to his officer…'twas like Moses leading all those people one after t'other. Suddenly every body in Bideford seemed to want to meddle in Hester Phipps' life. But that wasn't all.

Temperance Lloyd had started saying that she knew how I was making Ezekiel Judd's youngest lad sick, then making him well again. She claimed she'd heard me gloat that Judd would keep me in bed and board just so I would look after his son. The bulhaggle also spread about that she'd heard me talking to a black cat - which is rubbish as the moggy in our courtlage is a tabby with white paws. And to cap it all, on the last day of May, Mary Trembles started going around telling all how she had seen me fly under the middle arch of the Long Bridge on my broomstick the night before, crying out that I was away to fetch the Parliament's army!

Did anyone ask her what she was doing out after curfew? I'd stake my hat they didn't but anyways I weren't in any position to quibble bye-laws.

Now, Bideford is a small place, even with a garrison, and all this got to the constable sharp-ish and he went back to the Captain of the garrison and the sergeant-at-arms and they all went to the mayor who called the priest. Then, fast as lightning, I was dragged before them all at a long table at the back of the tap room of the best inn on the quay where the Royalist had put their headquarters.

The constable hauled me up and I faced all those men, and mighty afeared I was, I can tell you, barely able to walk and my right wrist so numb that I could hardly hold the Bible. They took that for a sign then. And not a good one either. I saw the vicar mutter something to the mayor who shook his head, his mouth all turned down and grim.

The captain-fellow had the constable fetch up the girls, and again each one put their story to the officers and all and there was some dudder when Temperance Lloyd had her say, I can tell you. But the captain of the fort wasn't having any nonsense and may God and the Saints bless him for that. He called up Daniel who had stood out for being a good militia-man and keen, so much so that his sergeant put in a good word for him saying he had been keeping his eye on Daniel and had plans for making him up into some special type of soldier. Anyways, when Daniel spoke they seemed to like his words.

I weren't allowed to speak at all but my knees were knocking so hard and my teeth a chittering so much I reckon I would have bit off my tongue if I'd even so much as started.

Then they brought in Ezekiel. The constable asked him about Abel and the old man wept that the boy had been so weest over the winter that he didn't think that his son would have lived without me coddling him, and that I was looking after the other childer so well that they all prayed for me each morn and eve.

The officer asked him about the night I was supposed to have flown under the bridge, but Old Judd said he'd seen that I had lain by Abel all night. Then the vicar ups and says that meant nothing as a witch would leave her familiar behind, in her own shape, to befuddle the innocent as she went about her black works - but the sergeant replied that, begging the vicar's pardon, he would rather wait upon the word of the lad Abel.

Now, at that, I cried out and the constable cuffed me round the ear. They fetched in poor little Abel, Makey carrying him in and setting him to the floor, keeping the boy and his pa separate in case justice should be spoiled but the little mite looked frightened out of what few wits he had.

I don't think the Captain had been told that Abel was not like other boys for when he asked him questions and got no reply the officer got mad. The constable had been trying to tell him, but I think the sergeant and the Captain were leery for it was well into the afternoon by then and they had missed their mutton, ale and bread. They were hardly attending to the constable at all. In one sliver of quiet I cried out,

'Sirs, please, he cannot hear. Abel cannot hear nor speak, Sir!' I could hardly recognise my voice for it scraped in the air like a broken fiddle. I got another cuff about the head for speaking but the soldiers had heard me and so had Abel. He squirmed out of Makey's grip and staggered across the floor, falling to my feet and clutching my skirts with his spoony-shaped fingers and what happened next was like one of St Mary's miracles.

For Abel spoke. He spoke badly and was not really understandable but a croak, a feeble noise that sounded more like an animal rang about the room.

'Thluv! Thluv!' he kept repeating and would not let go of me, though Makey pulled and the vicar tried to prize Abe's hands open. I was coming over all zaundy and about to fall on my face, when Old Judd jumped up.

'Your honour, may the Lord ov Hosts be praised, vor here are marvels! There is God's work here today!' he cried out,

'My son Abel God-be-Praised Judd could not speak. In all his eight years he has been silent. This lass brought him virst to laughter and it was like music to my ears. Now I cannot take this speeching as aught but a sign vrom God. This maid cannot be in league with the Devil vor how else could such a wonderous thing happen at her veet?' He fell upon his knees and began to pray.

That was the most words I ever heard Ezekiel Judd say that he weren't taking from a prayer book, and the message was plain. By now the room was a riot of noise, folk leaning through the servery crying out, 'Praise the Lord!' and such like, and Mary Trembles sniffling and hiccoughing while Susannah glared at her brother's back with a black look like thunder was coming. Temperance just looked odd, with shining eyes and rocking to and fro, mouthing something silently all the whiles. The officer had to bang the hilt of his sword on the table to get the uproar under his control again. The others at the bench put their heads together and after they had argued a bit, the sergeant-at-arms stood up.

He called over Ezekiel and made him stand close to the bench so that nobody in the room could hear what was said. My teeth were knocking together so hard my head ached. All I could hear was them rattling. Them and the heart-breaking whimpering coming from the corner where Makey had Abel in his arms clutched tight to his shoulder so he wouldn't see. Yet I was too mazed to cry.

Judd had his hand on the Bible and was nodding hard. The Captain got on his feet,

'By the authority invested in my by His Majesty the King, I call this court to order.'

A buzzing began in my ears. Who had decided this was a court and nobody told me? It was nought like the court in Bristol, but all of a sudden it did seem twice as deadly for I knew what would happen. They had decided to themselves that I was a witch.

The Mayor stood up and called forward Temperance again, made her hold the Bible fast in both hands and swear that she spoke the truth. He asked her again to tell the court what she knew of my cat, how sure she was of the colour and why she did believe ill of me. He said they had evidence which they would measure her words by and if she were found to be at odd she would be in some great trouble for she was swearing an oath, and did she understand? I thought my head would burst; my knees and wrists were so sore it was like they were on fire and still I had to stand.

In the end, it came down to the colour of a cat; not black but a tabby ratter that lived in our alley and liked to rub its shoulder on my skirts while I was pegging clothes out on the washing line to dry, the very same moggy that Old Judd had called after his wife, Hepzibah. In his eyes it could not be, had never been any witch's familiar and nothing would stand in the way of Ezekiel Judd's testimony on that.

The moment the Captain heard her nonsense a second time, he thrust his heavy stool back from the table. Taking the Lord's Book in his hands, he declared that the court was closed, that it was the bench's ruling that I was not guilty. He also decreed that, on the next Sabbath, the town constable would give Temperance Lloyd fifteen lashes of the whip at the cart's tail for lying upon oath. That, he said, would teach other silly women not to meddle or waste the time of men with more important matters to attend to.

What he said after I didn't hear for I was in a dead faint on the floor.

XV Mary: Cornwall August 1643

To hear news of the progress of King or Parliament offered me little comfort for there was no word from Ireland or Lewis. Time plays tricks upon my mind and the month of August 1643 felt more like a year for it was then that I was drawn into the machinery of war, and so commenced the journey that led me here.

Where to begin? I had escaped one marriage due to the changeable politics of the Chudleigh men: Sir George and his son, my erstwhile 'intended', James. The repercussions were as lasting as my Aunt's indignation. Now I was to discover that her step-son, my Roundhead cousin Alex, at his post on St Nicholas Island in Plymouth Sound, had spent time a-plenty considering the Chudleigh's change of heart while he also contemplated the implications for his wife Jane and his children. The sequestered estates of 'delinquents' provided the funds for both armies; Alex was putting his family's future at risk if he was backing the losing side.

Good news travels fast, and bad news even faster, and just two days after the fishermen brought us the news of Bristol, another small boat slipped into our cove at low tide. I was collecting seaweed for a tincture and was absorbed in my work, only hearing the hull of the skiff rasp as it beached onto the sand. Two men clambered from the little rowing boat and as one hauled it a little further from the waterline, the other, a tall, lean figure that I knew well splashed towards me across the rippled sand: Alexander Carew. His neck hunched into the collar of a scruffy cassock coat and a Monmouth cap pulled down on his chestnut curls, he looked much older than I remembered.

I was dumbstruck. Alex should have been more than twenty miles away, a garrison commander guarding Plymouth Sound, and subterfuge in a Cornish cove was hardly his remit. Before I could curtsey Alex grabbed my elbow and steered me to a gully between the rocks where we would not be seen from the shore, whispering,

'Have you been at Antony recently? When did you see Jane and the children last? Tell me are they well?' I could not reassure him as it had been weeks since I had last ventured from Penwarne. To visit Antony House was to remind my Aunt of her plans to alter my matrimonial status but since his wife and my aunt were sisters I could not believe that any harm could have come to her and told him so. What I heard next took my breath away.

'I wish to surrender St Nicholas Island to the King and I need your help to do it!' He put his hand to my mouth to stem the protests that were about to pour from my lips,

'Mary, it cannot be easy for you but I would not ask this if I did not believe that you hold the key to my future.' Taking my hand he continued, 'I have been thinking.' That phrase - forever loaded with consequences.

'Since the King has pardoned my Uncle George Chudleigh and cousin James for their imprudent opposition I have reason to believe I too will receive his grace. I have had time to regret the harsh words betwixt my father and I, God rest his soul, and with the King's cause so strong I cannot face the prospect of …well, let enough be said that I fear that my decision was a misguided one.'

I quickly recounted how his portrait had been cut from its frame after his distressing departure and where he would find it stored safely away, for which he kissed me on the forehead and squeezed my hand, but continued urgently,

'Word must be sent to the King's commanders. To the east to Exeter, to Sir John Berkeley ideally, as from there word will easily reach Prince Maurice and His Majesty. Alternatively I need to get through to Colonel Digby who I believe to be at Tavistock.' I cried out, forgetting the clandestine nature of our meeting.

'Hush, hush. Hear me out, Mary. For pity's sake, hear me.' I pulled my hand away, and leaned against a rock, warily waiting. What he proposed was an impossible folly.

He told me that he had noted how my step-mother had taken Penwarne family matters into her own hands since my father's illness though he added, 'God help me I have no idea why she feels she has the right.' It was a small but significant salve to my battered self-esteem. He rushed on,

'But that is where my strategy lies. I can arrange for a pass for you to travel to Chudleigh, to Ashton Manor…' I began to utter a protest but Alex stopped my lips again. 'Yes, I know that your aunt will have none of it but the authorities in Plymouth, and elsewhere for that matter, have yet to hear of Lady Carew's affront.'

My nerves being stretched to breaking pitch, this made me giggle unbecomingly for it sounded too much like the name of a tune one might play on the spinet or lute, like Lady Hunsdon's Puffe or Mistress White's Choice. Alex frowned at me but pressed on,

'Gossip cannot have spread so far, and my step-mother, your aunt, will have ensured that the embarrassing situation with James has not been made common knowledge. What could be more innocent than for a maid to be travelling to her suitor's family home, especially since the Chudleighs are already your relatives by marriage?' A hundred observations sprang to my lips, not least the fact that the countryside was over-run with soldiery and officialdom.

'Much of your journey will be by sea and even ashore you might be surprised at how little military you will see, cousin. The Lord Lieutenant cannot have his men everywhere, and besides, I shall arrange for you to have a pass to secure you through Parliament's lines. Then your kinship with Sir George Chudleigh will see you safe.'

It seemed simple. Was I so naïve? And why did Alex Carew need me and why come to Penwarne? I asked him. His explanation was straightforward. There was nobody else he could trust: these were matters better suited to the word than the pen. He would not commit his plan to paper. He had one servant whom he could trust to go to Tavistock with the message, but his real hopes lay in my hands.

What was I to tell my father, my sisters? He explained that I would receive a letter from Jane, asking me to Antony to keep her company and after that there would be little to explain. If Jane wished to go to Alex's mother's home, perhaps to take her youngest children to see their great-grandmama Chudleigh what could be more innocent than for me, a potential bride in the household, to accompany her?

This was awkward. If Jane, Alexander Carew's wife, was party to the plan then the thought that I would be undermining her hopes left me with much more of an obligation even if the plan was reckless.

'Mary! Jane really does need you. It is no lie for she is with child again and this time I could not bear it if ...' I stopped him with my hand upon his arm, my mind whirling with thoughts of my own. I took a leap of faith,

'Alex, I hear you. So for the sake of Jane and your children, born and unborn and for the good of His Majesty the King, I will do as you ask. But I would have a favour in return.' The tide was beginning to lap at our feet, and with time of the essence I rushed on, telling Alex of my secret, of Lewis Tremayne and the hopes I had of him returning one day to fulfil his promise.

'But I have had no word, nothing except a rumour that he serves in Ireland. If I do this service for you, Alex, promise me on your honour, that when you reach the King's side you will send news of Lewis to me and get word to him that I am still his Carew chick.' His words will stay with me forever.

'That I will do for with all my heart I cannot wish you anything better than to find your soul-mate, for Jane is mine and I would have no other. I cannot bear to think that because of my imprudence we are separated and that she could lose all. But it will be put to rights, with your help.'

The tide was well past the turn and he needed to leave. Alex hugged me tightly, saying,

'I have no words to thank you, Mary. Await the messenger from Antony. You will know Jane's handwriting. God speed you well!' I called, 'and you!' but he had already run into the shallows where the boatman and he pushed the skiff back into the waves. They took up the oars and rowed out to the sailing smack waiting offshore, the rising sails already filling with the wind that would take him back to Plymouth

Sound.

Two days later a packet arrived from Jane and I was able to announce at supper that I had been called east. Candace snickered and said she hoped Aunt Grace had a new suitor waiting, an aging and pious gentlemen with bad teeth looking for a young wife. She was ever the spiteful minx. I went to my father's room and kneeling, asked his permission to travel at first light the next day. The slight lift of his fingers marked his approval, and by breakfast I was aboard a small boat destined for Looe, from where I was to ride. I would be at Antony by nightfall.

XVI Grace: Bristol August 1643 – 19th September 1643

Gloucester did not fall, despite the mortar and all the King's men. We heard stories of scores of homes outside the city razed to the ground by the Gloucester residents, the buildings burned to a barren wasteland so that the besiegers would have no cover. It made Bristolians shudder to think what might have happened outside our walls. However, it could not make the impositions and deprivations any the less for knowing we had been fortunate. The city was full to overflowing, and the only creatures to find room were the lice.

I could barely think straight, moving from one task to the next in a daze. Grieving for my brother brought my spirits to a low point. The regular presence of Bartholomew was oppressive. Although he had stopped pressing for the banns to be read, his persistent self-righteousness was galling. In addition, my father began to show signs of a deep weariness, nothing specific but he had lost his usual robustness.

The *Ann* made a voyage to Kinsale in southern Ireland. Another voyage was made to France where support for the King was firm, though Fenwick reported that they barely escaped a parliamentarian fleet off the south coast of Devon. The returning cargoes were worth little except for the city's supply but the information from Ireland was valuable: there would be reinforcements for His Majesty's army by the turn of the year. Though there was no profit to be had, the grain and the gunpowder were essential and kept us on the right side of the authorities. Charting the progress of the voyages, my father's illness seemed to improve a little, invigorated I thought by his contribution to the Royalist cause or the pursuance of his old habits. If the ship was alongside he would became lethargic again. We had little enough food but after a few mouthfuls he would push his plate away, complain of fatigue.

Because of the business with the King's special voyage my father's 'shop' saw more visits from overseers of the supply lines and we seemed to be the favourite billet for officers en route with messages from one Royal army or another. Although we were not as cramped as many of our neighbours, it still stretched the resourcefulness of Matthew in obtaining fresh provender. Since the fateful voyage to Antwerp, gunner Sark had remained part of the crew of the *Ann of Bristol*. As the transfer of men and muntions, not to mention information, was the largest part of the cargoes the ship carried, he could to be found wherever Bartholomew Fenwick was doing business. He was even occasionally a guest at our table though Sark was no conversationalist. That there was an uneasy relationship between Fenwick and this taciturn stranger was evident. It seemed to hint at more than the collaborations of men fighting for the same cause. However, strange times make for strange bedfellows, and I paid it no heed for daily there were obstacles to be surmounted, worries to overcome.

Late summer heat in the first weeks of September soured the air in the city to such an extent that rumours of plague and the sweating sickness began buzzing round the crowded streets like flies. Our cook became ill with a raging fever and Jinty took over the kitchens. When the cook died, my confidante remained in charge for there was little chance of finding a replacement in the chaos of a city in conflict. My father was again ill and took no interest in the servants, leaving the matter to Matthew and myself. I missed my conversations with Jinty but there was nothing to be done about it. We would all have to manage as best we could. Fenwick was at the house daily while the *Ann* was in port, solicitous for my father's health, bringing another bottle of some strong wine which he told father had been a gift from a factor in St Malo but which, it seemed, was not to Fenwick's taste. I tried to excuse myself with household duties but could not entirely avoid Bartholomew's company without seeming rude for he mentioned marriage not once. I thought, too innocently as it transpired, that his failure to press forward his suit was in consideration of the circumstances surrounding us all.

With every messenger who laid his head down within our walls, we had news of the King's fortunes. Gloucester continued to refuse to surrender to His Majesty's demands and now there was word of a relief force from London, a brigade made up of the city's regiments of militia to support the beleaguered town. Would Ned be among the Parliamentarian units on the march? I had no way of knowing. I could not express my concerns to anyone, least of all my father whose condition continued to fluctuate but which seemed to deteriorate with each bout. I could not help but notice that the buttons of his doublet now pulled tight across his stomach even though he ate less than a sparrow might.

Looking back to that time is like watching a ball slowly rolling towards a stand of nine-pins. It began one morning with a domestic incident which in itself was minor. The potboy though still not of an age to be recruited, of necessity had been promoted to footman and had been carrying a tray of food to a Royalist infantry officer who had newly arrived from Dorchester.

The ensign was one of the first we had encountered who lived up to the foul reputation which, according to their opponents' news-sheets, the 'Cavaliers' had earned. He demanded more victuals and wanted them quickly. The boy, Tom, had been running to attend to the call when he encountered Fenwick in the passage to father's 'shop'. The clatter of tankard and tray and the curses over beer-stained clothes brought Matthew hurrying to attend the commotion. I looked over the banisters but could not see round the stairwell.

The altercation between our steward and my betrothed seemed heated but the exchange was in low undertones and hard to hear. I heard a slap, the boy gave a shout, followed by more disputation; one individual retreated along the hall. I returned to attend to one of the last of our wounded and thought nothing more of it.

Bartholomew did not appear for dinner. I assumed him to be at the quaysides. At table my father complained of overwhelming tiredness and said that he would retire for the afternoon instead of attending to business so I was alone, trying to make sense of the household accounts, when Jinty tapped the door. She was uncharacteristically reticent, asking to speak to me confidentially. What happened next was a blur. I recall her starting with an expression of concern, she seemed afraid yet she got no further than 'Captain Fenwick...' when the door burst open and the Constable of the Watch, with two armed men, pushed in bellowing,

'I am authorised by the Governor of Bristol to arrest Matthew Allerway for assault. Where is he? Search the place!' and the soldiers sped off towards the back of the house, quickly finding our steward who, unabashed, had come to see what caused the noisy intrusion.

They grabbed Matthew and he was unceremoniously bundled from the building. I tried to insist there must be a mistake, but the watchman would say nothing other than it was a serious matter, the Governor's orders and we would be better holding our tongue, or we risked being accused of obstructing justice. We were stunned but within moments, and before Jinty could confide any more, Fenwick strode through the door.

'I see the authorities have dealt swiftly with the trouble-maker. It will not do to have the stability of the city challenged by unruly behaviour and insolence. It could be the start of civil disobedience, insurrection of the most insidious kind. Servants in league with the enemy...' I could hardly believe what I was hearing. But it was Jinty who spoke first,

'Master Fenwick, they have arrested Matthew Allerway! He is the last person on God's earth who could be charged with civil disobedience! How can you have formed such a low opinion of such a well-respected man? Especially since you know very well to what lengths Matthew went to assist ...' Fenwick stepped towards Jinty, so close that the toes of his shoes slipped beneath the hem of her gown. His expression shocked me for it was both smug and menacing at the same time.

'Mistress James. So righteous,' he hissed, 'It would be better for you to keep silent, for you speak of matters beyond your station. You are merely a servant in this house and I suggest that you remember your place.' He glared at her, threateningly.

I can still hear the brass lantern-clock on the wall as it measured its slow tick-tock-tick. He turned around abruptly, striding to my side and placing a heavy hand on my shoulder.

'I will overlook your impudence for now. Go! You are dismissed. Mistress Godwynne and I do not need you.' Jinty had no choice, and nodding briefly, she left. We never finished that conversation.

I have often wondered if my life took a strange direction at that point. In those moments, though, my thoughts were in a whirl. Fenwick presented to the world the face of a respected man, one who had asked respectfully for my hand in marriage. Yet he had taken control with a malevolent arrogance hidden behind his smooth fawning. My father was ill, it was plain to see. Hal was dead and Ned could not speak for me because, according to everyone around me, he counted as one of 'the enemy'. Matthew was under arrest and I had no idea why. And now Jinty's support had been callously removed. I realised I was alone.

That evening there were no other guests as we took supper in the small, private chamber on the first floor, a concession to the family while the billeted officers took over the hall downstairs. Father was informed of the domestic crisis. He seemed so exhausted that it hardly made an impression. Fenwick ingratiatingly poured him wine, maintaining that it was not fitting that our footman-potboy should serve us. I did not dare suggest that Jinty could. He would not let me pour nor would he let me drink what he deemed was unsuitable for my delicate tastes. I was allowed a small glass of sack and nothing more. Conversation was non-existent, though Fenwick continued to talk none-the-less. It did not seem appropriate for me to enquire what he knew of Matthew's detention.

As a wet and windy autumnal dusk fell, there was a clamour in the hallway. This was common enough, for there were often evening dispatch riders arriving for the night. Booted feet thundered up to the first floor, a sword scabbard beating a tattoo against the stair-spindles. I half expected gunner Sark but after a peremptory knock the door opened on a trooper, lobster-tail helmet tucked under his arm, back and breast-plate and buff coat muddied from a hard ride in foul weather. He bowed briefly and introduced himself as Lieutenant Phillips, an officer of Prince Rupert's cavalry, having a missive for Mistress Grace Godwynne on the directions of His Highness the Prince himself. He then handed me a packet. It was addressed in elegant handwriting, closed with an impressive seal.

When I opened it, another letter, unsealed and unfinished slipped between my fingers. It needed no signature for the handwriting was familiar and dear to me. It was Ned's. For once Fenwick was stunned to silence, and stood open mouthed as my father slowly stooped to pick up the fallen sheet of paper.

The royal message unfolded before my eyes, my heart sinking with every word that I read. Its brisk tone had the formality one would expect in a Prince's correspondence and should any spy have opened the missive he would have found nothing of note. However, I was acutely aware that this belied the compassion with which the envoy had been sent.

Mistress Godwynne,

I trust that you will excuse the haste with which I write. The nature of the news contained within cannot be conveyed without pain.

My Lieutenant will give you details of the engagement yesterday at Aldbourne Chase where we made trouble for the Earl of Essex and his army.

I will say no more than among the captured soldiers of the London Trained Bands I heard one name which attracted my attention for it was associated both with maritime service rendered to His Majesty the King and with care and kindness to the sick and injured of His Majesty's officers in Bristol. As such it was of interest to me.

I had a cornet of horse make enquiries. Edward Godwynne was injured and I straightway directed my physician to attend but the wound was too severe for the soldier to be saved. In his snap-sack was the enclosed. Though unfinished it had been addressed to Wine Street which confirmed my supposition that you might be a relation.

I tender my deepest regret for this most sad news and most of all for the manner of its making.

The flourished signature was 'Rupert'. Below the name of the Prince was a scribbled sentence:

In remembrance of our last conversation I respectfully send you a gift. He has learned much from Boye and responds to the name Patch.

The officer stepped to one side and brandished the end of a soggy piece of rope at me. Behind the man's shabby, bucket-topped boots stood a slim hound. The dog's coat was completely black except for a white stripe down his chest. He ears pricked, he was attentively watching us all.

The gift from a Prince trotted towards me. He sat neatly on his fine haunches and, as he put up one filthy paw in the only canine salutation I recognised, my tears began to flow in a silent and unheeded stream.

I recognised that it were time to move on when Daniel Edwards marched off. The sergeant, being as good as his word, promoted Dan to Corporal in Major Somebody-or-other's regiment of foot. He was to be part of the Queen's guard. We'd heard that she was at Exeter and near to having her latest lying-in and that terrible threats were being made to her and the unborn babe by Parliament decrees. As if childbirth weren't difficult enough, poor woman.

Both sides are as bad as each other at throwing hard words, and I should know for I have seen it from behind both lines. Rumours were flying that the ships to carry Her Majesty off to France had been sunk in a sea battle off Topsham and that she would have to ride all the way to the Land's End because they couldn't trust the Barumites not to turn traitors and hand her over instead of letting her sail safely out of Barnstaple Water. So another Bideford lad was marched away to do his duty and for all I know he's still marching wherever the poor Queen goes.

But I can feel for that woman just brought to bed of a babe then chased from pillar to post in fear of her life. When my William heard I was to bear him a child he was as fearful as the King to see that I was protected.

'Tis true that the Queen passed time at Pendennis Castle, these very walls. Now wouldn't that make a fine tale to tell my children, that their ma slept in the very same place as the Queen of England. Mind, I'd stake my last farthing that she had more to eat in a day than we souls have had in a month. But there, I run ahead of my tale.

When it came to it my leaving some of it was me being pushed but some of it was me a-going, for just like at Kat Conybeare's I knew when I wasn't wanted. If I'm being truly honest, there have been places where I didn't feel comfortable enough to stay. It weren't nothing to do with the grafting for I'm a girl well used to that, nor was it the fish at every other meal, for I could see folks in the town who weren't half as well fed as Judd's brood. Mind you, Joy had to spend most of the earnings from whatever daily catch Makey, Zeal and their pa could net just to buy bread. Prices were rising something terrible and if we had another wet summer it would be no better come harvest time. No, I didn't leave a'cause of the hardships. It was Abel. Or the lack of him.

I came to be right glad that Judd's girls were more content to go out and about for me. After the Sunday of Temperence's whipping, wherever I went, every one of the townsfolk seemed to be gawping at me. They stared and they whispered even though the vicar had made a pronouncement in church that day. He'd said that I was clear and sheer innocent and they spiteful types were all misled. At least I think that's what he said, he used a lot of fine long words that bain't rememberable and anyway, nobody seemed to listen.

Nothing that any clergyman said would help little Abel either. I do think that the fright of that day was too much for that little heart. He being a sensitive soul, the day with all the strangers around and that miracle, well, I think it just took too much out of him. He got weaker and weaker and nary again did we hear a sound from him. He was always a poorly little childer and never rosy or nut-brown like his brothers but the blue tint to his lips weren't right. He would take nought to eat or drink, even the warmed milk with honey that I knew he liked best of all. He had not even the strength to play with his shells. When little Abel was slipped into the grave next to his ma I thought to myself, 'His speaking was one miracle which cost too dear, and if my soul is damned for believing that then, so be it.'

Now here I am all scummered with tears again and not an inch of clean hem left on this shift to make myself presentable! I'm just like each and every woman in these walls who has her frown-lines drawn in with enough muck for the cob wall of a barn.

Anyway, there it was. The Judd household had one less

mouth to feed and no need for another, the place seeming empty without that little lad. With Ezekiel's girls two years older and doing fine with their needlework and spinning, they were quite able to take care of hearth and home without my help. I suppose I had done too good a job but then they were quick to learn and biddable girls.

It was a few days past mid-summer morn when after the dawn prayers and before he set off with his nets, Ezekiel Judd sat me down and about as sentimental as I had ever seen him said,

'Maid, I doan't want 'ee to go believin' that Judd is ungratevul but since I has all'us been vore-right with 'ee it needs I must say what is on my mind. You knows that tiddn't vitty that the house have a woman and not a wive, for volks will talk. But the good Lord joined me with Hepzibah and I will take no more than one spouse. I cans't vind 'ee no work that the girls cannot turn their hand to, and my boys...well now that little Abel needs no nursing...'

I couldn't bear to see the old man going to so much trouble with words, so I finished for him and said that I was heart-sore to be about the place without little Abel around, that I had been pondering moving on but would be glad of a kind word to see me on my way. I think he was right relieved, for he said he'd see me 'vairly done by' then hauled up his nets and scuttled out.

Thus, there was I, packing up my bundle once again. I decided that Barnstaple was an easier route than to Torrington and at least I knew the town a'cause I'd been there for the fair. I would have to go by road for the tides weren't right to get Makey to take me by boat and anyway, I didn't feel it proper to ask.

I went to see the town constable to see about a pass to travel, and he sent me to the sergeant at the fort. He hadn't marched out with the soldiers for Exeter, and recognising me from my time with those troublesome maids, he gave me a piece of paper with his name in a black swirl at the bottom of it, which I stupidly folded straightway into my pocket smudging the ink. He tutted at that, waved me out. I think he was glad to see the back of me.

Early the next morning, the girls gave me a tiny Barum-ware dish tied in muslin. They had filled it with the mustard poultice for my joints. They hugged me, sniffing that they would remember well all their fireside lessons. Old Judd, bade me kneel to pray with them so I bent my aching knees once more. At the 'Amen' he gave me a hefty package, wrapped in oiled cloth, and whispered 'May God protect you.' I don't mind admitting that the parcel stopped any tears that might have flowed - it was heavy and all I could think was, 'Hester, that's another thing to carry!' until I caught a glance at the shelf beside the fire and saw that there was a dusty gap where the family Bible was wont to lie in the daytime. It was no burden to me after that, for all that I couldn't read one word of its pages.

For though he might have cuffed me often enough, whether I deserved or not, Ezekiel Judd was the first person who ever showed such care to me and I might not be the most God-fearing girl, but I learned then a bit about human kindness.

As I set off, Judd told me he had been to the church the eve before and said that I should pass by that way before making for the bridge. I didn't think I needed any more prayers but with God's book slung in the bag over one shoulder, it seemed the proper thing to do, though when I got there the curate definitely looked bothered to see me. He wasted no words, but handed me another paper. Judd, he said, had stated what to write and had made his mark on a testament to my good character that I might get employment wherever I went. The likes of me had never had such a thing and when he handed over this latest marvel, my mouth dropped open in surprise. I must have looked right mazed. I took the note, put it with my pass in my snap-sack, bobbed a curtsey and headed for the Long Bridge now with two bits of paper and a book to my name!

I had to show my permit at the barricado, but was waved through with nothing more than a wink from a tooth-less pikeman with a rusty helmet too big for him. I was just past the last of the shipwright's yards, wondering why some lettering was so important and if perhaps someday I might learn writing after all, when three figures climbed up from the river bank and planked themselves in front of me. Susannah, Mary and Temperance had taken the trouble to get past the fort and see me out of Bideford and I told them I thought that was too kind of them in the circumstances. They didn't like that one bit. I reckoned they expected me to be afeared.

Well, I wouldn't have let them have the satisfaction even if I had been, so I squared my shoulders, tried to ignore the stabbing pain in my wrists and bade them let me past.

'You may pass,' says Susannah, 'but hereby we lay this spell upon you.' She stepped up so her outstretched hand was near to touching my chest.Then up came Temperance and Mary and pointed their fingers at me too, joining in. The words still make me shudder for all that I know they cannot hurt me.

'By the darkness of night, may you suffer every day,

And the sun never set upon your pain.

Hot will be the burning fire in hand and foot

So with every step you will remember us!'

With a last hiss Mary thrust a tiny sack into my hand.

I took it though I could never tell you why. I should have thrown it in the Torridge, but I didn't. I only pushed between their jostling, bony shoulders, stuffing it in the bag at my shoulder. I just wanted to get past and quickly; I needed to put some miles betwixt me and Bideford. Somehow all the sweet thoughts that had followed me across the bridge had gone sour.

That day no packman came past me with hides for me to ride upon, no wagon with a lad to share his cider, only a dozen troopers on horses that shouted oaths as I lay into the hot hedge, trying my best to get out of their way. By the time I reached Sticklepath Hill and could see the road dropping towards the river Taw and Barnstaple Bridge it was evening. My skin was burned by the sun and my body hurt so badly that it was all I could do to put one foot in front of the other.

It was 25th June, a clear soft twilight beginning to fall. I had to get across the bridge before curfew, so bracing myself I was just about to stagger the last half-mile when a gentleman's voice spoke up,

'And where are you bound, young woman, for you look as though the troubles of Jehoshaphat are on your shoulders?'

Well, if it had been nearer dawn than dusk I might have had the wit to answer that I did indeed have Jehoshaphat on my shoulders, and few of his army of Judea as well. But the man addressing me wore the long black gown and narrow, white neckerchief of a clergyman, and I was a good and polite young woman and had a letter to say so.

'I am bound for Barnstaple, sir, to seek for a job in a quiet household. I have come from Bideford and hope to make the town this night but I will admit that I am weary, and have but a little coin in my purse.' That was honest enough, as I had never kept anything from Judd's income for it had not seemed right. All I had were a few pennies from Morwenstow, put by for a rainy day, and they were stitched into my hem not in my purse, but I didn't say all that to the gentleman. He stepped up and took my arm, saying,

'I am making for that town myself, and I am sure I can find a corner near a hearth to keep you safe this night. We will let the Lord take care of the morrow.'

So, limping and sore, but with his strength and stout staff to support me, I made it to Barum just as the peal of the town churches began to ring the gates closed. I wasn't to know that I had jumped from a frying pan well and truly into a fire.

XVIII Mary: From Cornwall to Devon August – October 1643

For all it was high summer, when I arrived at Antony the evening was damp and chilly enough for the servants to have been told to light a fire. I welcomed it for I had not seemed able to warm myself since Alex rowed away from Portmellon. Despite the homely glow, the conversation was desultory chitchat about the ailments of mutual acquaintances or commonplace observations about the children or the dogs. Supper was taken in almost total silence but eventually my Aunt could contain herself no longer. Her opinion as to the prudence of Jane's decision to visit Dame Elizabeth Chudleigh was expressed in her typically forthright manner. She did not approve. That Jane was pregnant seemed irrelevant, nor was it was the fact that individuals at the destination in question had changed sides. But they had ruined her matchmaking plans and that was far more significant. Any sensitivity to the fact that the family was that of her late husband's first wife, Alex's grandparents, was totally lacking.

Jane had snatched a moment when I first arrived to remind me that I should say nothing of our true mission to anyone. Now she barely responded to her sister's ranting and as Aunt Carew was making statements rather than inviting discussion, I remained mute, implying agreement and attempting to avoid any harassment. However, when my Aunt changed tack and began to speculate upon the possibility of a match with John Strode I could bear it no more.

I know that I should have deferred, been duly respectful, but I could no longer hold my tongue. It simply happened. I blurted out,

'I will have no matchmaking, Aunt, for you have none but your own interests in mind in the matter and I will be no pawn in your game!'

It was shocking; where was the dutiful niece? However, a young woman may take only so much.

I should have realised then that there was something strange in my Aunt's reaction. It was not what I expected. She did not explode with fury, but only sat back into her cushions with an inscrutable expression on her face.

'Perhaps Mary has a man in mind?' chirped Jane, trying to dissipate the tension, but unwittingly making matters worse. For from inscrutable, my aunt's eyes narrowed and her tone became malevolent. The room lost what little warmth it had and a shiver ran down my spine.

'While your father remains a cripple you, madam, will be instructed by those who know what is best for you. There may be those who believe they are a fitting spouse but I will not have it! Now my husband, of blessed memory, has departed this life and while your uncle George is occupied with his own concerns, there is no-one better placed than I to deal with the matter. I take it as a sign of ill-mannered ingratitude on your part to challenge me. But that is, I suppose, what one should expect of one with such a haphazard upbringing,' she finished, waving her hand dismissively.

There was little I could say except feign a headache, beg to be excused and leave the room. The irony of the insult only dawned on me as I packed my scant belongings, for was it not true that a large proportion of my childhood had been spent in my aunt and uncle's household? Only later did I discover the extent of the deceit concealed in her snide remarks.

Jane, her two youngest children and I left early by boat the next morning. There were no formalities, from the small quay on the river. However momentous the journey was in reality, we wanted to make our departure seem as normal as possible, or as normal as could be in the midst of a civil war.

The boat had been sent by Alex. He had used the credentials he still held, expertly arranging our voyage to Totnes. He had dispatched another faster boat to warn Dartmouth castle that we had permission to pass.

Teignmouth would have suited our purposes better but I was told we would have had more delay to wait for high water in that estuary. There was no room for delay. The voyage was already frustratingly slow, for winds were light and contrary. Eventually we slipped between Kittery Point and Dartmouth's quays, catching a rising tide up-river to Totnes. We had arrived just before the King's forces closed the siege. With Dartmouth still Parliamentarian, we were given clear passage.

From Totnes, which was under Royalist control and where we blatantly flaunted different family connections to secure lodgings for the night, it was another day of uncomfortable travelling in a litter for Jane and the children. I hired a quiet mare for myself, ponies for Jane's maid and the manservant escorting us. Again mentioning the Chudleigh name opened our route eastwards.

Guards challenged our paperwork at Newton but only perfunctorily. A sick and pregnant woman with two wailing infants, even accompanied by a small entourage, posed no threat other than a noisy and troublesome inconvenience to the soldiery. They had bigger matters on their minds. My nerves in shreds, I was nevertheless shocked to hear that Jane had pinched her children severely to provoke suitably impressive distress. Desperate times do indeed call for desperate means.

By the evening, our nerves and bodies wracked, we had reached Ashton Manor, our destination on the outskirts of Chudleigh village. It was August 19th. Jane went straightway to her bed and I was left to watch the children as their great-granddam, Dame Elizabeth, aged now but far from infirm, fussed and cosseted them. I could say nothing of my mission. I still remember the headache that I suffered that night, with blinding flashes and my temples so sore it was as if a hot poker had been thrust through my scalp. I lay awake till dawn fretting at the plan I needed to put in place to ride to Exeter and to Sir John Berkeley the next day. A packet from Alex, passed to me on the boat, lay under my pillow. The message it contained and which I had memorised seemed written in flames behind my eyelids every time I shut my eyes.

In the morning, our plan might as well have been tossed to the winds. A rider who had come looking for Sir George, misdirected in Ashburton, had arrived at Chudleigh instead of Totnes. He carried momentous news from a spy inside Plymouth's walls. The rider was not to know the implications of his message for two ladies in the household. The spy had reported how a courier had been intercepted trying to escape with a message for the leader of the Royalist forces at Tavistock. Interrogation had exposed an attempt to surrender St Nicholas Island to the King. Consequently Sir Alexander Carew, the traitor who had proposed to change sides, had been arrested by his former Roundhead comrades and was to be transported to Portsmouth thence to London. He would be tried for treason against the realm. Alex' other go-between had been captured; what, if anything, had Alex told him of my mission I wondered.

I tried to catch Jane before she slipped to the floor. She was taken to her bed and when I knew she was calmed I slipped to my room and burned that incriminating packet, grinding the embers to ash in the hearth.

Now there was no need for haste but what was I to do? Inactivity and lack of news frayed my nerves. I was afraid that Jane would miscarry and so busied myself, spending time tending her the way that I had tended my pets as a child at Penwarne. However, she and the babe were made of stronger stuff.

Jane insisted her next move would be to attend Alexander wherever she could catch up with him, but it was to be a month before any action was possible. To the delight of their great-grandmother, the proposal was for the little ones to remain at Ashton Manor, to be cared for by the maid who had travelled with us from Antony. I knew that Jane hoped that I would accompany her on her quest. For sure, with Aunt Carew at my back and a houseful of sisters taking care of Penwarne, I had no mind to refuse. By the end of September the plan was complete; contacts had been made, and papers had been arranged to allow Jane plus one maidservant to pass, on compassionate grounds, to plead her husband's case in Portsmouth. I was to be that maidservant. All that remained was to finalise our route.

We delayed, for the district was in turmoil with Dartmouth now in its fourth week of siege and Royalist re-enforcements passing to and fro across the skirts of Dartmoor to Okehampton or through to Exeter. Then the children caught chicken pox and we were forced to delay again.

I remember I seemed to have a permanently aching head. By the start of October, and with the risk of autumn gales potentially hampering any voyage, Jane had all but decided to take a litter and attempt the journey by road. Everything changed again when a trooper of Colonel Digby's regiment rode into the barton as we watched the children taking turns riding the pony in large circles around the yard. The horse's hooves scattered pebbles against our skirts.

The message was to all at Ashton Manor: with Colonel Digby's respects, Dartmouth had been recaptured from the rebel forces and was now held for His Majesty. However, Colonel Digby sent his deepest regrets that the town had come at a high price. Colonel James Chudleigh had fallen in an assault upon the town walls and had died of his wounds. He had been buried in St Saviour's Church on 30th September.

Her grandson James's death put our hostess into deep mourning. In other circumstances I might have now been donning a widow's veil. It may seem callous but I was beyond caring. All I could think was that with my bargain with Alexander ended there would no longer be any news of Lewis.

With the King's forces in control, Jane was resolved, deciding that the passage through Dartmouth would now be feasible. Despite Jane's protests and the need to wait for the extra papers, Dame Chudleigh insisted that it was proper for us to take a second maidservant, despite our attempts to be inconspicuous. As soon as a respectful time had lapsed we rode out of Ashton Manor. However, I was not to leave the West Country after all.

Travelling from Totnes, we had to change boats in Dartmouth, and waiting on the quay to board our ship I unashamedly eavesdropped on the conversation around sailors from a Bristol vessel. Loyal locals had gathered, wanting news of the progress of the war or just of doings beyond their battered borough, and there were distinct rumbles of disapproval when the seamen spoke of French re-enforcements for His Majesty's militia. The general opinion seemed to be that foreigners brought bad ways with their troops.

I noticed a tall, blue-eyed man with another individual, lank-haired and non-descript in looks but clearly superior from the expensive cut of his garb and the new sea-cloak he wore. They watched as the little crowd murmured among themselves. Then one sailor, slurring and the worse for drink, shouted out,

'If yoush fear the Frensh then look well to the defenshes of your town for there are Aye-er-ish troopsh to come to hish Majeshty'sh shide and then any man, woman or child who hash ever had Roundhead treaschery in their filthy heartsh had besht …'

The sailor never did tell what the townsfolk had to fear from the Irish for the well-dressed man raised his fist to strike him. I think he would have felled him with a blow except his hand was stayed by his companion. In the seconds that followed the sailor disappeared into the crowd, the two men grappled and the better dressed disengaged far enough to strike the blue-eyed one across the face, his signet ring catching a slash across the tall man's cheek. The wary crowd parted before him as he strode away.

The episode, over in an instant, captured my attention for one reason. The sailor had mentioned Ireland and the last news I had of Lewis was that he had been in that very country. Without thinking, I stepped boldly across to the man whose face now bled profusely. Offering him my kerchief and without thinking of proprieties I begged him to tell me what he knew of the King's Irish army.

He watched me with a wry amusement on his face even though his eyes, a startling blue, were watering with the sting of his wound.

'Mistress, I can tell you nothing more than when I was last in Kinsale we brought word back to His Majesty's agents that many troops and officers who have served in Ireland are preparing to return to these shores to fight for King Charles.' My expression must have changed and he misinterpreted the cause for he continued reassuringly,

'You have no need to fear that man's rumour mongering - he is one of my men, just a deaf old gunner enjoying the attention paid to his gossip. The word is that the troops will not come to the south but via west coast ports like Bristol or Barnstaple, maybe Minehead if we still hold the place.'

He nodded his thanks for the dressing for his wound, raised an eyebrow and with a gesture of his head offered me my kerchief back. I told him to keep it and he gave a brief bow as Jane caught my arm, pulling me away towards the steps to our waiting skiff.

The boatman had helped the servant-girl aboard and stowed our boxes, and now waited to row us to the vessel to take us east. But I had decided. Responding to the same outrageous impulse with which I had resisted my Aunt, I placed my hand over Jane's gently lifting it from my arm.

In a torrent of words, I told her of Lewis, of that first declaration, of my dream that he would remember me, of the horrible torture of Aunt Carew's matchmaking, and how now I had a glimmer of hope, of news. There was a remote possibility that Lewis Tremayne was on his way back to England. I must wait where he could find me. I could not go with her.

Jane called to the boatman, bidding him delay our passage. She received a curt reply that tides would not wait on ladies, no matter what their state - or estate. Grudgingly, he shipped his oars and passed another rope to a boy waiting 'on the quay. I remember Jane's hand was hot as she turned my face to look her directly in the eyes. Gripping my hands in hers, she whispered,

'Mary, why did you not tell me? I had no idea.' Then she suddenly went grey, and I truly thought that she was ill.

'Oh Mary, Mary…may heaven forgive me I have been so stupid! How could I know that my sister could be so cruel? After you left us that last evening at Antony, Lady Carew was furiously storming about, pulling papers and letters from this box or that and strewing them about her writing table.' Jane gestured as she poke, imaginary sheaves flung hither and thither. 'She picked up one bundle and threw them on the fire, and at the time, what she said made no sense: "Well, let this spite them!" She left them to burn and went to bed. When she had gone I pulled the bundle from the ashes. Some had been destroyed by the flame, but many were only singed. They were addressed to you!'

I was stunned. What was Jane trying to tell me? Even now my hands shake at the memory. Jane continued, abject apology in every syllable,

'I should have given them to you, but I panicked. In the rush I simply stowed them in my bag that night. I had completely forgotten them. Mary, forgive me! Go back to Ashton, go back to Dame Elizabeth. Look in the little trunk I have left behind and you will find the packets. I tied them up with some string but I have not opened any of them. Go, with my blessing, with my plea for forgiveness, and God be with you and with your love!' Kissing my cheek, she called up the boat, and carefully negotiating the wet steps, climbed in and the boatman rowed her away.

I did go back to Ashton Manor and in the little, unlocked chest in the room above the porch, I found exactly what Jane had promised. The sweep of the pen on the page was one so familiar; I had memorised it from the single sheet which I kept close by me everywhere I went and I would see it in my dreams most every night. In my hands I held over a dozen letters, most now stained with soot or scorched, all with broken seals, addressed to Mary Carew, Antony in the county of Cornwall. The letters were from Lewis Tremayne.

XIX Grace: From Bristol to the high seas September 1643 – January 1644

The letter from Prince Rupert and the news that it contained brought such despair that, at first, even the gift he had given me was no comfort. We had never kept house-dogs. I worried that the hound would wander off, keeping him with me on the leash at all times. I need not have troubled for by night-time, with or without the rope, he would stay close to my heels, carefully eating what scraps I gave him. To dog, the filthy halter seemed to designate that I was his and he mine, and Patch became like my own shadow. He was little trouble, which was just as well for I felt as lifeless as an empty puppet. Or a skittle toppled, rolling helplessly.

My father had taken the news of the death of Edward harder even than the loss of Hal and it was now evident that he was very sick. The barber-surgeon bled him claiming that the melancholic humours would be best dealt with that way, but it only served to weaken him more, if that were possible, and he slept most of the day. His face was the colour of a fading bruise, his stomach was distended and he would drink very little, eat nothing. I sat with him as often as household duties allowed, Patch curled beneath my skirts, his paw on my foot giving comforting warmth.

After his arrest, Matthew Allerway had been detained and to the horror of the household was conscripted into the pike-block of a regiment marching with Sir John Belasyse to join the King's army. We heard they fought at Newbury but never saw him again.

By the close of September 1643, it was clear that my father was near death. Fenwick was absent, the ship once more at sea, not bound for Ireland this time but on a run to Le Havre. I was grateful for that small consolation as Jinty and I took turns to sit with our patient. Late one evening she called me, greatly agitated. My father had asked for me and for the rector from St Peter's church. His voice was barely audible as he told me that he wished to make his last will and testament and to clear his conscience with God so that he might die in peace.

I could not gain-say him for I could not dissemble nor avoid the evidence of my eyes or my experience. When the Reverend and his church warden entered I placed paper, pen and ink them before them. As he began his task, my father was insistent that I listen carefully.

I was heiress to a considerable amount now that Hal and Edward were dead, but by the laws of the merchant fraternity the business could never be mine. Thus he wanted to make it plain that his wishes were that, as I was but eighteen years of age, I would marry his choice of husband as soon as was possible. He named my betrothed, Bartholomew Fenwick.

There it was, in thick, black ink on the pages of a document witnessed by two men of the Church. In the event of my father's death before the *Ann* returned to port, and lacking my trusted godfather, the legacy would be held in trust, to be overseen by Will Fitzherbert and Edmund Arundel and a notary to represent Fenwick. The words 'jointure' and some vague details were inserted at the suggestion of the priest. Despite that, on my wedding day Bartholomew Fenwick would succeed to my estate, becoming the proprietor, the commercial director, the factor and captain of the Godwynne enterprise. He would own all. He would own me.

My father believed he had done what was best, hoped that he had given me protection and security in troubled times. As the church bells of St Peters and St Nicholas sounded two hours past midnight my father let go the ropes which moored him to this life.

The trustees did not need to act for long. In accordance with his wishes and after as decent a period of mourning as I was ever going to be allowed, Bartholomew Fenwick and I took our marriage vows in front of Elizabeth Yeaman and William Fitzherbert, with Edmund Arundel and his wife as the congregation at 8 o'clock on the morn of All Saint's

Day, November 1ˢᵗ 1643. None of the household at Wine Street attended but in the shadows near the font stood Sark, a new scar livid across his left cheek and an expression of disapproval written large on the rest of his features. The priest took his silver, my husband curtly thanked all who had attended then walked me back to our home. With a sardonic bow he then took his leave. The *Ann* was to sail. He did not deem it necessary to tell me her destination.

So there were no hearty good wishes for our future; no bride-ale or festivities. There was no lifting me across a threshold for good luck, nor boisterous jostling for garters with well-wishing friends, nor even ribald teasing of the shy newly-weds. My nuptial bed was never decked with flowers nor with ribbons and was shared with a hound. And looking back, there was more love there that night than I saw in my marriage bed any night thereafter.

Bartholomew Fenwick was not my choice so perhaps I ought to have been relieved at his departure but I felt nothing. I neither regretted nor delighted in the circumstances for I was numb.

Bristol was thronging with troops, a stream in and out from Wales to Oxford, through to Somerset or the Welsh Marches, constant coming and going and always the need for provisions, food and munitions. Necessities, such as boots and breeches were so hard to come by that there were tales of soldiers sharing their garments and exchanging clothing for a bedroll when their sentry duty changed. Fuel was in constant short supply and that winter was bitter which went hard with all of us, though not so bad in Bristol as elsewhere for we had the trows, which sailed between the little coal ports of South Wales and the city. Christmas passed as a season of very limited good will for fleets, forces and citizens alike.

When the *Ann of Bristol* returned, it transpired that Fenwick - my husband - had explored the possibility of high profits from his old collier trade down the east coast but the politics of war had altered the perspective somewhat. So, harried by weather, Bartholomew returned instead with black powder from Nantes and complaints of pirates of every persuasion from Algerian to Dunkirkers and too many Englishmen who changed sides as quickly as a tide would turn. My husband: the hypocrite.

It transpired that our home was not the haven that a seafaring man required. Fenwick chose to remain on board the *Ann* when she was alongside. When he did visit Wine Street, he closeted himself in the 'shop' to maintain what control of his domain he could, writing at length in a battered book, supervising the strong-boxes which were manhandled in and out. I was now living in one room, the rest of the household functioning only for the benefit of the Royalist engine of war. The garrison quartermaster had put a master of the billet to fill the gap left by Matthew's arrest and Jinty was now little more than a tap-room servant. She and I snatched occasional companionable moments together. One day I even confessed that my nerves were being worn to shreds anticipating the night that Bartholomew would decide that it was time to enjoy his conjugal rights. Nothing Jinty said could have prepared me for the experience.

Re-victualing ships was a constant drain on the King's purse; neither soldiers nor sailors were paid on time, if at all. In mid-January a fleet under Captain Wake made Bristol's problems worse. They had been driven back on a Dublin run by weather and a mutinous crew, and for twenty-four hours, the town militia were busy dealing with the unruly consequences until a limited amount of back pay had been found, subduing sailors both on board the ships and under the tables of the inns on the quay.

My initial belief was that something about the exceptional disorder must have moved my husband to protect his assets for the next morning Sark brought a message from the ship. He looked truly discomforted when Patch trotted over to him and presented a paw in greeting, something I had only seen him do for my father and for Jinty. When my visitor ignored him, Patch came and stood close by my side, leaning against my skirts. Sark cleared his throat, his voice grating. He did not meet my eyes as he said,

'Master Fenwick bids me fetch you down to the ship. Mistress Jinty has instructions to collect your necessaries...I am to escort you immediately so, if you please, will you get your cloak. The hound is not to follow.'

I remember how my knees nearly buckled, and to cover my nerves I snapped at him that the dog would be at my heels no matter what he or my husband ordered. In minutes, I was wrapped in my heavy hooded cape with my muffler tight round my neck, stepping warily on the frozen cobbles beside Gunner Sark, Patch without collar or leash contentedly trotting between us.

The small stern cabin of the Ann was dark, the winter light dim. Bartholomew was peering over papers, his book and some charts, his breath white in the chill air. Piled behind his table were the boxes from my father's 'shop'. He bade me sit, barely lifting his head. Patch slipped in behind me as the door closed, hidden by the folds of my skirts. He slinked under the stool that I pulled towards me; I caught the glint of his teeth, bared silently under a curled lip. There was no raised paw for Bartholomew.

'Take off your cloak. You will not need it again tonight. Indeed unless you have better sea-legs than your father I suspect you will not have need of it,' he gave a vulgar snort of amusement then added, 'until you reach your destination.' Stung by the contempt as much as the statement I forgot the cardinal rule with my husband and spoke when it was not called for. I asked,

'Where are we going?' Attending to the fastening at of my cape, I did not see him cross the tiny space between us, so the blow to my cheek nearly knocked me onto the floor. A paw slipped alongside my ankle. His next words were loaded with a shocking cruelty,

'Understand me, madam! Where you go I will decide! Where I go is none of your business! Suffice it that I deem it necessary, for now, for my dutiful wife to sail life's voyage with me. You will not be returning to Wine Street so...' Leering closer to me, Fenwick glimpsed Patch, a low snarl now accompanying the flash of the hound's fangs.

Reeling towards the door, he roared for the bo'sun. My companion slipped round Fenwick's legs and out onto the deck, my pleas to hound and husband totally ignored. The door slammed shut and was locked. Within minutes, shouts told me that the banks-men were letting go lines. I could feel the ship beginning to work her way into the stream.

I was left alone all that day. That night is not one I care to recall. Muted, ardent dialogue accompanied the turn of the key. Dark, male laughter then briefly the dim light of a lantern silhouetted two men, the one being my husband, with his clothes awry and a physical inclination that was only too evident. The door closed.

Stand. Turn. Bend. Pain. Revulsion. Shock. Humiliation.

The next morning a thin boy brought a bucket of icy water, a set of shabby clothes that looked like his own and tossed me a bundle containing only a shift, my hairbrush and a handful of my monthly cloths. For better or worse, I was at sea.

XX Hester: Barnstaple July 1644

If I was hoping to better myself in Barnstaple, the starting didn't go well for all that I had the company of a gentleman of the cloth, Reverend Thomas Dyckwood. He babbled of grand relatives in some place in Cornwall...Foy-ee he said it was, and how he had a step-brother who was a preacher, well known. I should have wondered why a man so well placed had no horse or even a mule.

They let us in, the Reverend Sir introducing me and my papers all being in order. I was rubbing my blisters when my escort introduced himself so I was never sure which church he said he was a vicar to, though him throwing himself down on his knees and praying for the victory of the Godly over the Ungodly had the guards truly impressed. He seemed unwilling to look for church lodgings. I hoped there'd be at least a tap-room with a settle, a cold tankard of cider and some cheese but the guards were odd as if they were not sure what to do with us.

And that was all a'cause Barum town was all desperd upset on account of there being an uprising against the King's men!

Now, Hester Phipps has all'us got herself to places at the wrong times, though it was only once by choice, and that once was here in these walls. The best of the King's garrison in Barnstaple had left to join with the soldiery who were to protect her Highness, just like Daniel and the Bideford boys. The paltry few that were left had been set upon by the Barum folk who were hot Puritans like their neighbours in Bideford but more handy with their fists and pitchforks. So they had now taken the town back from the Royalists and not one cannon shot fired!

'Tis fair to say that there are few towns who lie comfortable with any troops, but those North Devon folk were particular angry about what gossip they had heard from the sailors on the quays. There were rumours that the King was bringing Irish brigands to fight in his army, the very same Catholics who had murdered a throng of good English Protestants across the Irish sea in '41. I need not tell you that Irish Catholics, brigands or not, would nary mix well with the Puritans in Barnstaple, Bideford or anywhere else for that matter. So the cry was 'Not within our walls!' and 'For God and Parliament!' with a few more private local scores settled too by a knock on the poll and a bucket-top boot up a backside. It was all nicely disguised below the grand politicking.

Once we were in the town, I thought we would go looking for the curate but the constable and his men, shirt sleeves all rolled up, were ushering folk off the street, and sent us into the nearest tavern. It only had one room for hire and that already had two occupants. Nonetheless, up speaks my cleric,

'Our Saviour was content to be born in a stable and the Lord will provide. I am a man of God' he boomed, quite impressive, 'and this young woman is in my care, so your one room will suffice, for God as will be our witness, there will be nothing to scandalise you good people done by my hand'. He had a marvellous, good way with words did Tom Dyckwood but it weren't his hands you had to watch.

I never asked what the lodgers who had already taken up the tavern's mattress made of two more strangers joining them. Our fellow travellers, an old packman headed for Ilfracombe and a one-armed rat catcher whose mangy dog lay on his head in place of a nightcap, had claimed their places but respectfully moved a little for the Reverend. I stood befuddled, no place for me, until a truckle bed was hauled from beneath the bedstead. My arse lay on the floor through the broken ropes and the mattress was no more than an empty sack, but I was so tired that I would have slept on a bed of nails and thanked you for it. There was no need for blankets for it was summ'at hot that night which was just as well for there were none, which was shocking for I paid two good pennies for a week in that room. Anyway, early the next morning the feather-bedders were still snoring, the rat-catcher's dog now lying on the packman's feet, so I quickly used the chamber pot and, taking the bag which held my papers and my new apron, I set forth to seek some form of work.

Finding my way round a town that was as flat as Bideford was hilly took a little while but once I was able to get my bearings from the quay I did better. The streets were buzzing like a skep of angry bees with scores of the militia and their pikes moving about much smarter than the lads at Bideford. The Barum men were all in step, a prayer-sheet stuck in every man's hat band. It was a change of the watch and sentries were moving out east to all the outworks and entrenchments. There was no King's army going to catch Barnstaple napping that was certain sure.

'Now Hester' says I to myself 'where in a busy place like this is going to need a hard workin' lass like you?' and, dodging the soldiery, I followed my nose to a pie shop. My coin wouldn't stretch to pie every day of the week but my stomach thought my throat had been slit, so I fetched out a halfpence and whiled away a few minutes with the baker Estmond's daughter while the shop was quiet. No work to be had there but a little gossip never did any harm.

She told me all about a serving girl who had scandalised the neighbourhood by taking herself off after a Cavalier corporal from Bideford, no banns, no ring, yet another example of the Devil at work in the town. But, thought I, where there's one lass in disgrace, there's an opportunity for another with good character, especially if she has a bit of paper to say so. With a few well-put questions, I bade my new friend Bess 'good morrow' and walked down to the quays. Perching on a pile of ropes for a few minutes I ate a piece of my pie, remembering it was most of a whole day since I had proper food. I decided I would save some as the tavern food was dear, so putting on the cleaner apron and wrapping the pie in the old one, I went looking for a Mistress Palmer in Cross Street.

Well, it was a fine little house and no mistake. Bess had said he was a merchant and until lately had been town mayor, so his wife was always house-proud and tidy. Mistress Palmer took the paper with Master Judd's mark upon it and said that she would speak to her husband and I was to wait upon her Monday next in the afternoon, but she spoke kindly and I made a neat curtsey and thanked her politely.

Reverend Dyckwood took me to church that Sunday though we kept a decent distance apart. I looked out for Mistress Palmer and her husband and she, noting me, gave a small nod of her head. That pleased me for it boded well, I thought. But other men's plans put Hester Phipps out again. This time is was Colonel Digby's fault.

The packman had gone on his way but Dyckwood, the rat-catcher and me were sitting that night in the yard of the tavern when there was right commotion start up. The alarum bell at South Gate was ringing, dozens of booted feet thumped past and there was a lot of loud hollering. I wasn't going anywhere near any trouble, for I was hopeful of the morrow's outcome and the prospect of employment, but the men ran out to see what was up, the rat-catcher's dog barking and yapping fit to burst.

News all about the place was that a rider from Crediton had overtaken a force of Royalist troopers with dragoons and foot-soldiers. It seemed they were intent on Barnstaple, to sack and burn it down on the orders of Prince Maurice. The word was spreading and every man for Parliament, and some few who weren't but daren't risk their neighbours' wrath, were arming themselves and organising barricadoes by Litchdon Green, seizing the small guns from the ship on the quay and hauling them to the castle mound. We waited all night and all the next morning. 'Twas worse than the waiting of Job, said Dyckwood which was strange for Ezekiel Judd's version of Job and Reverend Dyckwood's seemed at odds to me.

Just when I was thinking I might risk the walk round to Cross Street, the alarum bells began again. That pitched the landlord to bar the door and all the windows onto the street and frightened the ratter's dog off down the lane so his master had to go chasing him. That left me and the minister in the dimness and stale malt-air of the taproom. When he hid under a table I followed, asking if he should he be ministering or pacifying or something churchly, to which he replied 'God's bones, I should not!' then quickly added that he was sent as my protector and thus should be at my side.

The next hours were full of noise, more thunderous even than thunder, rolling round the narrow streets, and the crack-tat-rap volleys of muskets shots so sharp it hurt my ears. I felt as if I was already nailed in my coffin. As the clamour grew, my knees were shaking for we could hear that the fighting had spilled through the South Gate, there was such clashing and bashing, men shouting and screaming, with Barnstaple men raising their voices in singing psalms with more shouting and grunting and bellowing, some in languages I did not recognise.

The smell of the black powder was bitter, mixing with the stink of men and fear. I swear I heard a man die outside that very place, crying 'Jesu have pity!' for his body was there broken and crumpled against the door-jamb when in the umby light of evening we crept out. The bells were clanging again but this time they were for joy that the Royalists had been seen off, while at the main gate Colonel Lutterell welcomed in Lord Robartes and a parcel of troopers, with a promise of more reinforcements to come. I will never again smell a tap-room without feeling zaundy, though I have never been afeared of thunder nor lightening since.

In the morning, I helped the rat-catcher bury his little dog on the riverbank by Castle Green. The old man was more upset over losing that mangy creature than my pa was when my ma died and 'twas tragic to see it and I stayed with him a while afterwards.

So, it was later in the afternoon, when I had waited until I thought it was the proper hour after dinner that I called, only a day late, to speak to Mistress Palmer. Good as her word she had sought advice from her husband. I was told to get my belongings: I had a new position in that fine house in Cross Street.

With Jane gone, I had time to contemplate my position. I concluded that I could no longer tolerate my Aunt's ministrations, knowing as I did that she had wilfully put a distance between Lewis and I. The charred evidence proved that he had written every month, probably despairing of the girl he thought he knew. At best, he would think me rude, at worst he would have started to forget me. The most recent letter was dated February 1643, so there were eight long months in which he could have put me from his mind.

Jane's little ones, still with their doting great grand-mama, occupied some of my time for I had taken it upon myself to continue to teach their lessons as Jane had done but I could not stay at Ashton forever. It was in a conversation with my hostess that a solution presented itself, a way to elude my Aunt - at least for a little while.

Dame Elizabeth oft-times expressed her delight in her family, advocating the rejuvenating properties of time spent with the younger generations. She spoke with deep conviction, certain that my own grandmother would feel the same should I ask her. When she discovered how long it was since I had seen grandmama, Dame Elizabeth was insistent that I should visit Drewsteignton for the benefit of all concerned.

The very fact that Chudleigh lies on the skirts of Dartmoor as does my mother's family home made it seem so straightforward. Messengers were back and forth to the Royalist command posts in Devon and Cornwall so contacts in the right places could readily procure a pass for me. I again packed my belongings, this time with the letters tightly rolled in oiled cloth. I was sure Jane's offspring would be content and well cared for, so there seemed no reason not to accept the loan of a quiet moorland pony. With a burly manservant as an escort, I took the road north to

Moretonhamptstead.

The days were short and cold, the first frosts dusting the hedges. A message was dispatched to my grandmother, giving notice of my arrival. I joined company with some packmen on the second morning, which made the trek a little more congenial as well as safer. Their debate upon the 'falling-out' which ravaged the country was entertaining, a cheerfully ill-informed bickering. Their general conclusion was that it had 'little to do with the likes of us.' I wished that I could be as indifferent.

Dartmoor must raise strong women. Both my grandmother and Alex's were born in the years of Good Queen Bess, over four-score years ago. Both were only as agile as their years would allow but neither had lost their sharp wits. While Dame Elizabeth chattered about the here and now, her family being the centre of her world, my grandmother loved to reminisce about the days of Gloriana, though these were not the ramblings of an old woman. She would declare that she could write a history of the age that would improve on that of Richard Carew's, a tome that she had read and re-read. I did not doubt her for a moment. She could quote the text extensively since she had been given a copy by the author when her daughter, my mother, married his son.

I had been a child when I came last to the squat granite manor tucked into a sheltered valley. It was a different world then. Now I was a young woman unwilling to bear the yoke of family expectations and, while the notion of visiting my widowed relative was appealing because it put distance between me and Aunt Carew, I could not be sure that I would not be sent back with a flea in my ear for being disobedient. I need not have worried. Grandmother Hilman hugged me to her, then holding me at arms length and studying my face, declared,

'Hmm…an affliction of the heart, if I am not much mistaken. Well, if I cannot mend things then I expect I know a woman who can. Come in, be cherished and we shall put everything to rights!'

It had been so long since I had heard words of loving kindness spoken only for me that the flood of tears that began that moment only subsided after an afternoon beside a roaring fire, with hot spiced cider to drink and sweet honey cakes warm from the oven.

To my relief the scheming of the Dowager Lady Carew (Grandmother was apt to use full titles where appropriate) did not meet with approval. Over the next few days as I slept, recovered, confided and considered, Grandmother watched over me. She decreed that I was too old to address her with a child's label saying she preferred me to use her Christian name, Dewnes. From that day, I was with a beloved friend and not just a relative.

In Dewnes' mind, there was no question; I would stay at Coombe Manor and should the family require a reason then she would be happy to fabricate one: an aging grandmother was in need of a young companion and nurse. Who better to fill the position than her competent grand-daughter? Dewnes showed me the letter before dispatching it to my aunt at Antony. I could not help but laugh. The tone was impressive, imperious and totally incontestable. Dewnes was more than a match for Lady Carew.

There was a curt acknowledgment almost a fortnight later, civil and terse, agreeing to a situation that was already a *fait accompli*. The letter to my father showed a great deal more affection and was solicitous for his health, with suggestions for decoctions that might aid his recovery. John Carew had proved himself a loving and loyal son-in-law, of whom Dewnes had always approved.

The weeks passed very pleasantly at Coombe, low beams and small mullioned windows keeping the rooms dim, but fires in every hearth and well-stuffed cushions on the settles made for cosy living. I slipped into the domestic routine and soon felt at ease and at home. The relative seclusion of the manor meant that the festive season was quiet, but far more cheerful than at Antony for all that. Villagers brought the mummers' play and received generous hospitality. No Puritan edicts were followed in our locality.

January saw snow but we were prepared; it was very little hardship to us for it did not last. At the February cattle-market we mingled with moorland farmers, their wives grumbling about the latest requisitions and the lamentable price of everything, passing on the latest gossip from Chagford or further a-field. There was little troop activity to report although a proclamation by the Earl of Essex ordering all Parliamentarian soldiers to repair to their colours signified that the fighting season had resumed.

Our evening conversations by the fireside often returned to the subject of families, the great and the good. Dewnes would make outrageous observations, rock back in her chair and roar with laughter, her eyes sparkling with mischief. I had enquired about the web of Carew connections, her discourses serving as good medicine for my damaged confidence. One such conversation however, took a different turn. Dewnes began innocuously enough,

'My opinion of the Carews has diminished since Alice married your father. He was always the best of them, straightforward, no eccentricities. Of course, brave too; the loss of that hand never hindered him you know. It would have overwhelmed a lesser man to be so hampered.' I knew all this of course, but loved to hear Dewnes reassure me,

'Your uncle's first wife, Bridget Chudleigh, was a dear girl, a delight. His widow? Well, she was born under the fifth sign; typical of those women that are happiest being busy with other folk's business.' Applied to my aunt, that was a considerable understatement. What Dewnes said next shocked me,

'No good will come to the Carew family through that woman!' I shivered. Astrology was something many considered harmless nonsense, but the merest hint of witchcraft could condemn even a gentlewoman, the penalty immutable.

'Don't you look so worried, maid! 'Tis merely a statement, not a curse! Your father and I shared the same sentiments from the minute the betrothal was announced.' This was a fascinating insight into family relationships and one I would never have imagined. With characteristic briskness my grandmother changed the subject, taking me by surprise,

'Now, what are we going to do about you, my dear? You are not sleeping well, something patently obvious from the dark circles below your eyes, and it is not simply due to the lack of fresh air.' I had to confess that, as time went on, the absence of any information was draining my spirit.

'I cannot tell what to do, Dewnes. Though I am out of my aunt's clutches for the time being, to have any hope of being where Lewis might look for me I think I must return to Cornwall. I have no way of knowing anything!' Grandmother's expression was unfathomable. She simply replied,

'We shall see what we shall see,' then just as deftly she changed the subject again, 'I do think this wool is a better quality for spinning than the last sack, you know.' And with that the topic seemed closed.

The next day Dewnes was complaining how the low March sunlight showed the grime on smeared window panes when a woman arrived at the barton, neatly dressed but in workaday clothes. Loveday Yendacott and I were introduced. Dewnes treated her with great respect, drawing her near to the fire and finding a cushion for the chair. Refreshments were ordered and as the housemaid left, Dewnes spoke confidingly,

'Goody Yendacott, I have asked for your help for my grand-daughter is troubled and cannot sleep. I would greatly appreciate your advice, and perhaps a remedy?' I knew very well that my grandmother had access to her own stock of remedies, and to be truthful, it disturbed me that the ministrations of a stranger were being sought on my behalf.

'I'll take no payment, Goodwife Hilman, you understand me?' the visitor said, with no hint of deference. These women were equals. My grandmother replied just as directly,

'I do understand you, Goodwife Yendacott.'

'Then call me Loveday, and I shall call 'e Dewnes and we shall mark each other well.' I had missed something in the exchange, something subtle, but the atmosphere had imperceptibly changed, relaxed, the two women as easy as old friends.

'Mary, come sit with us, and bring over the tray of cakes, if you will,' said Dewnes, which I duly did, sitting on the settle opposite Loveday. She put down her drink and leaning towards me took my left hand, looking into my face as she did so, then back to my palm where she traced the lines with the tip of her little finger. I was taken aback, but did not pull away.

'You do not recognise it but you already have the answer to your question,' she muttered. Without thinking the one question incessantly on my mind flew to my lips, where was Lewis? I thought she was about to dismiss me, as I felt her grip release my hand, then snatching my wrist, Mistress Yendacott pulled my palm towards her again, her eyes scanning intently. She huffed and seeking in the folds of her skirt pulled out a pouch then poured forth six smooth, speckled-green river pebbles. These she threw on the slate floor between us, seeming to mark carefully the lie of each stone. We remained silent until she huffed again, and sat back, seeming satisfied.

'As I say, you have already been given the answer to your first question, but there is another which you should ask. The stones say he will come over and under the water, and should beware the man of two faces. Believe the words of a scoundrel for he tells of a steadfast heart.' She shook her head as if to clear her thoughts, took a swig of wine and finished, 'But I cannot see beyond the gates.'

I was uncomfortable at the stranger's ability to see into my deepest thought but also wondered if the strong drink before noon had turned her head, but Dewnes took Loveday's hand in hers, and gently kissed her fingers, murmuring,

'I thank you, Loveday, for Mary means the world to me and I have been much troubled by her unhappiness.'

'You are welcome, Dewnes!' replied the woman, pleasantly, as if nothing out of the ordinary had happened.

She put her hand into her pocket again and pulled out a twist of clean linen containing several little lozenges. She gave them to me nonchalantly, adding, 'Take one each evening. You will sleep far better for it.' Finishing her wine, flicking the crumbs of cake from her skirt into the hearth, she stood up to leave.

'God give you good day, Dewnes! And to you Mary, sweet dreams! I thank you for your hospitality but now I must go. Goody Tozer needs me at her confinement.' Both grandmother and Goody Yendacott bobbed each other a brief curtsey, which I hastily copied. As we walked our guest to the porch, the housemaid brought forward a well-laden, covered basket. I could not see the contents but from the smell, there was a least a batch of newly-baked honey cakes under the linen cloth.

'I would take it as a great favour if you would take this gift to a woman in the village,' said my grandmother, looking Loveday in the eye.

'She will be much comforted, I thank you,' replied Loveday and pulling up her hood, stepped out into the daylight. That night I slept more soundly that I had done since I was a child.

On the spring equinox, on a grey afternoon with low cloud blanketing Dartmoor, a clatter of many hooves and loud male voices rattled the doves from their perches on the gables. Somehow Dewnes did not seem surprised when a tall soldier, with chestnut-red hair and arrogance in every gesture, strode out of the swirling mist to bang at the front door, complaining,

'Hell and the devil confound it! I have ridden these by-ways more times than enough, and yet now I find myself in a god-forsaken hole miles from nowhere! Begging your pardon, madam!' he sketched a slight bow, 'Where the devil are we?'

'Good-day sir!' said my grandmother, calmly, 'you find yourselves at Coombe Barton and I will wager have taken the wrong turning in the village. Can I press you and your men to stay for refreshment? There are new-baked honey-cakes...'

The gentleman stopped in his tracks, eyed my grandmother warily, then bellowed to the platoon of horsemen, who dismounted and pulled off helmets and gauntlets. Dewnes directed him, 'Let your men take their horses into the barns where they might dry off a little. I will have the servants bring out food.' The horses were soon finding their way to hay-nets hung on the barn doors and the men stood at ease, conversation rolling in a deep rumble round the rafters. The stranger shook off his cloak, his manner brusque,

'Sir Richard Grenvile, at your service madam! My men and I are destined for Plymouth, and though my superiors directed me via Totnes, I had a fancy to take in my ex-wife's old home. We go to Tavistock and some plundering at Fitzford!' Catching sight of me he straightened, one quizzical eyebrow raised,

'And who is this?' he exclaimed with a disconcerting leer as I carried out a tray of clay cups to the barn.

'This is my grand-daughter, Sir Richard. Her name is Mary Carew.' The effect of my name on the cavalier was extraordinary, for he stopped as if stunned. Turning to regard me more seriously, he seemed perplexed,

'I have heard that name so often in the last two years that I would have become sick of it, except that the man who kept it ringing in my ears is a kinsman and a Cornishman.' Then he brusquely added, 'Yet a Carew is not of these parts. You should be across the Tamar.'

'My home is across the Tamar, Sir Richard,' I replied, my heart beating so hard that I was sure that he would hear it. 'At Penwarne, near Mevagissey.'

'God's death if that isn't a coincidence! Lewis rarely passes a day without speaking of you. You bear no resemblance to his description, you are fair-haired and much prettier and I shall tell him so when I see him!'

'And when do you expect to see him, sir?' My grandmother spoke where I could not.

'His orders were to sail from Cork a week after me so he

should have landed at Barnstaple this month past.' He drained his cup. 'But I cannot stand about here exchanging social niceties. Come lads! Move your saggy arses, we're away! To horse!' and with a sardonic bow, he mounted and led his troops away up the lane. Watching them disappear into the fog, Dewnes murmured,

'Well met, Sir Richard Grenvile. How fortunate for us that your attention was on Fitzford and not on gathering supplies for the new season's campaign!' and turning on her heel, she hooked her arm in mine.

'Let me think,' she said, smiling, 'Those two questions of which Loveday spoke…I know that the first question was where is Lewis Tremayne?' I nodded.

'And I would guess that the second question, answered by that irrefutable scoundrel, was 'when is he coming home?''

XXII Grace: By sea to Ireland and to Wales January 1644 – March 1644

There was no question that I was expected to wear the boy's clothes and it seemed to amuse Fenwick when I appeared on deck. On the first day I had rebelliously left my hair loose, a flare of copper which blew about and blinded me as the wind whipped it into ropes even though I pulled a wool cap over my head for warmth. I braided it into a clumsy plait and tied the end with some twine. It felt strange with cloth about my legs but was unquestionably more convenient in the winter weather.

I had a choice: to be cowed or to be defiant. Below deck, I doubted things could get worse; above deck? Well, I would find out, but defiance seemed preferable. I had spent time on ships, mostly on Bristol's waterfront. As boys, Hal and Ned often rode down the Avon on board traders, coming ashore when the gig pulled alongside to take the harbour pilot back to Portbury but I was not allowed on those adventures. Resenting the restriction, once I had contrived to go with them, for which we had all received a thrashing. Nevertheless I knew that I would find my 'sea-legs' more quickly on deck and I needed to know what was happening.

At first light, I found a position by the rail on the quarterdeck above the cabins and, in a crisp and cold NE wind, remained there for as long as was practicable. The business of sailing, tacking, navigation, all routine matters went on despite me, the lookouts alert for enemy shipping. Fenwick gave his orders then went below to a different cabin. During the day, I might as well have been invisible. Three more nights I suffered the same agonising indignity: never did I have to look into his face and only once did I fear that I might get with child, for he was careless. After the first morning, I fetched my own seawater.

Outside, everyone on board ignored me. All except the young boy who shyly brought me a dish of bread and cold meat with ale when I refused to go below.

Then there was Sark. During the day he was usually in evidence, often I caught him watching me, a frown on his face. I did not mind his expression for I had no desire to engage in a conversation with the gunner. It seemed to me that he and my husband were in collusion and I had made a dark assumption that the sinister male laughter of the night was associated with this disturbing man. Sark seemed just as reluctant to communicate. It was dusk on the third day before he cleared his throat and gruffly asked,

'If you should want to stand the dog-watch I can help.' I thought the reference to a hound was callous and cruel. I glared at him. He looked uncomfortable but continued,

'I should explain. There are those that say the dog-watch is named after a patch of sky where the dog-star Sirius can be found.'

Here was a strange situation for, though I could not be sure, I thought that Sark was placing an emphasis upon certain words. The bo'sun stood not far away but the wind would carry Sark's words away from him, and the two crewmen at the whipstaff certainly would not be able to overhear us. Nevertheless, Sark seemed wary.

Dog-watch, help, explain, dog, patch, found. There was only one way to find out if Sark was passing me a message. I replied,

'But Sir, do I get your meaning correctly? Explain more clearly, if you will for I thought the sky changes with the season.' He looked irritated, turned to me and glared pointedly,

'Safe to say, the dog-watch is half the norm because contented sailors may then be well fed at a suitable hour.' Safe, contented, sailors, well fed. That was the message. Patch was safe and it seemed that Sark had something to do with it. I could not hide my relief though where they would conceal a dog I could not guess; the *Ann* was not a big ship.

'Thank you, Gunner Sark. That is most happily understood.' He replied gruffly that he had matters to attend to, and left, his feet barely touching the ladder down to the main deck.

I watched him rehearse the gun crews repeatedly; a man professional and exacting, hard on any man who did not meet his standards, but now even more of an enigma.

I daily noted the sun's rise and set, privately guessing that we were heading for Ireland. I was right. At Cork our 'cargo', nearly one hundred soldiers, a few with their womenfolk, met us with their captain-of-foot, returning to fight for King Charles. I remained at my customary station watching them board from the small boats. Their officer climbed to the quarterdeck, snatching a second look before he addressed me. He was obviously both curious and acutely embarrassed. I could not help but smile.

'Good-day, er..ma'am? May I join you? I am Lewis Tremayne, Major in the King's army.' He grinned back; a boyish, impish look and I liked him immediately. Sark, who had been watching from the fo'c'sle, darted across the maindeck.

'Good-day, Major. I am the Master's wife, Grace Godwy...' I corrected myself, 'I apologise. The name is still new on my tongue. Grace Fenwick: I am pleased to make your acquaintance.'

Sark had climbed the ladder, nodded brusquely to the newcomer and established himself in a position on the opposite side of the deck to mine. An unexpected mischief overtook me and believing that it would annoy him, I invited Sark to join us, introducing him to the newcomer only as Gunner Sark. Lewis Tremayne, immediately engaged, took a professional interest in the merchant ship's armaments, forcing the other man to reply, then,

'So, whereabouts in Cornwall are you from, Sark? It seems a pity that two Duchy men cannot address one-another less formally; call me Lewis. What's your Christian name?' It would have been uncivil for Sark to avoid the question, though he was obviously very uncomfortable and kept his voice low.

'I prefer to work just with my family name, Sir, but my given name is,' he cleared his throat and finished,

'Tremenheere.' My expression probably reflected my surprise for I had not registered an accent. The colonel was considering the information,

'Hmm, there's a Tremenheere on the Lizard, near the old Tremayne lands at St. Martin-in-Meneage....' Sark interrupted him,

'No, no, it is after my mother's family where I was brought up, further west. I never use it, for folk think me Dutch or Irish. Either way I am taken for a rogue.' He frowned. 'Life has proved simpler as plain Sark!' he added wryly. It was obviously difficult for anyone, even Sark, not to warm to Major Tremayne who then asked,

'The Channel Islands are invaluable in the King's supply chain. Are you of the islands?' Sark shrugged a reply,

'I may be. It was my father's name. He was a sailor but I never knew him.'

I was intrigued, and a little surprised at how easily Sark had relaxed with Lewis. I had never seen him so at ease. That changed in a moment as Fenwick came up on deck and issued orders to make all sail as soon as was possible, sailors rushing to man the rigging and the anchor capstan. Sark looked skywards as he contemplated the clouds then he declared,

'The weather's turning; it's brewing from the south-west. It will not make for a comfortable voyage. You should go below Mistress. It will be rough when we leave the anchorage, wet and dangerous up here. Master Fenwick will have to be on deck this night I shouldn't wonder,' he added pointedly. Once more, I thought I sensed a meaning out of the ordinary but I was not ready to take Tremenheere Sark's orders.

However, his forecast was accurate, the weather was vile and eventually I reluctantly went below. Nor was Fenwick in evidence. Battered, the ship eventually took shelter on the Welsh coast, Lewis Tremayne discovering that we were off Pembroke, which according to his intelligence, was a town held by Parliamentarian troops but under considerable pressure from the King's forces. He was delighted to be engaging so swiftly with the Royalist campaign, expecting to be put ashore with his men to join the attack.

Yet men of war should be ready for surprises. And women too. At dawn of January 24th, a small fleet of five ships made their way into Angle Bay. There was no doubt from the pennants at their masts that they were Parliamentarian. We were trapped in a haven, and had no way to escape. To take the *Ann* out to sea would have taken her into the firing range of the two largest ships. The crew were edgy, but only Sark looked peculiarly worried. The bo'sun blew a whistle and the ship's company and the soldiers gathered on deck, the terrified huddle of camp-followers crushed at the rear and the sailors lining the ship's rails.

Fenwick appeared, looking complacent. My flesh began to crawl. The crew shifted imperceptibly. Fenwick climbed to the quarterdeck; I moved as far away as possible. Sark and the bo'sun joined him, the other officers remaining on the maindeck. My husband addressed the assembly,

'The fleet of Admiral Richard Swanley has, this day, arrived to assist the Parliamentarian forces struggling under the threat of the Royalist menace by land. He and Vice Admiral Smith intend to liberate these shores for God and Right, from the hold of Charles Stuart's minions.'

As I listened, my flesh began to tingle in alarm. The tone was all wrong. What was I hearing? There was worse to come.

'My ship has, for the last month, been acting with the knowledge of the Lord High Admiral as a spy-ship for Parliament's naval forces. My sailors are paid by Parliament and will fight for Parliament.'

I could hardly comprehend the extent of this treachery. The ring of seafarers around the unarmed soldiers tightened, each now revealing a weapon or cudgel in their hand. Fenwick nodded to men on the fo'c'sle, two flintlock muskets were aimed at Lewis Tremayne.

'Major Tremayne, I give you and your men this one opportunity to correct your error of judgement in joining forces with Charles Stuart, the tyrant-king. Pledge allegiance to Parliament and...' He did not have time to finish.

'By God, I will not!' Tremayne bawled, 'you traitorous cur! My soldiers...' He was unable to finish for three heavily built men restrained him, one dealing him a blow to the back of the head. I looked around at Sark. He might have been made of stone. Fenwick addressed the deck again, the soldiers now hemmed in tightly.

'Your officer has made his decision. I wonder how many of you feel he was mistaken? Join with the good Lord's army, or perhaps you like the life at sea? Take the pay of Parliament's Navy!' Not one man moved. Fenwick sneered,

'If you will not take the pay, then take the consequences!'

At a signal from the man who had betrayed my father's trust, a villain who had handed the *Ann* to the enemy, the bo'sun stepped forward to take over. The crew made to secure Tremayne's company but they were not about to go without resistance. For a brief while, the deck became a heaving mass of shouting, brawling men. The crew had the advantage of surprise and experience of the vessel; the soldiers were weak from the voyage. A shot rang out, and a man howled in pain. As the noise died suddenly, Fenwick spoke,

'You are prisoners, traitors to God's cause - and for all I know you are the papists bound for English towns to murder good Protestant people as you did in your own land. Secure them and take them below!'

The men were herded back down the companionway, many of them falling to shouts of derision. Sark stepped forward. The bo'sun moved with him. I think nobody had noticed me.

'Fenwick,' Sark growled, keeping his voice low, 'You will answer for this deceit!' Fenwick laughed; a cold, evil sound.

'Is that an observation or statement, Sark? Do not bandy words with me. It has hitherto been expedient to keep you by my side but remember what you owe to me. From now on I have the pick of Parliament's gunners. So if you do not like my naval regime, or my methods, you may join the infantry below.' Sark's next words made me feel sick, seeming as they did to implicate him with the man I now despised more than ever.

'You have yet to establish yourself, Fenwick, and just as you have always done, you still need me. I will continue to arm this wallowing hulk and make her a fighting ship. But take care, for complacency is a bad trait at sea!'

He turned on his heel, and went below. Trying to suppress the nausea sweeping over me, I retched and Fenwick turned, sharply motioning to the bo'sun to remove me. I was manhandled to the cabin. As the key turned in the lock, the man's brutish laugh froze me to the core.

Swanley's forces began an assault on the coast within hours, with sailors and a small land force taking the local Royalist garrisons by surprise and ships' guns pounding the little towns around the Haven. The bitter winter weather meant the invaders were suffering, but not as much as the captives below the deck of the Ann.

Conditions were inhuman, the stench becoming a physical thing around us. Food had been in miserably short supply but the cold did as much harm as the neglect. Men died, their bodies unceremoniously thrown overboard. I could do nothing, remaining under lock and key except for one hour every morning. I was fed very little and only given the means to look after my basic well-being. My monthly courses stopped. The rags I wore began to hang on my frame, and at night I wound my old skirt around me to try to keep warm. I saw nothing of Sark, or Lewis. Fenwick used the cabin rarely, me not at all.

For four weeks, we waited at anchor as the rest of the fleet operated along the west Wales coast. A concentrated attack finally saw Tenby surrender after days of bombardment. By my reckoning it was the beginning of March. One morning I heard unusual ceremony, shouted commands. The ship's boy arrived with the simple instruction 'Be ready', the bo'sun manhandling me to the quarterdeck some time later. There was biting wind, even in the shelter of the bay. The ship's company was gathered, the pathetic prisoners struggling up from the putrid squalor below decks, squinting in the light.

Beside Fenwick, his manner unnaturally deferential, were two men. I was to discover that one was Admiral Richard Swanley, a beaked nose, dark eyes and prominent brows giving him the look of a hawk. The other, more square-set, was his Vice Admiral, William Smith. A table and two chairs from a cabin were set before them. I looked for Sark, catching a glimpse of him at the starboard gunwale, watching warily. Then he went below deck.

He re-appeared escorting Lewis Tremayne, now untidily bearded with matted hair; yet his shoulders set straight as Sark released his grip, sneeringly muttering something in the major's ear before he shoved him towards Swanley. What followed was a sham, an ordeal and a travesty of a court martial, Swanley falsely claiming that the troops were Irish Catholics, and thus Parliament's implacable enemies. The worst was to come: a death sentence, after which Admiral Swanley stood up and with a cold brutality declared,

'These vermin stink, they stink of the blood of the innocent Protestants that is upon them. They aren't fit to dirty the hangman's noose.' With nothing left to lose many soldiers, weak as they were, yelled that they were no murderers, that they fought to suppress rebels, but it was of no use.

'Tie them together, back to back. Then I want them all washed, wash them of the blood they have spilled! The women included! I want the ship's boat in the water to make sure they are washed so completely that the Devil will be able to recognise them in Hell! Get on with it!'

I wept as the soldiers were seized, women too, all beaten if they resisted. They were tied as Swanley had directed; some were bellowing and screeching, others struck dumb with shock. Lewis Tremayne writhed and shouted until Sark took over his restraint and slapped him hard across the mouth. Elbowing the coxswain out of the way, he watched as the ship's longboat was lowered over the side.

Despairing I watched as Sark tossed a belaying pin into the boat and, a knife between his teeth, climbed down the pilot-ladder, a murderous expression on his face. Nobody offered to accompany him. Fenwick turned to speak to his commander, keeping his voice low and screening his mouth with the back of his hand. Swanley glanced in my direction and smirked, nodding in sympathy,

'Feel at liberty to do as you please, Fenwick! One less bitch won't be missed if you've had your fill of her!'

The bo'sun grabbed me and I was hauled, struggling, to where Lewis was sprawled and at hip and chest we were bound, our backs together. I kept screaming over and over as they dragged each obscene human bundle to a gap in the rail. The ship's boat bobbed between the pathetic pools of bubbling foam. I caught a glimpse of Sark's back as he leaned over the side of the smaller boat, knife now in his hand, intent on the figures in the murky depths, but soaked by the spray of forty pairs of screaming, praying, wailing humanity hitting the water.

We were not the last to be shoved from the ship, and we did not hit the ship's side as many others did, so I was conscious as the shock of icy seawater flooded over me. I was conscious as the shadow of the skiff loomed over my head, and still conscious as the boat, tipping ominously pulled alongside. Shipping oars, Sark's hand grabbed the ropes at my shoulder and the knife glinted, slashing. The noise around was sickening, unworldly, but I heard clear,

'Are you ready?'

A Cornishman replied,

'Onan hag oll!' There was a yell and the skiff tipped. It tipped too far, and another, unbound body joined us in the sea, a barrel falling with him. I realised that my arms were now free; I tried to move but the water made the cloth around my body so heavy. My mind was becoming numb. A pair of hands was beneath me, pushing me though the water. I surfaced to see the stern of the ship looming overhead. I could read the bright new paint of the name on the carved board high above but could not think why it looked so wrong: *Leopard.* Then I thought I heard the words,

   'My love, I am sorry!' before a terrible pain filled my head. After that, I knew nothing.

XXIII Hester: Barnstaple July 1644 – September 1644

Straightway after Mistress Palmer took me on I dashed in to tell the Bess the baker's daughter my good news then I ran back to get my bundle. But the whiles I'd been out some thieving, draw-latch knave had riffled what few belongings I had; my pass and the pie had gone, just the Bible lay broken backed and tossed aside with my apron. The taverner would give me back none of my unused rent either, the rogue. 'Lucky for you, Hester' I thought to myself 'that you have those few coins still stitched up in your hem.'

My new work was just as unkind to my poor knees as Bideford had been though my wrists ached less. I minded nothing about my labours except for one thing, which was clearing up around the cage of a parrot-bird in the parlour. The bird was supposed to be one hundred years old, though it did not look it, and threw seed and shit all around. Some clever wit had taught it to cry 'Whose mare is dead?' which it did when you least expected it. It had learned some other language too but, for sure, not from the Godly in that house, for a parrot-bird screeching 'Who's a poxy doxy?' sounds more like a seaman's than Alderman's, and it had probably heard a lot worse.

The town paid a heavy price for the Royalist's defeat with soldiery packed in every corner of the place to increase the defences. And the military bought their own justice too. A week or so into July a Lieutenant-somebody was hanged in front of the Guildhall at High Cross as a deserter and turncoat, a'cause he fought first for the Parliament then took twenty troopers with him to the King's side. They captured him in the attack on the town and if it had not been for Barum troops fighting at Modbury in '43, he might have lived to tell the tale, but he was recognised and so felt the hangman's noose.

Whilst Barnstaple was seeing its fair share of warring,

Parliament was winning battles up country. The turmoil reached us in North Devon and it put a stop to Barnstaple Fair. All the unsettling news must have put off traders heading for Barum and so the few country-folk who braved the roads full of riders were right folshid that '44 saw no show of a fair by anyone at all. But then again no huckster would come where customers had no coin to spend in his booth.

That week the weather broke too, with rain and rain upon rain. I was running to the pannier market one morning, though Mistress Palmer was not hopeful of much produce on the stalls, when the Reverend Dyckwood stepped out from behind one of the pillars under the overhanging rooms of the Guildhall. Catching my arm, he called,

'Ho! Mistress Phipps, I do believe you have been avoiding me!'

Now that was nonsense for I'd no time to spend avoiding anyone for I was kept too busy, and he was the last on my list. He stepped closer,

'I have something of yours found after you left the lodging; you must have dropped it - a poppet. Does it mean a great deal to you?' From the purse at his belt he pulled the little bag, which Mary had thrown after me, a clay doll tucked inside.

I had quite forgotten it but as he thrust the thing at me, my mind flew right back to the day I found a drawing on a rag in my basket for the shape was the same. In the legs were stuck pins where the knees should be, there were rusty holes at the hands where pins had fallen out. I snatched at it but was clumsy and the thing fell in the wet where the rain began to wash the shape until quickly it was only a clobb on the stones. Reverend Dyckwood caught and kept my wrist tight and drew me to him, speaking so none would hear,

'You have a side to you I would not have expected, Hester Phipps. Many would say that I have just witnessed a tool of witchcraft. A minister must protect his people from such evils. Come wench, explain yourself!' I did not like his tone, but I could hardly fight a man of God in the street.

He pulled me through an alleyway to the back of the inn, and up to the letting room. No packman or rat-catcher there now, just he and me. He seemed to have gathered himself.

'Hester,' he says, silky-voiced and quiet, 'Do not be afraid, for the Lord will be with you. But you must let me help. If you have Satan in your soul I can rid you of him…'

I cried out that I had been cleared fair and proper by a court and he could see the Constable in Bideford if he did not believe me, then blabbed the tale of the bridge and the curse. He went even quieter,

'I believe you, Hester, I believe you. You have a true heart, for I can see into your soul. But wickedness such as this, spells and hexes, cannot be battled by the pure soul alone. I will need to help you, cleanse you, purify you for the Lord. Will you kneel, Hester? Let me help you, Hester?'

Now, there I was in a cleft stick betwixt a walloping for meechin' away from my work, and a damning for a sin I didn't commit. I decided that a beating I could take but damning needed someone more fitty than me to put it right. I put down my basket, and knelt.

'We will pray for guidance from the Lord, and move as he wills it! Close your eyes, and pray Hester. I will prepare the Holy Wine and we will cleanse your soul!' I did as I was bid, and in a moment, him speaking all sorts of Bible words, I had my head tipped back and a cup of strong wine put to my lips.

'Drink the spirit of the Lord!' whispered Dyckwood. So I did. Three times he filled the cup for Father, Son and Holy Ghost he said. By the time the third was empty my head was a-swim so much that I could not keep my balance. The last thought I remember was that my knees were not hurting. The last words I heard were, 'Here will I cleanse you of all evils!' and then all was black.

I woke up on the splintered floor, my skirts around my waist. The hem was torn open and it was empty. There was no priest, nor vicar, nor man of the cloth in sight.

For shame, I cannot tell you how I had been cleansed, except that all the scrubbing in the world could not wipe away the mire. At that very moment, I was in the darkest place I could ever have dreamed of, worse even than these days in Pendennis fort. Nothing I said would stand against the Reverend Dyckwood, for who would believe me, a serving maid, and him a learned churchman? Running through my head were Old Judd's sermons telling me about the apostle's teaching that whatever a man sows, that is what he will reap. And the very word 'seed' brought on a dark, heaviness clinging to me, making me shudder so I could not stop.

I gathered myself, my knees so weak that I barely crawled out of the tavern, going as best I could, back to Cross Street. I couldn't guess what time it was but when I bumped into Bess, an empty basket on her arm it did remind me that I had lost my own, and I should have been back to my mistress long before. I could bear it no more. My tears started there in the street and I could not stop them.

Bess took charge for I doubt if I made any sense at all and she could see there was something terrible wrong, me with my hair all cawtched and hem torn awry so she took me back to the bake-house, where in the sweet musty warmth I spilled out the awful truth.

Even to my own ears, it sounded that I had been summ'at mazed to trust the man and I half expected her to give me a slap towards the beating I would surely get at Mistress Palmer's hand. But she did not. She was angsty for me and straightway went up the stair to the baker's rooms, and a moment later had fetched down her mother. Then her pa the baker came down, and I thought 'Hester, here is the crowd come to stone you, not just give you a beating!' but suddenly I had four doughy arms around my shoulders and kind words and there was I, awash with tears again and all a-bivver.

Bess' father helped me up to their tiny parlour above the bake-house, and sat me down with a cup of Geneva spirit, which I did not want, but he told me to drink, saying it would warm me through and stop the tremors. His kindly wife gently shooed him away and sat down on a stool beside me and taking my hand said,

'That man will pay for what he did, Hester. Good God-fearing Barnstaple folk will not stand by and see an innocent abused. No matter what his church, he will not escape justice. We will go to Mistress Palmer, for her husband will know what to do. But first, I am sorry but I must ask. Do you have your monthly bleed?' I nodded, afraid all over again. She asked a few questions then patted my hand saying, 'We have something which will help that' and sat with me for some long time just rocking me gently and quietly chattering about everyday matters until I felt calmer and the heaving sobs had stopped.

At the Palmer's house, I came under the protection of the women and there was more kindness. I still cannot say the word for my 'trouble' though it was spoken often enough that day. Master Palmer went straight-way to the Constable who raised the hue and cry, for Dyckwood was to be found and brought to the justice. I was sent to bed with a spoonful of a tincture of bay-berry and the next day my concerns about the consequence of a Dyckwood 'cleansing' came with cramps and blood and I wept again, this time out of relief.

Of course, they could find not hide nor hair of him, but as the town was all in an uproar a small matter of the rough courting of a lass would easy slip people's minds. For war was at the gates again.

We had watched as many troops marched off to Taunton. Colonel Luttrell the town commander had only been following his orders. Still, it left Barnstaple with a scanty garrison. Some Roundheads were sent to Ilfracombe for ammunition but the guns at that place had been turned against the men, and the officer was sent back with a flea in his ear. There were thirty cannons around Barum, on the quay or in the fortifications, with no shot nor powder and not too many soldiers to man them.

The rustle of rumour was at work again and Barnstaple folk were quaking but 'twasn't long before rumour became fact: the Colonels had no time to lose for the Cavaliers were on their way.

Time hung heavy in those next weeks, passing too slowly. I now had information about Lewis, though there was nought I could do with it. Because I had hope, I wanted to be off to Barnstaple, or Bideford or Bristol or anywhere where I might seek him, like a lovelorn princess in an ancient romance setting out to seek her knight in shining armour. What had Grenvile said? Lewis rarely passed a day without speaking of me.

However, women should not go adventuring. Neither does a well-bred girl roam the land in search of her gentleman. It was no time to leave the protection of Coombe Manor for there was no sign of an end to the conflict. Such was the harsh reality of '44; the situation between King and Parliament had been resolved neither by negotiation nor by battle and we had heard of the recall of troops to their regiments by both parties.

The winter stores seemed to run short much sooner that year and the weekly assessments had to be paid to whichever authority held the upper hand, there being little to distinguish between the commissioners of either party who collected the plate and coin from the hard-pressed people of town or county. Plymouth had not surrendered to the Royalists, Exeter remained staunchly for the King and the south-west soon became a focus for Parliament's army. We were to discover that even the remoteness of our quiet manor would not keep us safe.

Late in April Dewnes received a letter from Antony House, thinly veiled disapproval in every line. I was to be informed that 'matters' both there and at Penwarne remained unchanged, despite my absence. The implication was ominous. My grandmother and I discussed a strategy should Aunt Carew make demands.

'I will keep you safely confined, it barely needs nine

months, so that your hero can claim you and you may give your consent to marriage in your own right,' she laughed, waving her arms in dramatic gestures designed to dismiss the apprehension I felt when I recognised the handwriting from Cornwall.

'Then the Dowager-Bombast-Carew will have no more control over you,' she paused, 'though of course, it would always be pleasant to have your papa's approval even though it may not be necessary when you have reached twenty-one years of age.' She hugged me to her and conspiratorially added, 'So, where shall we build you a hiding place?'

Whilst I still feared the command to return to Cornwall, I need not have worried. Aunt Carew held no sway at Coombe. One brief missive from my sister Agnes added nothing of significance from home except that father's speech had improved a little and that Candacia had killed her pet linnet by leaving the cage on a sun-baked window ledge. I was not missed, it seemed.

We heard that the Queen had reached Exeter on May Day and once more I bewailed my inactivity, Dewnes tersely observing that since Her Majesty had the might of an army to protect her yet still she was in peril what sense did it make for me to take to the highways?

The next day the ancient arquebus that had hung over the hearth in the parlour was taken down and dispatched to the blacksmith in Moretonhampstead to be cleaned and to have adjustments made. Within the week Jan Leightfast, a small, wily-looking chap with a grizzled beard who my grandmother euphemistically introduced as a 'fowler', was standing in the sun in the middle of the courtyard demonstrating the loading and employment of a long musket almost as tall as he was. The refurbished arquebus was then unveiled, at which a surprised Leightfast spluttered an oath, rapidly apologising to my grandmother for the blasphemy. He inspected the piece.

'Tis a crude adaptation of an antique piece to the modern way of a flintlock, but am I to suppose there's nary a need for lit match-cord then?' he said, looking sceptical.

'Indeed that was my intention for I have heard flint and steel can be used to spark the pan – Oh, dear! Am I using the correct terms? – Well, I have heard it is easier for an amateur,' Dewnes replied artfully, 'but it would perhaps be reassuring for us ladies to test its proof?' Then she slyly added,

'And who better than your good self, Master Leightfast?' at which the poacher straightened his shoulders and hefted the gun.

With a bigger barrel, flared at the muzzle, it was far more unwieldy than his musket, and loading the powder, shot and wadding was an awkward and time consuming matter. Even he needed a forked rest to support the weight of the gun. To accompany the demonstration he delivered a wordy discourse on the development of the firearm and its efficacy against all manner of wild beasts and armed men.

The gun took such an amount of time to load that the attention of the farmhands wandered so, when the gun was primed and fired, the ear-splitting retort around the granite forecourt took nearly everyone by surprise. Two panes of glass were dislodged from the leads in the window above the porch, dogs howled and barked furiously and it took ten minutes to calm the mare in the stable. Where the bullet went nobody could say.

'Well, that was invigorating,' remarked my grandmother, taking a long look at the smoking weapon. 'Do you think I might have a try?' and at the expense of another piece of glass and a further round of canine confusion, she wielded the barrel with remarkable dexterity, though agreeing that a blank shot without musket-ball was perhaps prudent.

'How reassuring to know that one can teach an old dog a new trick,' she said, dusting the smouldering wool from her sleeve. She handed the arquebus over to me.

'Now it is your turn, Mary! You never know when you might need to use it!' I followed Leightfast's instructions; afterwards the smell of burned black powder stayed in my nostrils for hours, a great bruise showing on my shoulder by evening.

'It is not ideal but as every new gun is requisitioned as soon as stock and barrel meet it will have to suffice to protect Coombe as best we may,' declared Dewnes, at the supper-table. 'In an emergency I can't see us having coils of smouldering match-cord to hand, hence my request that the old piece have the adaptation of which Jan was so critical. I doubt if I could manage a pole-arm or pike but with our old gun, and if I give each of the maids a rolling pin with permission to use it on the nether regions of intruders, I think we may manage well enough.'

She spoke with a lightness that gave the lie to the expression in her eyes. I thought grandmother jested when I was also encouraged to dust off the antique bow and arrows which hung behind the door of the porch and, as Dewnes instructed, "pass the time at a lady's sport" as well as my household tasks. But her eyes retained the same dark look and I knew this was no joke.

Around midsummer's day, I received a letter from Jane with the news that Alexander was still imprisoned in the Tower of London with no sign of a trial, though she had been allowed to stay with him. His step-brother John, a lawyer with no love at all for the King's cause, had indicated that matters would go badly, implying that it was no less than Alex deserved. She missed Cornwall and her children, all of whom were now back at Antony. In case I had not heard, she told me she had been safely delivered of another daughter a little earlier than expected but now nearly six months old and thriving better than Jane could hope, adding that she suspected that she might be carrying again. The letter ended 'I hope that your predicament has resolved itself'.

How could I reply to Jane? Her situation made my own complaints seem petty. I did not know where her infant had been born but I could only admire the courage of women like my cousin and the Queen who had shared the perils of childbirth, confined and in straitened circumstances, and yet bore their anxiety with fortitude.

Packmen travelling the moorland roads brought us news and rumours of Royalists under Prince Maurice mustering at Okehampton, and Cornishmen who were now even more reluctant to leave their county to fight. The Roundheads had been victorious near York in early July, one tradesman selling a crumpled tract entitled 'A Dog's Elegy or Rupert's Tears', a scurrilous ridiculing of the Prince and his faithful hound which had been killed at the same battle.

If we believed that the war would be fought at a distance we began to think again, for it also seemed that the Earl of Essex was intent on eradicating the King's supply lines by taking control of the Duchy of Cornwall. They would need to skirt Dartmoor, or cross it, unless the plan was to enter the county along the north coast route. The King and a sizeable force were closing in behind this massive parliamentarian army, heading westwards but they would not arrive in time to protect us.

'You mark my words! They'll descend upon us like locusts, just when the cider has been pressed and the barley is beginning to ripen,' grumbled Dewnes as we podded peas for drying. 'The cheeses and butter will go, the chickens will be killed for the pot and where will that leave us next winter? Nothing for making honey cakes except the honey - and if they could find a good use for it I am sure they'd requisition that too!' It was a sign of tension that now my normally amiable grandmother was often tetchy.

We did not have to wait for barley to ripen though, and the apples were still tight on their branches. And Lord Essex did take a northern route, but not the north coast past the place Parliament were last defeated in Cornwall but rather he swept his army, ten thousand strong, around the northern edge of Dartmoor. For a brief period Okehampton, not fifteen miles from us, was his headquarters and daily foraging parties extended their efforts well onto the moor, for the supply train for the hungry Roundheads was counties away.

It was twelve months since the Bristol fight, and not now a genteel bottling of soft fruit to occupy me, but those essential tasks that would keep us all through the winter. I joined the village-folk in the few fields scraped from the moorland that would produce wheat. With Lammas-tide approaching and a good dry spell in the last dusty days of July, we all hoped that at least the harvest would be early.

We had been out all day, the men mowing and the women following behind to help stack the cut sheaves, children gleaning stray stems behind us or fetching small beer and bread for our dinners. Supper was to be provided at Coombe for those who wanted, and leading the farmhands back to the manor, Loveday Yendacott and I were ambling wearily across the walled yard towards the house when two boys ran, like creatures possessed, back from the direction of Drewsteighton shouting of soldiers and looters, beatings and firebrands.

Within moments, it seemed the whole barton was filled with shouting, heaving troops armoured with back and breastplates, more men on horseback, waving pistols and yelling commands. I grabbed Loveday's sleeve and pulled her into the house, glimpsing our own folk pushed out of the way by the mass of soldiers in tawny-orange doublets. I guessed there might be thirty but it seemed many more for they shouted, harsh and strident with unfamiliar accents. An officer with an evil looking weapon, half axe-half spear, strode towards the house. There would be no honey cakes in the barn to placate the Parliament's men.

Already the kitchen was rattling with un-natural clatter, with jeering and more uproar as the brew-house was wrenched open. Dewnes stood in the cross-passageway, momentarily speechless with indignation. Then,

'Go in there!' she pointed, pushing Loveday and I into the parlour. Taking her riding whip, she stepped towards the door, opening it just as the trooper, his leather buff-coat covered in dust, raised his fist, about to hammer the hilt of his sword on the oak.

I cannot say what happened for sure - whether the sight of the whip enraged the Roundhead soldier or whether the momentum of his swinging blow, unblocked by the door, was now unstoppable. Perhaps he merely saw an old woman as an obstacle to Parliament's triumph over tyranny. A scream echoed round the granite walls as sword cleaved shoulder and a terrifying silence followed.

For the second time in my life, my actions defied convention. I could not tell you how or why the ancient arquebus came to be in my hands but I can tell you that with an icily clear mind I took down the box of shot, the horn of gunpowder. Boots clattered in the porch. While Loveday tried to stem an unstoppable flow of blood, I re-enacted Jan the fowler's lesson. I grabbed the forked gun-rest and hefted the gun to my chest. I stepped out into the passage, braced myself against the wall and levelled the barrel at the cavalryman silhouetted in the doorway.

I heard a distant shot and my finger hauled on the trigger. Another shot made me jump, snatching at the mechanism that would bring flint to steel and spark that deafening cacophony and blow to hell the soldier who had mown down my beloved grandmother.

A click. Silence. There was another shot deafeningly close but not the one to pummel my shoulder or sting my cheek with hot powder, or fill my head with sulphur fumes. The arquebus had misfired. In my hands I had nothing but an antique novelty, deadly only in that it contained enough gunpowder to blow me to shreds if with some terrible irony a random spark ever made its way to the touchhole.

The Roundhead began to laugh, a cruel, foul belly laugh that was drowned out by a ringing, thumping explosion.

Again, the panes of glass in the window above the porch rattled but the gun in my hand remained heavy and cold. The smell of sulphur drifted past me as a breeze blew through the house from back door to front. A man spoke, quietly this time and in a familiar accent.

'Mary, do not turn round. My Carew Chick, do not move. It would be too cruel of Fate if you were to do more damage than the rebels or the Roundheads have managed these last three years. But I fear if you move one muscle that bloody cannon will blow us all to kingdom come!'

Strong arms, these dressed in a well-known west-country blue, lifted the weapon, and caught me as my knees gave way beneath me. More strong arms carried my grandmother to her room.

Tenacious to the last Dewnes did not die that evening, and driven by her indomitable willpower would speak once in a while, observing wryly that indeed my knight had come to my rescue but with a lamentable sense of timing as far as she was concerned. Her chortle was too painful and she did not laugh again. Her last words to me were whispered and disjointed but Dewnes Hilman's spirit filled every syllable,

'Remember, six months to elude Grace Carew. Remember, blacksmith's wife. Remember, my blessings, follow your heart.'

I sat with her until dawn, holding her hand as she slipped from this life to the next and all that long night the strong arms of the man I love were around my shoulders.

The bay where the Admiral had been holding his fleet was deep but narrow. Deep enough for Swanley's barbarity but narrow enough to allow two strong swimmers, who were expecting the ordeal, both towing a burden but lucky with the tide, to make it to the shore un-noticed. The ship's crew were intent on recovering the un-manned skiff, preparing the ship to weigh anchor and sail. If it were not for the horror of the drowned victims, one might almost think it was planned.

As I began to regain consciousness, I tested my senses one by one: sand and pebbles cold and hard under my palms, a light cold breeze, a warm weight lying on my chest. There was a distinct smell of stale fish puffing in my face. I could hear waves at a distance, gulls and the scrape of flint on steel. The taste of salt on my lips and bile stung my throat. I had a very sore head but I was alive.

The fish-breath and weight moved, and a scratchy tongue licked my face. I opened my eyes to see round amber-gold eyes staring into mine. I blinked and a damp, black, ecstatic dog leaped up and started barking wildly.

'Someone is very pleased to see you,' Lewis Tremayne's voice was close by, 'but perhaps it would be best to quieten Patch in case he draws unwanted attention?' As I rolled over, the water from my clothes dribbled cold against my skin and sending me into a spasm of shivering.

I called Patch who dashed to my side and at a word sat as close by me as he could, flicking sand about with his tail. Putting my arm around his bony shoulder, I revelled in his warmth and looked around. Sark was a few feet away, blowing on smouldering tinder to bring a fire to life, as Major Tremayne gathered small bits of driftwood from above the tide-line. A broken barrel lay in the shallows.

I got up and walked carefully to the fire, my shoes gone. My mind was woolly, a jumbled mass of fragmentary horrors, and I had no idea of how I came to be ashore. The fire began to crackle and spit as the officer laid sticks into the flames. Sark stood up and spoke,

'The fleet has sailed but we are in danger of being hunted by friend and foe alike, so there is little time to rest. We are on the wrong side of the enemy and must chase after the King's army until we catch up with them.' This was almost too much to take in. Snatches of the past few days began to come back to me.

'You hit me. You hit him.' I found forming any more coherent conversation impossible.

'Yes. Lewis knew I would hit him, and we had to make it convincing. I did not expect you to do as you were told. So it was necessary to make you compliant,' shrugged Sark. There was something bothering me but the woolliness in my brain meant that I could not fathom it. I focussed on what I could see.

'Patch. How?' I stammered. Tremayne chuckled but Sark replied,

'He was the least of my problems and far easier than you, though a tiny drop of poppy juice from the medicine chest helped. My gun crew wanted to keep him, fattening him up in case of dire emergency!'

My expression must have told more than a thousand words; humour was beyond me and so he quickly added, 'No, to be truthful, they were all fond of him, and knew of my plan, helping to get the barrel into the boat and rigging the line. He was a little sick when we broke open the cask but otherwise none the worse for his ordeal.' I nodded, hugging Patch closer.

'Where are …' I could not bear to think of those screaming bundles of humanity. Sark looked into the flames.

'I did what I could, cut as many free as I could…' The major walked over, put a hand on his shoulder. Then it occurred to me that Sark had other responsibilities.

'What will happen? Them. To…' I began falteringly. 'What will happen to your men?' The gunner stood up briskly, his tone pragmatic,

'They're full-grown and know the game. If they get paid

and get a gun-captain they respect they'll stay. If not they will take their considerable skills elsewhere. Come, try to get your breeches dry. Keep warm like this, swing you arms and jump from foot to foot.'

He demonstrated, and looked foolish, which enhanced my mood a little. He stepped over to move behind me. I was unresisting as he reached to undo the dribbling knot that hung down my back, explaining,

'You would be better if you loosened your hair; it will dry faster and you will be all the warmer for that. We will be heading west as soon as you are able. There must be a farm somewhere nearby that we can filch some shoes at least. We need to reach Carmarthen with all speed.'

So began an episode, which even as I tell it, sounds incredible to my own ears. The gentlemen were already on familiar terms, the result I supposed of one man saving the other's life. Lewis seemed happy to respond to Lew, and he shortened Sark's Christian name to 'Men', something which became a familiar jest for as we set off each morning he would call out, 'Forward, Men!' I remained simply 'Mistress'.

With no cottages nearby that we could safely approach, it was mid afternoon before a solution to the problem of apparel presented itself; a grisly find in a hedge, two bodies, neither of which had been plundered of anything but their weapons. My scruples had vanished. I set to stripping one body as the men dealt with the other. They turned away as I wriggled into cold, dry garments but I was so grateful for the clothes that I would not have cared had they cheered me on. Lewis gave me both pairs of the long boot hose; the socks came over my knees, yet effectively filled the shoes which otherwise would have been too big. We were all now wearing as many layers as was practicable.

Our speed increased immeasurably, my anxiety giving me strength from nowhere. I could not remember when I had last eaten. Coin in the dead soldiers' pockets bought us bread at a farmhouse near Whitland, Sark's Cornish passing close enough to a Welsh dialect to be acceptable. We found a dilapidated barn and I slept fitfully, waking to the cold light of a full moon. Sark's watchful shape filled the doorway, his breath a silvered cloud. Patch wriggled closer and I dozed again.

We crept into St Clears on a Sunday morning. While the cottagers were in church, we shamelessly stole the remains of a ham from a kitchen on the outskirts of the village, leaving two pennies from our deceased benefactors on the plate by way of compensation. Patch caught a rabbit that evening; in Carmarthen we traded it for a jug of small beer and a little information. It transpired that the remnants of the Royalist force were two days ahead of us on a slow if steady move to Shrewsbury, but the Parliament army was nowhere near big enough to harry their retreat so it had regrouped on Pembroke, now a good way behind us. My escort looked more confident at that news.

The ostler had no horses in his stalls, both armies having sequestered anything with four legs, so for the price of a pint of ale paid for by the other dead man, we camped on the straw. I fell asleep instantly with Patch curled close to my chest. Lewis and Sark still took it in turns to watch for possible danger, for there had been inquisitive looks in my direction but curious locals were no real threat. This area of Wales was for the King and so we had little to fear and nothing to lose.

Nevertheless, I had recognised that meddlesome folk might just cause us all trouble and, though I could disguise my looks with dirt, my hair was the problem. It was simply too conspicuous even knotted up under my hat, for I had no pins or comb to keep it neat. Tendrils kept escaping and even the most dashing cavalier could hardly justify my long, coppery locks. I remembered seeing Sark sharpening a dagger so while Lewis and he splashed a cursory morning wash at the pump I asked to borrow the knife. Dampening my head, I went behind the stables to the midden. There I bound up my hair, quickly weaving it into two braids then hacking them off halfway up their length. It took me some minutes and as I threw the last red-gold rope onto the dungheap I realised that I was being watched.

Shaking loose my new crop, I turned round. Sark, his arms folded, a shoulder leaning against the stable wall, was observing me. He had an enigmatic expression on his face. Before I could fathom it, he unfurled himself, stepped up and held out his hand for the knife.

'Stand still,' he told me, 'Close your eyes.' Warily I did as I was told then deft, cool hands gathered strands from across my face, and in seconds, a neat fringe had been cut to lie across my forehead, covering my eyebrows. Not another word was said, and when I opened my eyes he had already turned and walked off, leaving me with my new boyish locks just showing as I pulled on my woollen cap, the new anonymity strangely liberating.

Lewis had discovered that the Royalists intended to re-enforce Shrewsbury as a major garrison. He and Sark would offer their services there. For me, the only way to confront Fenwick would be through the Royalist authorities and, as I had no resources but an amenable escort, Shrewsbury seemed a good place to begin. Tracking their route, we were gaining on them with each passing day even though the roads were now mired in mud, hazardous with murky water disguising deep holes, though the mild weather with occasional sunshine was infinitely better than frosts.

In those ten days, we foraged the countryside, often under the instruction of Sark, who seemed to have a wealth of knowledge about edible roots or plants. We made a reasonable team. Patch worked; he was a keen and effective hunter using a wicked flick to break the creature's neck then waiting patiently for his share of any forthcoming meal. I quickly learned to skin anything that he caught.

Only once did I find that the knife in my shaking hand was stabbing indiscriminately at flesh, which in my mind's eye was not coney. Sark gently eased the blade from my fist that evening, a steady hand on my shoulder until the trembling stopped.

The worst miles were those after Llandovery, for that night we could only find shelter beneath a hedge and Patch had merely caught a lamed squirrel. I was so hungry that I was happy to eat my meagre share once we had roasted it over a lacklustre fire. I had been enjoying my boyish identity but the novelty of wearing breeches, even if they were practical, wore off when I developed blistered legs where the hard old wool had chafed. Sark found young shoots of comfrey near a stream, suggesting that the sap might ease the irritation, which it did.

We were fortunate that in every village along the route, rabbit was a welcome commodity. Folk ignored poaching when there was a chance of fresh meat, which we easily traded for space in a dry barn and, after one particularly good day's hunting before Knighton, fresh bread and broth and a place by a hearth.

Conversation en route was mainly between Lewis and Sark, for keeping pace with their long-legged strides meant I had little breath to spare. I could listen though, and despite myself was entertained, fascinated by the diverse topics on which Sark would initiate a discussion, for Lewis seemed only to have one subject upon his mind, the welfare of one Mary Carew. He had left this lady in Cornwall.

In those days, I imagined Mistress Carew to be proud and hard-hearted, an icy maiden as cold as her colouring was fair. Now the very thought that I should think badly of any woman, let alone Mary, makes me discomfited.

Lewis fretted that Mistress Carew did not reply to his letters, though I reassured him that might be because soldiering is notorious for moving men about; perhaps the correspondence had been lost? Speaking intently on another occasion he told us that he had declared his affections and indeed hoped to return to Cornwall to ask for her hand in marriage; Sark's effort to change the subject at that point was not subtly done,

'Well, I do believe that today is the spring solstice. The evenings are certainly drawing out!' It was hard to hide my smile.

On other occasions, their shared experiences of military life and officers led to a discussion of Lewis' commander in

Ireland, Sir Richard Grenvile. Lewis told us of the general's grief and anger at the news of the death of his brother Bevil.

'He's a fine, professional soldier but more than that he is a true Cornishman and swore then that he would play his part against Parliament to even the score for the Grenvile family. He left Ireland weeks before me, told me that when he "had a power he would go to the King". I did not understand his meaning but Grenvile always had a scheme or two. He'd give away nothing though, even to his Cornish cousin!'

'We Cornish have such strong bonds,' Sark chuckled, 'even great playwrights have recognised it.' I wondered what Sark knew of playwrights, but Lewis picked up the thread, 'What do we say? *A Godolphin never wanted wit nor a Grenvile loyalty.* ...though it's true that our Richard has always one serious want, the want of funds!' I remarked that I thought the man sounded a scoundrel. Both men laughed, Lewis wryly conceding,

'That may be true but he seems damnably proud of the fact! That reminds me, he owes me three crowns but I'll wager the same amount again that I never get it back! No matter! I love the man and I accept his faults.'

His attention wandered,

'I wonder if he is back in Cornwall yet, and would he have word of Mary? I could write...' at which point I slipped in a cart rut, yelping as I twisted my ankle. His deliberations paused while he sought a hazel staff that I could use as a support. By the time we were on the move, albeit slowly, Sark had introduced another topic and Patch had returned from another chase, this time with a partridge in his jaws. All melancholy was dispelled at the thought of roast bird for supper.

Shrewsbury was a town in chaos when we arrived, barricades three deep at the river crossing. There were hundreds of soldiers, the routes into the city under heavy guard. Lewis shamelessly deployed his rank and status, finally getting the attention of a sergeant-at-arms. The garrison of the castle, swollen not just by the influx of troops we had followed from the south, was also full with men from Chester and the northeast. The King's forces were mustering at Shrewsbury awaiting a leader, the new President of Wales.

With Patch on his halter for the first time since I boarded the *Ann* - I could not bear to think of the ship under any other name - I was jostled and buffeted by a mass of humanity the likes of which I had never experienced. I had never ventured out into such thronged streets in Bristol; this was so strange.

The crowds were overwhelming, the smell and noise bewildering and when I caught a glimpse of the bridge such a sense of homesickness swept over me that tears began to trickle down my grubby face. The stone arches so resembled our own Bristol Bridge, shops and timber-framed houses built halfway across a busy thoroughfare. A rotund woman carrying a large basket at her hip pushed past me jeering,

'G'orn! Dry yon tears lad, they say the King's men get their wages regular! Hey, but they'll not let you keep a hound when you join your regiment! You'd better send him home to yer mam!' and passed on into the crowd, laughing raucously.

I was unsure whether my anonymity was due to dirt or disguise but it had seemed welcome until the significance of her words dawned upon me: I had been mistaken for a boy. In that case, there was a real and dangerous possibility of forced recruitment. I remembered a proclamation of military regulations in Bristol early in '43 that women should not clothe as a man and wryly recalled that back then Jinty and I had scoffed at the very idea. I had given the matter no thought, for the clothes I had worn since leaving Pembroke were opportune finds and had been so practical. I assumed it would be simple to return to normality yet I had given little thought to what 'normality' might entail. Now I was betwixt hammer and anvil: I was in dirty, ragged clothes with no money to buy new; I was dressed as a boy but in truth a young woman.

Furthermore, I was in a Royalist town, a married woman whose spouse was at the very least a violent turncoat.

Nevertheless, he was my lawful husband to whom I owed obedience and without whose money, Godwynne wealth, I was destitute. To add to my problems I suddenly realised that I had lost my guides. I had no idea where Sark or Lewis Tremayne had gone.

A furore at the bridge-end caused a surge of people. Drummers and trumpeters created a wall of battering sound. Amidst the commotion, I only heard the disjointed crying of heralds shouting,

'Make way, Duke of Cumberland!' and 'Earl of Holderness!' ringing around the narrow streets. As the press of onlookers moved back before the escorting guards I was left isolated on the corner of an alleyway, more or less opposite the now empty approach to the Welsh Bridge.

Toward me rode a column of superbly dressed, well armoured men, at its head a tall man riding a fine grey stallion. Patch began to pull, began to prance and skip. Caught off guard, I let the leash slip through my hands and he dashed off towards the crossing, barking, the rope trailing between his feet. Patch began rearing up at the leading horse and I shut my eyes tight, dreading terrible consequences, a disaster resulting from terrified horse and aggravated rider.

Instead there began a huge wave of laughter, cheers and clapping. I opened my eyes to see a large white lion-dog with a mane of curly hair and a sleek black mongrel hound, their tails wagging so hard that their feet were barely touching the cobbles, circling and pawing and running too and fro.

'Ho Boye! Hey Patch! What frolics have we here? Stop your galliard! Come! Sit!' boomed a voice with an accent I recognised. I could barely believe my ears, my eyes too wet to see clearly. Patch dashed over to me, barked, and hurtled back to sit perfectly neatly at the feet of the cavalier's horse. My companions stepped warily from the crowd as the rider looked towards me, stood in his stirrups then flashed that most charming smile.

'I' faith, but here is a fine change! It is Mistress Godwynne, the most gracious nurse I ever met! God give you good day, madam!' he saluted me, then added with a grin, 'And my compliments to your tailor!'

Prince Rupert of the Rhine, the newly created Duke of Cumberland, Earl of Holderness, dismounted. He called both black dog and white to heel and to the utter confusion of his officers but to the delight of the populace of Shrewsbury, escorted a scruffy, tear-streaked boy and two disreputable fellows back across the bridge and up into the town. The Prince made it plain that Major Tremayne, Sark and I would dine with him that evening, and with cheerful liberality, he ordered a bemused secretary to dispense the appropriate authorisation and a bag of coin for each of us to purchase new clothes.

I was thus able to re-establish my female identity, purchasing a serviceable gown, cloak and shoes as well as two linen shifts, caps and some stockings. I decided to keep the boy's disguise for in truth I had become used to the feel of the garments and to myself I used the excuse that the doublet, at least, would serve for an extra layer of warmth should the weather become too inclement.

The conversation at table that evening was animated, the Prince thoroughly engaged while my companions described the events since Lewis left Ireland. He was in turns stunned to an angry silence then loudly proclaiming incredulity as we recounted our Welsh experiences. However, Prince Rupert was diplomatic enough not to enquire too deeply into my side of the misadventure.

Notes were made for directives; messages and information gleaned from our story to be dispatched immediately to Oxford where the King had his winter base. Lewis asked for other military reports. Already it seemed there had been a doleful beginning to His Majesty's '44 campaign.

My eyelids were growing heavy and I was wondering how soon I could excuse myself without seeming discourteous when the noise of Lewis whooping with glee jolted me awake. Sark too was applauding loudly. The Prince was giving an account of one welcome incident.

From his narrative, I recognised the name of Lewis' old commander, Grenvile.

'How long has he been amongst their number? I swear he left Ireland well before we did and I am sure he was for the King,' Lewis sounded intrigued. Prince Rupert's secretary confirmed that Grenvile had indeed been back in England since the autumn. He was initially placed under arrest when he landed at Liverpool and was taken to London, until he could persuade the members of the House of Commons that they could trust him. After which he had returned to his old allegiances, cheated Parliament of a troop of horse and a large sum of money to fund them and with the enemy's plans for the '44 spring campaigns had gone to the King at Oxford.

Lewis let out another hoot of laughter that startled the dogs under the table into frantic barking.

'So that's what he meant all along! I wondered what that sly old fox's plans were. Well, I'm to Oxford then, for I would serve with my old commander! Are you with me, Men?' Sark smiled ruefully, and shook his head, saying,

'I think not, Lewis, for I do not hold rank high enough to choose my campaign. I will go where I can best serve His Majesty, or at your Highness' direction,' he added, with a deferential nod of his head to Prince Rupert.

The Prince cocked his head on one side, pursed his lips and looked at Sark.

'Master Sark, your expertise would be welcomed anywhere for it is certain, is it not, that gun commanders with your experience are rare? Yet it is my estimation that the battlefield is not your chosen sphere. You being a man of a seafaring nature I do not think your talents are best deployed on terra firma.' The Prince stood. We all hurried to follow.

'I am promoting you. Now Captain Sark, your orders are thus: you are to go to Oxford, you will escort Mistress Godwynne thither.' His deep brown eyes looked at me, one eyebrow raised,

'Damn it, madam, I cannot think of you as wed to a traitor!

Mistress *Fenwick*...the title offends me!' While others may have thought him to be speaking in jest, in that moment I realised that, somehow, he had the measure of my circumstances. Turning back to Sark he continued,

'From Oxford you will join my brother Maurice's army which lies at Lyme on the coast of Dorset. There your skills will be appreciated.' His nod was an emphatic sign that he would countenance no argument. Sitting down again, he seemed vaguely surprised that everyone else was on their feet.

'Lewis Tremayne, you are herewith promoted to Lieutenant-Colonel. Your orders are to rejoin His Majesty's army. Do we know where Sir Richard is?' the prince asked his secretary. It seemed that Grenvile was back in the west, in command of the forces surrounding Plymouth.

'Hmm, then you will be travelling westwards. Where you serve, and with whom, will naturally depend upon orders from Lord Hopton but he may well decide to reunite you with your commander. My campaigns are for the north and while I would have you at my side, I have heard you Cornishmen fight best together and when nearest to your own land!' He smiled at both men then looked over at me. I was barely awake, Patch's warm body curled comfortingly around my ankles.

'But see, Mistress Grace is sent to sleep with this soldier's talk! Gentlemen, tomorrow is another day. I shall look to Mistress Fenwick's paperwork in the morning. My secretary will attend to you now to ensure that you have all that you need, but I bid you goodnight.' His hand upon my shoulder kept me in my seat, for which kindness I was thankful for I doubted that my legs would have held me had I been obliged to curtsey. However, I did take the white paw offered as His Highness' companion followed the royal commander from the room.

XXVI Hester: Barnstaple October 1644

When Mayor Peard offered his opinion that our town would defy the enemy and stand firm for the Parliament, Barumites weren't all convinced he was right. Bess and me doubted we could last long when the rumour-mongers started saying that it was 'Roarin' Goring' come to make his headquarters at Raleigh, not two miles away. This was the same Goring who would roister and pillage, spare none and put all to the sword. I do think that the truth was that the good people of Barnstaple, finding their waistbands loose and bellies rumbling for want of food could neither face a fight nor endure a siege, no matter who the commander was.

Anyways, cutting a long story to shortness, the good burghers decided that prudence at the right time was better than valour at any time so the Mayor and Corporation did draw up terms to put to the King's messengers. They asked that there be no pillage or extra soldiery in the town, nor any change to the church. They were afeared a'cause somebody had been spreading the word that Puritans would have much to fear if Parliament's army lost the war. His Majesty was gracious and happy to agree so long as Barnstaple surrendered. So that came about with no blows struck which pleased us ordinary folk no end. Colonel Luttrell, Colonel Bennett and their soldiers marched away with the flags flying and drums beating, but 'twasn't all that notable for there weren't many of 'em to leave.

That first night there was hell-up in Barum, for all the King's promises. There were so many troopers and soldiers that the town might as well have been pillaged. The streets were thronged. 'Twasn't from rowdiness, nor bad spirit I thought, but sheer numbers of folks looking for stores where in truth there were none to be had. The King's men had fought a hard fight through Cornwall and I did hear that every one of them had back-pay owing. I could see for myself the ragged state of their kit and all were poorly shod.

Matters eased a little when many of the troopers left to rejoin the main army at Exeter where the King was lodging. The Royalist commissioners set up their stall though, extracting money from anyone who appeared to have it and going hard on them who wouldn't pay up.

For this next bit of my tale I needs must remember the timing a-right and steel myself a little for 'tis no cosy memory. I think it was just about a month after Barnstaple surrendered, for the trees were losing their leaves in every autumn blow, so that would be October '44. Town life had mostly carried on; a few ships arrived from Bristol or Ireland; there were still markets but there was little to buy; soldiery still passing through. But when one morning there was a big disturbance outside the house, it brought Mistress Palmer to her door, she demanding the meaning of the noise.

In Cross Street were a dozen or so men of the Trained Band, led by the brawny shoemaker, John Tasey. In the middle of the throng, looking fair mazed, with a rope around his neck and his hands bound behind his back was none other than Dyckwood.

'Fetch the master!' she told me, and I was only too ready to go for the sight of that clergyman made me want to be sick. Her husband came at a run, and taking charge of a nasty situation, led the raggle-taggle crowd, which was growing by the minute, along the street to the Guildhall. Somebody had already fetched the Constable, and Justice Beaple.

Puritan Barum folk were not happy for they cried that this was the man who had falsified the word about the King and all his bad works. 'Twas amazing how Barnstaple was now a model of loyalty and a good way to prove it was to show how indignant it was at being hood-winked. I thought he had falsified a few words of God as well, but they were truly outraged and before long there were shouts of 'Hang him!'

The noise was bringing even more folk and news was spreading fast. A good-looking, dark-haired officer with a fair lady by his side had been walking past the Palmer's house in the direction of the quays. He pushed through the throng and started talking right seriously to the town officers and I saw the lady of quality look at me, not haughty, but with kind eyes. That did surprise me back then, but I have come to learn that quality has different faces.

When the Constable's sergeant cried out for silence and made his pronouncement I could have been knocked down with a feather, for there was to be a trial and no waiting for the assizes, war making things expedient or some such reason. More justices had been sent for, a jury would be sworn in and the court would gather in the Guildhall within the hour. While Dyckwood was hauled inside, I hid behind my master and mistress as the Constable came across and bowed, saying,

'Master Palmer, Madam, if it please you, I will need your maidservant to attend this hearing, for matters pertaining to …' and he used lots of long words. My mistress turned to me,

'Hester, do not be afraid. Did you understand what the gentleman was asking for I know he used language of the lawyers? It may not be easy for you.' I could feel the tears welling up for her tone was kindness itself. I saw the fair lady was still watching me, so I sniffed the tears back and shook my head.

'Dyckwood will be accused of perjury for his identity is not as he claims and there is that gentleman's word on it.' She pointed to the newcomer. 'There are other felonies as well as the serious matter of the…' she hesitated over that terrible word, 'assault which you suffered. The Constable wanted to know if you would stand in court to speak out against the accused. Take your time to consider…' I curtseyed to her saying, 'Ma'am, I will stand if the Constable thinks it needful.'

Nothing could be worse than what had already happened and all of Barum knew the tale anyhow, so if there was to be shame then I was already cloaked in it.

'Come along, Hester' I said to myself 'You'm been in a courtroom before and worse than this' so I took a deep breath and followed my mistress.

The story was that John Tasey had come across the not so very reverend Dyckwood when he returned to his workshop to find the scoundrel arguing the cost of new soles on his shoes with Joan, John's wife.

'I'll give'ee new soles!' cried John and instead gave his customer a good thwack round his head with a shoe-last. After that Dyckwood wasn't going to run anywhere, shoes or no. When he came to his senses, the militia had him roped and no escaping.

The dark-haired gentleman, hearing the commotion, had stepped up to ask what the problem was, he being one of the King's men in Barnstaple and having some authority a'cause of him being on the business of Sir Richard Grenvile. He had a right personable way with him too. When the Constable told him that Reverend Dyckwood was accused of a crime against a woman of the town the Colonel had grown angry and said,

'This war breeds monstrosity in wicked men but I suspect that is but one of his crimes and would be prepared to stand under oath and bear witness to that!' so the Constable says 'very well,' and that is exactly what happened.

I didn't know then that the Colonel and his lady were both from families who were something proper in Cornwall and because they were knowing all the gentlefolk there they could say for certain sure that Dyckwood was not who he pretended to be. It was true enough that the Foy-ee gentry he claimed as kin do have a relative, who is a famed Parliamentarian preacher, but the man who stood before them had never been ordained and it was nothing certain that Dyckwood was even his name. So much for his purification.

There being a mention of Parliamentary loyalties, there was more questioning of the Colonel gentleman about the possibility that the man was a spy, which caused some murmur, the turncoat's hanging being fresh in everyone's minds.

After some pondering the justices declared that the matter was a military one, requiring a court martial. That was smart thinking for it would also take the burden off them and the town, and so they straightway sent to Exeter to arrange it.

Which was why, when it came to the matter of the assault on Hester Phipps, when I was all girded and ready to do my duty, I was set aside.

In the end, Dyckwood was hung for being a spy. He did deny it and I do think that perhaps he was hung for the wrong sheep as you might say, but sheep or lamb, spying or assault, they stretched his neck and the townsfolk cheered as he dropped.

XXVII Mary: Drewsteignton to Barnstaple and back August 1644 – January 1645

As the heat of July hung on into August the King's campaign stretched through Devon and into Cornwall. That Lewis should discover my whereabouts seemed incredible for it had only been a simple aside in a conversation when he was reunited with Sir Richard Grenvile that had given a hint as to where I was.

Perhaps the irascible nature of that commander hid a flash of humanity. Perhaps it was a remark discarded without thought. Nonetheless, he had said that there had been uncommon Devon hospitality in a hovel in the hills above Okehampton, not the sort of place he would have expected to find the lady of quality upon whom his officer had expended so much breath. He had added that it was ungentlemanly not to have done the looks of that woman justice. Lewis had merely deduced the place to which Sir Richard was referring, knowing that I had family in that district.

He and his company were in the van of the King's forces moving into Cornwall, hot on the heels of the huge Parliamentary army under the Earl of Essex. They were hoping to force the unwitting Earl into an uncomfortable position in an unwelcoming county. Lewis had applied to lead a reconnaissance party and, having tracked the troop of Roundheads who appeared intent on troublemaking, was frustrated that he had still not been able to prevent the tragedy which had so effectively devastated Coombe's tranquillity.

The main body of the army was now some hours ahead of Lewis' men, so he could neither stay nor take me with him. Truth to be told, I was so shaken that I only wanted to stay in familiar surroundings. In addition, with the death of my grandmother, Coombe had been thrown into chaos. Dewnes' funeral would take place as soon as practicable but until my uncle John Hore, named as her executor, could be on hand to take over the running of the estate I was the only person the servants and workers knew and they needed me.

In the little time we had, I explained to Lewis some of what I had faced in the years since we had last seen one another, showing him the battered remnants of his correspondence and explaining the significance of the charring. It was difficult to read his expression but he hugged me close saying,

'I will return, my chick, I *will*. This present campaign cannot last long. Stay at Coombe and, when I can, I will come for you and together we will go to Penwarne to your father, and to Heligan to mine, and your Aunt will hold no power over you while I protect you.' In his arms I believed that it could be so.

'I will pray every morn and every night that God will keep you safe. Stay out of harm's way, Lewis. I could not bear to lose you again.' I whispered that prayer as I watched while he and the blue uniforms of his men marched away westwards and melded into the moorland landscape.

From that day Goody Yendacott came back to the farm daily, assisting with the wounds of the labourers, gently reassuring the maids who had been so distressed at everything that they had seen. She and I talked, and I do believe we grieved together in those days and weeks. My Uncle John, all silver whiskers and gentleness, arrived and with the legal matters resolved, a new routine settled around Coombe.

Dewnes had left me a small legacy, which now meant I had independent means and the freedom to make my own choice once I reached my twenty-first birthday. But in August of 1644 that was six long months away.

The weather and the fortunes of the occupying army in Cornwall changed for the worst towards the end of August. At Lostwithiel ten thousand soldiers, crammed between that town and the coast, had decimated the landscape leaving the populace close to famine. As September began, another battle on Cornish soil again saw the Royalists triumph and

168

the battered remnants of the beaten army, reviled and half-starved, straggled out of a vindictive Cornwall. The war had come too near to Penwarne for my liking.

On September 3rd I received a brief note from Lewis sent by messenger from Liskeard with the news that the King was moving towards Tavistock. Lewis hoped that we would soon be reunited, though currently Grenvile's orders, and consequently Lewis', were to pursue the fleeing Roundhead cavalry: Lewis added that his senior officer had instructed him to 'inform Mistress Carew of my satisfaction that Tremayne's topics of conversation now afforded some variety'. From that military man, Lewis added, it was tantamount to a blessing.

His Majesty had thought better of gracing the long siege at Plymouth with his royal presence and had marched back to Somerset leaving Grenvile to blockade the city. Initially Lewis was given the task of recruiting across Dartmoor, rounding up deserting soldiers and giving Grenvile the satisfaction of increasing the force that sat at Plymouth's boundaries, so there was an excuse for the occasional fleeting visit to Coombe. Later he was sent across Devon to chase the funds to which Grenvile's powers as High Sheriff gave him access for as the autumn wore on and the season for fighting drew to a close the priorities for Sir Richard seemed to tend more towards raising money than men.

In those snatched hours, we talked. He told me of his experiences, the perfidy of the sailing master that brought the troops from Ireland and the courage of a fellow Cornishman that saved him. I told him all I knew of the news from his home county; the small insignificant things that he said he had missed the most. And of course we spoke of us, our future and our dreams once the King and Parliament had settled their differences. Our parting became harder each time.

Arriving not long before breakfast one day early in October, Lewis was briskly informing me of the latest news between mouthfuls of cold meat and bread. It seemed that the general had been allotted a vast sum of money from the levy raised by the King's Commissioners, which Grenvile would use for soldiers' wages.

'Many folk call the man a scoundrel but he pays his troops and will not rely on free quarter for his men. That's why he can command loyalty,' said Lewis, adding wryly, 'That, and a propensity to run miscreants through first and determine their guilt afterwards!' I shook my head at his acceptance of such brutality.

'Is it thus everywhere, Lewis? Do all soldiers have such a dark side?' Lewis answered, momentarily solemn,

'The darkness is in every man's heart when his home and loved ones are threatened, Mary. And if a man says otherwise he is a liar!' But the shadow-mood was not to dampen Lewis' spirits, and I sensed he was keeping something from me.

'But, Mistress Carew, I am not here to discuss the horrors of war but celebrate. I have been promoted and with rank comes privilege. Go, pack a few necessaries and be ready to leave within the hour. I have orders from Sir Richard for Barnstaple. The man is strict and his commands must be obeyed: I am to do Sheriff's business for him in North Devon and have permission to have my lady accompany me!'

I was shocked. Though I knew women did follow their men on campaigns, I had simply not considered the idea for myself - or that Sir Richard Grenvile was the sort of commander to approve of a baggage train of women. I said so and Lewis grinned.

'If the stories are to be believed Grenvile plans to lodge his own mistress in his quarters if the siege at Plymouth carries on much longer!'

'But what will folk say? It might be well and good for your general, but we are not yet wed, Colonel Tremayne, and there might be talk of a poor, defenceless woman taken advantage of by one of those swaggering cavaliers!' He swirled me around, laughing.

'Then if there is to be talk, we might just as well give gossips something to speak about! If you insist I will let you bring a maid and tell everyone you are staying with my mother's family: the Dartes are respectable enough. Make haste, chick! I have even brought a docile mare for you to ride!'

In the event, nobody commented on the Royalist officer with four mounted soldiers escorting a young gentlewoman. A chamber was always made available to me for which Lewis seemed to have ready coin, and despite his jest and my increasing wish that it was otherwise, my privacy was sacrosanct, he kissing me a gentle 'Goodnight' at the end of every evening. Only when we reached bustling Barnstaple was accommodation more difficult to find for the place recently surrendered to the King's forces and a sizeable garrison was now billeted across the town.

Lewis begged accommodation with his relatives but found space for me with a merchant in Cross Street. As we arrived, we found ourselves amidst a throng of angry residents. My host and his wife were shielding their maid-servant who stood between them, ashen-faced.

A minister related to the Treffry family of Fowey was accused of raping the lass. Lewis and I looked aghast. Not Hugh Peters, surely? The name that was being spat around the lanes of Barnstaple was not however one that was familiar. And when Lewis returned from talking to the Justice of the Peace, there were also grounds to believe that the accused had adopted a false name and was impersonating a priest as well as abusing the young woman.

With some alacrity, the town Mayor had called for it to become a military matter for hidden identity equated to spying in his mind, and we were happy to be delayed in the busy port while Lewis gave evidence. I could not bear to watch the hanging but wondered rather how the young woman I had seen hiding behind her mistress was faring.

It is strange to think that our lives should grow so close from such a coincidental meeting. I would not forget the look on her face that day.

My own adventure ended too soon but not as it had begun, with a merry quip at the door of Coombe Manor.

Instead Lewis was brought urgent orders to go to Exeter, there to collect dispatches to be taken to Dartmouth. He could no longer escort me home, though he assured me that his soldiers were reliable enough. It meant another parting but this time in unfamiliar surroundings. Handing me the papers I would need to pass about the countryside, Lewis attempted to make light of it to cheer me,

'For years you had no idea of my whereabouts, chick, and it is but a few weeks until I shall be able to ride into Coombe again. Dry your tears for I cannot bear to leave you with them as my last memory.' I did my best, but once he had ridden from the town it was a long while before I could face my escort to make the ride back to Drewsteignton.

The year drew to a close, December seeing a long spell of deep cold, the ground frozen solid for many weeks. Before the end of the month, I received a letter from Jane which saddened me more than words could express. Alexander Carew had been tried for treason. Though Jane, heavily pregnant again, had managed successfully to plead for a stay of execution in order that her husband might put his affairs in order, my cousin had faced the executioner's axe two days before what should have been Christmas Day 1644.

In January, Lewis reported an attack on Plymouth's northern defences. However, the rebels had been reinforced by sailors from the Parliamentarian fleet anchored in the Sound and Grenvile's men remained thwarted. Nevertheless, January of 1645 did bring one turning point for it marked my birthday, my twenty-first. Since the work at Plymouth had left no opportunity for Lewis and I to travel westwards to seek paternal approval for our marriage, it seemed fitting that the banns for my marriage should be read at Drewsteington church.

The vicar had known my grandmother well and knew too of her approval of my choice of husband. Three weeks was all that was required, from 22nd January. Yet within two, Grenvile had received orders from Prince Rupert of the Rhine. The King's General in the West and his Colonel of Foot Lewis Tremayne, with three thousand men, were to march eastwards to Taunton with all speed and with no grounds for leave of absence whatsoever, be it for birth, death or marriage.

Although not a soul had registered any objection to my marriage, Coombe was not to see preparations for a wedding breakfast that spring. Not in the spring nor summer or autumn either.

For while Lewis served with the Royalist army in Somerset a messenger rode into Drewsteignton, seeking Mistress Carew at Coombe Manor. He carried a letter in an untidy hand that I recognised well enough. It was from Candacia. My youngest sister had written in haste, she said, but despite her brevity, there was the spiteful barb I had come to expect. Our father's condition, she wrote, which had been changeable at best and made even more vulnerable by my absence, had taken a sudden turn for the worst. The physicians could give little hope, and so I must return to Penwarne with all haste. I felt a chill run down my spine, a sense of foreboding and, I confess, the stirrings of the guilt I had suppressed for months.

The messenger was one from Antony where I supposed my father's condition to be as much a matter for concern as it was at Penwarne. The man had come prepared with papers authorising our travel. He was instructed to wait while I set Coombe in order and gathered my belongings then, with as much speed as possible, we were to ride westwards.

It transpired that my departure from Shrewsbury was in the wake of the Prince, for Rupert had been instructed to urgently attend his uncle and his Council of War. Sark continued as my escort, and we discovered we had developed a quiet conviviality grounded I supposed in shared experiences. His taciturn nature was not as I had supposed, founded on permanent ill-temper, but rather on the stillness of a man at ease with himself. If he thought there was a convivial conversation to be had then he seemed as content to converse as to be quiet and day by day I started to look forward to our journeying.

We reached Oxford soon enough with no mishaps. With the Prince's recommendations, Patch and I found accommodation in a tiny gable room, three floors above a mercer's shop. Sark did not tell me where he was to board and I had no idea when he would leave. Several days later, I received a small parcel containing a hairbrush and a note:

My sister used one very similar to this. I hope it meets with your approval. I travel today. Simply signed with an 'S' the message left me saddened that he had been dispatched to Prince Maurice's army without saying goodbye.

The city of golden stone was full to overflowing. I had grown accustomed to Bristol's clamour where Wine Street was the only broad thorough-fare; I had been stunned at the crowded nature of Shrewsbury; but Oxford was worse still. Food was short and prices horribly inflated by the demands of the royal court on limited supplies. The place stank, the threat of disease hanging in the air.

Even the court gentlefolk were housed in places no better than my own room. My landlady boasted that one of the wealthiest gentlemen in London, Sir John Harrison, was housed in the baker's garret next door, along with his two daughters. Ann, his eldest, a pretty dark-haired girl only a little younger than myself, met me outside our lodgings a few days after I arrived. She stooped to fuss Patch, and I may have looked askance at the bustling mayhem around me, for having introduced herself she suggested she walk with me while I familiarised myself with my surroundings.

Ann was an excellent guide, full of amusing anecdotes about numerous important people who she would pointed out as we strolled, my hound calmly trotting on his leash between us. I was mortified as we sauntered through the courtyards of several colleges, Ann telling me how she and 'Bella', who I later found to be Lady Isabella Thynne, had once scandalised the dons and students at Trinity College by attending chapel in what had been deemed inappropriate dress. Ann was unapologetic for she said it had been searingly hot and the fusty academics too prudish. I dared not ask what had constituted 'inappropriate dress.'

She soon confided that she was to be married the following week to one of the Prince of Wales' council, Sir Richard Fanshawe. There would be no grand celebratory masque or any feasting, for as she cheerfully informed me, they were as 'poor as Job'. It seemed not to matter one jot. She was completely overjoyed at the prospect. She had stopped to talk to me, she said, for Patch reminded her of Richard's own dog but now as we were firm friends she would seek me every day.

Ann, Lady Fanshawe, was true to her promise of friendship even after she had moved to the new accommodation that she occupied with her husband. It was Ann, bashfully aware on her own account, who pointed out to me that my thickening waist was perhaps not due to inactivity after my strenuous adventuring. Nor, she added, could it be excessive eating. I realised the stark truth that lay behind her diplomacy: she was telling me that my courses had not stopped for any other reason than I was expecting a child. Unhappily, the child was my husband's.

I had nobody to turn to, and no idea what to do. I had no home to go to, and without the generosity of the Prince, I had no money. My husband would assume - nay, would hope - that I had drowned and this so pregnancy was the stuff of a nightmare or a tragedy, the tragedy being the future of an innocent who was conceived neither in love nor with due respect for marriage vows. My reaction was to crumple.

My companion was stunned at the effect of her remark. My need to confide was overwhelming and she listened, sometimes encouraging me to continue when I found describing my experiences hard; sometime she offered insight or suggestions. Ann believed that to face one's demons was to defeat them. Bringing everything into the open, she said, would help me to regain my composure.

I knew Ann would keep nothing from him but I did hope that Sir Richard had been given a censored account of our conversations. He promised to make enquiries about grounds for separation in circumstances like mine though Ann said he suspected the church and the phrase 'till death us do part' were more likely to prevail, 'unless' he remarked, delicately apologetic, 'her husband's traitorous act bring him to justice and the executioner.'

Missives, messengers and a constant stream of troop movements meant Oxford teemed and seethed. Although I had not suffered any of the ill effects common in early pregnancy I now felt lethargic and unwilling to venture out into the crowded streets. If it had not been for Patch, I think I would have taken to my bed. In the fine, warm days of early June when her wifely duties allowed Ann would call on me, encouraging me to walk with her in the collegiate gardens, despite the fact that these bustled with courtiers, drilling militia and even now, in the midst of the clamour, undergraduates with papers and books tucked under their arms.

Returning from one excursion, I found a package had been left for me. Tightly wrapped in waxed cloth there were several seals on the mouldy string binding the bundle. The enclosed letter was easier to open. Ann, blatantly curious, hovered at my shoulder and I let her scan the few lines of a strong handwriting very different from the formal secretary hand my father had used in his accounts. I had already skipped to the signature at the bottom of the page. The letter simply read,

Mistress Fenwick,

I greet you from the town of Lyme where last month my skills were, as His Highness hoped, of some use. Nevertheless, the rebels have out-manoeuvred us and Essex has forced Prince Maurice to withdraw. He plans to move to Exeter. I will not stay with this army for I have permission to go to Topsham directly and there join part of the King's fleet.

Prince Rupert had the measure of you, I thought. You are no landsman. I read on,

The parcel which will accompany this letter should be tightly sealed. I came by the enclosed book by dishonest means but nevertheless I would justify the action in any court in the land. I confess that I had knowledge of some of the events it details. My perspective now being somewhat different I deeply regret that I stood by and did nothing to resist.

There followed two lines, firmly crossed out and illegible under the thick black ink but the letter continued,

As the fortunes of a seafarer and a man of war are uncertain, if you should ever find yourself in need of security against Bartholomew Fenwick, the evidence hereby incorporated may stand you in good stead and certainly, should you hear of my death, if you have not done so before then you should open the packet forthwith and put yourself in the protection of the authorities.

This was followed with '*Your faithful servant, Tremenheere Sark.*'

'What strangeness is this?' Ann pondered, 'for the man seems to hint at darkness and uncommon peril. Will you open the parcel Grace? It is too mysterious!' I handed her the packet and Ann impulsively broke the seals, pulling away the rotting twine.

I was not pondering the parcel, but more the implications of a signature, of a full name, of those words 'your faithful servant' and the feeling that the lines that were taken out were significant, related to a dim recollection, of something essential that I could not quite recall.

177

'Eugh! This is disgusting, absolutely foul!' declared Ann.

When I looked up, she was warily holding out, between finger and thumb, a leather-bound journal, salt-stained, battered and fusty. It had seen better days but I recognised it; I had often seen in my husband's hands in the 'shop' at Wine Street. The writing inside I recognised too, the inscription on the frontispiece confirming it was the property of 'B. Fenwick Master Mariner'.

The contents appeared to be a combination of sailing rutter with directions and coastal diagrams, details of voyages and cargoes and a journal including some accounts, but there were also diary entries with notes and commentary. I privately noted Ann's remark, wondering if she implied more than just the state of the tattered book, but Ann was uncomplicated and when I glanced in her direction, her expression was simply a reflection of the grubby item in her hand.

Patch wandered over to sniff inquisitively at the item, sneezed hard and yapped shrilly, which made us both giggle.

'Patch agrees with you, Lady Ann! This will wait until we can investigate it out of doors where the noxious fumes can be wafted away by city breezes, even if they are of only marginally healthier airs!' I casually wrapped the bundle back together, propping it upon the windowsill thinking to freshen the pages a little. The letter I folded carefully and tucked inside my pocket.

It was later, lying against my pillows in the lowering light of dusk, that I resumed examination of the folios of my husband's log book. Perhaps there would never have been a good time to open that volume, but that night I was taken, page by page, further into a living hell. Amongst the mottled pages in my hands was detailed the outlay of coin paid to a man, unnamed, at Bristol to dispatch one J. Vickery, sea captain.

In another diary entry it simply stated 'HG - achieved his end' but with a date which was heart-breakingly familiar as the same voyage on which Hal had died. The evidence I had in my hands was damning.

However, what I found written towards the back of the manuscript froze my very soul. There were various notions for affecting wine without it tasting tainted; a note on the efficacy of a tincture of a certain mushroom.

As I continued reading, a spasm of sickness overtook me and excruciating pain stabbed my stomach. I read the detailed effects of ingestion of the fungus poison and the symptoms that could be expected. To my horror there, written large upon the page, were the very symptoms of my father's illness. My beloved father had been given poison.

I never reached the entry that marked Bartholomew's Fenwick's marriage to an heiress, the self-congratulatory gloating acknowledging the achieving of his goal. Nor did I read any of his accounts of the wealth to which he now held the title for, by nightfall, I was in agony and, by dawn, my first pregnancy was over.

XXIX Hester: Barnstaple Winter 1644 – June 1645

Over that winter in Barum town, I discovered that a girl could have a mistress who was fair as well as firm and, after her kindnesses, I do believe I would have done anything for Mistress Palmer. Don't mistake me, for the household was one where I had to work hard but, though 'twas strange to say, my knees and wrists, for all the scrubbing and rubbing, had never been better.

There always seemed to be important people lodging with Master Palmer. He had been the mayor and was a proper gentleman. Mind, all the other houses had the billeting sergeant at the door, so the mistress and master were probably as well taking in officers and the like or he'd have filled their beds with soldiery anyway. But my employers were truly good as well as godly and I had never had such kindness anywhere, not even at home. I even got to like the parrot-bird.

His Majesty the King decreed that our town would be a proper garrison with a governor and all, so we now had Sir Allen Apsley and his officials. The town's local militia were whipped into shape, not that all the men were keen to drill, march and practise their weaponry. In a force that was to be set against the Parliament men, many in Barnstaple would be going against how they were truly inclined, including Master Palmer, though he seemed quite gracious about it. But that was the Palmers for you, always courteous.

My new friend Bess and me were right glad that we were in a Royalist town despite all the hardships, the shortness of food, the crowds of soldiery, and the forced labouring on the fort. For otherwise we had heard there would have been no Christmas in '45 with that Ord'nance of Parliament of twelve month ago, and we decided 'twas one bad thing about supporting the Parliament men for they would cancel the only thing that brought a bit of cheer to mid-winter.

She and I exchanged little New Year gifts. I had made her

a pocket decorated with black-thread needlework which took me hours. I used that green ribbon from Dan Edwards all washed and pressed like new to make the ties for round her waist. Bess had made me a little book, paper pages stitched together and with a cover of some blue fustian, all blanket-stitched in yellow. I thought to myself 'Now Hester! That makes two books you have and that's nearly a shelf full!'

When she gave me the parcel Bess said, all serious,

'Hester I have drawn on each page a letter of the alphabet which you must learn if you are to write, which is why this is my New Year gift, for I will teach you if you want to learn.' I hugged Bess then, and thought I was the happiest I had ever been.

We set to the writing each Sunday afternoon after church and we would put the world to right as I worked at my lesson. Bess seemed to hear more of the news than me, for I suppose the townsfolk would chatter in the baker's shop. I said the New Noddle Army was a daft name for soldiers and she said I was being a lummox.

She declared that Oliver Cromwell would be the Parliament's new hero, and I said if he was the sour-faced Puritan I had heard about then I would take a roistering Cavalier any day.

She also said the blond Cornish maid who had lodged at the Palmer's house after Dyckwood's hanging must have been the officer's doxy and I said most surely that she was not, for she was a right kindly lady and he not the type to chase a trollop. Then I told Bess of the tears on the day Mistress Carew and Colonel Tremayne had to part. She told me that I was a softheaded romantic.

Bess and me decided that we wouldn't ever get wed to a soldier, no matter how good looking. But in the meantime we had already come to suppose that 'tis the women who all'us have to pick up the pieces, feed the children and find the price of a loaf of bread and if it were down to the women we'd see to it that there'd be no need for an army, new, noddle, model or whatever kind.

By May Day of '45 Bess had taught me to write my name

181

by me copying the shapes she penned out for me. I still could no more read than fly like a bird but if ever I was given a paper again then I might recognise my own name on the page, and for a miner's daughter from Radstock that would have to do.

That year didn't go well for His Majesty and, with the Parliament army winning here and there, the poor King must have been sore affeard for his lad. Who knows what the Roundheads would have done with him if they'd caught him?

Our town had been visited by a grand gentleman called Sir Edward Hyde, who had liked the place and the next thing was news that the Prince was heading westwards, coming to Barnstaple! The town crier let it be known that Sir Edward had told the aldermen of the borough that he was right pleased with our readiness and miraculous fortifications and that with the excellent state of the place it was fit for the King himself.

Well, that's all very well, thought Bess and I, but he don't see the state of the market and the price of vittals to the common folk.

There was summ'at extr'ordnary in the work in the days before the royal party arrived, with cleaning and polishing and trying to find space for extra beds to be made up. The mayor, armed with his lists of who-was-to-stay-where, came to see my mistress so we knew that it would be Sir Richard and Lady Fanshawe who would lodge with us. The guests would be bound to bring their servants.

Now, there was the rub for our house had only two small rooms in the eaves. Mistress Palmer was right flustered about it all. But I spake up and said that it would do no harm for the royal servants to share the space we had which she decided would have to suffice for otherwise it would need palliasses before the fire in the kitchen and that would inconvenience the cooking too much.

Charles, called Prince of Wales and Duke of Cornwall, with all his Council of War arrived in the middle of June. These were the first courtiers I had ever seen. All that finery in one place! I thought these Cavaliers were indeed grand. With them came more soldiers, presenting arms, trumpeters heralding and speechifying at the North Gate and all the good households in the town then taking in guests of the best sort. Some whey-faced Puritan types moaned about it but most Barumites wanted to do their best, with the Prince staying at Dick and Grace Beaple's house at the end of our very own street.

Bess was so excited she kept finding excuses to pass the door, hoping to see him, and she took three baskets of bread in the first afternoon alone. Two days later, after breakfast, Bess and I were with a crowd watching on the quays, there being two wherries coming slowly up the Taw. She was fair mazed about the Prince and kept sighing on,

'He's all dark and handsome, they say!' and 'I would dearly like to catch the eye of a Prince'. I told her she was too old, for the King's son wasn't more than sixteen, and she looked so sourly that I laughed so much that I fell off the mooring post I was perched on.

Strange to say though, for all my being set against being a soldier's woman, here I am, for life do take some funny twists and turns. No more so than in Barum that summer.

Anyway, those boats coming up the river were bringing the court ladies, for the wives did not travel with the Prince's party which had ridden over Exmoor by the pack-horse ways. Instead, they came by sea from Minehead. There was a crowd on the quay to greet them, those menfolk who were expecting their ladies and some of us townspeople there too.

As the wharf-men tied the moorings, I left Bess and went to stand behind Mistress Palmer, who had me with her to carry our guest's smaller belongings, so I was quite near the front and had a good view. If I thought the finery was grand when the Prince arrived, then my chin nearly hit the cobbles when the court ladies stepped down the gangways. So much lace on their collars, hair all curls and ringlets, and some gowns that would take me a lifetime's wages to buy! Not one looked as though they had journeyed overnight on a ship let alone been harried from place to place with a Parliament army giving chase. I decided the ladies' maids who looked after them must work summ'at hard.

Though he bowed and greeted five or six women, Sir Richard finally stepped up to a lovely lady, quite small built, with beautiful eyes. I was just thinking to myself 'This must be Lady Ann', and getting ready to collect some box or another, when I espied someone else. I felt my cheeks start to burn and my heart began to pound inside my chest, and I believed in that moment that all my good fortune was about to be brushed away again. Who should be stepping down behind Lady Fanshawe, with a black, long-nosed hound trailing after her? It was none other than my old mistress from Wine Street days, Grace Godwynne.

Alongside her stood a man, attentive as if he might have been her husband, except I thought he was distant in a way too. I took note of the scar down one side of his face but then there were his blue eyes - I'd never seen the like. He escorted the ladies to those folk that were to greet them and then was gone for the ships were to sail again on the flow of the tide.

True to say, I was a bit abashed, and it got no better, for though Sir Richard and his lady wife were clearly on good terms with my mistress they also seemed happy alongside Mistress Godwynne. I knew there was no extra room for her lodging, the best there was being the garret in which I was sleeping, for the Mayor's lists had not detailed the better sort accompanying the party. I might end up sleeping by the fire after all, me and the hound.

As the woman who would have had me hang stood in our hallway I noted a wedding ring and soon heard the visitors introduce her by a new name. But Mistress Fenwick had been mistaken for a servant. Where was she to sleep? Where else were the great folk expecting but with me of course.

I was expecting to ride to Tavistock then directly through Liskeard, Lostwithiel and down to Penwarne because en route to each there were houses where I had relatives who would offer shelter and respite for an hour or even overnight. However, as we prepared to leave Tavistock, it was not the road to Horsebridge that we took but to Plymstock. When I challenged my escort he politely insisted he was correct, claiming he had his orders to ride for Saltash. He did not hand over the papers authorising my travel and was respectful but firm, giving me to understand that I was expected at Antony before I returned home.

Still I could sense nothing amiss. In the late morning of the third day, a grey and overcast April 1st, I rode into the courtyard of Antony House, now with barricades that had not been there when I came last. An elderly man with a crooked gap-toothed smile, familiar to me as one of my uncle's trusted gardeners, came forward to take my horse. Handing him the reins I remarked on his change of occupation to which he replied dryly that all the young men, grooms and all, had either enlisted or been conscripted into one army or another. Their tasks had been taken up by the women, or by the men who were too old to fight, or the jobs simply remained left undone. I looked around and began to note the signs, the hint of shabbiness, which would never have been allowed when my uncle was alive.

A maidservant waited at the open front door and stepping into deeper gloom I was directed into the great hall. At the head of the long trestle table sat my Aunt and ambling calmy from the parlour was Candacia. There were candles lit despite it being near midday and their light threw eerie shadows, the light from the hearth giving both women a vermilion glow.

The notion struck me: why was my sister not at Penwarne where she was needed? Already confused at the presence of my sibling, when at every step that I had ridden I had been anticipating calamity and dire news, I was completely taken aback at her apparent ease. What was happening here? What had happened to my father?

'Oho! So the prodigal daughter returns,' she sneered. The sense of malice in her look and her words felt like a slap. I had anticipated invective from my Aunt for her very bearing told me that I could expect no warm welcome, but such spite was beyond even Candacia's norm. Aunt Carew held up her hand and Candacia closed her lips on what she had been about to say next.

'Niece, we are overwhelmed that you should grace us with your company at such short notice. The missives from you or your dear, departed granddam have been so lamentably rare. Those we did receive implied that the well-being of the county of Devon depended upon your presence within the salubrious walls of Coombe Manor. I hardly expected you so soon.'

Fleetingly it occurred to me that Dewnes must have managed to inflict a substantial wound to my Aunt's pride for her to respond so bitingly. I took a breath ready to convey some regret that such an impression had been given but my Aunt did not intend for our meeting to be a dialogue of any kind. She continued icily,

'I do not doubt that you might be missed in such a place, but here at Antony ...' she ended, waving her hand airily, even discarding the words that said 'You mean nothing'. At one time, this would have stung and brought tears to my eyes but I was a different Mary Carew now. Aching and exhausted, I nevertheless refused to be cowed. In response I straightened my shoulders, looked her in the eyes as her callous tones rolled on,

'However, now you are returned we must see to it that arrangements for your betrothal resume. This war cannot be allowed to stop...' It was as if reality had never impinged upon my Aunt. The angry words as Jane and I left all those months ago, all the events in Cornwall and beyond seemed to have no relevance to her at all. Once more, my impulsiveness got the better of propriety and I interrupted,

'Dowager Lady Carew, I must stop you for I fear that I have missed something of great import. Tell me, what is the news of my father? Why am I delayed in going to his side when my sister's letter warned me that his condition is in such decline that I must make haste?' The look that passed between Candacia and Aunt Carew said everything. Candacia seized her moment. Her words were hissed rather than spoken,

'While you have been abroad, sister dear, we have suffered here in Cornwall. Men pressed into the tyrant King's army, privations worse than any nightmare. It would have been no surprise if father had taken another seizure or any of us been murdered in our beds, raped to within an inch of our lives!'

My mind was racing now, realisation dawning: my father's health never had been in jeopardy and somehow I had been duped into returning. In that moment I recalled too the ordeal of a young woman in Barnstaple and saw Candacia for the wicked, self-centred harpy that she had become. My aunt broke into my thoughts,

'It has indeed been difficult here since the troubles began but I think you will find that your dear papa is much as he was. How regrettable that you should have misinterpreted your sister's correspondence. I am sure she did not intend for you to be in any way distressed, did you my dear?' As my sister gave a fawning curtsey, I could not stop myself,

'From the wretchedness I have seen on my travels it seems to me that Antony has been scarce touched madam!' My Aunt snapped back,

'Where have you travelled? You know nothing! You have no idea how much more we would have been distressed had it not been for the solicitude of our friends, their respect for my dear husband's memory and our steadfastness to Parliament's cause.' I could well imagine how Aunt Carew would play upon the good nature of neighbours like the Edgcumbes, use the Puritan zeal of the Bullers to draw down protection, or deploy the long-established rank of the Carews to defy men like Robartes. She would do anything to preserve her own authority.

The contrast between Antony House and Coombe could not have been starker. However the time I had spent with Dewnes had given me confidence, taught me that I need not tolerate cold indifference from people who did not care for me. Lewis had returned to me; he would be at my side when all this was over. I would no longer be bullied by this selfish harridan but neither would I give her the satisfaction of grounds to criticise me; I must remain calm, polite, above reproach.

'I do not intend to trouble you at Antony, madam, and will be leaving forthwith for Penwarne for I do have concerns there and wish to see my father as soon as may be. Though I thank you for your consideration over the years, since January my marriage is no longer a matter for your concern. I will be able to discuss the matter with my father for if his condition has not altered, as you say, then he and I will understand each other very well just as we did before.'

The colour drained from my Aunt's face, the veins on her temples standing blue in the parchment coloured skin, her back rigid with fury at my defiance.

'You will not leave without my permission! You cannot leave for I am mistress here and the stable-hand will be whipped to within an inch of his life if he so much as thinks to saddle a nag for you!' I breathed deeply, replying quietly,

'I will not inconvenience you, Aunt, for I have money to arrange my own conveyance. My grandmother generously provided for me in her will. Please do not distress yourself.' Candacia looked on dumbfounded. I am sure she could not believe my challenge to the Dowager though the news of my independent means may also have robbed her of words.

Aunt Carew had hauled herself to her feet. Slamming the table with the flat of her hand, the clamour brought the maid running into the room; the command was spat out,

'Mistress Carew will not be leaving. Instruct the staff that ...' The poor servant looked abashed but at that moment a commotion in the forecourt heralded a visitor, one about to walk in to an awkward Carew crisis.

Seconds later the robust figure of Piers Edgcumbe strode into the room, and as if nothing had ever been amiss, a beatific smile transformed the Dowager's face, Candacia sank into a demure curtsey and I unclenched my fists leaving stinging imprints of my nails in my palms. I curtseyed too though the reprieve from the emotional outburst was making my knees tremble.

'Lady Carew! How well you look today! As I was passing this way my wife told me to call to thank you for the remedy you sent her. It was most effective. She wondered, was it one of your dear husband's concoctions? She would take it as a great favour if you would allow her to know the recipe.'

The banality of the conversation was in such contrast to the moments before that I felt a sense of hysteria rising at this ludicrous state of affairs, reminding me of my last meeting with Alex. Stealing a glance to where his portrait used to hang the feeling passed as fast as it had come. Piers turned to me and as a true gallant might, he took my hand,

'Ah, Mistress Mary! You have grown more lovely since we saw you last, has she not, Lady Carew?' I could not look at him, but kept my gaze firmly on the floor in case again I had the inappropriate urge to giggle. He gushed on,

'I did not think to meet you here though. Let me say, I was deeply sorry to hear of your grandmother's death - a most terrible circumstance indeed. You must have been terrified! We have had our anxieties here of course, but to date have suffered less than most - though our coffers are lighter for it. 'My aunt coughed, or perhaps it was a slight choke as she cleared her throat. As if as an after-thought, the visitor acknowledged my sister with a nod.

'I am on my way to Looe where Will Scawen has some problem with an issue of the Vice-Admiralty. He seems to want my opinion, though why I could offer anything useful I do not know!' he chuckled, modestly, 'And how long will you be staying, Mary?' I seized my moment.

'I was just informing my lady Aunt of my plan to travel on to Penwarne today, Sir. I am concerned for my father's welfare and fear I have been away too long.' He patted my shoulder.

'From what I hear your father has been making a steady improvement. Naturally, one cannot expect miracles, but I do not think you have any need for concern! And what a cheerful coincidence then that I had my instructions from the distaff side or else I would not have been able to offer an escort. If it is convenient for you, then we might set forth as soon as you wish. Do you have a mount?'

Oblivious to the undercurrent of tension his genial offer had renewed, he made polite conversation while I excused myself to make myself comfortable before the ride. In the mirror above the wash-stand in the small bedchamber to which I was shown I could see nothing to warrant the compliment, but patting my cheeks to encourage some colour into them, I squared my shoulders to face the inevitable skirmish with my Aunt. Our guest might hear a familial farewell, but the reality would be a battle royal resembling that at Marston Moor.

In the event, the need to retain her dignity and composure forced my aunt to courteous words she certainly would not have chosen to use had there not been a respected bystander. A decent horse was made available and with Piers' cheerful commentary ringing in my ears, we rode to Looe where I was offered accommodation. No less than a Judge of the Admiralty Court arranged for me to sail on a small vessel bound for Mevagissey as soon as the wind and tide allowed.

Alone that night I brushed my hair and contemplated the curious, circular journey which had ended, nigh on eighteen months later, in the place it had begun. I thought about Piers Edgcumbe's remarks: how much I had changed was for others to decide. But on one thing I was certain; for as long as I lived I would not forget this day of April Fools.

The long summer of '44 rattled into autumn, with relays of messengers and diplomats, the constant dialogue between monarch and parliament, the optimists who believed that words were stronger than swords. I felt as though all the incessant business of war was happening not outside my window but beyond a bubble which surrounded me.

The still-birth left me sadder than I could have imagined, weak and feverish. The evidence of my husband's evil duplicity I tried to push to the back of my mind for I believed there was little to be done about any of it. Ann, with no regard for her own condition about which she was quietly confident, came daily when I was most ill. She would bring small packages of food, simple fare but prepared especially to tempt me to eat, and decoctions from an apothecary whom Lady Rivers had recommended. The mercer's young son was engaged to exercise Patch for the princely sum of one penny a week, though it was not the coin that mattered, but more the kindness of Ann in considering the necessity.

My health seemed to fluctuate with the King's fortunes. In July there came a blow which set me back again. Ann wept telling me of the terrible loss of life at Marston Moor, but I was overcome by a black weariness when I heard that Boye had died alongside them and for days the comforting warmth of a gift from a Prince, curled snoring gently by my bed, was my only link with reality.

I was fortunate indeed to have been taken under the wing of Sir Richard and his lady. In time I grew stronger, Ann encouraging me to walk in the gardens of the nearest college, a few more steps each day, while she divulged the latest scandal, the day-to-day matters with which we distracted ourselves from the wavering fortunes of the King's army. By the time I was well the Lostwithiel campaign had been won but the Scots had captured Newcastle. And Ann was within weeks of the birth of her first child.

Although she had tended me, little I could do would help Lady Fanshawe when her son Harrison was born for nobody could have saved that little soul.

The callous machinery of war meant that, for the first time since they were wed, her husband was now to depart with the Prince of Wales bound for Bristol. In the weeks after the little coffin was buried in St John's church, Ann could not bear to leave her rooms. Her sister Margaret and I took to turns to stay with her for she was terrified of being alone. Hourly my friend looked for missives, anything to reassure her that Sir Richard was safe. We heard constantly of the movements of the armies, each with its baggage train and the clusters of camp followers lumbering along behind: there must have been as many reasons why those women chose to follow the drum rather than stay at home.

Thus it was that, in May of '45, the chain of events began in Oxford that saw me embrace the same role, the one that led me here.

Ann received a message and money calling her to the side of her husband. More animated than I had ever known her, she insisted that I accompany her with Margaret and their father for, as she declared, if they were to reside in the city of Bristol where better than at the house of a good and dear friend?

Certainly I had no reason to decline, for with Sir Richard's letter had come a short missive in a hand with which I was beginning to feel familiar. The content purported to be a brief report on the state of my old home in Wine Street; run-down, chaotic, and managed against all odds by an irascible Jinty on minimal resources reluctantly made available by Fenwick's notary. It also told me Sark had chosen to sail with a west-country fleet on a ship called the *Dolphin*, which regularly worked the munitions run up and down the Bristol Channel. I sensed it conveyed something deeper too. The signature remained '*your faithful servant, Tremenheere Sark'*. I thought that for a man once reluctant to use his Christian name, he now seemed liberal enough with it on paper.

We arrived in my home city on 20th May and Wine Street was indeed in a state of chaos, the return of the nominal mistress of the house making no impact whatsoever apart from in turns reducing Jinty to floods of tears and an uncharacteristic panic. Sixteen months might as well have been sixteen years, for hardships had taken their toll on everything except her embrace, which had lost none of its strength.

There was nothing of consequence left in the house, very little that I could rescue that had sentimental value. Our small garden, unkempt now, was commandeered by Patch as the canine luxury of a space where I could toss a stick for him to fetch and he could dig small holes to bury the bones he was given by a doting Jinty. The scraps were boiled clean of meat but were the best she could do as a reward, she said, for within a week he had cleared an infestation of rats.

Sir Richard Fanshawe deployed all his powers as secretary to the Prince and duly arranged that his own lodgings should be the house belonging to a certain traitor whose name was known to him. I was now an observer at the heart of a busy diplomatic world, people coming and going at all hours with intelligence, commissions and information.

By the end of May we had settled to a routine, one that was almost familiar. A dispatch arrived from Sir Edward Hyde regarding a hundred barrels of gunpowder to be transported by sea from Barnstaple to Bristol, to be followed only days later by the man himself who had taken the same route back to the Prince's side. He brought with him one whose expertise he applauded as 'that noted artillery expert recommended by Princes': Captain Sark.

Within minutes of Sark's arrival an ecstatic Patch had dug up two bones which were duly dropped at Sark's feet, and which from then on constituted a relay game of throw and retrieve to the echo of barking and laughter whenever Sark happened to call. I liked the sound.

Explaining the comings and goings and talking about the business of the port came easily when Ann wanted to know about the city around her. After we had watched the *Dolphin* sail for a second time, as we dodged up Swan Lane from Tower slip to avoiding the working quaysides, Ann lobbed a remark which made my stomach lurch and crushed the breath from me,

'I do believe there is a woman in Bristol whom Captain Sark holds in high esteem, the very reason he visits the port.' I turned around sharply causing her to bump into me, slipping on the cobbles.

'I beg your pardon,' I said, as much by way of apology as hoping I had misheard 'but I do not catch your meaning. Which lady and how do you know?'

In those moments I had discovered that it mattered to me very much that Tremenheere Sark did not have a lady of esteem in this city or anywhere else, and that what had knocked the breath from me was a bolt of nothing less than pure jealousy. Momentarily Ann looked startled, then took my shoulders in her hands and held me at arms' length.

'Why the dismay? It's you, you goose!' she laughed, 'And, Grace Fenwick, from the look in your eye each time Captain Sark has called at or departed from Wine Street, I would say that esteem is more than returned!'

A thunderbolt could not have hit me with more force and I must have seemed a dolt, but from that moment, it was as if a curtain had been drawn from before my eyes. That night, in fitful sleep I dreamed a dream, a version of which had often haunted my sleeping. In the dream, I could not move or breathe as I sank in silent dark waters swirling around me. This night though there was no nightmare feel, for though my feet were bound as tight as ever, my hands were free and I could hear, and what had lain hidden in my memory now rang clear: not just 'I am sorry' but also 'My love'. The waters were now sky and I was not falling but flying; no longer darkness surrounding me but bright blue, the blue of Sark's eyes.

Conditions in Bristol were getting worse. It was no better supplied than Oxford; the rats and the summer heat continued to be a problem and with them came a disease - a plague or something very like. The sickness took strong or weak, man, woman and child and from the first sign of a fever to a choking death, nothing seemed to halt its path. Physicians across the city warned those who still had their health to keep away from the last breaths of the dying for that was when the miasmas were at their potent worst.

The Prince was taken to Bath where the air was said to be more wholesome. Sir Richard rode back to his wife on the first day of June to warn Ann that she must to be ready to pack at very short notice. As soon as sufficient vessels could be found the ladies of the Prince's entourage would sail westwards, while the gentlemen rode for Wells and Bridgewater, thence to Dunster and onward as necessary. Ann came to find me, the tracks of tears marking her face.

'Ned Hyde has declared that we must all leave for the sake of the Prince's health! It is no longer safe here! But ever since father commanded me from our house in London to Oxford two years or more ago I have never been where it has felt more like my own home than here, and in you I have a friend as close as my own sister. Richard rides with the Prince so once again I am to venture on alone. Grace, I cannot bear it!'

I could say nothing for I could offer no solution. My own situation was now twice as precarious. Thanks to Ann, I was informally under Sir Richard's protection but I hoped that my identity had not been revealed. If it were to be made known that I was with their party, my very survival would depend upon the attitude of a lawyer and the machinations of his client.

However, daybreak delivered a new imperative: instead of the ordered, supervised routine of our kitchen it remained cold and still. Jinty lay unconscious in her bed, her breathing laboured, her pulse erratic. My mentor and indomitable friend lay close to death.

All morning I sat outside her room until Margaret and

Ann persuaded me of the stark reality; our refuge was a haven no longer. Three vessels had arrived, two the common smacks which plied the channel and one slightly larger ship with a name which sang in my heart, the *Dolphin*. Boxes, bags and the few belongings the Fanshawes and Harrisons now owned were being carried down to the quaysides, set to wait until crews could stow them aboard the ships heading for Barnstaple.

It was Ann who persuaded me then that to remain in Bristol was a folly. She was passionate as she about spoke of Fate and lives destined to be led.

It was Ann who found Patch's lost halter, then held open my battered cloak-bag as I snatched only as much as I had carried from Shrewsbury. I wrapped the boy's doublet around Fenwick's book and tucked beside it a well-worn folio of Shakespeare's works, which was all I had salvaged of my father's belongings.

Ann led the way to the quayside I had known since I was a child, as I wept for the loved ones I had lost. Reaching the vessel it was Ann, who was acknowledged by the master and led away to a cabin that had been made ready.

However, it was Tremenheere Sark who held me that night. His arms were tight around me as the *Dolphin* left the quiet waters of the river Avon and I betrayed my marriage vows.

XXXII Hester: Barnstaple Summer 1645

Looking back I do think that month in the early summer of
'45 was summ'at strange for all around me were grand folk
and royalty. Daily there would be some great gentleman,
from hither or yon, riding in to do business with the Prince
and his Council. Barnstaple streets, filled with soldiery, had
banners on houses so you couldn't see the sky between
them. Flags flashed colourful in the summer sunshine where
they hung to show which mighty personage boarded there.
Another excitement was a rider, with a trumpeter this time,
bringing news of a big fight somewhere in the middle of the
country, which men said would end the war. And there was
I, plain Hester Phipps, right in the middle, with it all
happening on my very doorstep.

The mistress, Lady Ann and Mistress Fenwick - she that
had been Grace Godwynne - would pass the time in sharing
experiences, sometimes sitting in the garden. Not long after
they arrived, on one sunny afternoon, my mistress called me
from the kitchen when I was making massard-cherries into
pies for the supper table. I supposed then Mistress Fenwick
had explained how it was she and I were known to each
other, and I was now sore afeard that this was when I would
be turned on the streets as a thief.

But instead there were smiles as I stepped out towards
them, sitting on their stools in the shade. I did my best
curtsey, which was even still a tad wobbly for I was all
nerves. I was so surprised that I could barely stammer a
reply when Lady Ann spoke to me directly,

'Hester, Mistress Fenwick has been telling me that you
survived a ship wreck? Do tell us about this misadventure
for I am determined to voyage with my husband and so I
must know the ways of the sea.'

I must have looked mazed and when I caught her eye
Grace Fenwick looked a little sheepish and smiled. I knew
then that something about our lives had changed. Mistress

Palmer told me to sit down beside them. So, cross-legged on the grass and just as I had told the tale to Grace in the darkness of the garret, I told them of the storm and the wreck and how I had come ashore, and, though I shall never know why he did, I thank God that He had kindness for me that day.

Lady Fanshawe was thrilled with the tale. She bade Grace to tell again of her own adventure on the high seas, which she was reluctant to do, but when I heard what she said, and when the lady added some of the dreadful happenings which Mistress Fenwick was too distressed to recount, then I knew why those dreams came which most nights seemed to disturb Grace's slumbers.

The first time was not long after she arrived; I heard her sobbing, almost silent but so wracked though she did seem still asleep. So I shuffled across and held her till she stopped shaking again. I felt heart-sorry for her then. For here was a woman who one day had everything and the promise of more, then the next had found herself with more than she bargained for and yet nothing at all. And it seemed to me that it was in no way any more her fault than Dyckwood's wrong-doing had been mine.

'We are all sisters of misfortune in this wretched situation,' declared Lady Ann, 'for my husband and I have only Richard's pens, ink and paper which are his secretary's stock-in-trade and twenty pounds to our name, but we must make of it what we can.'

I thought to myself that she was mistaken in counting us all as sisters, but misfortune was perhaps as good a commonality as any. Mistress Palmer said she was touched least by the brutality of the war, but Grace Fenwick told her she must not rate too low all the troubles of price rises and billeting and the constant fear of blockade or pillage: everyone was suffering.

We sweated through June and into July. News from everywhere was sounding bad for our King. It was just into that month that the town erupted with another troop of horsemen, for into the seething streets came Sir Richard

Grenvile. Now, I knew all about his reputation for his family had been the talk of Bideford, threats of the dread Grenviles used against many a Puritan's child when they behaved badly. Anyways, there he was with men and a mission. And with him some of the western lads who had long been loyal to the crown, including a pock-marked fellow with a winning smile and the words to charm the birds from the trees, William Mattock of Cornwood on Dartmoor in the county of Devon.

I tripped over him as I was coming from the dairy in Joy Street and my language wasn't sweet for I near lost a whole crock of cream a'cause of his big feet. But there, the path of true love don't run that smooth they say and it was as good a beginning as any. He was in church the next Sunday and did give me the sweetest grin I had ever seen, but his officer was to ride off back to Ottery St Mary the next day, and I decided I would think no more of him.

Then Bess called me as I passed the shop two days later and told me that some scabby cavalier was asking if she knew the whereabouts of a lass with black hair and eyes the colour of honey who fetched cream in a brown jug and wore a deep green skirt and yellow bodice. Bess said she told him that every housewife in Barum had a brown jug and he'd best be off, or at least watch his step, for husbands didn't want their wives chased around the town's streets. That made me right disheartened for that would be the end of that, I thought. She could see it and jostled me with a hug, continuing,

'But I told him too that if he cared to wait at the quay this next evening I would see what I could do!'
I had to pick up my green skirts and dash to get my chores done and when supper was cleared away, I begged leave of my mistress and went to the riverside.

I liked Will well enough at our first meeting but 'twasn't long afore that silly face became so dear to me. His boyish giggle is so unlikely in a man built like the side of a barn, with the strength of a miner which he was before the war, and the resolve of a pikeman in the King's army which I

199

discovered him to be. And I liked well that he was all'us mindful of his manners for all that he stood almost twice my size.

It turned out that Grenvile had left some troops with the Prince for there was word that soon the party would be moving west to the safety of Cornwall, and Will had been one of those to stay and by that good luck, we were brought together. 'Twasn't all to be plain and smooth, but I was ready to take the rough with the ready and anyway, that autumn as the leaves fell I could see there was one in a more sorry state than I.

As the weeks moved on, living cheek-by-jowl with Mistress Grace, we rubbed along fine, all the old times like water under a bridge. And living so close I could not help but mark the changes. Though she wore a ring on the proper finger of her left hand, I did not think that Mistress Fenwick was anything like as joyful as a wife should be to discover that she was expecting a child that would be born before the leaves of spring came full on the trees again.

XXXIII Mary: Penwarne in Cornwall April 1645

My return to Penwarne that spring was more joyful than I had dared to hope. For, no matter what malice prompted my Aunt's remarks, I had maintained a regular correspondence with home. My other sisters were delighted to see me and keen to hear of my experiences at first hand. My father, while still severely physically impaired was indeed improved, his speech slow but quite intelligible. He could now grip a pen in his left hand again, which was a great joy to him for it put him back in control of the affairs of business which required his signature instead of Uncle George's or the lawyer's.

That first afternoon was spent in the great hall full of spring sunlight. I sat close to my father's chair with my sisters curled on cushions by the hearth or on stools around us, the numerous house-dogs lounging in between. That is all except Candacia who remained sulking at Antony House. Jane's tragic news had naturally been conveyed many months before, but Bridget in particular wanted to hear every detail of the mission I had undertaken, deeming it to be a courageous assignment on behalf of his Majesty. Bridget ever did grasp things a little awry but I felt no pressing need to put her straight.

The account of the companies of soldiery, whether Cavalier or Roundhead, had sent poor Agnes near to swooning. Despite my fears, even during the campaign that ravaged the Fowey peninsular in the previous summer, very little had touched Penwarne lying, secluded, in its hidden valley. Though soldiers had passed through Mevagissey, and recruiting officers called at St Ewe and Gorran, Jonathan Rashleigh had collected our contribution of silver and pewter to the King's mint but nobody else had thought to bother a small manor where only a cripple and his five daughters resided.

I was careful in describing my friendship with Loveday

Yendacott, or mentioning her special talent, since anything that had the breath of magic sent them all into a silly panic and, besides, it also required me to reveal more of my involvement with Lewis than I wished yet to convey. Until I had chance to speak to papa alone to explain, to seek his consent, I did not want any sisterly prying whether well intentioned or not.

How often do we prepare a situation in our minds, imagining conflict and crisis, when in the reality it transpires that there is none? I had rehearsed my conversation with my father so many times, dozens of different ways with as many differing outcomes both happy and heartbreaking.

I took an opportunity the following day to speak to papa alone. Respectfully, I did not mention the malice of Aunt Carew, but I detailed the numerous suitors whom she had considered. As I described her disgust at the Chudleigh's change of loyalty a small twitch moved the left hand side of papa's face to correspond with the twist of his mouth on the other. He chortled,

'George Chudleigh was ever two scats astern of everyone else, it just takes time for him to realise it. Faith! I would like to have seen her face when she heard! I am truly sorry to hear about James though.' There was a pause as he wiped his mouth, then, holding my hand in his he continued,

'I have no doubt my sister-in-law has been interfering in other folk's concerns since the day she was old enough to talk, but her tongue is her burden. We should feel pity for her. You are home now so have no more worries on that score. So, tell me, who is the fortunate young man?'

I was bewildered at my father's perceptiveness. He gave a chuckle, nothing more than wheezing, rapid and throaty, but a sign that he was truly amused.

'A man is not a father of five girls without learning to read signs. I may not have long enough on this earth to wait for you to summon the courage to tell me and thus I have to ask!'

So I knelt, my head on his knee and spoke of Lewis, the letters, his promise and the truth of what happened at

Coombe on the day my grandmother died. I did not, however, speak of last autumn's adventure to Barnstaple even if it was an innocent expedition. It was sufficient that papa had acknowledged that my affections were engaged without the outrage that a father was entitled to feel in the circumstance. Although I was of age I hoped for my father's approval too.

'Come child, come close.' He tugged my hand and I stood beside him. 'Come, buffet me with kisses and in exchange I will give you my heartfelt consent.' I could not stem my tears - of joy, of relief and more - as he continued slowly,

'When you were but - what - six years old, Jane Tremayne and your mama, God rest their souls, used to watch the children at play, jesting that Lewis and you made a pretty pair. I'll warrant they would have delighted in this news and I cannot think of a finer young man to take care of my little dreamer.'

It seemed that I was indeed to be a bride and would be wed with the blessings of my father if not the whole of the Carew dynasty. I would be married from my home to a man I had loved for as long as I could remember. It seemed that it was a match made in heaven and all I needed now was the groom.

XXXIV Grace: Bristol to Barnstaple June – July 1645

On that voyage to Barnstaple, my world turned inside out; my heaven and hell were transposed. Duty, virtue and conformity were like chains holding me to a life of cruel indignity while betrayal, adultery and transgression were my liberation.

The ship's limited accommodation was made available to the ladies by a man I recognised: the master of the ship was Pasco Jago, though at that point he did not know me. Unbidden, Sark had designated his tiny cabin, little bigger than a box, to be mine. My bed was his.

Ann feigned disinterest in anything but the adventure of being at sea, while her sister Margaret and the other women on board were laid low with sea sickness even though the voyage was smooth and uneventful. So two days and nights were all we had together, stolen time between Sark's duties. As the ship waited for the tide off Barnstaple Bar and before we had stepped out onto the deck, Sark - I had become accustomed to just that one name - had taken my face in his hands and kissed me gently.

'Do you know the work of the playwright Shakespeare?' he asked me; I nodded, remembering my childhood.

'My father often read his work, and Ned and I would enact his favourite scenes'. Sark smiled gently,

'Then when you read 'Twelfth Night' think of me, of us, and know that I was yours from that first eve in Bristol, but like Orsino was deceived.' I wondered if his interpretation was the same as mine but he continued, quoting,

'What relish is this, how runs the stream? Or am I mad or else this is a dream? Grace…'

I put my finger to his mouth to stop him. Words were barely necessary for the reality of our situation was stark; he would sail and I must bide where good will would support me for my husband was a fortune hunter and a traitor. Sir Richard Fanshawe had informed me back in Bristol that lawyer's expertise could only ensure that my husband and I could separate on proof of his cruelty. I might have a weak claim to a little part of his wealth but neither he nor I could marry again for we could never be un-wed. Nonetheless, from that day my father's book lay beneath my pillow the page where the play subtitled 'What you will' began marked with a little ribbon.

Stepping onto the quay I was stepping into another world of reversals. A face I recognised loomed from the party on the quay and my tongue dried in my mouth. The thief and convict Hester Phipps and I stood face to face.

The Fanshawes were to stay with Master Palmer and his wife but they had not anticipated an extra member in the party. With accommodation so scarce there was little alternative but for me to share a space in the cramped and crowded townhouse attic with my old servant.

To be truthful, I was now to all intents and purposes a lady's companion and little more than a servant myself. Lady Fanshawe's friendships were of no consequence to the strangers around us except in that it caused some consternation that she insisted that I be put up in the same residence.

In the very first hours, I worried about being lodged with my former housemaid; it was a change of fortune indeed and I feared that past acrimony would make our position impossible. I knew that I had no right to condemn her any more for, as God was my witness, I had no moral high ground now! And He had judged her. I did not know how but He had saved her life from hanging, decreeing salvation. Who was I to gainsay that?

However, Hester set to finding old sacks for Patch to sleep upon beside the kitchen fire and soon made me comfortable, shyly telling me of her miraculous escape from drowning and even confiding that she had a suitor. I begged her call me by my name, for I was no longer her mistress and eventually overcoming her self-consciousness, she did.

That night my nightmares returned, dark and haunting, and in the weeks that followed, that compassionate soul would often stroke my hair and her voice, crooning my name, comforted me in the worse episodes of my dreaming.

I had daily seen the affection between the Fanshawes, and now recognised the same between my host and his wife and even between Hester Phipps and the common soldier who came to court her when her labours and the call of the drum allowed. My future seemed so cold by comparison.

Yet, amity and shared adversity brought friendship and the need for levity, and in the sunshine-bright days we found things to laugh about. One day, after hearing of an incident involving two court ladies and an unsavoury exchange of words, Ann and I behaved extremely badly; we spent the afternoon, while nobody was listening, teaching the ancient parrot in the Palmer's parlour to say 'Who's the Countess of Puddleduck?' It learned remarkably quickly and croaked it very well.

Hester and I chuckled about the prank that night as we readied for sleep. I said that I hoped that she did not get the blame, to which she replied that as she knew nothing of countesses of any kind Mistress Palmer could not suspect her, but if the Lady Fanshawe could not keep her face straight then she would surely give herself away.

While we had voyaged, the fortunes of King Charles' army had taken a dreadful turn with a devastating defeat at a battle near the Leicestershire town of Naseby. The King was in retreat towards Wales, his campaign in tatters. The young Prince was safe for the time being but it had been an astute decision by his advisors to move westwards and for a while, there was talk that the King himself might take ship across the water to join his son in North Devon.

The rumour gained force when at the end of June, on a high tide in the early-morning, a familiar vessel drew alongside the quay. On this voyage, the *Dolphin* carried a different royal passenger, it proving a cheerful reunion for Sark and for Prince Rupert. The latter's familiarity as he embarked had caused considerable conjecture amongst the crew.

In Barum, eyebrows were raised when, on the morning

after his arrival, I was requested by name, with my hound, to attend the Prince at breakfast. The foreigner had a reputation for being unconventional, renowned for tactlessness and a quick-temper, so his hosts thought better of contradicting their royal lodger. It was to be a brief but cordial interview before the Council resumed their deliberations. Sark was there before me. It had not been possible to spend any time alone together for the ship had required attention and to now be constrained by courtly etiquette was almost too much to bear.

'What are the ship's orders? Do you wait for His Highness?' I whispered quickly, Sark shook his head, mouthing a reply 'Sailing tonight'. Then Patch, recognising two of his most favourite individuals in the world, banished all convention. He leaped into the Prince's lap, his tail cutting a swathe through the platter of new baked rolls set for the royal breakfast, only bounding off to pounce at Sark. The Prince yelled at the top of his voice,

'Manners, you rogue!' and Patch, stopped in his tracks, then practically tiptoed to the royal personage and sat at his feet, ears flat and paw tentatively raised. There was a roar of laughter, and dog and prince commenced a rough-and-tumble on the stone floor until a roll, snatched up by Sark, was used as a blatant bribe for Patch to come to heel and behave. The Prince looked mildly disappointed. A gentleman-at-arms stood, open-mouthed with astonishment, beside the door. The Prince gestured to him to leave saying,

'I wish for privacy with these good people. I will call should I need anything'. The man withdrew.

As our royal host stood up, brushing the dust from his breeches, his dishevelled brown curls touched the beams of the low ceiling.

'What it is to miss these moments I cannot express,' he sighed, his expression full of melancholy. But the moment of reflection was fleeting and bowing to me, he gave a dazzling smile,

'Mistress Fenwick! Your servant, madam, and well met again. Sark tells me you were persuaded by Lady Fanshawe to abandon Bristol. I regret to say it but in the circumstances I believe that you chose the correct path.' He waved us both to a narrow window seat for there was little enough furniture in the room. I wondered how much the Prince knew of our liaison; Sark's closeness was making it difficult for me to breathe evenly. I was glad we had Patch as a diversion.

'Your Highness, I was deeply sorry to learn of Boye's death. It must have been made even more distressing by pamphleteers making such scurrilous material from your loss,' I blurted out to cover my embarrassment, immediately regretting it as tactless and foolish. However, the Prince acknowledged my remark with a nod,

'Mistress, you are one of the first to wholly understand it and I do thank you. It is only when one has had such a companion from boyhood that...' and he shrugged his shoulders. Patch wandered across and sat on his boots. The Prince absentmindedly played with the dog's ears as his thoughts drifted then, his tone suddenly genial once more, he asked Sark about his change of career.

'Did you fall out with my brother Maurice?' he chortled, reaching to the table and breaking a roll, stuffing some cold ham into the cavity. He waved us to eat but I politely declined, pretending I had breakfasted already.

'No, Sir,' replied Sark, 'I knew all along that I was unlikely to be able to offer my best services ashore.'

Diplomatically put, I thought, you hated being ashore. Sark noted my expression and smiled a little, then continued, 'His Highness, your brother, was happy to release me to Sir Nicholas Crisp's fleet. He was in need of experienced men and with my seafaring and artillery experience and Prince Maurice's commendation I was offered the position as mate on the *Dolphin,* for which I shall be eternally grateful.' Again he glanced in my direction and I felt my face flush.

The Prince also looked up at that point, the edges of his smile curling upwards, one eyebrow raised above his dark, sparkling eyes. It struck me then that he had probably had the measure of us all along. Had he been as astute as Ann, I wondered? How much had Lewis realised? My blush deepened.

'Have you any news of Colonel Tremayne?' asked our host, almost reading my thoughts. It was too disconcerting and I remained distracted while Sark and he discussed Lewis' possible whereabouts, the movements of some of Grenvile's units and the defence of the west.

A loud tap rattled at the door, and an ensign announced that the Prince of Wales was ready to resume Council. Rupert, taking my hand, put my fingers to his lips.

'Well, Mistress Fenwick. I bid you farewell again. God keep you safe. And bon voyage, sir! We shall have to see what Sir Nicholas can do about sinking that felonious husband of hers! It would rid the nation of a number of troublesome matters!' and, to my dismay, he winked audaciously at Sark, who I was gratified to note also coloured from collar upwards.

The Prince and Patch took proper leave of one another, and after we had said our respectful farewells to our royal friend, Sark escorted me to Cross Street.

'I cannot promise to be free but should you have chance to come to the quay later we may have a little time to talk. I will have sailed by first light.' I nodded, not able to trust my voice. Observing propriety in the busy street, he only kissed my hand then turned towards to the river.

We spent an hour that night under the full moon, talking quietly about anything and everything except the future, a cooling breeze washing up the river with the rising tide. The next morning the masts alongside the wharf were those of another ship and a new sheet of paper, a promise in a sonnet written in a beloved script, lay folded inside my father's book.

Rupert rode east to gather troops to harry any Parliamentarian units he could find but we heard worrisome stories of strife between the Prince and Lord Goring. There followed reports of carnage at Langport. Cromwell's mounted 'Ironsides' had ridden through a town set ablaze by cannon-fire and had cut down retreating Royalists. Somerset men had taken up where Cromwell left off, hunting demoralised fugitives and taking horrible revenge for the devastation caused by months of occupation. We had heard of it happening in Cornwall; it came as no real surprise that it was repeated elsewhere.

For Barnstaple, the effect was to spur the Prince of Wales' Council to consider their options. By the time scouts were bringing news of the enemy's approach on Exeter, the time and date were set for the withdrawal west into the Prince's Duchy of Cornwall.

It seemed that Hester's soldier, part of the contingent left to guard the Prince, was an enterprising lad as well as a besotted one. Speaking somewhat prematurely to his officer he had made cogent representations as to why he should be allowed dispensation to wed his beloved, not least, he said, because he would be doing the right thing by the lass who he feared was with child. He persuaded the captain that Hester could wash, sew and nurse and would be an asset at any campfire. Knowing the man's taste for stewed rabbit, he could be overheard regularly describing the delights of Hester's particular recipe for jugged coney when the officer was in hearing. Because he had basically ground the poor fellow down with his oversized persistence, the captain of pike finally sanctioned his Dartmoor giant's marriage and William went to the church to organise the matters there.

Hester herself remained to be convinced that a good mistress and a comfortable fireside was something she should give up for the life of a camp-follower and the sixpence a day of the pikeman's wage. And she was highly indignant at the impugning of her honour. None the less, when William Mattock went down on one massive knee in the middle of the Friday pannier market on 4th July, Hester Phipps agreed to meet him after the morning service on the very next Sunday when they would be wed.

I was witness to the ceremony and watched as the minister wrote the date and place of their wedding in Hester's prized old Bible so she should have it in 'special words' as she called them. Ann gave one of her silk ribbons as a garter. Mistress Palmer wrapped a small brass skillet in a near-new huckaback towel, with a wooden spoon and two wooden bowls as a practical and portable wedding gift. Her husband gave the newly-weds two shillings, telling Hester that it was 'to serve them for a rainy day though God willing, you will never have one.' Will, bless him, shed a tear at that.

Their married life began with Hester still in the attic room with me and Will on night watch. Three days later the Prince, his guard and all his entourage left Barnstaple taking the road to Bideford, en route to Launceston. With them went my friend Ann, Lady Fanshawe and my confidante Hester, carrying her rudimentary kitchen in an old basket.

However, I chose not to travel with them. I said my goodbyes, put on my boy's clothes, packed everything else into a battered leather cloak-bag and my hound and I joined the *Dolphin* as she rode once again on the high tide alongside Barnstaple Quay.

What God might have joined together the Prince of Wales' guard duties managed to keep asunder, but me and Will said to ourselves that we had a lifetime together so what mattered a few nights more? Then the Prince and his Council decided it was time to be off, what with Fairfax and the New Noddle Army giving the poor souls in Langport a thrashing and Exeter being the next place on their list. 'Tisn't far from Exeter to Barum, really, and 'twas all a bit of a worry.

There weren't too many wives following behind the Prince's guard, for it weren't the sort of unit to want a baggage train but Lady Ann put in a good word for me. I reckoned Will's sergeant and captain were right afeared that Will would turn nasty, him being a big lad, so they let me taggle along behind the wagons with my sail-cloth snap sack, basket and the brass skillet slung over my shoulder.

You know, I never thought I would be given anything when I was wed for I've never know'd anyone who'd got the wherewithal to give that much away. As for Master Palmer's two shillings? Well, nary me nor Will had a dry eye at that kindness! I had lost money to one shifter by hiding my coins in my skirt hems so this time I sewed it up in his doublet instead for I reckoned our silver for a rainy day would be safe enough with my girt great fellow protecting it.

So, Hester Mattock and the Prince of Wales and all his grand company set off, though the gentlemen rode to see the fort at Appledore as well as the one East-the-water at Bideford, which I was right proud I could tell Will about, even though some of my memories of that town weren't too wholesome. I looked for Ezekiel Judd or the girls in the crowds who gathered to see royalty pass by, but I never glimpsed anyone.

The baggage train made its way towards Great Torrington, rumbling on so that the Prince would find everything prepared for his arrival wherever he decreed we would stop. It took some time for everything to cross Taddiport Bridge for the mules took against the whistling and calls of some lads who were wading in the river and the fellows leading the carts could neither get them to go forward nor back. The bridge was too narrow so nobody else could pass either way.

It was early evening when we arrived at Holsworthy, the Prince having overtaken us some time previous. The troops were billeted around the town, Will yet again on night watch. I do think that his officer was mocking us, but my patience was longer than his jesting and I didn't mind that I had the bedroll to myself in the corner of a barn.

There seemed no hurry to get to Launceston. When we did reach the town they call the capital of the Dukedom soldiery was billeted everywhere. The fields around were trampled and cropped near to bare earth by the horses of whatever army had been there, for it weren't just the people who needed to be fed and there had been troops of one side or t'other here since the beginning of the war. You wouldn't have blamed the townsfolk for being bitter.

Anywhere you went folks were finding it hard to rub two halfpennies together. No matter what the tax collectors could say or do, those at the bottom of the heap still had less than those at the top, and if there b'aint anything to pay with then that's that.

We found quarters down near the ancient bridge, not Polson but the Prior's Bridge, which was fitty enough and for the first time we had a space to ourselves. The old maid who had the place was deaf as a post and so rarely got out of her bed that I began to wonder how she managed before I arrived. I seemed to be tending her all day. She had a poor sort of cot in the only room with a fire and so our bedroll was to be put on the upstairs floor. Not that it was much more than a platform in the rafters reached by a worm-holed ladder but nonetheless it was better than we'd ever had.

Will put a posy of willow-herb and valerian and some ragged-robin on our bed that first night which smelled so sweet and looked so pretty that I had to go back down the ladder for a jug and water for to stand them in, then he went all coy on me when it was time for us to lay down. Lud! That summer scent will never be the same. The very thought of it has me swimey and sighing. Shame on me! Now, where was I?

Well, the old woman's hut might have been a lovers' bower but 'twas also right at the bottom of the town. Have you ever been to Launceston? Lanson they call it in these parts. My! That hill is a trial if you have to walk it several times a day, which I did. Up with Will to keep him company, then back with fare from the market, or wherever I was able to collect the makings of a meal. Sometimes Will would get some basic rations and then might bring part of his bread, or maybe cheese home. Ale had to be got and milk for sops for the old woman. She seemed to live on warmed milk, old bread soaked in it and some honey if it was to be had. By the end of the day, I might have climbed past the castle four or five times and back again and that ruin on a hill so steep you crick your neck looking up at it.

The warring wasn't going too happily for His Majesty. By and by, our leaders knew they would have to gather all the western men together or there would be no army at all. Will came back most days with gossip about Grenvile doing this or Goring saying that and the ordinary soldier just wondering who was really in charge and where his next pay would come from.

I spent my days mending if I wasn't climbing to the town. Will's clathers were shredding and him not likely to get any more. Nobody was getting uniform by then. His boot-hose were more darn than knitting and his breeches would have been shameful if I'd not been handy with the needle. I earned a few halfpennies for pin-money doing the same for others too, Tom Phillips paying me with a bunny he'd snared. I put it in a broth that fed us and the old woman for three days, she deciding that she'd manage a plateful for all she had no teeth.

Poor Tom! Now, there was a man with many a tale to tell.

Will and he got along fine for they were both tinners. Tom was a Zennor man from down west towards the Land's End, and had fought for the King since the early days of the war. I said that showed he had a lucky streak a'cause he had dodged bullet and blade for so long. He was no volunteer back in '42 but had stuck it out anyways. He had tales of the fight at Braddock Down, and would sit atop the castle wall with anyone who had the time, re-living every move the armies made when they last fought at Launceston's Polson Bridge in '43. He'd been with the forces besieging Plymouth for as long as he could remember but with a change of commanders there had been orders to change units around too and he had landed up in Lanson. But I have never seen a man go so raging mad as Tom did the day he heard of what befell in St Ives late that autumn.

I remember him ranting that it was all very well for the Prince of Wales to declare that his Duchy of Cornwall was trusty and well-beloved and well affected to His Majesty but it weren't the case where Tom came from. In the sea town called St Ives they weren't so sure. Grenvile and several companies had gone westwards rounding up deserters - though they said he was 'recruiting' willing soldiers. They found St Ives barricadoed, a party of a couple of hundred townsmen and folk from local villages all armed and angry. Then the town folk saw they were outnumbered. It was terrible what happened next. The King's General b'aint known for his gentle ways, but to hang the constable of Zennor, who was Tom's cousin and who Tom said was right Godly, well, 'twas brutal.

Old Tom wasn't too able-bodied and I would say his terrible fit of anger that day might well have brought on the palsy that, in the end, did what bullet and blade could not.

Come November Will had been to Exeter and back as part of the Prince's escort. I'd not travelled with him then. Being newly with child, I was as sick as a dog all day, and at least in Launceston I had a roof over my head, for all it was a leaky one and there were mushrooms growing on the walls. Now we were on the move again and this time I was to go too.

The Prince went first to a grand lord's estate at Bockernnick or someplace with a name like that, where Essex had been trounced in '44, and then he and his fine gentlemen pressed on west to Truro. But in the meantime, Grenvile saw to it that regiments were changed about, including Will's. There was to be a new officer and who should Will now find himself with but a Colonel Tremayne.

Well, blow me but I recognised that man from Barnstaple! He was the fellow with the lovely lady who had stayed with the Palmers. He'd been promoted in the meanwhile but I was certain then that he was the very man who saw to it that my tormenting priest was condemned. 'Tis for sure a wonderous thing how His Majesty's cause has made so many diverse sorts cross paths, and no mistake!

Anyways, Colonel Tremayne and Sir Richard - Will said I had to call him that now - were from then on Will's proper commanders. Most of Grenvile's companies were set to watch the border between Devon and Cornwall, which is mostly along the river Tamar. With the way our luck went Will was put on duty at a place called Bridge-rule, as big a coincidence as you like, for it was barely a day's walk from Morwenstow where I first came ashore into Cornwall. Not that I wanted to go back there, mind.

If I recall rightly, 'twas at the beginning of December and we were billeted at a decent farm. One night we were at the kitchen fireside, Will was in his thinking mood, taking a pipe of tobacco, which he did now and again when it came with the rations or if someone else offered him the weed. Certain sure our pocket couldn't afford the stinking stuff. Anyway, he was saying how he'd have liked it better if he'd been stationed at t'other end of the river's defences which would have been nearer to Tavistock.

'D'ye really miss Dartmoor and the mining?' I asked.

'Aye, 'tis home, and 'tis what I do,' he said, simply with a girt puff on his pipe. 'Furthermore, I've a share in the brew-house in our village with my mother and I've a mind to have in my hand right now a pot of my own brewed winter ale to cheer up these damp nights!' Now I wasn't so sure of brew-houses, for I still could not go into an alehouse and take the smell without feeling ill, my memory going straight back to that time in Barum. I thought I might be happier as a miner's wife, but I didn't say nort to Will to spoil his dreaming, girt soft lump that he was.

Christmas passed by with no great feasting, though there was merriment for some as they took what little pay they had to the local inn and made as much of it as the innkeeper would allow. There was no debauchery for Sir Richard had made it known that there was to be no unruliness by the troops on pain of...well, my husband said that they would regret disobeying their officer's orders.

For a New Year gift Will made me a tiny bell, carved and polished out of holly wood with a clapper made of an acorn. 'Tis such a pretty thing and made the stockings I had sewn from some rough linen I had bought with my pin money look very unseasonal, though Will was as pleased as anything.

Then two days after that we were on the move once more, not so comfortable for me this time for I did ache summ'at bad and with starting to show the babe was less at ease, my bodice tighter after I had come to be quite thin. Will was right teasy about the orders, for other brigades were sent over to Plympton, which was near to his home. But his lot was to stay under the command of Major General Molesworth at Okehampton. There was one consolation; Will was made a sergeant of pike, so when he got his pay, if he got his pay, there'd be a little more in our pocket.

When we had word that Sir Richard had been locked up for disobeying the Prince and his Council it nearly broke Will's heart and I do think, if it hadn't been for me and the matter of his honour, he'd have slipped off back to Cornwood then and there and to hell with the consequences. Trouble was that old Fairfax and Parliament had different plans too and so by the end of January, despite some terrible cold which we thought would put paid to any army's movements, all the towns on the northern skirts of Dartmoor like Drewsteignton, Moreton'amsted and Bovey were all in Fairfax' hands and Dartmouth was theirs too.

I was right proud of Will, for with his advancement he seemed to have learned all manner of military cleverness so when he said,

'Hester, there's only one man the Royalist army will follow now!' He knew I was bound to ask,

'And who is that, my handsome?' He replied, sure as anything,

'Sir Ralph Hopton' and he was right.

Later, when he announced there was only one route for the Royalist army to take to come up on the enemy unexpected, and I asked him what that would be, I was not surprised that when he said 'Back the way we came!' he was proved right again. In the middle of a sodden, cold, February that's where we were sent, right back to Great Torrington.

I think the worst of it was that from Launceston to Kilkhampton, and from Bradworthy to Langtree, wherever the ruddy cavalry had been before us, a-prowling an' a-pillaging and living up to their wicked reputation, the villagers came out with their staves and clubs and anything that would hurt if it landed on flesh and bone. So for us of the poor footslogging King's infantry there was no quarter to be had anywhere and not one jot of kindness on the way.

Summer was on the way and May and June saw a drive to raise funds for the King's western army. However, folk who were impoverished before the war were even less able to pay now. Farm livestock had already been appropriated for garrisons around the county to feed men even if their pay fell short and there was little hay for the animals we had left. Spinners in their cottages found wool supplies low; weavers had no yarn with which to work and nobody could afford the cloth they did make. 1645 was an unkempt year and women darned patched onto patches. Millers had little or no corn to grind and stocks of seed-corn had been depleted as demand for flour had risen in the last winter. The spring sewing had been thin, a risky measure by anybody's reckoning. The miners could not sell their tin because Parliament blockaded the trade. Cornwall's spirit was close to breaking.

To raise morale local leaders rode about the countryside and villages encouraging tenants and townsfolk. The demands on the time of able and active gentlemen like Charles Trevanion were as heavy as demands on their capital. His visits had been intermittent since his appointment as Vice Admiral of the South coast but early one May morning, before he was due to review the local militia, he arrived at Penwarne. The problem of how to contact Lewis had occupied my thoughts ever since I had left Coombe. Our old family friend offered me a solution.

Sharing cold meat and small beer with my father, Sir Charles talked of riding to Launceston and papa, knowing of my concerns, enquired if his old friend might carry a letter on our behalf, consigning it to official channels if the opportunity arose. Sir Charles agreed without hesitation and I was told to quickly write my missive, our neighbour tucking the packet into his leather pouch. Miraculously the letter found its way by military dispatches and three weeks later I received a reply, reassuring and real, with Lewis' request that my father should ask to speak formally to John Tremayne about our marriage. Lewis confirmed that he had sent a letter to his father too, adding that as soon as was practicable he would apply for permission to ride west.

That day papa wrote to Lewis' home, but an informal meeting at the church gate after the service the next morning prompted an invitation to Penwarne, which John Tremayne was happy to accept. There was little to discuss for as my father had predicted Lewis' proposal could not have been more welcomed at the neighbouring manor. The debate over the notion of my dowry was cheery and amicable. Both parties knew the reality - there was no capital. The war had drained every gentleman dry, so a portion of the Penwarne estate was secured for me in a legal settlement which would be drawn up by lawyers.

My only qualm was my future father-in-law's assumption that after we were married we would live with him at Heligan. In our daydreaming, Lewis and I had pondered the thorny problem, planning our move into a smaller house at Kestle Wartha, the usual arrangement for the eldest son and his family while his father was alive. It was a handsome place though not large, more or less halfway between both homes, and I felt I could be happy there. Lewis' father was a dear man but the notion that we would share his house left me feeling anxious; I was again being managed. I believed that I was sure of what my future husband planned but creeping doubts began. Would he give in to his father to keep the amity between them?

These things occupied my thoughts and you may think me a silly, shallow girl, but in that summer of 1645 the progress of the King's war concerned me far less than it should have done, except that it put Lewis at risk. Naseby was a blow to the Royal fortunes, but Lewis was not there. The report of the full horror of the battle of Langport where Lewis' company had fought came well after a rider brought a one-line message: 'In haste but in safety, LT' with a scrawled post-script adding that he had rejoined Grenvile's regiments.

In '45 I was not hulling raspberries when Bristol surrendered for the second time.

The chaotic movements of the Royalist armies in Devon; the frantic efforts to summon reluctant Cornishmen to the local militia; the Prince of Wales' withdrawal into his Duchy, all these only served to confirm to me and to the war-weary folk to whom I spoke daily that King Charles' cause was as good as lost. As the autumn turned russet and gold it only remained to see where and how the matter would end.

What did I do with my days? I tended the frail as I had always done, sometimes at Penwarne but occasionally looking after folk in the hamlets around. I worked the still room drying herbs, making potions, distillations and the like. I tended our hives, making sure I told the bees the news as my mother had taught me and her mother before her.

As inclement October blew in, I sewed hangings for my marriage bed helped by my sister Agnes, whose painstaking work was very fine. On some new linen, which I lined with some old curtains found in a chest, we embroidered borders. In the corners we depicted three hands for the Tremayne name or lions for the Carews. Elsewhere I stitched our joined initials with simple leaves and flowers. I had little choice of fabric but was content with the woollen threads in green and black and a pale yellow which we had dyed ourselves. The furnishings were nearly completed when I received a message from Lewis in the first week of November.

Dearest Chick,

Time is short so I must be brief. My Officer intends to withdraw his regiments from Devon to the Cornish side of the Tamar. The eminent Young Gentleman and certain persons around him will find this unacceptable.

I may have more opportunity to come home then but I think it would be well to get the banns read as soon as may be done. My Officer will surely be called to consult with the great men at Truro and I will accompany him on that journey so will be able to call at Penwarne if only for a short

time. I am in the north of the county so not close but we have heard the enemy are going to winter quarters at Ottery so we hope that we will also stand down for the season. We can be wed but I am afraid it will be with little notice or ceremony. I hope you will not be offended but know that I am as ever, as always yours,
Affectionately
Lewis.

He was right. We had three weeks until a furious Council led by Sir Edward Hyde demanded that Sir Richard Grenvile attend the Prince in Truro to explain his actions. Lewis rode into Penwarne in the deepening gloom of a dank November afternoon, his horse lathered in sweat. He was euphoric and in buoyant mood.

'Sir Richard has been summoned before the Prince but does not intend to stay longer than protocol dictates. I have two days, no more, so here I am! Tomorrow shall be your wedding day, my dearest Mary!'

I was jubilant. A messenger was sent to the parsonage. Lewis spent some considerable time alone with my father and emerged calm, a little pensive but definitely happy. We were to be married at the church at St Ewe early the next morning and a wedding breakfast would be served at Penwarne on our return.

Our nuptials were not secret but the ceremony was a very quiet one, with only Lewis' eldest sisters Lizzie and Amy accompanying their father with papa and my sisters, all except Candacia who had remained at Antony, to witness us saying our vows. Our wedding night was tender, our parting very sorrowful. But that day I was given the keys to Kestle Wartha. Despite my apprehension, it was indeed to be our home.

I was charged with setting the place in order and while Lewis remained away with the army Agnes lived with me. We cleaned, deployed the maid, houseboy and two elderly farm-hands to their tasks and revelled in the scent and glistening shine of freshly bees-waxed furniture.

However, Lewis' optimism was unfounded. There was no

stand-down through that winter for, contrary to the earlier intelligence reports, Fairfax and his New Model Army were more active than ever and despite the icy blasts, the campaigns were on-going. In January my husband, leaving the business of defending the Tamar's banks and bridges, came home but only for three days: the Royalist army was 'preparing to march in to the lion's den' he said, though for the army in the west there would be no Daniel. Grenvile had been arrested for insubordination and the Cornish troops were losing heart.

'The way they slip off back to their homes is akin to watching a pile of salt dissolve before your very eyes. I have no heart to discipline them for I would like to do the same,' Lewis confided, feet stretched out before the parlour fire. 'But it is essential we make a move against Fairfax, though Lord Hopton has very few options. Men are already on the march to Stratton and I think we will be moving troops to Barnstaple before long.' Oblivious to all else for a few precious hours, I sat curled beside him and merely bade him say 'Good-day' to the parrot at Mistress Palmer's house if he was passing.

Lord Hopton's forces never made it to Barnstaple, for the army mustered at Great Torrington awaiting supplies from Launceston. And that was where Lord Fairfax' army discovered them.

I have heard the battle for that hilly town retold so many times in these last five months, for soldiers relish the memories of fights they have survived, the honouring of their comrades who did not. Suffice to say the wet terrain, the escarpments, the barricades and the earthworks did not deter the ten thousand men of Parliament's force against an army half their number. It was only luck - a mistaken direction to the wrong bridge - which left the lanes back into Cornwall open for the sorry remnants of the King's western forces to escape. And behind them Great Torrington church, a powder magazine still full of barrels and a holding point for two hundred Royalists, the Roundhead's prisoners, exploded sending flames high into the night sky, lighting the fugitives' way.

So came the collapse of the once mighty King's western army while Fairfax pushed relentlessly west. We had stragglers returning to Gorran with reports of Fairfax paying two shillings to every Royalist soldier who would go home. The blacksmith of Mevagissey was among them. The smith's wife, once she had ceased her weeping, gave him a black eye for never sending any word of how he fared. It was the smith who also told of how Cornish folk were aiding Fairfax' men to make barricades on the roads; their aim was to force the war in the county to a close. If it meant taking a stand against their former comrades then weary Cornishmen would do just that.

On the 9th of March, late morning in heavy rain, two horses clattered into the stable-yard. Lewis dashed into the house and threw off his cloak, filthy and dishevelled. With him was a young woman who was heavily pregnant and soaked to the skin and a man so large he seemed to fill the hallway completely.

'Mary, my love! This woman needs our warm, dry hearth and Will and I would benefit from a little of the same, but we cannot tarry so we must be quick!' and he led the bedraggled pair through to the kitchen, the men's swords clattering noisily on the wainscot. My house maid, barely more than a little girl, looked terrified.

Exasperated I called out,

'Lewis, stop! Enough haste. Take a breath and tell me, what is going on?' I turned to the girl; 'Come, sit here and wrap this around you! What is your name for my husband has forgotten his manners!' I handed her a blanket that had been ready to be put away in the press.

'Take off your doublets and we will set them by the fire while you at least drink some mulled ale'. I told the serving girl to fetch more blankets, and as she ran off Lewis began to spill out the news,

'This is Hester and her husband Will Mattock. Will has served with me since…well…long enough!'

I thought I knew the girl's face but for some time I could

not place her. I took her hand, rubbing it to chafe some warmth into her fingers. 'You are welcome, Hester!' She smiled at me, a broad and winning smile, though her teeth were chattering so much that she could hardly speak.

'We have been chased through the county and I have brought Hester for you to help her. You should both be safe enough here. I left my company as they were pulling back on Probus, barely ahead of Fairfax' cavalry. There may be a set-to locally or, more likely, we shall see Hopton pressed to accept a treaty of surrender.'

I gasped,

'Then the war is over? God be praised! Let us hope so and you may at last come home!'

Although Will and Hester added a fervent 'Amen' I sensed that it would not be so straightforward. Lewis changed the subject, offering Will another drink, seeking out some new-baked bread and cheese.

'Lewis, tell me. There is something else.' He turned to me and putting down his cup took my hands in his.

'My chick, I cannot come home yet. For some of us the war is not yet done.' I pulled away. 'I must go to Pendennis to await my orders. While there is a breath left in me and there are men who have sworn to stand for the King, my duty is to fight for His Majesty's cause.'

I could not believe what I was hearing and could not control my anger. I began pummelling his chest, crying out,

'And what if that cause was lost months ago? What then? How long am I to wait? How many times must I lie awake and worry that you will never come home?'

He recaptured both my hands in his. As he did Hester quietly spoke,

'Mistress, I have fought these last weeks to convince my Will of just that thinking. But these men are of a breed where right-ness and good-ness run through their veins. I would swear that if you cut them they would bleed honour not blood.' She gazed up at her man, an unfathomable expression on her gaunt face. 'They love us, and we them, but it is not an easy place to be. Yet if they were lesser men they'd not be them we love,' She sighed, long and deep, then she simply added 'And so we pay the price.'

I looked at her, a little colour creeping into her cheeks, perhaps embarrassed at saying so much. It was then that I recognised this diffident woman. I had seen her at Barnstaple, the victim of a dishonourable man. Immediately the sentiments of Hester's sincere testimony at my fireside made me pause.

As suddenly as it had flared my resentment ebbed away. I straightened my shoulders and looked my husband in the face, my hands on my hips like a fishwife. If he was going to leave, then he would do so knowing I too was strong.

'Lewis Tremayne, if you so much as allow harm to one hair on that head of yours – or his,' I pointed at the giant perched ridiculously on my hearth-stool, 'I will personally do what Fairfax, Cromwell and all their minions have failed to do and thrash you at Kestle's granite gateposts!' He hugged me to his chest where I was able to smudge away my angry tears.

The next hour we spent in gathering what we could in the way of clean clothes and some food, and then the men were gone, leaving Hester and me to get to know one another as we watched the puddles dry upon the floor.

Boy's clothes again and on board a ship yet I might have been in a different world for such were the joys of those next months. When Jago discovered my identity he was fulsome in his greetings, his great black beard splitting with an enormous white grin and the threads of his thrum cap jiggling with laughter. He was perfectly happy to have the daughter of an old acquaintance and her hound aboard and not one whit disturbed at a woman's presence whether I dressed in breeches or skirts.

'Jago daren't be superstitious about females on board,' whispered Sark, when I remarked upon the welcome. 'Since you sailed from Bristol last month we have signed on a new cook!' and he pointed to the maindeck where a broad-hipped woman, who could only be described as burly, was working.

Her skirts were hitched up at the sides into a broad leather belt so that the three layers of her multi-coloured hose gave the impression of striped tree trunks where her legs should be. She was gathering eggs from the chicken coop, which was lashed to the foot of the mast.

'It's his wife. He worships the very ground she walks on,' he told me 'and she sailed as bo'sun on his last ship.' He continued, speaking ever more quietly, stony-faced, 'They say she sank three of Parliament's fleet just by spitting at them…' I was about to exclaim then turned round to see Sark, lips compressed, clearly teasing me.

As *Dolphin* worked for the King up and down the western coast, from the Royal magazine at Bridgewater or occasionally Bristol, I stood watches with Sark, learning as any ship's new boy might about stars and navigation, finding that the calculations that Sark began to teach me came gratifyingly easily. In our brief spells of leisure, we discovered a shared love of the written word. He had a well-worn copy of a Spanish novel, a questing romance from which he would read extracts, and though I could not understand a word, I loved to listen and he would translate, sketching out the knight errant's adventures for me.

Sark often framed a rhyme, mostly silly ditties about nonsense, but he could pen a decent poem too. He gave me a battered booklet, saying he had won it at a game of cards from Jack Suckling, a Cavalier who, before the war, had been fleeing England on a ship that Sark was manning. Thinking to please him I secretly committed all its contents to memory. One day, as he scanned the sky for change in the sea-state, a verse sprang to mind, spilling out before I had time to think of the consequences,

'Out upon it, I have loved

Three whole days together!

And am like to love three more,

If it prove fair weather.'

Sark looked over to where I was practising knots with a piece of string. He responded with another quote, a different tone in his words and voice,

'Is there no respect of place, persons nor time in you? Three days, Grace? Is that all? My eyes tell me differently. When were you going to tell me?'

I looked up sharply. It hardly seemed the time or the place, but out here on deck with the crack of canvas and the swell against the sides of the ship, we were less likely to be overheard than in the cabin.

I had suspected even before I left Barnstaple but nearly three weeks on I was now sure that I was carrying Sark's child. There was no sickness, no discomfort just the absence of courses and familiar sensations which I now recognised for what they were. I had never felt so well but I had also donned blinkers to the reality of my existence and hesitated to break the news.

I realised that in so doing I had deeply wounded the man who I would love not for three days nor six but forever. I went to stand near to him.

'There could be no proper time, but it was not for anything other than I felt no need to say, to make demands, to …'

We stood, not touching.

'Time thou must untangle this…' he began to quote, then, 'Grace, we are living a borrowed existence and your future is now more ambiguous than ever. I can offer nothing to you, to our child, except an insecure life on uncertain seas…'I interrupted him,

'If you would offer me that, then I will take it with both hands for as long or as short a time as God permits and I will take each new dawn as it comes. None of us can know our future but to mark the past with regrets is something we can avoid. My love, I am truly sorry I did not tell you before. I do not want to be sorry again.'

A shout from the look-out tore any more words from between us. The alarm was raised; enemy ships had been sighted ahead off the port bow. We were tacking out to sea to be able to take Gore Point and cross Porlock Bay, intent on another powder run into and out from Bridgewater. However, the sighting of a fleet looking to engage with a large number of vessels in the distance was enough to make Pasco Jago wary. He paced the decks, side to fo'c'sle and back to the stern, making assessments, watching the wind in the sails, judging his advantage.

'Discretion and valour are uncomfortable bedfellows, Sark!' he bellowed, 'Change course and let us put some sea betwixt us and they for I do not like the view here!' And so the crew set to with sails and sheets and the *Dolphin*, with the advantages of a smaller ship's speed turned about and made off, working the wind back the way we had come. In our next port of call we discovered that Bridgewater had fallen to Fairfax just before we had been due to arrive and the engagement we had narrowly avoided had resulted in the capture of sixteen of King Charles' vessels which had been waiting to carry the King from Wales to North Devon. Jago's instincts had been correct.

There was now a constant edge to our voyage. Not only were there the natural perils of the sea to be faced but also the patrols of the enemy's navy. I knew well enough the dangers posed by capture. Then there was the ever-present threat from foreign pirates, Algerian or Dutch or any independent-minded opportunist. Their raids on shipping and the coasts of Cornwall and Devon used surprise and the distraction of the authorities to their advantage. Sark and Jago seemed impervious to the menace of the enemy but pirates were another matter altogether.

In spite of this, the hazards rarely served to make the atmosphere on board tense, often quite the opposite. Any discovery of advantage over Parliamentarian vessels became the topic of many a lively discussion; feats of nautical derring-do became the foundations of legends; wrecks were sometimes a matter for conjecture as to the cause, more often the remarks were simply men paying their respects to fellow seafarers.

Jago had many tall tales that he cheerfully repeated, his wife disparagingly rolling her eyes heaven-wards at each retelling. His favourite, with which he would torment any slothful crew members, was about the Royalist Sir John Mucknell who Jago swore nailed recalcitrant sailors to the mast by their ears. Sark would nod reflectively, arms folded, looking at his boots waiting for the moment when Jago required him to say,

'And how did he get them off the mast, Captain Jago, sir?' to which Pasco would sneer in gruesome glee,

''Ee used 'is sword, lad! Used 'is sword!' and miming the action would shout 'Snick!' at the top of his voice! I have seen grown men turn green and run to the gunwales at that performance though it could not shock me. Jago was genuinely distressed when he heard of Mucknell's ship being wrecked off Scilly that summer.

The Bristol Channel was a more difficult place for the *Dolphin* to ply her trade once the city that I had called home was forced to surrender, so in the autumn of '45 our sailing master decided to return to his old haunts along the south coast. Privateers like us were still operating out of the Fal under Pendennis Castle, doing what they could for the tin trade, for munitions and the Royalist cause, most of the fishermen around Cornwall assisting by slipping between the blockades if the bigger ships could not. We were well aware of the decline of the King's fortunes. Jago decided that the further west his ship was stationed, the safer he would feel and so the voyage to the Channel Islands became our new regular run.

However, in October, riding a strong south westerly from Jersey, we were beset by the very devils of the seas, Algerian corsairs. Their galley was swift and Sark warned me that should we be boarded the situation would be dire indeed. We could expect no quarter.

Jago was however, an expert seaman and when the Turk was spotted he had manoeuvred the *Dolphin* so that he would be able to gain advantage of the wind, though we could not outrun the brigands. And we had guns. Pasco Jago had invested in more small guns than large cannon, so the ship was perhaps better and more effectively defended that our opponents expected. Six swivel guns were set up: two on the poop, two more were placed for'ard with two on the main deck alongside the bigger six-pounders. All the swivelguns were portable by two men, each gun had another man to help load them and all had been deployed on the starboard side as the Turk approached.

I was 'manning' one on the stern. Without all hands there were not enough people to deploy all the guns, and I had watched Sark train his men so often from the quarterdeck of the *Ann* that I could have shouted the commands as well as he. And shout I did, for as the Turk drew closer, Jago's plan was for us to be as noisy, as offensive and as prickly as any vessel could be.

So looking like a very portly, stumpy sailor, my face blackened down with soot from the galley fire, I yelled as many obscenities as I could recollect from my childhood haunts on Bristol's quays, my hand upon the canvas bags of shot beside the gun. Jago's wife was one of the team on the other gun near me, and several times I caught her, eyebrows raised, glancing my way. She had gathered her skirt hem and pulled the fabric forward between her legs, tucking it into her broad belt: the effect was to give this mountain of a woman enormous 'breeches', making her more mobile and more imposing than three of her shipmates put together. And she was angry, more angry than I have ever seen any woman in my life. She pulled her battered broad brimmed hat tight onto her head and began to scream. Not a womanly scream of fear, but a deep, keening, undulating howl which as a background to the shouts from the crew sounded fearsome even to my ears. She seemed to be able to maintain the wail hardly seeming to draw breath. With Patch joining in with continuous, frantic barking the din was horrendous.

Before the Turk got too close, and not quite within range of the guns, Sark ordered the forward guns to fire single small cannonballs, warnings to the raiders that we would not be an easy prize. Jago was watching the how the wind changed with care, very aware that our sails could be emptied if the Turk positioned us to her leeward side. He was not about to give her the chance.

The noise as the two guns fired was thunderous; I hardly expected it, somehow thinking that because we were in open sea it would not be that loud. There was a jeering from the Turk as the shots splashed into the sea, but nonetheless the galley altered course a little, away from their direct line of attack. Jago gave a shout, a direction, and Sark ran back to the stern, overseeing another round of shot from our guns. I rammed the cartridge home as I had seen so many times before and the ship's carpenter aimed, following the slow progress of our attacker with the muzzle of the swivelgun.

Instinctively I turned away and knelt, crouching over my stomach to protect the baby inside, holding Patch close to me.

'Give fire!' yelled Sark. As the air was buffeted with the blast I felt my child kick strongly inside me for the first time and a wild elation swept over me. The fact that our shots had raked the starboard bow of the Turk and had splintered a couple of the huge oars added to it, and I redoubled my shouts, this time making Sark look askance. I grinned and he grinned back. Patch, quite untroubled by the explosion, maintained his contribution to the mayhem.

Amidships three sailors were preparing two more rounds. They fired and we could see more lethal shards of wood shower across the Turk's deck.

Now it was our turn to jeer, though Mistress Jago kept up that intimidating keening and Patch barked, his tail excitedly circling like a windmill. Then along our ship's side a cheer began, building to a roar, for the galley began to veer away, her course set for the open sea. I watched for what seemed a very long time, my heart pounding not with fear but with exhilaration. In due course, as the *Dolphin* stowed her guns, the ship returned to normal and, breathing a communal sigh of relief, we headed for the Cornish coast.

Later in our tiny cabin, I told Sark of the baby's quickening, a little afraid of how he might react. He put his arms around me tight and kissed me hard and long, and when he let me go looked so happy that all my concerns fled. Then I remembered I wanted to ask Sark something.

'Do you know why the master's wife was so fearsome and so furious? I have never seen anything like it before and probably do not want to witness it again!' He began to chortle, harder and harder until I could not help but join in too though I had no idea why. Breathlessly between the gales of laughter he spluttered,

'Collops!' That made us laugh even harder. 'Goody Jago,' he gasped 'was frying up collops of bacon when the Turk appeared. The engagement meant they all were ruined and there's nothing that will irk that woman more than food that goes to waste! It was all the collops!'

And we fell about laughing once more. When a roar came from through the cabin wall, an emphatic request for quiet, I needed to bite the back of my hand until I could bring my mirth under control. I fell asleep exhausted, a sporadic bubble of hilarity welling up every time my mind thought of one particular word.

As my condition began to be more apparent, Goody Jago's demeanour altered and we would chat affably while I did my share of galley duties. She had two sons, both seamen like Pasco though she had no idea where they were;

her four daughters had each married innkeepers in ports along the south-west coast. There was no fear or mystery in childbearing for Mistress Jago. My assumption was that she would be my midwife and I was content.

The winter sailing pattern was less arduous; nevertheless we faced storms often enough for me to dread them even though I had good sea-legs. Fortunately, Jago wanted his ship maintained. The Fal provided many safe anchorages for the repairs to keel and mast, and to make the most of the shelter we regularly dipped between the rotund twin forts, proud Pendennis, high on the rocky promontory on the west, and St Mawes, pugnaciously crouched low down on the opposite shore.

The ongoing care of sails and rigging was part of everyone's duties. I had always hated sewing even under Jinty's benevolent eye, but with a sailmaker's palm to protect my hand I found mending canvas far more to my taste and loved to work with hemp ropes, quickly learning to making the knotted weight for the end of every line.

But the winter ended not with a renewal of the old tactics or the resurgence of the maritime game of cat and mouse between Parliament's navy and the King's fleet. February brought the collapse of the Royalist cause. Pendennis Castle, broodingly overseeing the river entrance from its high promontory stood ready to safeguard the Prince of Wales. The *Phoenix* anchored in the sheltered waters below to ship the Prince and his council to France when there was no hope of His Majesty's fortunes turning.

At the beginning of March, the heir apparent arrived, stayed but a few days, and was forced to flee. Facing south-easterly storms, the *Phoenix* had needed to sail west to ride several tides in Whitsand Bay off Sennen. Consequently, the Prince had to take horse towards the Land's End to board her, the precious passenger making first to the Sorlinges and thence to Jersey and to safety. We played our part in the exodus, taking a small group including an old friend, Lady Fanshawe's father Sir John Harrison and his daughter Margaret, to St Malo.

On our return we were told to make ready to work our ship's boat up river to Truro where Lord Hopton planned to send as many essential goods as he could down to the fortress on the headland. It was said that this would be a stronghold so well prepared that the defenders could hold out for twelve month or more. We know now how badly that plan was flawed.

Men toiled to move some of the guns, powder and shot from St Mawes Castle across the broad waterway. It had the armament against any fleet but was too vulnerable from the rising land behind to be defensible for long. The governor, Hannibal Bonython, did not accept Sir John Arundel's invitation to join him across the water. When Cornwall surrendered on March 12th, St Mawes could only hold out one day longer.

The next morning Sark was helming our boat as it made the run downstream on the ebbing tide. Sir John had calculated that this would be the last opportunity before Parliamentarian troopers took control of Truro and beyond.

As the oars pulled the boat past the ferry crossing at Tolverne, two women calling and waving from the shore had attracted Sark's attention, their distress evident. One was calling out a name, one which convinced him that he should bring them both on board; the name of a man who had marched into Pendennis Castle just twenty four hours before.

I began to think that I could have marched in my sleep in the weeks after Torrington. There was little or no baggage train to speak of after that fight for we were mainly making shift for ourselves.

At Torrington Will's officer had established me and the few other women who still followed the drum in Taddiport, in a billet overlooking the very same bridge I had crossed seven long months before. Our shelter was not much more than a shed but it had a good roof and a'cause it had been 'entin' down for days and we was all sopping wet, we were content enough not to be getting soaked. Several women grumbled, for we weren't to be in the town across the river and they said they were right afeared of what might happen, or afeared of missing something more like. I was not.

I reckoned that the Colonel knew what he was about. Will said we were on the best side of the Torridge to be farthest away from the attack, which he supposed would come from Chulmleigh. With Will's new soldiering expertness, he was shown to be right. It worked out that Colonel Tremayne did a fine thing in leaving us over that side.

Once it all started, Will said the fighting from the barricadoes on the east went right through the town with horsemen, knee to knee, mowing foot-soldiers down with pistol or sword, and push of pike like herrings in a salt-barrel, all squeezed in between the narrow streets.

'Twas a terrible baptism of fire and I do mean that quite truthfully for I have never seen such a sight as when, while dozens of men were scrambling as fast as they could down from the town and across the narrow bridge, there was an explosion that battered my ears so they were still ringing hours after. It was a night with fast clouds and a near-full moon but still the sky lit up like a mid-summer day and the air thumped so it made your chest pound. The light looked hellish. The top of the town began to burn, though not as much as I reckon it would have done if all the cottages' thatch had not been sodden. As it was, the church was blown right apart and hundreds of our men with it. When I heard the news I fell to being sick for nothing about my time in Bideford or Barnstaple, for all the soldiery and the scaring, had made me think that such a thing could happen.

We heard the yelling and the orders for retreat and a girt hammering on the doors. Now, when there are guns and swords and trouble about, nobody has to tell Hester Mattock twice to move herself!

Will had seven men left of the thirty in his unit, Colonel Tremayne following with perhaps three times as many, and we all struggled through the lanes, knee deep in mud sometimes. Will said he saw soldiers throwing down their weapons as they ran even though that would normally get them hung for insub-something, bad soldiering anyway, if they got found. When I said I thought Will's men were too afraid of him to do that he just shrugged and said he'd carried six pikes when the boys couldn't manage, and gave 'em back when matters cooled down a little. The men who tossed aside their kit aren't with the army now and in all likelihood won't ever face court-martial. If they've reached their homes at all, that is.

So our long retreat began, and my marching feet sore with latchet shoes so worn 'twas only the laces and wishful thinking that held them together. My skirts were heavy for they were full of muck and were like board if they dried. I could break the caked mud off in clods. Enemy cavalry chased units on the Holsworthy road but knowing the district better than they did, Colonel Tremayne bade his men use other lanes, more northerly towards the coast, the way we'd come before. The locals might defy us but if we were going to get the rough end of a clubman's stick again, then the Roundhead cavalry would find little backing either. In the event, nobody troubled. It seemed with us retreating we weren't worth the bother of coming out in the wet and bitter cold for.

There were some of our cavalry set to watch at Morwenstow. I was right glad we didn't stop there. We went trudging on to Stratton where I did get one night's rest on a straw mattress. As we moved out Will said to look behind us, pointing to the hill that the Cornish boys made famous in '43. Though my eyes b'aint that good at a distance, I agreed it was a mountain.

We pushed onwards, for Lord Hopton had announced that the foot-soldiers would regroup at Camelford. I had just got our clothes dry if not cleaned when we broke up quarters yet again to leave for Bodmin. Will reckoned we weren't much more than a day ahead of the New Model Army. I could not call them noddles any more for there was little humour left in me by that time.

One good thing was that Colonel Tremayne had taken to my William. I do think he is a good officer for he watches all his men, knows them by name too. He learns a little of their ways or something of their family and where they are from. That's why they follow him - and who wouldn't? He's a fine looking fellow if you like your men average size, a bit on the thin side and dark curls wearing off his brow even though he's not even thirty years old yet.

Anyways, when we had to flee Bodmin he took Will to one side. The good Colonel promised that he had it in mind to see to it that I was taken to safety for the sake of the baby. When our Royal army truly was in full retreat west to Truro he was as good as his word. Colonel Tremayne said some place on Hopton's route was not far from his home. He would take us there. He said his wife would see to it that I was protected while the men went…well, suffice to say that Will and I had our first spat that day.

I yelled at him, wanting to know why he could not just lay down his arms so that he and I could do what hundreds of others had done: take Fairfax's two shillings, add it to the two that Master Palmer gave us, and the pair of us go to his home, to Cornwood. After all his dreaming, I would have thought that was such a clear-cut course, with an infant on the way and all. But no, not for my William.

Awkward at first, then bolder, Will made the longest speech I think he will ever make, explaining why he could not go home. I wept like a child to hear him. From that moment, I decided to myself that I never shall question his design again.

Well now, I'd often enough had sore feet, and plenty of times had aching bones but, my Lor'! On the pillion of that nag I was sure that my insides would be all shook out! Will is no horseman and the pair of us was jiggling up and down like apples bobbing in a barrel, and neither in time with the horse's back or hooves or any bit that kept a rhythm. On top of that, my babe had started kicking like a mule, and I was weary enough to drop. It was windy and wet and Kestle Wartha barton could not come too soon for me.

If I had been able to think while my head was shaking up and down, I might have wondered about the lady Colonel Tremayne had married. As it was, Mistress Tremayne was no stranger. I realised that she was the same fair lady that I had seen all that while ago in Barum and later she told me she reasoned that she knew my face too, remembering soon enough the circumstance of when we met. She was so gentle from the very first, and if matters had gone the way Colonel Tremayne had planned I would certain sure to have been happy being in her employ.

But there are plans and there are plans and Mistress Tremayne was not a woman to be directed where she would not go.

I had just about dried off after that ride, and we had done our parting from our men, when there was a frantic pounding at the door. A servant came to Mistress Tremayne from her father's house which I gathered was not that far away, insisting that she gather herself and her sister and, for safety's sake, go very quickly to her husband's father at Heligan. Word was about that the scouts of the Parliamentarian army were all around Tregony and the rest were expected to follow within the day. I didn't know how near or far that was but the messenger was terrible urgent.

Now, I cannot say if many wives would choose to go to

their in-laws if their fortunes took a turn for the worst and they had a choice. But I would for certain sure stake the two silver sixpences that still lie stitched in Will Mattock's doublet that none but Mary Tremayne and Hester Mattock could be quite so contrary as to ignore what was sensible and follow their hearts.

XXXIX Mary: Kestle Wartha to Pendennis Castle 9th - 13th March 1646

If four years ago anyone had told me I would defy my husband and that it was possible to act contrary to my family's counsel then I would have called the prediction misguided at best. I now have had experience enough of my own to know that these turbulent times can force extraordinary transformations in a woman's fortunes.

Over spiced cider and warm honey cake, Dewnes' favourite cure-all, we settled in front of the hearth and Hester began to recount her adventures. We were completely engrossed, Agnes aghast at Hester's tribulations, so the pounding at the door made us all jump. It was a lad, bearing a note from Lewis' father. I was bidden to Heligan for there were fears for our safety as the military situation locally was deteriorating.

In that moment, my impulsive streak became evident again. Perhaps I should blame the Mevagissey blacksmith's wife? She once told me she would rather be with her man on bread and water than apart from him with all the riches in the world. I imagined her voice as I made my decision on that March afternoon because I knew that I could neither take refuge at the manor nor return to Penwarne. I felt sorry for what I was about to do for deceit was not in my nature. If my instincts about Hester were correct and she felt as I did, then I had a very different plan.

I helped Agnes as she packed then sent her, with the little maid, back to Penwarne with an excuse that Hester needed to rest and I wanted a little more time to gather my belongings and would indeed to go to Heligan to Master Tremayne after the morning service at St Ewe the next day.

Instead, I sent my servants to the Sunday service with a message of my indisposition with a woman's ailments. My message suggested that I would still supervise the gathering of my necessities on the following day, gambling that the vicar and my father-in-law would be too embarrassed to come themselves to ensure that I followed their instructions. I knew they would not allow any of the girls to travel in the circumstances and perhaps Fairfax' men might take their time to sweep through our district. Once the coast was cleared I told Hester what I intended to do. Her response did not surprise me,

'Nothing ventured, nothing won!' was her pithy reply and so we sat down to consider our plan of action.

We decided that we would make our way west, join with our men, to face together whatever Fortune had in store. However, we had yet to work out how we were to do that, without the papers that were now obligatory. Nor had I taken much time to consider the practical issues of transport. My head was a-buzz with thoughts, all of which needed some pragmatic consideration. I wondered what grandmother Dewnes would have done. She was bold. She was enterprising, and she was certainly a little irregular. I needed to employ the same devices.

Sunday was dismally wet, making the parlour dark, so we lit two branches of candles and took out the creased paperwork with which I had been issued when travelling back from Barnstaple in the autumn of '44. Hester looked over my shoulder.

'Do you write, Hester?' I asked. She shook her head.

'I can recognise and write my name. My friend Bess taught me my letters when I was in Barum but I never did get any further, madam.' I looked at her directly.

'Hester, you must call me Mary. If we are to manage this escape then we must be equals in it! Firstly though, this permit is a thorny problem.'

Hester took up the paper and turning this way and that, placed it carefully on the table, tracing lines with her fingers.

'Wait, if you will...' and she slipped from the room returning with a well-thumbed hand-made book, self-consciously explaining,

'This was what I did my copying from in Barum. Without it I cannot truly help with any words.' Opening it, she traced the shapes of the lettering, comparing it to the document.

'Madam, Mary…I perhaps do not see lettering as you do but if I trace these lines and if I were a better or perhaps a worse scrivener, I could see how these shapes could be made to look a little different.' She was diffident 'Though whether they'm the right words I could not say.' I began to see what she meant.

In the next hour we carefully wrote out what we thought might serve as an official document using the words we could not change, planning what was required to alter what was there. We had only one paper and we could not alter the signature. One mistake would ruin everything but it was a chance we had to take.

Putting on some old kid gloves I took a deep breath and picking up a quill, its tip a little worn, I dipped it in the ink. The abbreviated 'October' was difficult to alter to 'March'. '1644' was written with unusually open figures. I lost my nerve and decided to return to the date later. Now, how was I to deal with the thorny problem of the surname Carew? The C was easy enough to add a stroke making the stem of T. I slipped in a form which could be mistaken for an 'r' and the 'a' only needed a line across the middle to look enough like an 'e'. I looked at Hester. The fine leather of the gloves began to feel clammy.

'The 'r' should make a good enough 'm'. Lor'! This man's writing is barely tidier than my scrawl! Look, perhaps here on the 'w' you could finish off the loop and make an 'a'…' I did, and then, a little more confident used what was left to strike in a tail for a 'y' with an 'e' flicked upon the end.

The pass now read that Mary Tremayne could travel with her servants. However, the problem was that the destination was 'Coombe and the environs'. I could not see a design but Hester did and drew on our imitation to show me: add a stem to the start of 'Coombe' and there was a 'K'. Eventually we were done apart from the date.

The more I looked the harder it seemed. Eventually Hester said 'Do what you can, as best as may be and we shall see how we fare.' And so I did. The result was without doubt a messy attempt at forgery.

Tears sprang unbidden and unwanted and in despair I threw the quill down on the table and curled sobbing by the fire, pulling off the ink-stained gloves. Hester quietly leaned across the papers. Picking up the ruined pass she blew gently across it, shook it a little, placed it carefully back where it had lain. Taking up the sheets detailing our workings she tore them into pieces, throwing them into the heart of the fire.

'Twouldn't do for anyone to see those, Mary. But look! It seems to me that this sec'tary was in a hurry and careless with his ink-pot. And any ignorant trooper would read how a misled and heart-broken wife had cried at her husband's questionable loyalties.' And as I picked up the drying sheet I saw what she meant. Tear stains and blots of ink now made the alteration indistinguishable or certainly unremarkable compared to the rest of the script. She pointed to the gloves, adding,

'Best burn those too and then none shall ever be the wiser' then laughing heartily added 'There's not one stain upon your character, Mistress Tremayne!'

I returned then to a notion that had come to me as we began our forgery work. If we were to change places, it might be possible for a humble maidservant to be accompanying a worried, pregnant gentlewoman to the nearest apothecary. It was a little implausible if you knew the truth but if you were Hester's imaginary trooper, a London roundhead and one who had no local knowledge of the gentry, then perhaps a panic-stricken, garrulous maid would speak for a self-conscious mistress too embarrassed by her delicate condition and the discomfort of her malaise. And maybe they could be excused for being in a hurry.

Hester embraced the illusion whole-heartedly even conjuring up a pretended condition, which we decided should be rare and dangerous to both mother and child. I set to organising clothing.

We worked and waited for the pounding on the door, anticipating all manner of horrors. Hours then days passed. I had the boy fit up the little cart ready to harness our mule. There was nothing more prestigious, the soldiers having taken anything that could be ridden. The mule, formerly at Penwarne and named Jack, had been overlooked simply because he was too old to be of useful service.

We had no idea what was passing in the locality, for I think most folk now kept well within their walls for fear of any trouble, so it was on 12th, Thursday, that Hester and I decided we could tarry no longer.

I lent Hester a bodice on which we had been able to loosen the lacing. She wore her own skirt which we had brushed and cleaned but which we cut and stitched with one of mine to look as if it had a finer petticoat beneath. She tied up her hair under my newest cap and looked quite the part with my cloak about her, muffler and hood at the ready. I had also found her some shoes that were a good enough fit.

Wearing my oldest, workaday gown I donned an old cassock coat of Lewis'. I had a basket of plain food packed and we put some spare clothing in a small bag, shifts and the like; we would sit upon some blankets, necessary because of the delicate condition of my 'mistress'. At the last minute, Hester could not bear to leave behind the modest belongings with which she had arrived, so we attempted to disguise them with the women's garments, stuffing the wrapped metalwork to the base of the bag.

I set the lad to make our transport ready. The cart was truly little more than a bed of planking about a man's length long and an arm span wide, with two biggish wheels to see it through the deeper ruts in the Cornish lanes. It was usually carrying sacks of this or that, but it would have to serve for Hester and I to ride upon, driving the cart as best we could. I had never handled a mule or a wain, and Hester was distinctly wary of the beast for it had snickered at her and shown its set of crooked brown teeth. I tried to reassure her but with little success.

Telling the servants we were riding to Penwarne, I bade them take care to secure the place that night and set the men to tasks that would keep them from noting that we would take entirely the opposite road to the one they might expect. With forged pass to hand and a modest amount of coin hidden beneath our clothes, we set off.

Progress was slow for the roads were truly mired. It had stopped raining but the ruts and holes were filled with water. With the low mist clouding the horizon we were like wary foxes, our ears pricked, alert to the threat of strangers. We had gone very little distance at all before we heard the sound we had been dreading; the thump of the hooves of a significant number of horses reverberating along the high, hedged road. They were approaching from the west.

There was barely room for a second cart to pass. The troop of horsemen, all wearing armour and carrying the short musket common to mounted forces, cantered three abreast, meeting us with many shouts and much jostling of horses and riders to reposition the unit along the hedge. The officer came to a halt beside the cart, his sword rattling frighteningly close to my ear. He was not pleased and when he spoke, my heart sank. His accent told me he was most definitely a West Countryman; my gamble now was from where?

'Halt! In Parliament's name! Whither go you? Oh, begging your pardon! I bid you good day, mistress!'

He had caught sight of Hester and, marking that she looked as though she was of the better sort and was with child, had remembered his manners. She groaned in a genteel fashion.

'My mistress ails sir and we hope to reach Tregony today for to see the apothecary and a midwife there. They have not been able to travel for fear of the ungovernable behaviour of the cavaliers, Sir,' I wailed in what I hoped was a suitably deferential but desperate tone, adding swiftly, 'My mistress has her papers, Sir...' He hesitated, but perhaps his mind was not on bureaucratic niceties.

'Move on here! Parliament has no argument with...er...such as you, no argument with innocents. I need no papers but I will have your names...'

I think nerves had put the devil in me that day for in that

moment I recklessly answered,

'This lady is Candacia Carew from Penwarne, cousin to John Carew, that fine Parliamentarian gentleman and lawyer of London. My name is Margery Butland, serving maid of that same manor, Sir.'

Hester moaned again, this time most dramatically, at which point the riders received a brusque order to ride on. As twenty dragoons jostled past, we were spattered all over with muddy water, which quashed any hilarity at my mischievous reference to my spiteful sister.

Jack, unsettled by the press of animals refused to budge for nigh on half an hour and I was afraid the company would ride back to discover our duplicity, but eventually with some gentle words and firm hauling on his harness, which came at the expense of my shoes and stockings, we were again on the move.

We struggled down the steep lane into the valley and out again at Tubbs Mill. I had decided to take a route that via several junctions could have taken us legitimately to Tregony. In fact, I hoped to use by-ways to reach Tresillian then make our way to Truro.

Another company of troopers' soon confronted us. They were coming from the direction of Ruan but, worryingly, there were foot- soldiers as well as cavalry. This time the officer did snatch up our papers, glaring aggressively at us. He only thrust the battered page back at me when Hester moaned.

'What's wrong with your mistress, wench?' he drawled. I answered swiftly and I hoped humbly,

'It's an uncommon malady of women in her condition, sir.' He was not rebuffed.

'Well? What ails her?' I felt the sweat prickle beneath my arms, and I must have coloured for I was hot with nerves. Hester spoke: I hardly recognised her voice,

'Good sir, the apothecary named it as frebitachio fundamentata. It is a...' she did not finish her explanation for a gruff voice piped up,

'Cor, my missus 'ad that! Right sore it was an' all.'

Another joined in,

'Aye, I've heard of it too. Poor woman!'

Pikes wavered as the tough facade of a professional military fell away and discipline dissolved into a discussion of ailments, ills and whose bruises were the most impressive. With yet another voice muttering darkly from the back of the group that 'we was told it was a disease for catchin' too if you stands too near' the exasperated officer snapped an order, glared ominously at Hester's slumped figure and waved us on.

By late afternoon, the mule, now very temperamental at working far beyond the norm, constantly needed to be led and consequently I was forced to alter our plan. We would push as fast as possible to Philleigh and down to Tolverne where, if we could reach the place by dusk, a ferry would carry us across the Fal, shortening the journey by some miles. That way we might just reach Truro before Fairfax' army did.

However, the conquering forces moved like the puddles of water we had watched on my slate floor, swiftly merging, and by the time we neared Philleigh two units had become ten. My nerves were frayed to shreds and we were both exhausted.

When we saw a rowdy gang, possibly dragoons, canter arrogantly through from Polsue towards Gerrans their 'standard' filled my heart with such anger and bitterness that, despite all my weariness, a potent energy surged through my body.

A large flag had been crudely attached to a broken pike; buff linen, stitched in green and black and yellow, unmistakeably one of my bed hangings. Everything I had endured came flooding to the surface and I would have confronted the men there and then and taken the consequences but Hester grabbed my arm, gently shaking her head.

'T'iddn't fitty, Mary. T'iddn't right. But 'tis no use you standing up to such as they. 'Tis said that Fairfax decreed after Torrington that such malice and disorder was undertook on pain of death. If it's so then they will get their just deserts. Come, let's move on!'

It was too busy in the village to loiter and we were too conspicuous. I gave Jack a little fuss and pricking up his ears he seemed to understand the need for haste. By dusk we had reached the river.

The ferry had just disgorged a dishevelled tinker who set off up the lane, clanking and rattling the few pots hanging about his pack. The ferry could not take our cart yet I had not thought of what to do with Jack. So while Hester capably organised our baggage I called the tinker back and to his amazement bade him take the mule and cart adding,

'His name is Jack. Be kind – and if he becomes too stubborn, try tempting him with cheese!' I tousled Jack's scruffy forelock and ran back to where Hester was standing. The ferryman was impatient.

'God 'a'mighty, wench! Some of us 'uv bin toilin' since dawn. This 'ere is my last crossing of the day! Yer mistress says you carry the fare so loose they strings and open thy purse!'

Perhaps I was too tired, perhaps it was a twist of Fate, which in those moments seemed so cruel, though hindsight tells me it was not so. Try as I might, I could find no coin. I could not find my purse and for my life, my mind a blank, I did not know where I had put them. Hester had searched, scrabbling through the basket, but it was too late.

'Bliddy wummin! Ye'd best not call me on the morrow for I don't do charitable work! No coin, no passage!' The surly boatman tied up his craft and stumped along the shore to the hovel that served as his home, emphatically slamming the door behind him.

Drained of every ounce of energy neither Hester nor I could move a step further. A little shelter stood a short way up the lane, accommodation of a sort for waiting passengers. Thus with no other plan but to sleep if we could, we nestled down in a corner, wrapped the blankets around us and waited until morning.

In the dripping dankness of dawn, boats were hurrying

down river on the tide. Many were carrying soldiers; all had an air of urgency. We dragged our belongings to the jetty, no sign of the ferryman yet. As one slightly larger boat navigated the bend in the channel, bringing it closer to the east bank, on impulse I began to wave to attract attention. Hester joining me began calling,

'Ho there! Ware, sirs! Here! Assistance here for Mistress Tremayne! Help us, please, help!' I do not recall what I shouted.

The boat seemed to slow down and turned, negotiating the flow of the tide with oars and sail. Then it pulled alongside the short wooden wharf. Strong arms took our bundles; strong hands helped us on board. A tall blue-eyed man, his cheek bearing a scar the making of which I had witnessed, cleared a space for us to sit. As if in a dream, I heard him say,

'Mistress Tremayne, we are well met for I know your husband. Rest assured that for the time being you are safe. Before long you will be in his care for he is at Pendennis Castle and that is where we are bound.'

XL Grace: Pendennis Castle 13th March - May 1646

Now the castle gates are closed. Not that I have seen them, for we berthed at Crabb Quay and it was by another gate that we entered, climbing the path from the east shore up the steep sides of the promontory almost surrounded by sea, on which this huge, grey fortress of Pendennis stands.

Nevertheless, in these five months I have sometimes been to stand behind those other massive doors that fill the archway, beside the chain that lifts the drawbridge. That entrance to this fort now haunts my day-light imaginings and my nightmares too. I have stood, and I have wondered what lies outside, beyond, in the future. But I move too far ahead in my tale; my mind is wandering.

Onboard the *Dolphin,* as we awaited the return of the ship's boat in the pearly light of that March morning, Goody Pasco and I gutted the fish we had caught on our lines. She was humming tunelessly, a sure sign she was at ease, so I was taken by surprise when she suddenly asked,

'Will you go to Bristol for the birth?'

I had not thought about 'where' the babe should be born, but was just grateful that I seemed in good health, the baby kicking inside me. I suppose the innocent in me had assumed I could stay with the ship. In reality I knew childbirth was neither safe nor without peril, but perhaps I believed that I had faced worse?

'I hoped…' I began. But she took my face in her massive hands and kindly and calmly said,

'You must get 'ee ashore for yon confinement. Jago himself would tell 'ee that even his seamanship can't all'us keep us safe. No, nor the good Lord neither. By lookin' at you it'll be before this month is out so you should make up your mind sooner rather than later, for circumstance leaves 'ee with few options, young 'un.' Patting my cheeks softly, she turned away. The subject was closed. I was shaken; I needed to talk to Sark and urgently.

I was still unsettled when the shallop pulled alongside and Sark climbed up onto the deck. As the crew set to securing the boat he came over, breathless and animated.

'We have just delivered the most intriguing cargo to the fort and you will never guess what it was!' he chuckled, 'and it will be more than Lewis Tremayne bargained for too, I shouldn't wonder!' Noting my expression he stopped and taking me by the shoulders, quizzed 'What ails? You look...weary.'I had no idea how to broach my subject, so blurted out my garbled response,

'I have to go ashore. Goody Jago says it is not possible to have the babe on the ship.'

He led me to the quarterdeck, where I leaned against the rail shivering slightly in the damp morning air. Maybe taking a pair of extraordinary passengers to Pendennis that morning had given Sark a new perspective for he spoke quietly but with confidence,

'Then we shall go ashore, Grace. There is a place that is as secure as may be for the likes of us!' and he pointed to the squat fort on the horizon. I could hardly believe my ears. Could it be that simple?

Sark then told me of their passengers. On the boat had been Hester, and alongside her, to the utter dismay of her husband, was Lewis Tremayne's wife, Mary. I have much to thank Hester for but I suspect that Sark's decision that day was based, quite significantly, upon what he saw and heard early that morning.

Later that day with Patch at my side, I found myself hauling my bulky body onto the little quay in the shadow of the castle and onward up the steep track through the cleared scrubby ground to the drawbridge and narrow gate used by all those arriving by sea. Before I entered, I looked across Fal haven to St Antony Headland and on out to the sea where I had found freedom and I pondered on the workings of Fate.

Sark's reunion with our old friend was a mixture of boyish camaraderie and commiseration, Lewis fretting about his wife's arrival,

'Ye Gods, Men! She has no concept of what she has done! I told her she would be safe at Kestle or, at worst, she should go back to Penwarne or to Heligan! Why did she defy me?' Sark rocked on his heels, avidly concentrating on the toes of his boots. I could see that he was reluctant to comment. When he did it was succinct but sincere,

'Ask her! Although even if you do not enquire, I suspect you will hear soon enough!' I was intrigued. This woman of whom I had heard so much obviously had great courage.

Hester, with characteristic frankness, had simply told Will,

'Mary Tremayne weren't biding at home, so neither was I! Us'm decided we'll make our fortunes alongside our men. When you and me promised 'for better, for worse' I for one meant it: without you 'tis worse, so I'm making it better!' Will could say nothing in response. Picking up her rattling bundle, he took his obdurate wife off to the crowded wooden guardhouse in which he had been billeted.

Colonel Tremayne's endorsement of Sark's expertise meant that Sark was swiftly absorbed into the garrison. We were given a space, no more than a small slither of planking, beside one of the westward-facing guns on the upper gun-deck of the circular, granite keep. His duties would revolve around the cannons all across the site, but this one became our bedfellow.

I never heard the gun by which we lived fire a shot although every other array of cannon around the site was regularly deployed, if only to keep the enemy awake. During periods when the prevailing winds meant enemy ships were not in the bay to present our gun with a target the great wooden shutter that closed off the gun-port would pitch our space into semi-darkness, but that was not often. When it was open our bedroll had to be carefully stowed for the weather blew in on the wind.

I took to wearing our blanket as much to keep it dry as for the warmth. The old woollen rug smelled of tar and hemp, salt and the sea; Goody Jago had handed it to me as I climbed down into the boat. In the folds she had wrapped a muslin bag containing oatcakes and salt beef, practical and pragmatic but nevertheless gifts from her heart.

The castle with its inhabitants was like a small town only in smaller confines, cramped and crowded. The overall impression in those first strange weeks was that it pulsed with the beat of drums that rattled out orders; it throbbed with the march of feet. Over one thousand souls, all with a common purpose, fell or were directed into the routines and duties giving purpose to our days and making the fortress run like clockwork.

The Governor cannot have found it agreeable to see more dependents arriving with the paltry supplies from Truro: oxen, beans, flour, peas, pipe tobacco, pregnant women. It must have been a bitter blow, but Sir John Arundel, dignified and honourable, would never stoop to complain of such things especially to those concerned.

It was simple enough to seek out Colonel Tremayne's men even in the teeming throng that filled the site and to find Hester was my priority. Being reunited with her brought back the security of my days at the Palmer's home but also the joy of a new confidante, the calm and competent Mistress Tremayne.

I quickly came to rely on Mary for encouragement as Hester and I moved nearer to our respective accouchements. I was now desperately uncomfortable, the weight of my body dragging me down. I was unsure of when the infant would be born and Goody Jago's concern had been infectious. Hester would try to distract me, spending hours teaching Patch new tricks.

It was a bright spring morning just after our arrival when we heard of Fairfax' ultimatum to Sir John Arundel. Hester and I were leaning our backs against the sun-warmed wall of one of the storehouses, Patch lolling on the stones at my feet. Looking across over a wide sandy cove, the view would have been attractive had it not been for the earthworks and smoking activity of the enemy on the rising ground less than a mile away. She languidly spoke, eyes closed, face turned to enjoy the first warmth of spring,

'Can 'ee believe it? We've been here less than a week and the Parliament would have us out! I've only just got settled in!' she chuckled. 'How long do you think we'll be here? I don't make wagers but I'd guess six weeks.' It was an innocent question but I felt a shadow over my mood.

'I do not know; I do not care to think beyond today. In truth, I have nowhere else to go,' I replied baldy then asked, 'Do you want your infant born inside or out of the castle walls?' She looked a bit taken aback,

'I'm here and while I am, that's where 'twill be. So you and me, we'll just get on with it, won't us? And anyways I don't know for sure when it'll be, do you?'

Her jovial realism was just what I needed and my black shadow-mood receded as she chattered on,

'Mind, from your shape I doubt if you will be too long. Mary said yesterday that she would offer her services to the churgeons as a nurse and I was summ'at pleased when I heard that.'

I told her how I had heard that there were old stables that would be cleared and scrubbed out as an infirmary though happily there were few ailments yet, only foot sores from poor shoes and the occasional cracked rib. Then I confessed that I had been too embarrassed to go near the surgeon so Sark had spoken to him for me. Certainly, my miscarriage had not given me any insight into how this delivery might be. I privately hoped that Hester and Mary, who I was already coming to like very much, would be with me with enough knowledge to do whatever mystery was necessary for a proper birth. It seemed Hester read my thoughts,

'Well, perhaps I might double my prayin' when it's my time, but till then I hope I can look to my friends to help me through it!' and she looked over to me, hesitant and self-conscious. I squeezed her hand to reassure myself as much as her, while Patch moved to sit on her feet.

March had come in like a lion and as the weather-wise predicted it would, went out like a lamb, and my time did indeed come at the end of the month. I was safely delivered of a son. For nigh on two weeks I was allowed to stay in a bed in the infirmary, Sark attending me in every spare moment.

Lewis and Will were invited to meet our boy and when the surgeon and my 'midwives' Hester and Mary decreed it suitable, I was allowed to go to the makeshift chapel facing St Mawes. There, with four godparents, Chaplain Taylor named my baby Henry Charles Sark. He had no nursery, no proper crib, but one team of gunners, all soft hearted, suggested they swap with Sark's fellows. We would still have only a sliver of floor beside a cannon but not one that suffered with such draughts. Little Hal was to become the delight of his father, his mother and the artillerymen throughout the castle.

Such joys were not long lasting and there was no such happiness for all. I shall forever regret not being able to help Hester as she had helped me, for although it was a good six weeks after my delivery and I was on my feet again, neither surgeon Wiseman nor Mary nor I could save her infant.

The surgeon, confessing to having very little knowledge of birthing, was able to save the mother but the babe was still-born, a boy whom they called William for his father. In a shroud made from my good shift, he was buried on May Day morn upon the shore of the Fal, seashells to mark the little grave. The chaplain recorded his name in Hester's precious Bible as his memorial.

The days lengthened and one personal tragedy was engulfed by the misfortunes of all; the stark reality had become evident. At Sir John's insistence, a full measure of the provisions within the walls had been made. The resulting inventory circulated by the quartermasters made plain the true condition of the stores. The garrison was told that the assertion of Sir Edward Hyde that there were supplies for twelve-month was disastrously overstated. It was more like six weeks. The already slim rations had to be cut. The salt beef given to me by Goody Jago did not go far in feeding Sark's men.

It was around that time that my milk began to dry. I think it was not so much the lack of food but a great sadness that overcame me, drying the nourishment for my son. Mary came to me, tentatively suggesting that there might be a remedy. She had a message from Hester, who was reticent to speak to me for fear of hurting my feelings: Hester had offered to become wet-nurse for my baby. We both wept when he suckled for the first time, I with a humble thankfulness for her kind heart and generous spirit and she for the love of two infant boys, one lost to her, one gained. Neither Sark nor Will ever spoke of the subject for it was a matter for the realm of women.

Fleas, lice, sores and boredom were the perils of May that year. The enemy fired their cannon but their range could barely touch the cliff let alone the walls of the fort. The oxen which had been sent from Truro in March were slaughtered and those women who were available spent hours scouring barrels to salt down what meat was not consumed by the garrison. The flesh would not keep long for we ran out of salt.

A noxious stench began to pervade everywhere and even a freshening wind, which should have helped by bringing in clean summer air, brought only blustery gusts, which were unsettling, a constant noise which let no man or woman or child rest and making everyone edgy and peevish. My nightmares returned; now I sank in the blue waters of a deep chasm, the entrance to which was closed by two huge, iron-clad gates.

XLI Hester: Pendennis Castle 13th March – May 1646

Even the gates to the entrance of Bristol gaol weren't as big as those of the main gatehouse at Pendennis fort. A'cause I had all come in by water, by the back door, so to speak. I never saw them open till me and Mary watched one day when the guard was changed. I waved Will off to his duties out beyond these massive walls, out on the hill-top where the livestock used to be kept and which was too near the enemy lines for my liking.

Will all'us said it was safe enough for there were great earth banks built up which the soldiers could move behind to look down over the marsh betwixt the headland and the enemy. One day he drew the shape of the whole of the King's defences around us in the dirt outside the barrack-house for me.

Now, to my eye I said it looked like a lock, the wall like the outline of a lock-plate and the girt round keep looking like the keyhole. Mind, all we women could see from inside was the huge drawbridge and all the blacksmith work on the studded doors nigh on the height of three grown men. We women b'aint allowed out there.

Grace and me, having babies to come, spent time considering what we would do and how it would be and I said to Mary that I thought Grace was a little nervous of it all, even though she was the most daring of us. I was right glad that Grace and Mary took to each other. Mind you, I can't imagine anyone who wouldn't like Mistress Tremayne.

It sent me cold to think of what Grace's evil husband had done and it seems that 'tiddn't fair sometimes how things turn out. So I thought as how I could make some distraction and taught Patch to roll over, legs all a-waving, if I called out 'Black Tom Fairfax is coming!' It made for a bit of fun. I could give nothing as a reward except a girt fuss and ruffle of his daft ears but Grace would slip him a tiny portion of oatcake if he did two tricks at once.

That was in the early days, back away before we knew how bad it would get. There's not much to smile about now, I can tell 'ee, and no oatcakes either.

Mary fetched me quick when Sark told Colonel Tremayne that Grace had gone to the churgeon. It was like a sisterhood, we three, but 'twas Mary that was like a rock to us both. See, she was the only one who did think anything through straight. I had never seen a birthing before but we had plenty of hot water and a darkened room and heat and two strong fists for Grace to push against and there he was. A fine son. Nobody seemed to know or care that his pa was not her real husband and I do not truly believe Grace had given the matter much thought either.

Henry Charles they called him. My Will was right honoured to be named a Godfather, pleased as could be that his Colonel and Grace wanted him. And his promise was …well, Will all'us was a man to take his duties serious an' all, God bless him.

He could hardly wait till we held our own child and when the churgeon thought I was beyond my time William got summ'at twitchy, but I told him there was nothing to be had but patience for the churgeon said infants had their own way of knowing when 'tis the time to be born. And so we waited.

When the backaches started I was right relieved I can tell 'ee, but now I worry if 'twas something that I did that brought things to the saddest pass. Perhaps I should have prayed more through the pains and not have been so bold with God's name in the past. Maybe that was His chastisement … but they said the little wight never took a breath. Not one.

It must have been my fault. I thought so in the miserable hours after the Chaplain left with my husband cradling the body of our boy. We called him William. I could only weep after they eased him from my arms and wrapped him in clean, new linen. He would've been dark like me but maybe had Will's ears.

Mary stayed with me hour upon hour. I could not sleep,

but talked and may have rambled for I am not certain sure how long I was in that dark place. I remember crying out that I needed to tell her something terrible important and I believe I dreamed or may have spoken of the ship-wreck and of my shameful history in Bristol. The bad things which were my troubles in Barnstaple she did already know, but who of us would put at risk the good-will of a friend by such a confession? I did. In my raving, I little knew what I was saying though perhaps it needed it to be said.

Once I remember Grace coming, bringing me the last of her oatcakes; she said it were so that the meal-worms would not have them, but it cheered me - and I made her promise to give Patch the few crumbs that lay where I could not finish them.

The churgeon would not let me out of the infirmary, although the space was filling up with soldiers, their sores festering. And there were some children who began to suffer cramps and could not be soothed except with a little poppy juice in watered wine. I kept to a little truckle bed tucked into a corner of the room, not even allowed to attend little Will's burial.

Mary would always come and sit with me when duties meant that my man could not. Gentle as a dove she listened as I spoke and made some sense of my story; and it felt as though a great burden had been taken when I knew she had understood that I was a convict, sentenced and all, and yet she did not sneer at me. There was nothing to judge, she said, for God knew each soul and He knew mine and who was Mary Tremayne to question that?

'I have been very stupid, Mary!' I remember saying. I thought of Ezekiel and the great Bible he had gifted me in Bideford all that long while ago. It struck me then and I mumbled,

'I must have brought all the troubles down upon myself for the good Book tells us that wickedness gets its just reward. That's why my baby was taken from me.' She put her arms around me, and comforted me, hushing the tears that flowed again for I could not stop them.

I do not know for sure which day it was, though it was not too long, for the milk in my breasts still soaked my shift despite the bindings. Mary was telling me the daily state of affairs when, sudden-like, I said,

'What of Mistress Grace? I have not seen Grace these last days.' Our friend looked discomforted.

'What? What ails? She's not ill, the babe's not ill? I could not bear it if Grace's little lad was lost to us too!'

Mary, trying hard not to make me afraid, told me how food was going shorter and that Grace's milk had dried so there was nothing for the bairn to suckle, adding how Grace had not wanted to add to my burden of grief by bringing her own babe to my bedside.

'Bring him here! Bring the boy! I have milk aplenty. If she'll trust me... that is to say...'

I could not finish but I don't think I needed to, and it never occurred to me to ask Will, but it just seemed that I had something that I could freely give and maybe God would see some good in that. And that was how I came to nurse young Henry Charles.

I got stronger by the day though the state of the fortress worsened. Still, I didn't mind too much; my soldier could be somewhere worse and I with him. For certain, it didn't smell as bad as Bristol gaol, or not until July it didn't anyway. The thing I hated was the fleas for they bit upon the places where there were no lice, and there was not one body which was free of them.

Washing was a notion something outlandish; and there was nothing in the scrubby undergrowth around the walls that even reminded you of fleabane to make a rinse with a'cause the soldiers kept the slopes scythed so no Roundhead could creep up under cover. It got to June and the quartermasters started measuring our water too, so there were better things to do with it than wash.

For a few days Will tried puffing his evil smelling 'bacco smoke over me for one great gentleman here had been heard to say that it was a sure way to stop the bites, and 'bacco was handed out ready enough from the stores. Will even got a new clay pipe when John Brownsell sat upon his old'un but I reckon the great gentleman was a-fibbin' for all that happened was me and little Hal coughed a lot and a hot ember burned a hole in my skirt.

I was right glad that I had been still a-bed when they slaughtered the oxen and the women were given the task of salting the carcasses down. Mind I don't think any one of us regretted the roasted meat we had for two meals or the broth that came occasionally in the days after.

Grace and I took turns at minding Henry, and otherwise each taking a share of the nursing or cooking or whatever duties the quartermaster thought were fitting. When little children got a tad fretful I liked telling them stories of giants and mermaids and would have drawn pictures but we had no paper. So Will dug up a square of turf behind the windmill, a quieter corner where the youngsters liked to play. He filled it with sand fetched from the cove by Crabb Quay, not deep, for it weren't much of a sandy place, but enough to be drawing in.

And before long, using Bess' method, little fingers used the box to draw their copy-shapes in. And I thought it mighty strange that while Hester Mattock, with her Bible and her very own letter book, was teaching little girls their alphabet, the soldiers taught the little boys to clean a musket.

XLII Mary: Pendennis Castle, Cornwall 13ᵗʰ March - June 1646

As a little girl, I had heard much of Pendennis Castle: from the old stories about the Killigrew's lawlessness as governors to Nick Slanning's pride in the place. Never did I think that I would find myself there. It might seem strange but as I entered the fortress on Pendennis headland, I could hear Loveday Yendacott's words in my mind. I dismissed them, for the small entrance by which we made our way into the place from the boat did not strike me as particularly awe-inspiring, but rather represented security; Lewis was here, I was safe and I rarely looked east across the Roseland, towards home.

Nevertheless, on the first day that Hester and I stood by the main gate to watch our husbands march with a guard detail out to the earthworks overlooking the enemy lines, I suddenly recognised the significance of that strange pronouncement. The realisation made the hairs upon the back of my neck stand on end.

The gates; Loveday Yendacott must have foreseen these gates, but had only said that she could not 'see beyond' them. Standing there, the towering entrance was blocked. Now none of us could see beyond the gates.

There are nigh on two hundred women and their children here but we three women, our fortunes brought together by love and war, have formed an uncommon friendship in these months. Hester knew Grace Fenwick before she was wed and yet she had been shocked at the circumstances of her marriage.

Grace was quite matter of fact about it, for, as she said, a daughter has very little choice if her father has made up his mind about what he believes is best. I ruefully agreed, privately thinking there but for the grace of God go I. Hester had been more subdued than usual when we discussed the subject, then shyly observed that for all her lowly background she had in fact had the easiest courting of us all. Grace always seemed so self-contained and assured and I could not help but envy her that confidence; she had seen adventure and while I had certainly defied my family's dictates, it had been from the safety of Dewnes' walls. I had not truly crossed any line. I could not help but wonder whether I would regret my actions. I thought not.

Hester too had experienced adventures but of a different kind. She spoke of so many of her burdens in those fevered hours after her delivery. Poor Hester, she carried such guilt and I did not know what to say. Despite her miss-spent past, she had followed the path expected of women everywhere, first as a servant, then as God willed it, as a wife. I was sure, too, that one day she would be a good mother. It was what I hoped for myself.

At least my upbringing had given me some skills, which made me useful to Lewis, his men and to our surgeon Richard Wiseman, for the hours spent tending broken wings gave me the patience and the strong stomach for nursing. At first there were few ailments, sores and blisters mainly, so the birth of Grace's child then Hester's saw the first true test of my metal. I cannot describe the desolation of that room as the surgeon laid the silent, still infant in Hester's exhausted arms.

Lewis and I shared a small partitioned cabin within the larger barrack blocks at the centre of the fort. His men had dwindled to forty-nine in number, including his armourer, the ensigns, officers and lieutenants. All worked a rotation in the cramped quarters, lucky if they had straw paliasses to serve as beds. Men on duty slipped exhausted into the spaces left by their comrades. With the gallantry of a true Cornish gentleman, Captain Dinham insisted that he would sleep well enough alongside one of his lieutenants and so, when I arrived, he moved in with Tom Lower who had to squeeze up his bedroll for my benefit.

It was impossible not to overhear conversations, which meant I was privy to some of the military intelligence that flowed into the castle, either from the Parliamentarian lines or much more rarely, by small boats that managed to slip through the blockade.

We were considering some such news when Hester realised that the man now commanding us at the fort was my great uncle. She was totally bemused when I talked fondly of Sir John Arundel, the parties at Trerice and his standing in Cornish circles. I had told her that when Fairfax first sent his demand to the Governor of Pendennis Castle I marvelled that the enemy should think he would need two days to consider a decision; the splendid old man I had known since I was a child would need no more than two seconds.

'I feel all of a dudder knowing that I mix with such lofty company,' Hester said, wide-eyed. I laughed but I could understand why she felt so, for we were in truly uncommon circumstances.

A month later in April, when Fairfax had handed his task to Colonels Fortescue and Hammond, Lewis told me that Vice Admiral Batten had offered passage to Weymouth or to France for those prepared to take it.

I began to tremble dreading the possibility of exile, but Lewis laughed and put his arms around me reassuringly saying,

'There, there chick! If you had heard their responses, you would have no fear! There was much serious debate of course, or as serious as Henry Killigrew can ever be! He asked what the fare would cost, to which Sir John replied it would "be in Cornish stone and mortar". Do you know what Henry replied? Hah! It was so typical of a Killigrew and just what you would expect of the man who pressed for the firing of his family home purely to inconvenience the Parliament's commanders!' I shuddered to think of the charred remains of beautiful Arwennack House, but could not help smiling as Lewis posed theatrically, pretending to puff pensively on a pipe,

'There he was, purporting to take great consideration and then weightily pronounced, "No, I do not have that coin. And besides, soldiers are notably bad at finding their sea legs; it is a well known disinclination!" It was a precious moment! Dick Arundel simply said that it was not the season for travel!'

Lewis was not so buoyant by the end of May when he and the other colonels and their captains, Oliver included, had to reach a verdict on the future of the horses. There was no food for them. Around the emerald hedgerows of the Roseland and Helford, the bright Cornish sun brought early summer but here it burned any scrubby grass not trampled by drilling feet or scouting sentries. What patchy grass had managed to grow had been cleared weeks ago; the fodder had been used up. So once more, the women boiled seawater brine to try to preserve the butchered Hercules or Dobbin or Spirit. I knew of seasoned cavalrymen who went hungry rather than eat meat after that.

On an early June evening, balmy and still, Grace, Hester and I sat together behind a storehouse where we had found a quieter corner. Our men were on duty, or in Lewis' case at a council with the senior officers. There had been great excitement, for a lookout reported a signal from a boat out beyond the blockade, lights that promised that a small, fast vessel would run in under cover of darkness. If that was successful, there was hope that one might also slip out.

We were imagining our own version of the list the commanders were compiling as they discussed the supplies to be procured, a request for aid. The message would be sent to the Prince of Wales in Jersey.

'For me there would be new, kid-leather boots and cherries, lots of juicy ripe cherries!' dreamed Hester, the baby snuffling contentedly at her chest. Grace frowned, muttering,

'I'd go barefoot if I could have a clean shift and a large, juicy bone for Patch. He is too thin already and his talents as a foraging hunter are wasted here for there's not a rabbit for miles around! Mary, what would you have His Highness send?'

I could not think. The words that spilled out were nonsensical and yet I could not stop them,

'Loveday Yendacott and her runes!' Fortunately, my

companions could follow my thoughts, for I had spoken to them of my increasingly frequent nightmares, the lingering imaginings already blurring from sleep to waking, the torment of the unknown, of my fear and the terrifying dreams. I sobbed,

'If only the runes could banish the terrors!' but it was a hollow expectation and I knew it.

The focus of my dream was always Loveday, the runes she used at Coombe that day always lying in her open hands but I could not see them, and everywhere she pointed all I could see were gates. She walked away, and I would begin to dig, scrabbling away at the walls, trying to follow. Running through the tunnel I had made I would look to see the gates from the outside only to realise that I was completely alone in a strange place. I would wake up trembling in a cold sweat, a stale taste in my mouth.

This was my dream, which recurring, began to feel more like the truth than my days, which slipped further and further into the realms of unreality.

XLIII Grace: Pendennis Castle June - 2nd July 1646

The long days of June were hard, the days of July worse still. The mood changed from cheerful defiance to a dogged determination but I began to think even that was faltering. The gunners that Sark spoke to remained as loyal to the King as ever, but Sark said their particular confidence came from the sizeable magazine of powder and shot. There must have been nigh on a hundred barrels back then for, though Pendennis has been extravagant with the artillery barrages, there were no concerns that ammunition was even close to running low.

Nevertheless Sark looked weary. We all did; we do. Despite the summer sun or wind weathering us, skin is looking pallid. Or is scabbed. The surgeon talked of men soft-brained by lack of food, forgetful, dispirited. He might have mentioned the women too.

I shared some of my scraps with Patch, yet in the hard bright light of every sunny day I came to realise what food I had could not sustain him. I think perhaps he must have caught a rat or two to feed on but I have heard Jago tell tales of desperation that makes men less fastidious about what they eat. And everywhere the men are hungry, very hungry.

I find it hard now to distinguish one day from one-another. I remember it was a bitter blow when one jackanapes in the enemy lines thought to use an antique longbow, a hunting relic filched from a poor cottager somewhere no doubt, to loose some arrows across the forward lines. Tied to the arrows were jeering messages including 'news' that the King now 'lay on a thistle bed in Newcastle'. We had already been told in May that His Majesty had surrendered to the Scots at Newark.

I cannot think now how we knew. Did Colonel Fortescue, Fairfax' deputy, send word with the official correspondence? Aye, maybe.

The sharpshooters vowed to redouble their efforts to pick

off our tormentors. Then surgeons began to tell the officers that soldiers could no longer stand for full watches. They were too weakened by hunger and were dizzy and drowsy. Therefore, colonels made new timetables of duties and reformed their lists. I have seen Lewis with his papers, but I think it is as much to occupy his hours as for castle business. And the long summer days are full of hours, too many hours.

Sark seemed to have an inner strength which made him seem resilient, though his temples were greying faster than his years warranted. Even in this he found a jest, pleased that his greying tresses stuck fast, for 'at least there was hair' unlike Lewis who was rapidly losing his, a shiny pate showing through the increasingly wispy brown locks. Mary said it was because he rubbed his hand across his head, a nervous action he had employed ever since he was a child,

'It is a wonder he has any hair at all! And especially when you know his brother Philip, whose head had been like an egg since he was twenty-three years old!' But these were petty matters made serious and used to distract our thoughts from what we saw and felt day by day.

His arm about me, Sark had once been considering a notion for a poem encouraging me to join with him in his wordsmithing. But my brain would not respond and I remained withdrawn, merely listening while he played with phrases. I had already discovered that even if I picked up my father's book the most familiar of Shakespeare's words just seemed to drift across a page leaving me unmoved. That was if I could see the distorted letters at all.

'I shall call it 'Verses made in Pendennis Castle when it was besieged by sea and land'. What do you think?' he said. I shrugged, replying that I hardly thought it a title that would sell a pamphlet; it was not a catch-like phrase that tripped from the tongue. I did not mean to sound harsh but I suspect I did. He persevered with a line or two,

'Penelope, fair Queen, most chaste Pendennis.

Of all forts...no, it needs something more...Royal forts...' and then, giving up, he rose and tossing silver-point and paper aside, made his way to the door and down the narrow spiral stair, leaving me alone. I picked up the papers and in one corner saw a tiny, perfect sketch of Hal, swaddled, sleeping. Was else was there to do but weep?

The truth was that I missed our son in every moment that I could not be with him and that was much of the time, for he cried so lustily when he was hungry that he needed to be where Hester was at hand. There had been no question of rearranging accommodation so Hal stayed with her and thus, in the hours when sleep would not come, I could not even hear his breath. And while that left me heart-sore, in those dark midnight hours I saw a reality where my child had little or no future with either of his parents. Sark never said what he felt.

One morning early in July, as our food dwindled to the most minimal of rations each day and the chances of any boat slipping beneath the guns of Admiral Batten's fleet grew slimmer, Mary came to find me, Hester hurrying in her wake. Both looked wan, Mary in particular for she spent many hours every day in the dim light of the infirmary where hour by hour the numbers of those whose health was failing grew ever larger. Mary was out of breath and her hands trembled,

'Where have you been? We have sought you everywhere!' I shrugged.

'Well, I am here!' I snapped.

Though my intent was to use another tone the unkind sound of my own voice shocked me, yet I could not control the sullenness and withdrew rather than apologise. Hester started to un-knot the makeshift sling in which Hal was snugly enfolded against her bosom. It was how she commonly carried him as it left her hands free, a real boon for more often than not her arms were full of little children; she seemed to have a way with them. Even though so many were now listless and often distressed, you could locate Hester if there were children laughing. Now her hands were placing my son in my arms, and her hands were wet with tears.

'What is it?' My own tears I never counted, but Hester's

were another matter, stinging my skin like a brand. 'What is it? Why the tears?' I looked from one friend to the other and as Mary sank down on the dust beside me Hester knelt behind me and put her arms around my shoulders,

'There has been a mission devised and volunteers have been requested.' Mary stammered 'The…the… Cornishmen who know the region have stepped up, and those most suited have drawn straws to swim…' Her resolve faltered. Hester swiftly ended the agony,

'Lewis volunteered but Sark has fought to take his place! He argued that he is a better water-man, and knows the creeks and bye-ways as a native and, besides, Lewis is needed here to do…oh…summ'at…giddy up his men! Oh damn it! My words were never clever but I cannot think!'

The baby jumped in my arms as Hester raised her voice. She leaned across and soothed him, while I looked at Mary, trying to make sense of the words. Her eyes were like two dark blue pools in a milk white face and as she looked into my eyes, her soul was plain for all the world to see. She whispered,

'…encourage… she means encourage, Grace. Men, I mean Sark is due to swim out from the North shore tonight. They say he will make for Trefusis Point, from there to use all his wiles to take a message to the Prince in Jersey or France, for he and his council need to know how hopeless the castle stands without relief.' I still could not respond.

'Grace, your man will part with everything he loves for the sake of a King's ransom and his soldier's honour! 'Tiddn't fitty! 'Tiddn't *right*! You must stop him!'

Hester's face was awash with tears again.

Perhaps Sark tired of me? Perhaps his duty to his King or his commitment to his men drove him? I don't know if even he could have told me. But I knew enough to say,

'I cannot' I replied bleakly, 'I cannot offer him anything more important than his sense of duty or pride or honour. Sark is right. He is uniquely qualified to take this mission; Lewis is the man his regiment have followed for years and now they are following him into Hell. If they are to come back from that place it will only be because Lewis Tremayne led them.'

I took a deep breath, my mind clear for the first time in many days. I would not change Sark's mind even if I could. For beside me sat a woman who had a future with the man she loved, and the man I loved was about to gift it to her. The least I could do was to give that gift my blessing.

On the second night of a sultry, stifling July, with no moon to throw tell-tale highlights on the eddies of a watery wake, a tall man, his hood concealing the ice fire of blue-eyes, slipped from the postern gate and along the eastern shore of Pendennis Headland. With him loped a flicker of white on a shadow. A second figure and a third carried a musket tightly wrapped as a long and slender parcel, and another smaller package, the waxed wrappings glistening dully in the dim light of a pierced lantern.

At the parapet a hundred feet above I watched, blind in the darkness, stretching my senses to follow the man and the wraith through the landscape.

As the figures reached a gun emplacement on the earthworks traverse, the packages would be handed over, then slung on the hooded man's shoulders. The duo would each grasp his right fist with theirs in their familiar silent, salute then, without a backward glance, the man and the shadow would melt into the night, slipping to the waterline. Gone.

One eerie, melancholy howl echoed round the shores of the Fal on the languorous night air and maybe some Roundhead soldiers round their camp-fire shivered just a little, glancing surreptitiously over their shoulder in case in Cornwall a will-o-the-wisp bayed like an inconsolable hound.

Here would be no happy ending for Grace Fenwick. I had known all along that dreams are illusions. Fortune's wheel turns and we must endure the consequences.

XLIV Hester: Pendennis Castle July 1646

I sometimes think back on what I had to endure in Bristol gaol and wonder was it as long as our time here? I could not say for my mind is getting a tad fuddled now. We have been in this fort so long I'm sometimes past remembering what month it is. If 'tweren't for Chaplain Taylor and his sermons on a Sunday I wouldn't know what day of the week it were either, though I know we are well past the longest day now by some weeks. 'Tis all a bit of a worry for Mary says that two barrels of the horsemeat opened yesterday were rancid, though they'll use them for broth despite that. The water in the wells is turning brackish too. We need some rain.

Still, Sir 'Jack-for-the-King' Arundel keeps us all going with that lively way he has when he comes about the place. Mary says the man is summ'at around his three score years and ten for he was ancient when she was born. It still 'mazes me to think our Governor is her Great Uncle but then she will tell you all the families around here are bound by kinship. Radstock was a bit like that, only there weren't so many wedding bands worn in the doing of it. Did I say Radstock? Or did I mean …oh, I don't know!

I sometimes think of what has passed here, of my little babe, but care not to dwell on that for it does upset my William so, and anyways, to brighten my days there's little Henry Charles. Everyone calls him Hal, nigh on four months old now and a quiet little mommet most of the time. Though don't get me wrong, he has for certain let me and Grace know often enough that he has a pair of lungs on him. Once he starts his hollerin' half the gunners in the place come running to see what ails their lad like they were all his…father…nay, I dare not talk of him, for it brings tears to speak of his father.

I couldn't tell Grace nor Mary but I do get summ'at leary through there not being so much to eat. But my Will's a lovely man and he will give me more than half of anything in his ration for he says giving it to me is like feeding two souls not just one and if Hal is to fight for His Majesty then he needs his vittals.

Well, the babe has no teeth yet but Will never did know ort about infants so he wouldn't know that now, would 'ee? So, I sup the broth or chew the gristle and the milk still comes for the little 'un, which is as well for I don't know how I could face his ma if it dried.

Lord, but I am so tired! It's not that I am a busy woman to warrant it either. I only play with the children or perhaps do a little sewing.

Just last week I decided that I would try to fix the seams on my old bodice a little, make it a bit more respectable. Grace helped me unpick a thread or two from the frayed edge of her shawl to stitch with and one of the lads made me a needle from an old bone. Took him a whole day but he did it. He's a right jester is Dick Hodge, saying he had such a press of work with this and that but he thought he could find me a few minutes.

And one week on from making my needle Dick is in the infirmary. I should try to pass the time of day with him if they let me go to visit Will today. 'Tis such a crush in there and barely space to move about. The churgeons have had to make one of the barrack rooms into another place for them who are ill a'cause there just weren't enough room in the old stable-block by the end of June.

That's five days Will's been in with the very sick folk already, and they said he's bleeding as he shouldn't and I haven't been allowed in every day.

I like to make myself a little more presentable if I'm going to see my husband, see, for I think it cheers him up – 'tis why I needed the needle and thread. I nipped in a bit off the side-seams while I was at my mending. But it's loose again for all I pull the lacing as tight as I can. I used to be what Will called his 'bowerly, comely wench' too. Not so bowerly any more. I do hope he don't hold against me a'cause of it.

Grace and Mary and me we sit around a lot. Grace is

summ'at quiet most of the time but we'll talk of this and that though 'tis not so comfortable for our mouths are all sore with the ulcers and our tongue stick to our lips. They both speak much of their nightmares, and who's to be surprised at that, really? I don't seem to have dreams, me. When I get to sleep I just want to sleep, and nothing has ever stood in the way of Hester Phipps rest. No, that b'aint right…I'm Hester Mattock.

Sometimes some of the other women come to sit with us, their children on their laps as they listen to my old stories, the same old stories that the little ones like to say the words along to, learning them by heart.

But there's not so many as there were, for both childer and dames are as like to be in their beds, too feeble to move about very much. Mary says she spends as much of her time attending them as the soldiery. Her and Master Wiseman and …now, I cannot for my life remember…what is the name of those other two churgeons? …oh, no matter… for 'tis Master Wiseman looks after Colonel Tremayne's men anyway. He - and Mary - have so many to see to from dawn to dusk.

I do think 'tis time Mary took more rest, for she has been taking dizzy turns, not quite zaundy and swooning full out but unsteady on her feet. Yet she won't hear of anyone telling her husband, saying that Lewis is a Colonel and engaged on castle business, which she says is a more important matter. More important than his wife?

Yesterday she can't have been so busy though, for Mary came to find me bringing Grace too, and they said that the chaplain wanted to see me. I was just idling so off we went up to the keep to the governor's lodgings.

My, that's a summ'at unket place, all grey stone, round and dark and with so many passwords to remember that if I lodged in that part of the castle I would never get about, not with the way my memory is now. Anyway, Grace got us through it. She used to bide there but since Sark went off to… well, since then she's brought her bedroll in with me. I think she's more content being nearer little Hal. If she cries out in the night, I soothe her to sleep just like in the old days at the Palmer's house in Cross Street. Or was that in Wine Street? Oh, Lor', 'tis so hard to recall.

So anyways, in a tiny room above, he had a little chaplain's table and he says to me, very kindly,

'Please sit, Mistress Mattock. I need to speak to you of …' and then he used all these fitty words so fast I could not keep up with the sense of it. I looked at Mary and she put her hand round my shoulder, gave me a squeeze, saying,

'Hester, William has asked Chaplain Taylor to write something for you, for your future. It's very simple but it makes everything right. If you go Cornwood…no, when…' and then poor Mary couldn't finish, sniffing and rubbing her eyes with her sleeve. That sleeve weren't too clean either. Funny what you notice sometimes.

Then the chaplain took a piece of paper from a pile, and turned it round so that I could see. On the bottom of the page I recognised a bit of the sort of mark that William makes when he writes his name, with two others below it. One the first line I could recognise G-o-d and G-r-a-c-e which I was a little pleased about for it showed my learning to read was coming along with my friends' help.

What bemused me, though, was why my William had needed to sign this paper and I said so out aloud.

It was awful quiet in the keep. Like there was nobody there except me. Then Grace took my hand with her one that wasn't cradling the baby, and Mary put her arms about my shoulders and gentle as a summery breeze said,

'Hester, this is your husband's will, and says that you are his lawful wife, that you are bequeathed what is his in Cornwood when he is…'

The silence went on and all the while I was thinking that of course my husband's Will's and I'm his wife for the vicar at Barnstaple had the bond to prove it were so. But perhaps another piece of paper would do no harm, for his ma no doubt would like it. Very faint, I could hear the Chaplain calling my name,

'Hester, Hester, are you listening?' I was. I nodded.

'Sergeant Mattock, William, is very sick. The surgeon believes it to be the bloody flux; he can do nothing for him. William wants to make sure you are taken care of. It has given him great of peace of mind to know that he could ensure that there was something to leave for your future.' His voice went summ'at croaky and he cleared his throat, 'You know, I have always thought that the best ale I have ever had has been made by the women…'

So I have another paper. There isn't any of my writing on the page even though it has my name upon it, and it only has two words in Will's hand right at the bottom. I wouldn't know otherwise but Grace assures me that it says 'William Mattock' though I know t'isn't pretty like his usual design. I keep it in my Bible, tucked in at the page where it tells anyone who cares to look when I was wed, of the life my son and of his father.

When we leave here, I expect there will be another sheet, the official type that I've needed for every journey I have taken since Bideford, so shall l put them all together. And along with my little blue book from Bess, that's near enough a whole shelf-full of paper.

Now, as I lie await in the in the dark night, I wonder if I should dare to or even whether 'tis proper that I should ask Grace if, when they let us away from Pendennis fort …well, whether she would come to that Dartmoor village my Will was so fond of? I b'aint never seen Cornwood but 'tis where Will has given me a home. As God is my witness, I will confess I am afeared like I b'aint never been before. About being on my own. And the unknown.

But while I think on this, somewhere else in the castle of Pendennis a Colonel of His Majesty's army has had to write another list. He is writing a fair copy of one that was drawn up near a month ago.

At the bottom of the second page he'll pen three names, three Devon villages with a lad from each of them; Whitchurch, Ditscombe and Cornwood.

First, two men will get their names marked upon the pages as sick: John Brownsell, that clumsy, careless fool and

Richard Hodge who his friends knowed as Dick, a wit with a knack for working bone tools. William Mattock is the last upon the crumpled paper.

Added later, beside the names will lie two strokes of the pen; heavy curling lines link the words together. Alongside them will be written one word that tells a story on its own: 'Dead'.

As I lie here the hours are dead, time seems suspended; my mind deceives me so that one day merges into the next, compounding the burden. It seems the angry sun that in the spring promised so much, in August has abandoned us. Even the winds have turned contrary and unseasonal, and blow away any hope of relief from Royalist ships.

Parliament's men call us the 'obstinate enemy', though few men here now have the vigour to even man the earthworks. Occasionally someone, desperate, will slip across the lines. The Roundhead Colonels should keep them here for each one inside is working for their cause by using up our provisions. Lewis' newest list lies beside the bed with 'Run' penned in fresh ink against another name, Rob Clarke. Nonetheless, the enemy do not seem to know how dire our straits have become. What honourable deserters! They leave but don't betray the castle's condition.

Yet one look at any man, woman or child should tell Colonel Fortescue that food is scarce. The apathy of hunger blankets everyone, many who were not strong to start. Sleep will not come, though daylight hours will see us drowsy. Our throats have become too sore to swallow and skin is pustuled - where the lice leave room. Some now bleed and there are those that say this will mean plague. The shoreline, where our men once fished or knocked off limpets to fill their bellies, is now raked by sharp-eyed musketeers, braced against the enemy ships' gunwales.

My mind gets easily confused these days. I thought the King of Spain came by... but no, that cannot be right! It must have been an *agent* of the King of Spain. My husband told me that el señor requested that the officers of the castle go to serve his master in Flanders. Uncle John...I beg his pardon...our Governor, thanked him graciously, replying that presently his regiment is fully engaged. However, when free they would, if our own monarch does not need their services, be happy to serve his Highness of Spain. 'When free' is only a little lie. When free, presently, soon, in a little while, when all is done....these are all the little lies we women have spoken hourly, daily, to the children, to our husbands, to ourselves for nearly five months now.

Lewis comes to me, looking so tired, so care-worn. I think it is much worse since he was chosen as one of Sir John's delegates to make the fortress' representations. It may be that Lewis was picked because of the trust the Governor places in good officers but it is just as likely that it is due to our close kinship. Richard Arundel would go, but it might not be seemly for the Governor's son always to do the work of a messenger, however imperative the task. Jospeh Jane has shared some of the burden but for Lewis it has been tormenting because for a while this war of attrition became a personal quarrel.

I am convinced it was because of the family affinity with our Governor that the wretched commander of the besieging forces tried his despicable tactic, alleging that a certain Colonel Tremayne had taken two civilian prisoners and had brought them to the castle, treating them harshly. Faith! There's not enough food for those already here! Why would Lewis bring in more?

It was no mere coincidence that my gentle father-in-law was the lever by which that Roundhead scoundrel thought to undermine the garrison's confidence in its officers.

Fortescue had Lewis' father arrested and imprisoned in the gaol at Penryn and through June and July, the colonel bombarded Lewis with demands. Naturally, Lewis responded that the allegations were false and he knew of no law that allows for the imprisonment of a father for what his son is said to have performed.

Poor John Tremayne has been released, but it was too harsh of them and took too long.

I am sure the letters by the official routes are designed to taunt us.

Yet has there not been correspondence by other routes too, by desperate, secret routes? Sir John insisted that another letter, a more ardent plea, be sent to the Prince. Did not Grace Fenwick pay the cost of that carrier? Was that last month or in June? My mind churns so wildly I cannot remember.

I used to do what I could in the infirmaries where there are now near three hundred folk, sick with lack of nourishment. I got weary though and sat with Hester and Grace sometimes. They knew of my discomforting turns, when I could not see because the world seemed to spin this way and that. When I felt that ill I could not even stand. They would see to it that I reached my bed and for a while, and for the love of me, they did not tell my husband.

Lewis and all the Council now debate strategy for daily there are letters and dialogue with the enemy commanders in the ruins of Arwennack House. Lewis told me after he first visited the Killigrews' old home that the walls are badly blackened even where the manor did not burn down, though now the smell of charred wood fades a little. Perhaps after five months it should.

Two weeks ago, we heard more ships had joined the fleet that watch the Carrick Roads and guard this headland. Lewis came to me one afternoon with news of a strange happenstance,

'My chick, how goes it with Grace these days?' I thought it kind of him to ask but odd, for I had seen him pass the time of day with her that morn. He continued, 'There has been an incident with which I find myself so discomforted that I cannot tell what to do so I need your guidance.' He sat beside me and told me how it was.

Joe Jane was the duty messenger that day. He was awaiting a response to some particulars when the captain of one of the new vessels at the anchorage arrived to pay his respects to the command ashore. Joe had shamelessly eavesdropped as he stood by. The ship was the *Leopard*, the captain's name Bartholomew Fenwick. Of course, Lewis would have known the significance of that vessel. All Grace's friends did. But Joe did not and so he innocently made a report of this intelligence on his return.

'I cannot tell what to do for the best,' Lewis said. 'I could send out a polite enquiry; I could demand that Parliament take steps against one of their own against whom there is ample evidence for murder, a crime even by Roundhead's standards. I could leave well alone and let him get away scot-free...' At these words, I shook my head, agitated on Grace's behalf.

'No, do not do that! I would not rest knowing that her tormentor lies outside these walls and we have done nothing to protect her. What would he do to her? Where will she go? She has nothing. Do what you may, I beg you...' My head swam again. I had begun to suffer fits more often, but I hid my face in my hands. He left, promising to investigate.

Lewis might have taken my pose as I hoped he would, as a sign of a woman's natural anxiety for her friend, except that Hester, with Grace close on her heels, stopped his way just as he was returning to his duties. For my own good, I was straightway carried here to the infirmary.

That is where I have lain since. I have had too much time to think, to let daylight-dreaming flow into my nightmares, and to wonder what will become of us. There is more talk of choosing exile and joining the Prince of Wales abroad. There are even rumours that our notoriously quarrelsome colonel Digby and a hundred hotheads plan to blow the castle up rather than surrender.

Exile terrifies me, but what if Lewis should decide to join Digby and those madcap men? What then? I must again wait just as I have waited before.

Accordingly, this is where I remained when, on Friday, 7th of August, that momentous day, my husband and Joseph Jane were dispatched to Arwennack House. Their task was to demand of Colonel Fortescue, as Lord Fairfax' deputy, whether he and Admiral Batten had the authority to make good any promises made under negotiations.

For Sir John Arundel, Jack-for-the-King, had resolved that the time had come to discuss terms for the surrender of the fort of Pendennis Castle in Cornwall.

Alongside this most weighty of responsibilities, greetings

were conveyed in a note to one Captain Bartholomew Fenwick of the *Leopard* from a man with whom he was once acquainted. That man, who, most remiss, had neglected to give his name, had sent word to Fenwick that he was now at leisure within the King's fortress of Pendennis. He enquired politely after the health of Captain Fenwick's wife.

The said Captain Fenwick, not wishing to enter into correspondence, merely sent a verbal reply regretting that his acquaintance found himself in such straitened and unfortunate circumstances.

Thanking him for the consideration, he added that he had been a sorrowing widower since God had seen fit to take his dear wife from him. She had, he said, tragically died of the plague in Bristol only weeks after their marriage. According to that eminent captain of the Parliamentarian Navy, our dear friend Grace Fenwick could not possibly exist.

Now I simply bide my time, anticipate the opening of the gates which I am told is only hours away.

I have not been told what awaits me but I pray that the enemy will not separate me from my husband for I do not know that I can walk from these walls alone when the time comes. Rumour has it that provision will be made for the likes of me, but God willing, tomorrow I will go with Lewis wherever our destiny leads, be it to our Cornish home or into exile.

The hands of men have drawn ink upon the pages of a document that will bring to an end a routine five months old. That routine has filled my hours and dominated those of every man, woman and child in this fort: individuals who have endured misery with dignity and courage for the sake of our King and in defiance of rebels.

And yet, I ask myself, who will care in one hundred, five hundred or a thousand years from now?

The Castle's Epilogue

Still Pendennis Castle endures. This granite fortress is uncommon; it watched and listened while one thousand souls lived, loved and died while still they held to their principles. These loyal individuals would only speak the word 'surrender' on terms so honourable, that the walls of the citadel still echo with their pride and courage.

There are three women. One fears her present, one ran from her past, and the third has an uncertain future.

A wheaten-haired wife has followed her hero; the walls gave her sanctuary. She has busied herself with day-to-day distractions with no thought for her own well-being, only to find herself weeping for her friends.

There is a woman with hair the colour of a sunset; her slate grey eyes will always look to the sea. This harbour has felt many tides since she watched for a wake and listened for the howl of a hound.

The girl with eyes the colour of honey is older than her years. She has come farther than any of her companions and still has far to go.

The castle held these three women. They made their choices. Choices they have yet to make will be far beyond the stones of this stronghold.

When a sea mist shrouds the Carrick Roads and muffles the cry of the gulls look to the headland. As a buzzard flaps its lazy path into the distance perhaps you will stop and listen, for then you might hear those mineral memories of an August long ago.

THE END

Steph Haxton, Newlyn, Cornwall August 2013- July 2014

Author's Notes
THE MAIN CHARACTERS

Fictional characters are those indicated by an asterisk. All others in the novel are historical individuals though I have only included a manageable number of biographies below.

Where my fictional characters meet real ones, I have tried to make the situations in which I have placed them plausible. Personalities are based on research where possible. Any fictional surnames are based on church records in the localities in which I have put them.

*Grace Godwynne, born July 1625, an intelligent and pragmatic red-head, is the only daughter of a successful Bristol merchant. Perhaps indulged more than many daughters might have been Grace has also been fortunate to have the benefit of an education at home alongside her brothers though she did not attend a school as they did. She could be expected to make a good marriage and bring her literacy and numeracy to running her own household but as a daughter, she cannot inherit her father's commercial concerns.

*Henry Godwynne, her father

*Ann Godwynne, his wife

**Henry (Hal) Godwynne and Edward (Ned) Godwynne, Grace's brothers

*Pasco Jago, master mariner of Dartmouth

*Jinty James, Lady's maid to Ann and Grace

*Matthew Allerway, Steward of the Godwynne house in Wine Street

Robert Yeamans, merchant of Bristol

*Elizabeth, his daughter

*Bartholomew Fenwick, master mariner

*Tremenheere Sark, master gunner and seafarer

*Hester Phipps, a servant. Born in Radstock in1624, the daughter of a miner, Hester is expected to make her own way in the world. Shrewd and resourceful but, as yet, a little immature Hester may not have had an education but she is astute and quick witted. Black hair and light brown eyes give her a swarthy, gypsy appearance and perhaps her capacity to adapt and think on her feet stems from some Romany in her ancestry

Mary Carew, born 22nd January 1624 (this is a fictional date for the purposes of the novel; it has not been possible to identify her actual date of birth). The eldest daughter of John Carew of Penwarne, niece to Sir Richard Carew of Antony, she is a gentle soul, a romantic dreamer born into the privileged elite of Cornwall. The Carews are an old and highly respected family, part of the upper echelons of the Cornish gentry and in their time courtiers and politicians linked to the powerful families of the West Country

John Carew of Penwarne, her father, 'Carew the One Handed'

Richard Carew, his son (Diccon): died in 1640; a stone at Penwarne Manor commemorates the date, but he is not buried in the local area, hence my speculation that he went to war

Agnes (some records show Ann), **Bridget, Grace, Candacia**, Mary's sisters

*Master Cobb, tutor

Sir Richard Carew of Antony

Lady Grace Carew, (nee Rolle) his second wife

Alexander Carew, Sir Richard's eldest son from his first marriage to Bridget Chudleigh

Jane Carew, his wife

Sir John Arundel of Trerice, born 1576, Governor of Pendennis Castle; nick-named 'Jack-for-the-King'.

*Captain John (Jack) Vickery

*Kat Conybere

*Thomas Yeo

*Isaac Lerwill

Lewis Tremayne, eldest son of John Tremayne of Heligan. Legend has it that he swam from Pendennis to Trefusis Point during the siege of Pendennis Castle to fetch relief for the garrison. As he was a signatory to the treaty of surrender in August 1646, this seems unlikely

Sir Richard Grenvile, Royalist commander

Sir Bevil Grenvile, his elder brother; raised and led a

regiment for the King

Charles Trevanion of Caerhayes, raised and funded a regiment for the King

Prince Rupert of the Rhine, nephew to King Charles, famous for riding to battle with his white hunting poodle, **Boye**

***Ezekiel Judd**

*******Make-peace, Zeal-of-the-cross, Joy-to-come, Hope-for-good, Abel Judd: his children**

***Antony Jones**

Susannah Edwards)   These women were

Mary Trembles   )   tried and executed

Temperance Lloyd)   for witchcraft in Bideford in 1682

***Lieutenant Phillips**, Royalist cavalry officer in Prince Rupert's regiment

Dame Elizabeth Chudleigh, Alexander Carew's maternal grandmother

Dewnes Hilman, Mary Carew's maternal grandmother

Thomas Dyckwood

Elizabeth (Bess) Estmond, presented a petition for financial support to King Charles II

William Palmer and his wife, merchant and three times Mayor of Barnstaple, Ann Fanshawe's host

Ann, Lady Fanshawe, her memoirs cover the period depicted in this novel

Sir Richard Fanshawe, her husband, secretary to the Prince of Wales

The 100 year old parrot is reported in Ann, Lady Fanshawe's memoirs

***Loveday Yendacott**

***Jan Leightfast**

Admiral Richard Swanley, Parliamentarian naval commander, noted for his ruthless dispatch of troops and their womenfolk en route from Ireland

William Mattock, a Royalist soldier listed as one of Colonel Lewis Tremayne's men at Pendennis during the siege in 1646. The document T 1621 at the Cornwall Record Office (CRO) lists his home as Cornwood, a village on the skirts of Dartmoor as well as his true fate

Thomas Phillips, of Zennor in West Cornwall. On November 20th 1642, Thomas Phillip made his will as 'being pressed for the wars in the King's Majesty's service and doubting my return'. Richard Grenvile hanged his cousin

John Brownsell, listed on the CRO document T 1621 with William Mattock

Captain Oliver Dinham, listed as one of Colonel Tremayne's officers in CRO document T 1621. Born in St Ewe parish in 1625, he was baptised on 2nd May (This last information is thanks to Steven Dinham)

Thomas Lower, listed in CRO document T 1621

Richard Hodge, listed in CRO document as above

Robert Clarke, listed in CRO document as above

Colonel Richard Fortescue, Parliamentarian commander of the troops besieging Pendennis, left in charge by Sir Thomas Fairfax

Historical Notes

This novel began as a set of ideas for a living history presentation, morphing into a dissertation and then to the notion of a full-length story. The final version is a very different beast from the initial scribbling…but in 15 years, I have changed too. That's literary gestation for you!

The whole idea of wrapping characters round the story of Pendennis' siege in 1646 has engaged me for a long time because the unknown, un-named women who stuck with their men through terrible times seemed to need acknowledging. History can recount so few women's stories because the facts were not recorded and can never be known but perhaps an historical novel can light a candle for them?

So having been the spinner of a fiction, but a historian at the core, I hope the following historical facts will prove interesting. I am always learning so if there's new information out there I would love to know. You can contact me via my website http://www.stephhaxton.com

My plotline is perhaps biased towards the Royalist cause but because the destination was a Royalist fort it was possibly inevitable.

The title of this novel is taken from a letter written in the summer of 1642 by Margaret Eure, aunt to Ralph Verney, whose father was killed defending the King's Standard at the battle of Edgehill. She was lamenting the approach of the civil war and the effect it would have on women:

"In my poor judgment these times can bring no good end to them: all that women can do is to pray for better, for sure it is an ill time with them of all creatures for they are exposed to all villainies". Ralph initially supported Parliament at the start of the war, but went into exile in 1643.

The Cornish language: *kernowek*. By the middle of the seventeenth century, the Cornish language was in decline and Mark Stoyle (*West Britons* (2002) University of Exeter Press) provides a useful map. He estimates that in 1600 Cornish was likely to have been spoken only west of a line between Fowey and Padstow. So, although Sark could be justified as bilingual, readers will perhaps grant me author's licence regarding the language Hester encounters in Morwenstow. Her misheard Cornish is roughly translated as:

Gowek gast = lying whore

Ma pleg = If you please

Meur ras = Thank you

The words spoken by Lewis Tremayne:

Onan hag oll = One and all (The motto of Cornwall)

The Sorlinges: the old name for the Isles of Scilly

The Civil Wars of the mid seventeenth century (1642 - 1651) touched every part of Britain and Cornwall's role was perhaps unique in this conflict between King Charles I and his Parliament. Historians have debated long and hard over the causes: unreasonable taxes, religious change, an obdurate monarch challenging Parliament's constitutional rights all played a part.

It remains that a combination of factors which might have been different for every region - or individual - brought about this 'war without an enemy'. (William Waller)

By 1646 the King's cause was lost and the die-hard Royalists were beaten back to defend two outposts with the remote hope that His Majesty's supporters abroad might raise a force to retake control; Raglan Castle in Wales only came under siege in early June 1646 and surrendered on 19th August.

However, the Governor of Pendennis Castle, Sir John Arundel, at least 70 years of age, refused Fairfax' demands on March 18th. Fairfax had offered him two hours to form a response but Sir John replied,

"having taken less than two minutes resolution, I resolve that I will here bury myself before I deliver up the castle to those who fight against His Majesty and that nothing you can threaten is formidable to me in respect of the loss of loyalty and conscience."

That spirit fuelled the following five-month siege for over 1000 men, women and children in the fortress on the headland overlooking the entrance to the river Fal. Pendennis finally surrendered on Monday August 17th.

The Royalists who were detailed in a list of those who

surrendered include: 'commanders, officers, gentlemen, *ladies, gentlewomen*, [my italics] clergymen and all others with their retinue.'

"On August 17th 1646 at Two of the clock in the afternoon Sir John Arundel of Trerice, Esquire, Governor of the Castle of Pendennis, with his family and retinue and all officers and soldiers of horse and foot, and all the train of artillery, and of the ships, as well as reformado'd officers as others; and all gentlemen, clergymen, and their families and servants, will march out of the castle of Pendennis with their horses, complete arms and equipages, according to their present or past commands and qualities, with flying colours, trumpets sounding, drums beating, match lighted at both ends, bullets in their mouths, and every soldier twelve charges of powder with bullets and match proportionable, with all their own proper goods, bag and baggage, with a safe convoy unto Arwinch Downs."

Second clause of the terms of surrender of Pendennis Castle, T 1629, held in the Cornwall Record Office (CRO)

Further clauses detail £500 (approximately £48,000) which was made available for the support of destitute soldiers and for the succour and nursing of the sick and wounded. A contemporary news-sheet of August 31st reports that:

'the number of soldiers who marched out were 800. A further 200 sick were left behind; 200 women and children, their provisions remaining little and bad, their spirits and resolutions great and desperate.'

It goes on to list the various ranks of the Royalist officers and their number, giving the total garrison as above 1000.

The news of Pendennis' surrender was of such significance that the three messengers who brought the message to Parliament were rewarded with £20 each, the equivalent of over £900 today, perhaps 2 years wages for a 17th century soldier.

The list of Lewis Tremayne's men exists and can be seen at the Cornwall Record Office in Truro, document reference number T1621.

Lewis' father was taken prisoner by Fortesque, on

apparently trumped up charges. Letters from the resulting correspondence are in the CRO collection, reference number T1624-1628.

The drowning of Irish captives: The episode depicted off Tenby was based on a real event. In March 1644 Admiral Swanley did indeed execute the Irish contingent of prisoners taken during the fight for Tenby and west Wales. The savage brutality depicted in the book is an indictment of the man and the Parliamentarians who failed to voice any condemnation of the barbarity, and indeed Swanley and Smith were given gold medals and chains as rewards.

(See John Rowland Powell &C V Wedgewood (1962) *The Navy in the English Civil War*, Hamden; London)

The battle of Lostwithiel 1644: for a wonderfully evocative story and brilliantly accurate depiction of this campaign read *The King's General* by Daphne du Maurier.

Ann, Lady Fanshawe: Ann Fanshawe wrote her memoirs as a tribute to her husband, Richard. It also records for their son an account of his father's role as secretary to Prince Charles, later King Charles II, as a diplomat and ambassador. From 1645 she travelled with him, and consequently gives a vivid account of the adventures she encountered. The piracy episode and the fact that Grace dons boy's clothes is based on Ann's diary. She details her stay in Barnstaple in some detail - including the parrot. However, she does not record what the bird was taught to say. She also changed a pass with a little adroit forgery to make good her escape from London in 1659.

The witches of Bideford episode is inspired by the story of Temperance Lloyd, Mary Trembles and Susannah Edwards, tried in 1682 for witchcraft. The accounts I have been able to find do not specify their ages at their trials, hence their teenage troublemaking for Hester.

The blacksmith's wife: The words attributed to the Mevagissey blacksmith in chapter XXXIX were actually extracted from a letter from Elizabeth, Lady Bourchier, wife of the Earl of Rutland to her husband.

The poem '*Verses made in Pendennis when it was

besieged by sea and land': The poem, which I have attributed to Sark, was composed in Pendennis during the siege; it likens Pendennis to Penelope, besieged by harassing suitors while Ulysses was absent, the author is unrecorded.

A Sketched Map of some of the places featured….not to scale

ACKNOWLEDGMENTS

So many people have helped in the process of this novel's evolution. At every stage, I have met with enthusiasm, and every spark of encouragement has meant I finished the book - eventually! An especially big thank you to everyone who didn't roll their eyes or laugh when I said I was writing a novel. Anyone I have forgotten, please accept my apologies.

It all began years ago with a comment by John More, historian and tutor at the University of Exeter and for that and his generosity with his time and critique, I am enormously grateful. He and the equally inspirational Ella Westland finally helped me nail the title. As Ella also showed infinite patience correcting erratic punctuation and spelling, as well as facilitating my first unbiased review from Hazel Dunn in Mevagissey, the map is my tribute to her. John Hurst has been a quiet powerhouse, not quite as vociferous as Margaret Perry, but both have been incredibly effective. I only wish that she too had seen the finished work.

Huge thanks go to Claire Chamberlain for a superb cover design created from my nebulous suggestions. Roger Alway has been my seafaring expert, steering me in the right direction. If it isn't right it's because I didn't ask Roger. Chloe Phillips at the Cornwall Records Office has been brilliant all through, reading an early version and sharing my enthusiasm for Civil War Cornwall. Sarah Turner read and painstakingly copy-edited the mss, a task over and beyond the call of friendship. Michelle Smith discreetly set me straight on repetitions in an early draft and I duly took note. Similarly, Maggie Fogharty tactfully encouraged me to prune the cast list.

Nathan and Vicky Harvey were delightfully hospitable at the beautiful Penwarne Manor. I hope they think I have done justice to their lovely home. Staff at the Morrab Library in Penzance; the librarians at Bideford Library and Deborah Gahan at the Barnstaple Local Studies Library were all so generous with their time and expertise.

Steve Phillips (Prince Rupert's Regiment of the 'Sealed

Knot') gave me the advice I needed regarding uniforms while Sarah Williams and the gorgeous Evie were the experts on historical poodles. Jean Nankervis provided an interesting character from Zennor who deserved a place in history and Liz Harman gave me a lot of advice on the Cornish language, pointing me in the right direction for help and translations.

At Mevagissey Parish Church Reverend Marion Barrett made an inspired comment when I couldn't find any burial record for Richard Carew which I was then able to build into Diccon's story.

And of course Professor Mark Stoyle's phenomenal research and publications have underpinned so much of the history behind this novel.

All of my friends have egged me on but my family have been more tolerant than most. Thanks go to Julia for observations on the taste of wine with poison in it, freely given with not a raised eyebrow as to why I wanted to know, and to Derek who gave great advice on Biblical references with the vaguest of directions as to the required context.

Thank you Stuart: drinking coffee and wandering Tehidy woods with you pushed so much of the plotting along.

Thank you, Fern, for the unwavering encouragement, for a hero called Sark and the inspiration for Grace, Hester and Mary.

Thanks go to Mum for the hours spent listening to my ramblings. At least you didn't have to type this one up! I hope you think Dad would approve of the finished item.

But most of all, my love and thanks to Ramsay for everything I could possibly need to complete this task, from exploratory detours across the west-country to my under-foot heating, but most especially for his reaction to the finished article.

This book is a tribute to all the un-named, unknown women and children at Pendennis Castle in 1646.